Keeper's Gift

JAY ANTHONY

Copyright © 2016 Jay Anthony.

All rights reserved. No part of this book may be used or reproduced by any means, graphic, electronic, or mechanical, including photocopying, recording, taping or by any information storage retrieval system without the written permission of the author except in the case of brief quotations embodied in critical articles and reviews.

LifeRich Publishing is a registered trademark of The Reader's Digest Association, Inc.

LifeRich Publishing books may be ordered through booksellers or by contacting:

LifeRich Publishing
1663 Liberty Drive
Bloomington, IN 47403
www.liferichpublishing.com
1 (888) 238-8637

Because of the dynamic nature of the Internet, any web addresses or links contained in this book may have changed since publication and may no longer be valid. The views expressed in this work are solely those of the author and do not necessarily reflect the views of the publisher, and the publisher hereby disclaims any responsibility for them.

Any people depicted in stock imagery provided by Thinkstock are models, and such images are being used for illustrative purposes only. Certain stock imagery © Thinkstock.

ISBN: 978-1-4897-0647-8 (sc)
ISBN: 978-1-4897-0649-2 (hc)
ISBN: 978-1-4897-0648-5 (e)

Library of Congress Control Number: 2016900077

Print information available on the last page.

LifeRich Publishing rev. date: 02/16/2016

> "And fare thee weel, my only luve!
>
> And fare thee weel, a while!
>
> And I will come again, my luve
>
> Tho' it were ten thousand mile!"
>
> "A Red, Red Rose"
> —Robert Burns

ACKNOWLEDGMENTS

My thanks to Colonel Burt Dall for his technical advice on the US Army and, in particular, Korea. He was there; I wasn't. Also to Geri Martin, who gave me much encouragement and motivation to complete this story. And last, but not least, my thanks to Angie Raitano, Angela McDonnell, and Lois Dupre Shuster for their insight and help, for which I am very grateful.

This story is fictional. Most of the names of characters are fictitious and any similarity to those living is purely coincidental. The reference to some events and places, such as the Berlin Airlift, the Korean War, and the Headquarters in Wiesbaden, are real. During the period depicted, there was a Liaison Squadron in Heidelberg, and many of the pilots were "flying sergeants." The reference to the aircraft flown during the Berlin airlift and some of the perils are authentic as far as the author can recall. Any references to how the military operated and the units involved are fictitious. The "happenings" in this story are not real and are the figments of the author's imagination.

Some of the locations in Germany, the United States, and Korea exist. The El Bordegon restaurant is authentic, and I had permission to write a little about it. Sadly, they are no longer in business—a great loss to those who visited it. Regarding psychic phenomena leanings, I leave it up to the reader to dwell on what is, what isn't, and what could be.

CHAPTER 1

Pfaffengrund, Germany (Outside Heidelberg)

Five L-5 Piper Cub aircraft of the Fourth AAF Liaison Squadron were preparing to taxi onto the runway for takeoff from Heidelberg for a two-hour flight to Bad Kissingen, Germany. Corporal Pat Duran was a passenger, sent on a temporary duty trip as an administrative clerk. Technical Sergeant Dick Levans was piloting the aircraft. That was good news for Pat, because Levans always let him fly the plane for a little while once they were airborne.

Levans was one of the many "Flying Sergeants" still active in the Army Air Corps. The pilots were leftovers from the War and still flew with the Fourth Liaison Squadron. Levans revved up the engine, testing the pressure, magneto, and temperature. All instruments were go.! The lead aircraft started to roll and was soon airborne. Levans advanced the throttle and released the brake, and the L-5 rolled, taking off the ground in less than a minute. One by one, the aircraft group gathered into a small formation at six thousand feet. Pat had on his radio headset and heard the pilots talking to each other.

Captain Frank Johnson, who was flying the lead plane, told the formation to spread out because the turbulence was bouncing his aircraft up and down. Captain Johnson was a fighter pilot, and it had taken him two weeks to get checked out in the small L-5 aircraft. This amused the flying sergeants of the Liaison Squadron.

"This is going to be about a two-hour flight," Sergeant Levans advised Pat. "I'll let you have the stick in a while."

"Roger that!" Pat answered.

Pat tried to relax. Looking down at his left hand, he reached over and turned the gold band on his ring finger. His thoughts immediately went back to the Easter Sunday on which he'd first met Lily, and he remembered all the little details.

She was walking toward the streetcar station in Heidelberg. I was walking behind her, and I was eager to meet her. Boy, how stupid I must have sounded to her, trying to get a conversation going.

"My name is Lily and I am going back to my home for an Easter feast," she said.

I was surprised that she spoke English that well, and I gave a little laugh.

"Is that right, an Easter feast?" she asked.

"Back home, it would be a feast for sure," I said.

God! I was so dazzled when I first saw her. She looked so fresh and neat ...

dimples and some freckles, light green eyes and honey-colored hair. When I asked her if I could ride on the streetcar with her, it was because I didn't know what else to say.

"You speak English well," I complimented her.

"My sister is married to an American civilian, and I learned to speak English."

I remember that I felt a little foolish asking questions, and I tried my best to get to know her. She had a good laugh when I asked what the little sign in the streetcar said. I remember pronouncing the German "Nicht auf den Boden Spucken."

She told me that it meant do not spit on the floor.

After we arrived in Handschuhsheim, just west of Heidelberg, the streetcar proceeded to turn around, ready for the return journey back into town.

I walked Lily to her house on that Easter Sunday afternoon, expecting her to tell me goodbye and that would be that. Instead she asked me to wait, and she disappeared into the house. After a few minutes I heard her call me. I looked up at Lily at the window, and she invited me to come upstairs. I did, and Lily's family invited me to spend Easter with them, welcoming me.

Pat looked out the window at the other aircraft. They were flying up and down—fifty feet up, and then after a short while, fifty feet down.

"A lot of turbulence," Levans remarked. "Wait till we fly over the hills and those quarries. Sometimes you get a real surge of hot air." He grinned at Pat, obviously not concerned about the rough air.

"Hey, Pat, I got a question for you. I know you're not married, but you're wearing a wedding ring. What's the scoop?"

"I got a ring for my girlfriend and a matching ring for myself. It was a birthday present for her, and her parents don't say anything about my staying with Lily at their house."

"Yeah, I kinda figured it was something like that. I saw you with her last week at the Serviceman's Center. She sure is a pretty one!"

"Thanks! I'll tell her you said so."

Pat thought about Lily and their relationship again. The first night they'd spent together and all the days afterward was just like they were married. They'd been together three months, and this was the first time that he'd be away for a week.

A sudden updraft caused their aircraft to rise, and it shook Pat out of his daydreaming.

"It's starting to get a little more turbulent," remarked Sergeant Levans.

The five aircraft passed over one group of mountains, and the air smoothed out.

"Pat, you still awake back there?"

"Yeah, just daydreaming."

"You can take the stick now. Keep your eye on the lead plane and just follow him along."

"Roger that!" replied Pat.

Westy Cragmore was flying directly behind the aircraft Pat was in. He was not paying too much attention to the weather conditions. One of the oldest sergeant pilots in the Army Air Corps, Westy often bragged, and other pilots later confirmed, that he had flown and piloted airships before the war. It was also rumored that Westy was older than his records revealed. Westy was a rugged fellow. He gambled, raised hell, drank till he stumbled, and was known to "hang one on." Last night had been no exception. Westy had a German *Schatze* and had been out partying with her until late, so today he was tired and hung over.

Things could happen quickly when flying, and this was one of them. A blast of thermal air lifted Westy's plane a few hundred feet, and it caught him unaware. Startled, Westy, in a fit of anxiety, felt sharp, stabbing pains in his chest. It was not the first time he had experienced these pains, and he had kept it quiet, never told anyone, least of all the squadron flight surgeon.

The heart attack came swiftly and without any warning. Westy tried to call out on his radio, but the pain was so intense it took his breath away, and he fell, forcing the joystick forward. His plane nosed downward, gaining speed until it hit the back of Levans' plane.

"Let go of the controls!" yelled Levans, taking the stick from Pat. The aircraft did not have any rear stabilizer; it had been chewed up by the propeller of Westy's L-5.

"*Bail out! Bail out!*" Levans yelled, as he tried to keep the plane level.

Pat clawed at the door latch as the plane headed in a nosedive. The rushing air pushed against the door, and Pat had to shove with all his might to keep it open. He managed to tumble out, and as he did he pulled the ripcord. The parachute line flared out, and the rear tail section caught the shroud lines, snaring Pat's parachute. In those last few seconds Pat's inner voice screamed his love for Lily. *I can't die, I can't leave her … This can't happen … Jesus, Lord!*

Both planes crashed in central Germany, and then there was silence. Pat did not feel pain in the experience of death. That he could be dead and still be aware of it was very confusing.

CHAPTER 2

"Goodness, this is not correct! This is a big mistake." The man speaking was holding a clipboard. "Westy Cragmore and Richard Levans are the ones scheduled. But this young fellow, Pat Duran," he said, looking at Pat, "is not on my arrival list. Good grief—and he's awake and looking at us!"

Two-ordinary looking men around fifty years of age, both dressed in what appeared to be white linen suits, approached Pat and bent down to peer at his face. Pat was aware of them. He could see them all right, and hear them too, but when he tried to ask who they were and where he was, Pat could not feel any words coming out of his mouth or hear himself talking.

"Yes, of course. We understand. My name is Brewster," the man said as if he'd heard Pat's thoughts. "And this is Ames," he added with a smile. "But let's get things sorted out first."

Brewster reached down and took Pat by the hand. At his touch, Pat felt a surge of energy, and he seemed to float out of the airplane wreckage. Turning to look back, Pat saw the airplane wreckage, fire, and crushed and mangled bodies. *Boy*, he thought, *that fellow in the chute is sure a mess.* All at once, the impact of what he saw came to Pat.

That is me! he screamed—or at least he tried to. Again, no sounds emerged from his mouth. *Oh my God! What has happened to me?*

"Now that is the awkward part we will have to sort out," Brewster said softly as he took Pat's elbow and turned him away from the crash site.

As Brewster talked, Pat felt a gentle breeze. Then, though he experienced no sense of movement, he found himself with Brewster at a very nice cottage with a patio that was surrounded by a variety of beautiful flowers. The cottage overlooked a pretty little village and it also had an abundance of colorful flowers.

"I don't understand," Pat said, and this time he heard his voice speaking.

"This will be a bit hard for you to understand, Pat," Brewster said. "You see, Ames and I were to receive two new arrivals over here, not three. It clearly says here on my sheet Richard Levans and Westy Cragmore. We were not expecting Pat Duran."

"Am I dead?" Pat asked. "Are you some kind of angel?"

Brewster chuckled. "No, I am not an angel, just a worker. I help out with the new arrivals," he added. "But your situation is different."

Brewster cocked his head to one side. "Quite so!" he remarked after a moment if in response to someone, but Pat couldn't see or hear anyone else.

"I have been told to get you settled down and comfortable, at least for now, and I will arrange for an appointment to see what is to be done."

Pat stared at him with a confused look on his face and asked. "What can be done?"

"Well", Brewster responded, "I believe that those of the higher plane of authority are looking into what can be done to correct your present situation. That is all I know."

"Well, that's something positive, I guess," Pat mumbled.

"Are you in any pain or discomfort?" Brewster asked.

Pat tried to gauge the severity of his injuries, sure they would be extensive, but to his surprise could not feel any ill effects. "No, I feel okay," he ventured, "just a little tired."

Brewster brought Pat into the little cottage and asked him to sit down and relax in an overstuffed recliner. Pat sat back in the chair. His thoughts were peaceful, and he felt totally relaxed. In a few moments he was lost in a deep and long sleep—a sleep that would last a very long time by earthly standards.

"We must get on with our job now," Brewster told Ames, a tall, slim, and quiet arrival attendant." Brewster was much shorter with white hair cut short, almost like a crew cut. Brewster was in charge.

"We will leave our temporary arrival for now," he went on, "and we will have some help in deciding what is to be done. One thing, for sure—whatever it is won't happen quickly. You know what a stickler Reception is with new arrivals."

An Army Air Corps flying safety accident investigation followed, and after hearing from the other pilots, it was surmised that Westy Cragmore had suffered a heart attack. An autopsy performed at the medical facility in Wiesbaden confirmed it. The incident and news of the accident passed.

Lily, after not hearing from Pat for two weeks, became obsessed with the thought that Pat had left her for another woman and was not coming back. It was not for another two weeks that she learned from her brother in-law, Frank, that there had been an aircraft accident between two airplanes from Heidelberg and that three people had been killed. A few days later she learned the names of those who had perished. As she'd feared, Pat Duran was one of them.

It would be a long time before Lily could cope with even the most basic things in life. She was devastated and heart-broken. It was hard for Lily to continue working at her aunt's hairdressing salon and listen to unwanted advice from the patrons. More than ever, Lily wanted to escape the questions the customers asked about her boyfriend, her lover, her American *Schatze*. It was too difficult to answer nosy questions, which only upset Lily more, and she was constantly near to tears. *No one,* Lily thought, *appreciates the depths of the sorrow I feel over Pat's death.* Lily tried to lose herself in her work and her aunt, Tante Marie, respected that wish and tried to see that the customers did not bother Lily.

Taking a break one afternoon, Lily did the family grocery shopping and went into Heidelberg to the big market platz. Lily was pleased to notice a greater variety of vegetables and some fruit now, more so than ever before. She bought some vegetables and some cooking apples. As she was leaving the market platz, Lily met the head teaching nurse from the university. She hailed Lily, and they hugged each other.

"Where have you been, Elizabeth? I hoped to see you—that you'd at least visit us now and then," said Sister Menckler.

After leaving the university, Lily had decided to use her middle name; it felt a little strange to be called Elizabeth again, but she smiled fondly at her former instructor. Lily then rushed out a breathless explanation about working at home, the hairdressers, and … her voice trailed off and stopped.

Sister Menckler again hugged Lily. "*Leibchen*, I know what happened at school. I found out because it happened to Freda Guetz, and we got the swine expelled." Continuing, Sister Menckler said, "Now this Don Juan is doing his medical training in the Darmstadt prison. The Guetz girl saw Intern Fleager follow you into the linen room, and she heard the commotion but didn't say anything to anyone until he attempted to rape her."

Lily's face flushed with embarrassment, but Sister Menckler took Lily by the arm and hustled her along to have a coffee and *schnecken* at the Gruenwall cafe. As she enjoyed the delicious pastry, Lily remembered Sister Menckler's weakness for sweet things—cakes or candies. As they settled down and had their coffee and pastry, Sister Menckler brought Lily up to date on the current training program.

"You know, you could come back and continue your training. You have completed one year, and you had very good marks. I was telling Herr Doktor Friedman, the hospital Administrator, that I would like to have you back in the training program because you are such a good student and I think that you will become a very good nursing sister," she said with a chuckle. Then her expression grew more serious.

"I have to tell you also that Herr Doktor knows the situation—why you had to leave—and he will clear the way for you to continue."

Lily was flabbergasted. "I don't know if I will have enough money for the training and books," Lily said, hesitating. "I have to earn money for these things, and I cannot ask my family because they have so little now."

"*Leibling*," Sister Menckler said, "the hospital is very short of staff. They are desperate for nurses, but they also need nursing assistants. Some of the first-year trainees work at the hospital part time and earn money while they go to school. It's like taking a double laxative—you get twice the action—at school and at the hospital. It's a great way to increase your knowledge and nursing skills," she finished.

Getting up to go, Sister Menckler suggested Lily visit the school office and complete the reentry paperwork.

"Will you do that?" she asked.

Lily nodded and smiled.

"Good, that is great!"

Lily quickly gathered up her shopping bag and ran for the streetcar and the ride home.

CHAPTER 3

Lily had a pleasant surprise when she arrived at the school administration office and requested an application to reenter her nurses training.

"Your name, please?" asked the clerk.

"Lily ... I mean Elizabeth Feldmann," she said.

"Ach so! I have word from the administrator himself that you are to complete what is in this folder. If you would kindly take a seat over there at the desk and fill in the forms, I will take you in to see Herr Doktor Friedman."

After completing the forms, Lily was ushered in to see Herr Doktor Friedman, whose face lit up when he saw her.

"So, you come back to us?" he asked with a big smile.

He told Lily that in one week's time there would be a position for work in the hospital. "Nursing Sister Menckler has asked that you be assigned to assist in her ward. You will receive the same wages as the other assisting trainees, two sets of nursing uniforms, and one meal each day and one midday refreshment."

This is something new, thought Lily. *One has to eat, and if the hospital gives me my main meal, I will be able to have some extra money.*

And so, Lily restarted her medical nurses training. Lily learned so much from Sister Menckler. The trainees looked upon some of the other supervisor nursing sisters as "holy terrors," but Sister Menckler was a special human being—wise, compassionate, and understanding. *What a sense of humor she has too.*

Lily plunged herself into her studies and spent most of her spare time studying the medical books, anatomy, and chemistry. Many times as Sister Menckler was making her rounds at night she would find Lily deep into her studies. When Lily had questions she would ask Sister Menckler, who was quick to explain in detail.

The next two years of training at the Heidelberg school passed very swiftly for Lily. By now she had completed her third school year. During that time she also worked alongside Sister Menckler at the hospital, and managed to save some money as well. Lily reached that point in her education where she could be considered for advanced training in Wiesbaden as a surgical nurse. Not everyone received that opportunity. She wanted to be a surgical nurse and not a practical nurse. It was no surprise to anyone when Doktor Smitzer, head of training at Heidelberg, announced, "Elizabeth Feldmann, I am very happy to inform you that the medical staff here have selected you first in your group to go to Wiesbaden."

The train ride to Wiesbaden was pleasant and not a long journey. She was in luck that the school had a dormitory set up for students—both for nursing and internship. Everyone had her own little bedroom with a desk and chair for studies. The women shared the multiple showers and bathrooms. There were three large rooms for community use: a lounge, a games room, and a large kitchen area with stove, icebox, and a sink for washing up. There were also small metal lockers in the kitchen area for the nurses to keep their individual food, snacks, and beverages.

Elizabeth reverted back to using her first name. She was very intent on her advanced training and pursuing more of the surgical aspects of nursing. In addition, though, her past experience with hairdressing proved to be an unexpected blessing. The hospital, which provided food and shelter, also paid twenty-five Deutsch Marks a week as a wage for working shifts in the hospital, and this meant that some of the trainees had money to spend, while others in the same situation as she. She had all her hairdressing tools—scissors, combs, curling iron and curlers, lotions, and her old but reliable electric hair dryer.

The word got around that one of the trainees could do hair—and do a nice job. Because of her skill, Elizabeth acquired several pairs of nylon hose, a knitted scarf and gloves to match, a bottle of wine and extra money—whatever the girls could afford. Elizabeth did shampoos and sets, and she also cut and trimmed hair. Once in a while she gave a permanent wave and a variety of hair styling. One of the training heads asked a supervisor if she noticed how nice the young nurses were looking. She then learned that the talented Elizabeth was doing the hairdressing for the trainees in her spare time.

Time passed quickly, and before Elizabeth realized, she was in her last year of training. She would soon be sitting for her final examinations and would, she hoped, receive certification as a full-fledged nursing sister.

One day following her shift at the hospital, Elizabeth was summoned to the hospital surgical office and asked if she would be willing to "hire out" her services as a private companion nurse for a wealthy American patient who was presently in the hospital.

"You speak English very well, and everyone recommends you. The hospital does not really have the extra staff to accommodate the Americans' request," the registrar said, "but this American is a very important person, and we would like to be of help. Since they are willing to pay extra for these services, we thought that it would be a good opportunity for someone who speaks English."

Lily learned that her services would be required in the evening, after supper until eleven p.m., and again in the morning from eight to ten thirty. *Strange hours*, she thought, but the hours worked out well with her training schedule.

CHAPTER 4

Elizabeth met her American patient that evening. Her name was Mrs. Bernice Templeton. She had undergone surgery for removal of a cancerous growth. This was being followed with radiation treatments. Mrs. Templeton did not look good. Her skin had a washed-out pallor, her hair was askew, and she was in great discomfort from the radiation treatment.

"Hello, Mrs. Templeton. My name is Elizabeth Feldmann. I am in my final year as a surgical nurse at this hospital, and I understand that you have requested me."

Mrs. Templeton just stared at her for a time, but then finally she smiled and said, "I'm so sorry for not answering you right away. I think I must have been in a daydream. For a moment I thought I knew you." Perking up, she said, "Wait till my George sees you."

Elizabeth didn't know what to make of that remark, so she busied herself making Mrs. Templeton comfortable and applied special cream to Mrs. Templeton's radiation-burned body. Mrs. Templeton gabbed away to Elizabeth, and they both knew that the chemistry between them was good.

"Mrs. Templeton, if you don't mind, would you like me to fix your hair? The nurses do not have time to do that, but I'd be happy to it. I have all my hairdressing tools with me."

"Are you sure, Elizabeth? I have a devil of a time getting it to look halfway decent."

Elizabeth chuckled and said, "I was a hairdresser with my aunt for a few years before nursing school. I also cut other nurses' hair and do hair dyes, perms and sets for them. I earn extra pocket money, and when someone doesn't have any money to pay, we then barter for things. I did a perm for a nice pair of nylon stockings once."

As she was talking to Mrs. Templeton, Elizabeth took out the scissors, comb, and hairdressing tools she had in her big bag. She deftly clipped and snipped here and there—all very quickly. She then took away the towel and got rid of the hair clippings. Mrs. Templeton was amazed at how quickly and efficiently Elizabeth cut her hair. Next was what Elizabeth called a "dry shampoo." A very short time later she applied a hair setting lotion, waved her hand hair dryer around Mrs. Templeton's hairdo, and the job was completed. She tidied up her patient and gave her the mirror to view the hairdo.

"Why, it's incredible," Bernice Templeton cried, "It's gorgeous! My hair hasn't looked this good in years!"

The door opened at that moment, and George Templeton entered his wife's private room.

"There you are, George! Come and meet my nurse, Elizabeth Feldmann," Mrs. Templeton said, her eyes sparkling. "Isn't she just a little darling?" she asked, her eyes intensely set on her husband George—studying his reaction and facial expression.

For a second or two George Templeton did not respond, but then he warmly greeted Elizabeth. "I was told that you are one of the best choices for this job and that you speak English well." It was more a statement than a question.

"Yes, I do speak English," replied Elizabeth, instead, she volunteered, "I am senior to many of the other trainees, and since I speak English, I was asked."

Bernice Templeton interrupted and said to her husband, "Look at what Elizabeth did to my hair ..." She turned her head so he could see more of her hairdo, a huge smile beaming on her face. "... and in a very short time too! And Elizabeth bathed me and applied that lotion on my burns, and I feel so much better."

It was obvious to George that his Bernice was in great spirits, and he saw that the senior trainee had a positive and good effect on his wife. George felt some weight lifting from his heart and shoulders.

George Templeton was the Deputy Air Attaché for the United States, and his office was located in Frankfurt in what formerly was the I. G. Farben Building. George had been quite concerned about his wife. She'd had a very serious bout with cancer, and for a while it was "touch and go" with Bernice's life in the balance. The doctor said that if Bernice would only rally herself, she would take a turn for the better and be on the road to getting well. George had tried to talk to Bernice and give her encouragement to get better, but she was feeling very low and had said, sobbing, "To hell with it, George! I'm tired of living, and I miss our kids. What do I have to look forward to?"

Already under a great deal of stress himself, George Templeton went to pieces emotionally, and with tears running down his cheeks he sobbed to Bernice, "I don't know why we lost our kids, but I can't lose you, too. I don't know what I would do without you."

Bernice had loved her children. She had always been an active person who gave her time to worthwhile projects and charities. But she was a lonely mother who sorely missed her children, who had been killed in a car accident. They were on their way home from visiting their cousin in North Carolina. A good friend, Edward Cantrell, was driving Jennifer and James home. It was getting dark, and that night a wet mist fell on the road and froze. It was hard to tell just when the "black ice" set in, but a semi-trailer coming toward them lost control and jack-knifed into their oncoming car. Ed Cantrell and the two Templeton children were killed almost immediately. It was a terrible shock to the Templetons. George had decided it best for him and Bernice to get out of the country as a diversion. Bernice had tried hard to overcome the heartache of their loss, but there was hardly a night that she didn't silently cry herself to sleep, mourning the loss of the children. She had been physically and emotionally run down, and when she was stricken with cancer, Bernice was ready to throw in the towel.

The moment of truth came to Bernice as she listened to her husband sobbing. Bernice had not considered the impact on George. She had been wallowing in self-pity and not thinking about her husband. At that point, however, Bernice started to rally herself, and she told George so.

"Darling, I'm sorry. I will try very hard to lick this thing. It would be nice if I had someone here with me, though, like a night nurse," she said. "I feel like a mess after the treatments. I get nauseated and can't eat."

George promised to look into getting someone and talked to doctor Freidman, the hospital administrator. who told him that they had a senior trainee who might be available. "And this young woman speaks the best English I have heard in a long time," he volunteered, "Even better then I speak!"

"Fine, that's fine," George Templeton said. "I expect to pay extra for her services, and the hospital too. You have all been very good to my wife and me, and I appreciate it very much."

He thought about how Bernice had responded to the night nurse, and he was delighted to see that she looked a hundred percent better already.

What a shock, George thought. *Elizabeth Feldmann looks like an older version of our daughter Jennifer.* He wondered if Bernice had noticed the resemblance also. George stayed with Bernice until after Elizabeth left at eleven o'clock. As soon as the door closed behind her, Bernice and George turned to each other.

"Looks like Jennifer—"

"—resembles—"

"—I nearly fell out of the bed—"

"—thought I was seeing things."

There were some tears from both George and Bernice.

"Oh, George," Bernice cooed, "I am so pleased with this girl. I know this is only the first night with her, but I feel like she belongs with us. I feel so good when she touches me, speaks to me, and does my hair."

George was pleased to see the radiance in Bernice's eyes and her expression.

"You know," he said, "as soon as you finish your treatment here we have to return to Frankfurt. I have talked to the ambassador and the air attaché about transferring to Washington and going back home."

"When do you have in mind?" Bernice asked, her mind racing ahead.

"It could be as soon as six weeks away," George said thoughtfully. "I have already called Four Winds and talked to Bill and told him to get the place shipshape and up –to-speed," he said with a chuckle.

Bernice looked up at him with an inquiring look. "And?" she asked.

"I could tell he was excited about our coming home. I could hear Queenie's voice in the background, asking questions. Bill told her not to get her knickers in a twist!"

Bernice had to laugh. Bill and Queenie Cranfield were the caretaker and gardeners for the Four Winds Estate. She visualized the commotion George's call would make. At the main house she could just see Chester and Martha Somers scurrying all over the house and sending their daughter, Penny,, to shop for all kinds of things.

George was watching Bernice and saw a slight downcast expression. "Honey, what are you thinking? You do want to return home, don't you?"

"Yessss, it would be nice. But, oh, it would be out of the question!"

It was obvious to George that Bernice was wrestling with her thoughts. "Out with it, girl!" he demanded.

"George, darling—dearest," she went on, "What if we asked Elizabeth to go with us to Frankfurt and then later when we go home, she goes with us?"

Bernice had that look that George knew so well. *She is going to do a number on me*, he thought.

"Sweetheart," George said, "let's see how it goes, and if you still feel the same way and I agree, and then we can ask Elizabeth. Agreed?"

"Yes, darling, you know best," replied Bernice.

In a pig's whistle, thought George. *She will have her own way!*

He started to work out the details in his mind ... *just in case!*

CHAPTER 5

In the following weeks, Bernice Templeton completed her treatments, and the attending physician advised George that he could take his wife to Frankfurt by the end of the week.

"I am very happy to see how much she has improved in just a few week's time," he said. Continuing on, he asked, "You are satisfied with Apprentice Nurse Feldmann?"

"My God, yes!" replied George. "She has been a marvel to have around. My wife has become very fond of her."

George hesitated for a moment, deep in thought, and then he asked the doctor, "Is Elizabeth Feldman soon to graduate as a nurse?"

"Not for about six more months and then she must sit for examinations and there will be actual clinical and surgical evaluations to be made. But this one will be one of the best. She will pass for sure!"

"Thank you, doctor," George said. "I must leave to return to Frankfurt now. *Auf Wiedersehen!*"

A few hours later George returned to his job, but his mind was busy thinking about the plans he had yet to make. George talked with his wife on Tuesday, and it was no surprise to learn that she had not changed her mind. In fact, she was more insistent than ever about talking to Elizabeth to see if she would come to Frankfurt with them, and then on to the United States.

"Bernice," George asked, "are you sure this is what you want?"

"If it is possible, yes!" was her immediate reply.

"Okay, then, I will bring up the subject with Elizabeth."

"No!" replied Bernice. "We'll ask her together. I spend more time with her, and if I sense that she might not want to go with us, you can jump into the conversation to reinforce our position."

The evening meal was removed, and at the stroke of six thirty Elizabeth came into the room. *She moves with such grace*, Bernice thought.

"Good evening, Mrs. Templeton, Mr. Templeton." She nodded to George and then turned to Bernice. "How are you today, Mrs. Templeton?"

"I am feeling much better, thank you," Bernice answered. "We were told that I am to be discharged from the hospital on Saturday and allowed to return to my home in Frankfurt. George is making arrangements for our return to America in about six or seven weeks."

"Oh, I am happy for you," Elizabeth said. She was a little saddened for she had become very fond of Mrs. Templeton and sorry to see their relationship end.

Bernice was a master at reading body language, and she caught the slight expression she was looking for. "Elizabeth, dear," she said, patting the place next to her on the bed, "come here."

Elizabeth came over to her and sat on the edge of the bed; her eyes were wide and had an inquiring look.

"Elizabeth, I want to ask you something that is very important to George and me. You know that we are going to return to Frankfurt and then, soon after, to America."

Elizabeth nodded.

"Well, my dear, I know that you are almost finished with your training here, and then you would go into a full career as a nurse somewhere in Germany. George and I would like to ask you, how would you feel about coming with us to Frankfurt and then on to America? Before you answer, please hear what we have to say."

George entered into the conversation at this point. "Elizabeth, I have made many inquires, and while you are almost finished with your nurses training here, you will be able to finish it in the United States. I have talked to Ralph Templeton, my cousin, who is a director at Johns Hopkins Hospital in Baltimore, Maryland. He assures me that you will get to complete your training, and at one of the finest hospitals in America. Elizabeth, we will pay you a very good salary and provide for your food and shelter. We have a big house near Hereford, Maryland, and we have a lot of room. Furthermore, we will pay for all your training and anything you need if you will agree to go with us."

Elizabeth stood up and turned away from Mr. Templeton, tears running down her face. She tried to formulate some questions but she could not control the tears.

Seeing Elizabeth so distressed, Mrs. Templeton got off the bed, gathered her into her arms, and said, "Oh, Elizabeth, we didn't mean to upset you. It was selfish of me to be so insistent, to ask you. It's just, well, I feel I need you to be with us and help me face the next few years. But I'm sorry. I didn't want to upset you. We care very much about you, and we felt this bond between us, and I hoped …" Bernice's voice trailed off.

"Oh no!" cried Elizabeth. "I was so touched that you thought enough of me to want me to join you. So many things have happened these past two month. My sister and her husband have returned to America, and they got permission for my mother and father to immigrate to America with them. They are going to stay with my sister Hilda in San Francisco, California, I think. I was feeling that my family was leaving and that I would have no one here in Germany."

"Elizabeth, darling, we want you to consider George and me as part of your family. We no longer have our children in this world," Bernice said.

Elizabeth had heard the heartbreaking story from Bernice Templeton, and she was touched and reached out to hold Bernice's hand.

Wiping away the remaining tears, Elizabeth said, "My only real concern now is finishing my training and becoming a certified nurse. I have worked so hard for this, and I must be able to make a living for myself."

"Have no fear, Elizabeth," George reassured her. "We will take good care of you, and you will not regret it!"

Elizabeth looked a little doubtful and said, "Mr. Templeton, I know you are a good man and that you mean well, but I know that all the things you are saying would cost much money. I know it is not my business, but you can't earn that much money. Can you?"

Mrs. Templeton roared with laughter and slapped her side. "Elizabeth, my dear, my George is what we call 'well off'. We have a very large house—an estate really. George's father was a very wealthy man, and he left it to his sons. Yes, George can pay for all the things that he is talking about."

Elizabeth was almost in shock, her mind racing a mile a minute.

George then sat Elizabeth down and, extracting his little notebook and wrote all the details he needed to start the ball rolling.

Other Factors

Following the end of the war in 1945, the Russians took control of Eastern Germany, with Berlin being divided into four sectors—under Russian, British, American, and French control. In the spring of 1948, the Russians blockaded all roads, railways, and any traffic from and to the West to get the Western powers out of Berlin. The Western Allies were in the process of overcoming the Russian Blockade by an airlift. This became known as the Berlin Airlift. At Wiesbaden's Camp Lindsey, Headquarters Command for forces in Europe, the word went out placing all American Air Force personnel on alert. Around-the-clock activities were underway at Wiesbaden Airfield. Aircraft would land, be refueled, loaded again with critical supplies, and then move into line for take-off back to Tempelhof.

During this time of international tension, George was trying to get all the documents processed and a clearance for Elizabeth. Things would be a little tight!

George had his hands full and had to visit Headquarters Command to confer with the commanding general. Larger aircraft, such as the four-engine C-54 were being flown into Wiesbaden and Rhein-Main from all over the world. The C-54s would take over the lion's share of hauling supplies into Berlin. Flying hours piled up, and aircraft maintenance was becoming critical. Burtonwood RAF Station became host for the Air Depot Wing in Lancashire, England. The base was reopened to the Americans to provide the facilities for major engine two-thousand-hour overhauls. Day and night, aircraft continued the airlift into Berlin. George Templeton's office was involved when one of the twin-engine C-47s crashed onto a mountaintop while the pilot was attempting to land at Tempelhof Airport in a pea-soup fog. All three Air Force members were killed, and the coal it was carrying was scattered all over the top of the mountain.

George received approval for his return to the United States, but the emergency situation with the Berlin Blockade meant that he would not be able to leave as scheduled. He would have to wait at least a few more months, until he could train a replacement to fill in for the extra work involved.

Arrangements were made for the hospital school to prepare the necessary transcripts that Elizabeth would need when she resumed her training in the United States. Elizabeth got all her things together and said her good-byes to her friends at the hospital. Elizabeth had one regret, however, and expressed it to Mr. Templeton. "In Heidelberg there is a head nurse, Sister Menckler. If it were not for her, I wouldn't be here. I could not leave the country without saying thank you and good-bye to her. There doesn't seem to be time if I am to go to Frankfurt and then to America."

"Look, Elizabeth," Mr. Templeton said," our planned time to leave and return to America has been delayed for awhile longer. On Saturday we will all leave for Frankfurt, which is an hour's drive. We will get you and Bernice settled in, and then I will have Max Gruber, the attaché's chauffeur, drive you down to Heidelberg. You will be there before suppertime. I will make reservations for you and Max to stay over and come back on Sunday evening. How would that be?"

"Oh, Mr. Templeton, you are too much really. What an angel!"

Elizabeth pulled George's head down and kissed him fully on his mouth. George flushed but felt a joy he thought had gone for good. It was like having his daughter Jennifer giving him a kiss when she was so joyful about something.

"Okay, it's settled then."

Saturday morning came, and so did Max Gruber, driving a big, long, American Packard limousine. They all got into the limousine—along with their luggage and all belongings—and were on the way to Frankfurt by nine o'clock in the morning. They arrived in Frankfurt and pulled up before an old-fashioned but elegant building. A servant answered the door, and another hurried to carry in the luggage and belongings. The dwelling was a townhouse, three stories high. It was a little narrow but spacious in depth and tastefully decorated. Elizabeth was very impressed.

"This is where you shall sleep," Bernice said, showing Elizabeth a very lovely room on the second floor toward the back of the house and facing the garden in the rear.

It had a beautiful view, and the window had richly appointed drapes. After sorting out her things and packing a small travel bag for her trip to Heidelberg, Elizabeth came downstairs and joined the Templetons, who were seated in the morning room ready to have tea, coffee, and pastries.

"Please come and join us," called Bernice.

She introduced Elizabeth to the two members of the household staff, saying, "If Miss Elizabeth requires anything or asks for anything, please see that she is accommodated."

Elizabeth had coffee and a cake. The coffee was rich and aromatic, and with a good heaping teaspoon of sugar and a spot of fresh cream it was delicious. Elizabeth also loved the cakes. They were rich in flavor and nice and sweet, not at all like the coffee and cake she got at the hospital.

"Where did you get these lovely cakes?" Elizabeth asked.

"We have our cook bake them here at the house," replied Bernice. "Do you like them? We have plenty on hand. Perhaps we should pack you a little snack for your trip to Heidelberg." Turning to the maid, Mrs. Templeton asked her to prepare some sandwiches and several pastries for Elizabeth's trip.

"Oh, Mrs. Templeton, you are too good to me. I would like to ask …" Elizabeth hesitated.

"Go on," prompted Mrs. Templeton.

"Nursing Sister Menckler, who I am going to see, has two loves in life. The first is nursing, and in that she is the best! And the other love is a good pastry or chocolate candy," she said with a chuckle.

"Well, by all means, let us make this trip worthwhile!"

Mrs. Templeton spoke again to the maid, who quickly went to the kitchen and returned with a round, covered box. It looked like a hatbox. Taking off the lid, Elizabeth saw at least a dozen assorted pastries. Then Mrs. Templeton handed Elizabeth a blue box that had the name Cadbury's Milk Chocolates.

Opening the small box, Elizabeth saw that it contained one pound of assorted chocolate candies. The smell of the sweet chocolate was almost intoxicating.

"Oh, Mrs. Templeton, I don't know what to say. Sister Menckler will either hold me for ransom for some more, or she will want me to take her along with me."

"You take those things with you, Elizabeth, and you tell Sister Menckler that you will stay in touch, and that should she visit the States, she would be welcome to visit. You tell her that," insisted Mrs. Templeton.

"Oh, I will, I will!" cried Elizabeth. "I just can't believe the way everything is happening."

CHAPTER 6

Max Gruber appeared at the door of the morning room and gave a polite cough.

"Shall we be going now, Fraulein Feldmann?"

"Yes, you'd better get started," Mr. Templeton said. Reaching for his notebook, he extracted a piece of paper and gave it to Elizabeth. "This is your reservation for the hotel in Heidelberg. It is already paid for and it will include any meals or anything you want while you are there. If you care to have friends dine there with you, and then feel free to do so. Oh, yes," he added after a quick look from Mrs. Templeton, "I want you to take this." He handed Elizabeth five hundred marks of the new German currency. It was worth about one hundred and fifty US dollars. "Consider that a beginning 'travel allowance'—we wouldn't want you to be without funds for anything you needed while you are away," he said.

Elizabeth didn't know what to say. She looked at Mr. Templeton and then over at Mrs. Templeton, who spotted the tears forming in Elizabeth's eyes.

"It's okay, dear," she said. "You go and enjoy your trip. We will see you back here on Sunday evening. Max will have you back before suppertime … We are planning a special meal in your honor."

Elizabeth was still choked up with gratitude and hugged both the Templetons before she got into the limousine. She felt somewhat giddy as they drove off.

Max reached out and turned on the radio. The Armed Forces Radio was playing the big band music that was so popular with the Germans and the American troops. One of the most popular numbers was being played, and Elizabeth sang along.

"Give me five minutes more, only five minutes more, only five minutes more in your arms. … lala la lala la …" she sang and hummed along.

As they cruised along the Autobahn, Elizabeth drifted off to sleep. The limousine was like a comfortable armchair on wheels. She felt the vehicle swerve and then heard the sound of the tires rumbling as the limousine crossed over the cobblestone roadway. Elizabeth realized that they were leaving the Autobahn and coming into Heidelberg. She was now wide awake and looked to see if she noticed any changes. After all, she had been away for a year! Max knew where he was going, and he pulled up at the entrance of the Kirchstadt Hotel. Elizabeth knew that this was the best hotel in Heidelberg and that it was reserved only for American officers and their families.

Elizabeth looked at the reservation paper Mr. Templeton had given her to present at the front desk. Max carried in her bag and waited beside her at the desk. A clerk came up to Elizabeth, and it seemed that he detected from her appearance and clothing that she was most likely a German citizen. In a somewhat arrogant manner he asked Elizabeth in German what she wanted here and informed her that the hotel was not for Germans. Elizabeth responded in English, rising to the challenge.

"I believe you are holding reservations for me," she said as she handed over the reservation slip to the snooty clerk.

The clerk frowned and read the slip of paper. It appeared he was about to give Elizabeth a hard time when another person glanced over the clerk's shoulder, interrupted, and spat a few quick words in German to the clerk that sent him scurrying. "You idiot," he said in German, "this is a reservation made by the US Attaché office. I don't care if it's for Hermann Goering! With that paper, he too would get a room!"

Elizabeth and Max could hardly keep from laughing out loud but just smiled politely. The accommodations were excellent, and Elizabeth made sure that Max was also taken care of. She then called the hospital to learn where Sister Menckler was.

"Sister is at her ward right now. She will be finished in about forty minutes," the telephone operator said.

"Would you kindly ring me through to the ward?" Elizabeth asked.

She heard the phone ring, ring, and ring, and then finally a slightly tired voice that Elizabeth knew so well answered. "Yes? Sister Menckler here."

"Sister Menckler, I understand you are looking for some new nurses to train."

"You are mistaken, *fraulein*. The one thing I don't need right now is more nurses to train," she replied in a haughty voice, clearly agitated.

"How can you say such a thing?" Elizabeth went on, trying to keep from laughing out loud. "Someone told me that you are an angel who helps the trainees to become super nurses in a very short time."

"Who is this? Your voice … your voice sounds familiar … I know you! Wait a minute—is this some prank by one of the first-year trainees? I will put you into cleaning bedpans if I find out."

Elizabeth couldn't hold it any longer and roared with laughter. "My dear Sister Menckler, calm down! It is Elizabeth Feldmann. I am here in Heidelberg!"

"Elizabeth, you rascal, you really had me going there! I was sure it was some of those new young trainees. I was prepared to find out who it was. But why are you here in Heidelberg? You have not completed your training in Wiesbaden. I can count the months, you know," Sister Menckler said.

"I came down to visit you. I know you will be finished with your shift in a short while, and I would like you to have your supper and maybe a glass or two of wine with me tonight. Okay?"

"My, my! We are coming up in the world. Hot meals, a glass or two of wine? Are you coming down with fever, or are you marrying a man with lots of money?"

"Neither, my dear friend, but I have something very important to tell you, and I also have something for you. A little present! A car—a very big American car—will come to the main entrance of the hospital to pick you up. Max Gruber is the name of the driver, and he will bring you to me at the hotel. I will have him there to pick you up at half six, okay?"

"Mein Gott, at my age I have to dress and go out for dinner," she complained, but Elizabeth knew it was only in jest. It was seldom that this dedicated and hard-working head nurse had the opportunity for the nice things in life. She was a person who gave twelve to fourteen hours a day to her profession.

Sister Menckler arrived with Max, who took her to Elizabeth. After much hugging and kissing, the two women went down to dine in the elegant facilities. They were both in awe as the waiter seated them at a table that Elizabeth had reserved. Apparently the word got around that this party was to be treated as VIPs. The menu was in English. Sister Menckler, after putting on her glasses and studying the menu, was none the wiser about what to order. First of all, her English was not that great, and second, she wasn't familiar with the fancy dishes.

"I will do the ordering," Elizabeth said. "How is your appetite?"

"I only had some soup and bread for lunch. I could eat something substantial."

Elizabeth ordered a bottle of Rhine wine and an appetizer of pickled herrings. Next, she ordered a medium rare T-bone steak for Sister Menckler and *Wiener Schnitzel* for herself with German home-fried potatoes and a salad for both of them. The appetizer and wine came. The waiter put out fresh, warm dinner rolls and a side dish for each of them with several pats of real butter. When the steak on its sizzling platter was placed before Sister Menckler, Elizabeth started to laugh at the expression on the sister's face.

"My God, you could feed half the nursing staff with this piece of meat," she said. "Are you sure this is not horse meat?"

"It is real meat from the beef cow ... enjoy it," Elizabeth said.

It took a while for the pair to finish their wonderful meal. Once Sister Menckler had cleaned everything off her plate and wiped the juices with her last piece of roll, Elizabeth ordered coffee and dessert. Settling back in her seat after enjoying the Crème de Mint frappe, Sister Menckler said, "I am ready to go to heaven! I always said, when I go, I want to go with a full stomach. It will never be as full as it is now." She groaned.

Elizabeth asked for the check and signed the dining chit that was offered her and gave the waiter a twenty-mark tip, which brought an appreciative smile to his face. The tip did not go unnoticed by Sister Menckler either.

Elizabeth took Sister Menckler to another part of the hotel that was arranged with tables and chairs for lounging and having cocktails. They ordered a Cointreau liqueur as an after-dinner drink, and Elizabeth told Sister Menckler the news about her training, the Templetons, and her going with them to Frankfurt and the pending trip to America.

"Mr. Templeton has promised me that I will continue my training in America. He has told me of a hospital called Johns Hopkins in Maryland, I think."

"Oh, I have heard of Johns Hopkins. It is a very fine hospital," Sister Menckler said.

Elizabeth answered many questions and realized that she was starting to repeat herself. She passed on Mrs. Templeton's invitation, should she ever visit the United States, to Sister Menckler.

"The Templetons must be very nice people, Elizabeth," observed Sister Menckler. "I am so happy for you on one hand, and on the other hand, if you eat every day like we ate tonight, you are going to be bigger than a Valkyrie warrior."

It was time to call it a night, but before it ended, Elizabeth presented Sister Menckler with the hatbox of pastries and chocolate candies. Sister Menckler was beside herself, and she hugged Elizabeth, wished her well, and implored her to write often and tell her how much weight she put on.

Max Gruber waited for Sister Menckler and gave her the VIP treatment on the ride back to the nurses' quarters. When they arrived, several of the nurses were outside having a smoke. Everyone wondered who was coming in the big American car. Max came around to open the back door, and out stepped Sister Menckler, hat box and all. The nurses stood with gasping mouths as Sister Menckler entered the doorway.

Passing the staring nurses, Sister Menckler said, "Nurses, close your mouth. You'll all get sore throats!"

CHAPTER 7

Elizabeth spent part of the morning in Heidelberg. She told Max that she wanted to ride the streetcar to Handschuhsheim where her parents used to live, look around, and then come straight back to leave for their return trip to Frankfurt. Elizabeth took her seat on the streetcar and watched the familiar scenes as the trolley made its way across the bridge and the Neckar River, heading out of Heidelberg toward her destination. Looking up, Elizabeth read the words *"Nicht auf den Boden Spucken."* She remembered how Pat Duran had asked what the words meant and how to pronounce them. She recalled that every time they rode the streetcar home, Pat would practice pronouncing the words.

Tears gathered in Elizabeth's eyes. She thought that she had got past feeling the loss of Pat, but just seeing those words printed there brought back the memories of Pat, especially that one night when they returned late on the last trolley. That was when Pat began to stay every night. They'd lived a fairy tale life. Their love was to be something special, something lasting. Elizabeth had to shake away those thoughts and found that the streetcar had arrived in the town platz. Everything looked the same, but Elizabeth knew that to her it would always be different.

She entered the hairdressers, and her aunt screamed when she saw Elizabeth. She knew all the news because Elizabeth had kept her informed. She wrote her a letter every week, even if it was only a few lines. *Tante* told Elizabeth that she had a letter from Hilda and Frank in America.

"Your mother and father are both well and enjoying the weather in San Francisco."

After a short while, Elizabeth said that she must return to Heidelberg and take her ride back to Frankfurt. She left with smiles and best wishes and a few wet eyes too.

Max Gruber was ready when Elizabeth returned, and they set off on the trip back. The drive back from Heidelberg was quick and uneventful. Since it was nearly past lunchtime, Max and Elizabeth stopped at a small German fish and chip shop. The lunch snack was not too filling, and Elizabeth treated herself to a small draft Lowenbrau. Max had the same, but with a little salad on the side and a bigger glass of beer.

"How far are we from the Templeton house?" Elizabeth asked.

"Thirty-three kilometers," answered Max.

Before she knew it, Max turned the car into the Templeton driveway to the house. Elizabeth thanked Max for driving her on this trip to Heidelberg.

"Think nothing of it, Fraulein. I enjoy getting out on the autobahn and seeing what 'Fritz' can do," replied Max.

"Fritz?" inquired Elizabeth.

"*Ja Wohl!* The *Amerikanish* Packard. I call it Fritz," was Max's response.

Elizabeth didn't need to ring the doorbell. The door opened as she approached the entrance, and the maid welcomed Elizabeth with a friendly smile and greeting.

"The Templetons are out just at the moment. They will not be away very long, and they said that if you come back while they are away, you should freshen up from your trip and they will see you at five o'clock."

"Thank you. I would like to rest a little," she said.

She had not really had a chance to see her bedroom properly or unpack all her things, so Elizabeth decided to set about doing that now while she had the free time. She noticed a door in her bedroom and, opening it, found her own private bathroom. No bathtub, but a modern shower. Elizabeth liked a shower. She had got used to taking a shower at the hospital nurses quarters. Elizabeth was very efficient and did things quickly. She sorted out her clothes, hung them up, put things away in drawers, and was done. The bathroom had an ample supply of large Turkish towels and other linen. She got the shower going and had the luxury of continuous hot water. *And what lovely soap,* she thought.

Elizabeth didn't have too many clothes other than her nurse's uniforms. What clothes she did have were several years old and were beginning to look a little worn. It was quite warm so Elizabeth decided to put on a blouse and skirt she had not worn for a year or two. The outfit looked a little young for Elizabeth, but cute and appropriate for warm weather. Elizabeth put on a pair of brown American loafer shoes her sister Hilda had passed on to her. Hilda had thought they looked like schoolgirl shoes and had not worn them very much. Elizabeth hadn't worn them at school as she always wore white shoes.

Elizabeth wakened after a short nap. She had heard the slamming of car doors and assumed that the Templetons had returned.

Elizabeth had asked for, and received, a recommended schedule of activities for Mrs. Templeton from the doctor. Checking over the list she saw that "rest" was an important part of the recovery process. The doctor also noted the importance of good nourishment, vitamins, and a little exercise (walking was recommended), and there was a footnote stating that she was to keep her spirits up and avoid becoming negative.

Coming downstairs in her summer outfit and loafers, Elizabeth knew she looked shorter and decidedly much younger. Both George and Bernice Templeton just stared at her as she came into the reception room. Alarmed, Elizabeth asked, "Is anything wrong?"

George Templeton was the first to recover, and he hastened to tell her that all was well. "I have to tell you this, Elizabeth. Coming into the room just now ... well, you look so much like our Jennifer, that for a brief moment we thought ..."

Looking from one face to the other, Elizabeth could see their expression, and she just reacted in her own compassionate way and went to hug Bernice Templeton.

Mrs. Templeton was a little choked up with emotion, but recovering, she said, "Elizabeth, aside from the fact that you do resemble our Jennifer, we both feel good to have you with us. I think you have that 'touch.'"

"Oh, Bernice, cut that out!" George turned to Elizabeth and said, "Bernice met this woman one time that claimed to be a healer and had that 'touch'. Cured her of her headache—or was it an ingrown toenail?"

Bernice waved him off with her hand and sniffed, "I'm sure you wouldn't know about such things. You men!"

Elizabeth didn't know whether to comment or not but then decided to anyway. "I believe what you say could be true. I knew an old woman from the small town where I used to live. Some people called her a witch, but I know that there were others that said she cured several little children of high fever, just by laying her hands on their heads. I can't remember her name, but I can recall her face. I saw her several times when I was a little girl, and I heard my mother and my aunt talk about some of the things she did to help people." Looking at the Templetons, Elizabeth said, "Yes, I think some people have something, maybe from God, that they can help others with. I believe this!"

"See! I have an ally with Elizabeth." Bernice snickered.

Elizabeth took this moment to take charge, as this was the reason for her being with the Templetons. "And, Mrs. Templeton, I think that you have been running around all day making yourself tired. I have my notes from the doctor, and he said that just because you feel good now doesn't mean that you do not need to rest."

With that, Elizabeth went to Mrs. Templeton and checked her pulse. It was a little fast, so she asked her to please sit down and relax.

"Can I bring you a cup of tea?" Elizabeth asked.

Bernice declined and urged Elizabeth to sit next to her on the couch.

"I am so happy that you are here with us and delighted that you are going back to America with us, too. While we are waiting for dinner, Rudy will serve some wine to sharpen our appetites. I want to tell you all about Four Winds, our home in Hereford."

CHAPTER 8

"Mr. Templeton's father used to visit a place nearby called Gunpowder Falls and the Pretty Boy Reservoir. He saw this piece of land nearby that turned out to be over thirty acres, and he bought it. Later on he had an architect design a house and had it built. Sidney B. Templeton, George's father, never lived in it. It took three years to build, and everything that went into the house was the best."

Going on, Bernice said, "It was to be a new family home, but George's mother expired from a severe attack of influenza and a failing heart."

"How old was she?" Elizabeth asked.

"She was sixty-two at the time, and Sidney Templeton lost interest with the house when his wife took ill, and he gave the house and property to George and me later on, as a belated wedding present. He was a very generous person."

"How did the house get its name?" Elizabeth asked.

"The house was given the nickname of 'Four Winds' by our Jennifer and James. Jennifer said that because the family was always traveling, each of us was like the wind, going here and going there." Cocking her head to one side in memory, Bernice continued, "Our James—he preferred to be called Jimmy—said if we are all like the wind, we should call it 'Four Winds.' The name stuck, and one day George had a large woodcarving made with the name 'Four Winds.' The children were delighted with the large wooden plaque, and it was attached to the entrance way."

Mr. Templeton added, "We made a visit to Asheville to see the Biltmore Estates, and we borrowed some ideas from there to use for 'Four Winds.' We planted a variety of trees along the way from the main road up to the house. We also added some fruit trees to the property, but I don't know much about gardening and trees, so we hired a caretaker and his wife—the Cranfields, Bill and Queenie. You will like them," he said. "Bill is an Englishman, from the old country, and his wife, Queenie, is Irish. We have an expression that when someone can grow things in the garden, we say they have a green thumb. Well, the Cranfields definitely have a green thumb and can grow anything, and Bill keeps the place in top shape."

"Don't forget about Queenie," interjected Bernice.

"Oh yes!" George said. "Queenie has the best herb garden you can imagine, and she can do almost anything with flowers and shrubs. As far as I am concerned she is an expert when it comes to wreaths and floral sprays."

Continuing on, Bernice said, somewhat sadly, "We also had some animal pens where Jimmy kept some chickens, ducks and pheasants. They were his as long as he looked after them. After the accident, we got rid of most of the animals, but Bill kept the chickens and pheasants. We are never short of fresh eggs. And speaking of food …" Getting up, Bernice indicated that dinner was ready. She saw the nod from Lisa, who retreated back to the kitchen.

The meat was brought into the dining room on a wooden trolley. The steaming vegetables were brought in and placed on the sideboard, while Rudolph, whom everyone called Rudy, carved slices from a standing beef rib roast. He served each one a plate with the meat, and then Lisa followed, serving parsley new potatoes and, because it was in season, fresh young asparagus with hollandaise sauce. A lovely au jus complemented the serving of beef. The table fare included hot rolls and butter, condiment dishes of horseradish, pickled beets, pickled chutney, and other items totally unfamiliar to Elizabeth.

Mr. Templeton viewed and sampled the bottle of wine Rudy brought. "Very nice, go ahead and serve the wine," he said.

The meal was excellent, and Elizabeth had to fight the temptation of having seconds. *Sister Menckler was right*, she thought. *If I eat like this all the time I will wind up looking like the* Hindenburg! Dessert was a dish of fruit, cake, custard and whipped cream—"trifle," Mrs. Templeton called it. It was delicious, and Elizabeth detected the flavor of sherry wine in it. Coffee followed.

Elizabeth was observing Mrs. Templeton and saw that she was looking a bit tired. Soon after they left the dining room, she went to Mrs. Templeton and suggested that she rest in the great easy chair and relax after her large dinner. It was more of a command than a question. Bernice started to object, but Elizabeth said, "Mrs. Templeton, you hired me to help you. If you are not going to take my advice then I am of little use to you."

Mrs. Templeton got the point and agreed. "You're right, Elizabeth. I'll do what you say, and I will go to bed early tonight too."

George Templeton was happy to see Elizabeth take charge as she did. He too thought that Bernice was overdoing things a bit, trying to make everything nice for Elizabeth.

CHAPTER 9

In the days and weeks that followed, Elizabeth got Bernice into a routine that was less tiring for her. She paid special attention to making sure everything Bernice ate was nourishing and appropriate. Elizabeth had asked George Templeton if it would be possible for him to acquire a large volume of cold pressed castor oil that would be used for special hot packs for Mrs. Templeton. A few days later he found a liter of the cold pressed castor oil. Elizabeth made special hot packs by saturating a flannel cloth with castor oil and heating it, and then applying it to Mrs. Templeton's back and in the front. Bernice pretended to complain that she felt like a hot jellied eel with that stuff on her, but it did feel good, and her skin that had previously been burned from radiation treatment quickly healed and took on a smooth, healthy appearance. Getting the oil off was difficult, but Elizabeth made a solution of baking soda in warm water and was able to wash it away. The result was very refreshing and comforting for Bernice.

And so the days passed into weeks until one evening George Templeton came home with the announcement that all the paperwork was completed. He handed Elizabeth a passport and visa to enter the United States.

"We will be leaving Rhine-Main airport near Frankfurt next Tuesday for a direct flight into Baltimore . I have all the flight reservations confirmed, and the movers will be here on Friday before we leave. We will be flying by commercial airline."

"If Mrs. Templeton directs me," Elizabeth said, "I'll do whatever packing is needed. It would not be good for her to overexert herself."

The Templetons both smiled at her, and then George said, "That's a good idea, but you don't need to worry too much about her overdoing. Since most of the furnishings were provided with the house, we don't have to pack or move much, just our personal items."

Bernice raised her finger to catch George's attention. "Darling," she said, "I hate to be a pain, but there is something that we have to see to."

George raised an eyebrow in answer.

"And, what is that?" he asked.

Bernice gestured to Elizabeth and said, "We need to get Elizabeth squared away in the clothing department. She is in desperate need of a new wardrobe."

George looked up to the ceiling and slapped his head, "Christ, I wasn't even thinking about clothing! You're right. I can get her into the big Frankfurt military Post Exchange with you, Bernice. What we can't get in the PX we'll shop for downtown in Frankfurt. I'll have to stop by the American Express and cash a check for some German Marks, so we'll have plenty of cash."

"Splendid, darling, I like the way you work things out so quickly," she answered sweetly.

George beamed.

The following day the Templetons spirited Elizabeth away to the land of the big Post Exchange. Having diplomatic clout, it was no problem bringing Elizabeth in with them. Bernice winked at Elizabeth when she told the clerk that she wanted a lot of things for her daughter, who had just finished school. They spent three hours shopping in the PX. Max next took them to a big department store district in Frankfurt's up and coming shopping area. In one exclusive salon, some of the clothes were modeled for Elizabeth and Bernice to see.

George yawned and shifted his feet. It appeared that shopping was a tiring task for him, though for the women it seemed to be therapeutic, as they didn't get tired.

"George, honey," Bernice suggested, "on the first floor is a cocktail lounge and coffee bar. Why don't you go down, have a drink or a coffee, and we'll join you as soon as we're through here.?"

"I'll do just that. Good idea!" And saying that, he left the women.

"Oh, Mrs. Templeton," Elizabeth cried in shock. "These clothes are so expensive, and you and Mr. Templeton have done so much for me already. I could never afford this, never in a hundred years."

"Sweetheart, let me tell you something, and listen well," Bernice said. "It is just as important for you to be properly dressed and have a decent wardrobe of clothing as it is for us. If you do not look good, people will think that we are unkind to you and that we are slave drivers. Besides," she sniffed, "we enjoy having you look finely dressed. Can't you see that it is a lot of fun for George and me to do this?"

Elizabeth's tears started coming again, and Bernice shook her head, but she didn't look truly upset.

"Elizabeth, what am I going to do with you? Please, be happy. Enjoy the shopping, the clothes. Share the joy of receiving while George and I enjoy the giving!"

"Mrs. Templeton," Elizabeth said with teary eyes, "you both will have a free ticket to heaven—for sure! But surely I have enough things? We will need a truck to carry all these things," she said, worried that Mrs. Templeton might have too much to carry.

"Nonsense. The clerk will send everything downstairs, and when we are ready, Max will take them and put them in the car."

The shopping now completed, the two women joined George Templeton at the coffee bar. Bernice ordered a coffee and a brandy for both Elizabeth and herself. It was nearly four o'clock. The day had flown by so quickly. The women, now sitting back having a break, were feeling tired. Max loaded up the car trunk, and the extras went into the back of the car with Bernice and Elizabeth while George rode up front with Max.

Max, never one for many words, asked, "Is there anything left for people to buy in the store?"

George chuckled, and they headed back to the house. Elizabeth's new wardrobe took every bit of two large suitcases. The extras were packed in an overnight bag.

When it came time to leave, all of the household staff lined up to say good-bye to the Templetons and Elizabeth. Mr. Templeton gave them each an envelope and thanked them for all their good service and honesty. None of the German help looked into their envelopes until after the Templetons left. Lisa gasped at finding one thousand German Marks. All the other staff found that they had the same amount.

When they arrived at the Rhine Main airport, Max and George handled the luggage until the airport baggage handlers took over. It was time for Max to depart. George gave him a hug, an envelope, and said, "Max, take good care of Fritz. I hope that you will serve the next American diplomat as well as you have served me."

Max said his *Auf Wiedersehen*. Examining his envelope, Max found the sum of two thousand German marks.

Checking in at the First Class counter at the Rhine-Main Airport, Elizabeth, who had never flown in an airplane, learned that they would be going on a Pan American Constellation aircraft. It was a large four-engine plane, the latest big-propeller aircraft for transatlantic flights.

Elizabeth asked Bernice if she had flown very much, and Bernice said, "Sure, nothing to it! But to be honest, these transatlantic flights take a long time. George told me recently that there are big jet aircraft that are being proposed for future air travel, probably a few years in the future."

George explained when Elizabeth looked at him quizzically. "Boeing is working on plans for a new jet airliner that will make future travel faster. Aircraft like that will fly at twice the speed of propeller driven planes, I venture."

Boarding for the flight to America was announced. First Class passengers were permitted to enter and be seated. Next came anyone with children or disabilities. Last, came the remaining passengers. Elizabeth and Bernice sat next to each other while George occupied the seat across the aisle. When all the passengers were aboard and the emergency information and seat belts were demonstrated, the aircraft departed.

The seat next to George was vacant, so he could really stretch out. Once they were airborne and reached cruising altitude, the flight attendant served cocktails. Bernice opted for a Bloody Mary but settled for wine, same as Elizabeth, when she saw Elizabeth frowning at her. For George it was a traditional Scotch and splash of soda water.

The flight was a little bumpy until the aircraft reached its high cruising altitude. Elizabeth, who had been busy insuring that Mrs. Templeton was comfortable, realized that she was airborne and flying very fast through the air. She was not frightened, and nor did she feel sick. The flight was occasionally bumpy but generally was comfortable indeed. A voice over the intercom announced that the aircraft was flying at an altitude of twenty-three thousand feet and at a speed of 325 knots. After the novelty of the first two hours and a lovely meal, they all settled down and soon dozed off.

The aircraft landed at Shannon Airport in Ireland to top up on fuel before crossing the Atlantic. Within thirty minutes the aircraft was on its way again.

The wheels gave a slight screech as the aircraft touched down at Friendship Airport in Baltimore. It was several minutes more until it could taxi to its berth. After exiting the aircraft and approaching the entranceway to the reception area, they spotted an official holding a little sign that said "Templeton".

"I am George Templeton," he said, advising the official.

"Please come with me," the official said, leading the Templetons and Elizabeth through a side door and straight through to the immigration booth.

"Passports, please, and your visa also, miss," he said.

After examining all their documents, the immigration clerk stamped the passports, gave special instructions to Elizabeth, and said, "Welcome home, Mr. and Mrs. Templeton."

"Thank you," replied George. Still escorted, they entered the baggage area where a porter gathered up all their luggage, which was immediately cleared by customs. They departed the baggage area, which was part of the international flight arrivals and restricted to visitors. Once outside the doors, a high-pitched British voice caught George's attention.

CHAPTER 10

Waving furiously at them was Bill Cranfield. Bill hugged the Templetons, and it was plain to see his look of concern for Bernice.

"Bill," Bernice said, "this is Elizabeth."

"Well, I'll be," was all Bill could say.

The Templetons could see Bill, too, had instantly seen the resemblance between Elizabeth and their daughter Jennifer. Bill recovered his composure and said to Elizabeth with a naughty wink, "And she's a smasher, too!"

Bernice tapped Elizabeth on the shoulder and said with a smile, "It's a compliment. He thinks you are good looking."

They had a porter bring out all the luggage on a big rolling trailer, and George asked Bill if they were going to be able to get everything on board.

"Fear not, guv'nor," he replied, and he led the group to a large Cadillac sedan.

Just then the Four Winds' old Ford station wagon pulled up behind them with Chester Somers behind the wheel.

After he'd greeted everyone, they loaded the luggage into the station wagon, and Chester drove off. Bill got everyone situated in the Caddy, and they set off for Four Winds.

The estate had a caretaker's chalet next to the five-car garage. The estate boasted its own electrical generating system, in case of electrical failure and outages. While the Templetons were not extravagant, they purchased quality, and what they had was the best. The main house at Four Winds had three levels, not including the basement. The ground floor entry was by way of a grand entranceway. Five steps led to the entry and foyer. The oval-shaped foyer displayed a curved stairway. The floor was ivory and gray Italian marble that continued up the stairway.

On the ground floor was a large library/reading room with a desk. The other rooms were also spacious, including a living room with a miniature grand piano, a great sized family room, and a dining room with a table that could seat at least ten people. The kitchen was equipped to handle a variety of cooking requirements, and a closed-in patio provided a pleasant area to enjoy fresh air without worrying about insects. There was a "powder room" and a "gents room" on the first level. The house had five bedrooms on the second level, each with its own bathroom. There were also three guest suites as well as servant quarters on the top level.

The house was custom built and well taken care of. Chester and Martha Somers handled the household chores. Their daughter Penny also helped with the linens, laundry, and house cleaning. The entire Four Winds staff loved the Templetons, who treated them like family and paid them very well. They all looked after the estate as if it were their own.

The Christmas before the children's accident all four of the Templetons played host to their employees. They cooked for them and served them in the great dining room, using the best china. They finished up on Christmas Eve with presents for all and singing of carols.

"The Templetons are one of a kind," Bill Cranfield often remarked. "You don't find folks the likes of them these days. Fancy me telling them at the club that the guv'nor and his family served the help like we was real gentry!" Bill hadn't lost his British ways, even though he had been in America for over twenty years.

If old Bill missed anything about England, it was his local pub. The village club in Maryland had a bar that was the closest thing to an English pub he'd found. Bill was responsible for getting a dartboard put up, and before long, dart teams and activities had picked up. Old Bill was resourceful and purposeful. He was easily accepted and respected by the local community, and he was also a source of information on what was going on "up at the Winds." Old Bill could spin a yarn or two and would have the locals laughing for hours.

Bill's wife, Queenie, was somewhat laid back and always chastising Bill for his "sinful ways." Queenie was of Irish–Roman Catholic upbringing. She helped with chores at the house and in the summer helped with the garden and harvesting. Queenie was the real "green thumb"; little Jimmy used to brag. Jimmy had been impressed with Queenie's knowledge of plants and flowers. She grew an herb garden and even gave Martha Somers a tip or two on the use of herbs for cooking and baking. Queenie also was an expert at making wreaths and sprays for the holidays.

George asked her to make several Christmas wreaths for the house and a spray or two for inside. Queenie made two large wreaths for the front door and also a special wreath for over the fireplace. This wreath had sprigs of scented herbs entwined in them and so gave off a lovely aroma. George insisted on paying Queenie for her labors, but she set the "guv'nor" straight.

"It is a present," she said, "and you will have the good grace to accept it as such!"

George backed off—having met his match—and thanked Queenie. In the spring, however, as an Easter present, the Templetons presented Bill and Queenie with first-class round-trip tickets to England on British Airways so they could visit family and old friends. Bill and Queenie had always talked about going back one day for a visit, but it seemed they never had enough money saved or something came up. Bernice said she thought that making travel arrangements was just not the Cranfields' thing and that if they were ever going to go, and then George would have to do something—so he did.

Getting the Cranfields ready for their trip was worse than getting a couple of newlyweds launched. Bill and Queenie gave everyone at least three courses of instructions on everything.

"Don't forget to water. Oh yeah, make sure the hens have feed and enough water," Bill said several times.

Everyone at Four Winds had to assure Bill and Queenie that they would be able to manage for the two weeks that they would be away. Queenie, usually not one to show much emotion, started to cry.

"Queenie," Bernice Templeton inquired, "you are coming back in two weeks aren't you?"

"Aye, I am that!" sobbed Queenie.

"Then why are you crying?" asked Bernice.

"Ooh, I don't like the idea of leaving," sniffed Queenie.

Jimmy chirped in and threatened to tell everyone how Queenie had chickened out of taking a vacation.

That got Queenie's back up, and she bristled at Jimmy, saying, "You just wait till I get back, Little James. I'll bring one of 'em Irish paddles and warm your backside!"

That broke the ice, and everyone laughed and finally got them on their way.

Now two years later, the caretakers and staff had received the news that the Templetons were coming home. They also knew of Mrs. Templeton's delicate condition and had been told that the Templetons were bringing along a young, fledgling nurse whom they met in Germany and who would be a resident at Four Winds. That news sent the household staff scurrying into a major household spring cleaning to make everything was in tip-top condition for the Templetons' return.

"Here they come," yelled Penny from upstairs. "I can see the Ford wagon coming up the road, but I don't see the other car yet."

Chester Somers pulled up to the front door, and Penny was there in a flash. "Dad, where are they?" she asked.

"They're coming," he assured her. "I left straight away so I could get the luggage here first. Where's your ma?" he asked.

"I'm right here," Martha said, coming down the steps to help with the luggage.

"Martha, wait till you see this Elizabeth. Just you wait," he chuckled.

"Tell us, Dad," begged Penny. "Come on—tell us what's she like. Is she pretty, does she have a face like a horse, or what?"

"God, you womenfolk!" complained Chester. "Like I said, you just wait. You'll get a pleasant surprise."

"Chester, old son," croaked Queenie, coming around to the front of the house, "what is all this wait and see business? Has the girl two heads or what?"

"Ah, come on, Queenie, just wait. I'm telling you I was surprised, and so will you be," responded Chester.

Everyone grabbed luggage from the station wagon and brought it into the house.

"I don't know which ones belong to anyone," wailed Penny.

"Just line them up there, and we'll sort things out after they get here," Chester said.

A horn blared a few times, and Queenie, who had the sharpest ears, recognized the sound. *That will be the Caddy honking*, she said.

And sure enough the car wound its way up to the front door. Everyone ran outside to greet the Templetons and to "inspect" Elizabeth with great curiosity. Queenie was the first to reach Bernice, grabbing hold of her and hugging the breath out of her. Tough old Queenie was shedding tears worse than a waterfall.

"It's so good to see you," sobbed Queenie. "I just can't help it, Mum. It's so good to have you back home again."

"Oh, Queenie, you are a right softie," Bernice said with a smile. "You would think we were away for a lifetime instead of two years."

George and Bernice were swamped with hugs and slaps on the back from the others while Elizabeth got out of the car.

"*God's truth!*" Queenie's commanding yell stopped everyone in his tracks when she first saw Elizabeth's face.

Although Elizabeth was now twenty-six years old, she had a small frame and slight build that gave her the appearance of a much younger girl, and she looked close to how the fifteen-year-old Jennifer had been. It took a moment or two before everyone caught their breath and rushed to welcome Elizabeth. By now Elizabeth was neither surprised nor offended by the reactions caused by her resemblance to the Templetons' deceased daughter, Jennifer.

It took a while to move ten feet from the car to inside the front door.

"Folks," cried George, "let's get into the house and we will have plenty of time to answer your questions." That finally got everyone moving.

It was an hour more before all the luggage was sorted out and brought to the rooms. Queenie went into the kitchen to help Martha rustle up some tea, coffee, and cakes for a quick refreshment. Chester and Penny helped with putting things away.

Penny took charge of Elizabeth, showing Elizabeth her room and explaining the facilities. Penny liked Elizabeth right away, and although she was quite a few years younger than Elizabeth, she thought they might become close friends. Elizabeth was quick to read the look of friendship in young Penny's eyes, and she reached out to give Penny's hand a little squeeze.

Elizabeth was in awe of the lovely home and the exquisite decor and furnishings. *Mrs. Templeton did not exaggerate,* she thought. Elizabeth's room had a big, four-poster bed. The covers matched the drapes and coordinated decor of the room. The wallpaper was of a gold background design with a contrasting pattern. The room had a sideboard with drawers, and an elegant mirror graced the top of the unit. The closet door opened into a space for clothes to hang on three sides of the small room. It also had shoe racks and shelves for other items. The other door led to her big private bathroom. The decor and features were definitely female oriented.

She wondered if it had been Jennifer's room.

The bathroom had a big sink and a countertop that included a lighted, framed mirror for makeup. There was a bathtub as well as a separate glass-enclosed shower stall. The bathroom featured light pink tile. The bathroom was bigger than the bedroom Elizabeth had in Heidelberg.

Elizabeth found to her surprise that the house had an intercom system, and she heard Bernice talking to her.

"Elizabeth, in order to talk to me you have to switch the 'talk switch' to speak," she said.

"Oh yes, I found it." Elizabeth laughed. "There are so many new things to get used to."

"That's okay, dear, it will take some time to know what's what," Bernice said. "We are going to have some cocktails in a few minutes, if you would like to join us. Then we are going to eat out on the back patio. Martha and Queenie have been busy preparing a special treat for us. I hope you're hungry."

"I'll be down in just a few moments as long as I don't get lost in this big house."

The rest of the week went by in a flash. There were many things to do to get settled in. George was busy arranging little but necessary things. He took Elizabeth down to the Motor Vehicle Bureau to get her application for a driver's license and a learners permit. Next, he contacted a local driving school to set up a full driving course for Elizabeth.

"You will need to be able to drive back and forth to school and the hospital from home," George told Elizabeth. "Baltimore is really not a safe place for a young lady at night, alone. I want you to be able to drive safely to wherever you are going.

Elizabeth was capable of quickly reading and digesting the Maryland driver's manual, which covered all the road symbols, signs, and requirements. At first, though, it was a little confusing, since of course in America, the road signs had English words like "entrance" and "exit," not *Eingang* or *Ausgang*.

Elizabeth soon passed her written test for road signs and rules and was ready to take to the road with her driving lessons. George told her, "You are going to need a car to drive for your lessons, and later on to drive back and forth to the hospital."

He ordered that the five-year-old Ford Fairlane be fully serviced inside and out for her to use. Elizabeth felt like she was driving a boat, not being used to big cars. She soon got over the feeling that she was going to bump into everything. One thing that was in Elizabeth's favor was that she was a quick learner and very well coordinated. She was also a good student, and the driving instructor commented to George that she was doing exceptionally well.

At the supper table one evening, George and Bernice told Elizabeth that they were going to spend the coming weekend in Washington DC this coming weekend, and they asked if she would like to go with them.

"We plan to go Friday evening and eat out," Bernice said. "We have reservations at the hotel for Friday and Saturday night, and we will come back home Sunday evening."

"Oh, that would be very nice!" Elizabeth said.

Browsing through the library downstairs later, Elizabeth found a book on the District of Columbia that contained information and pictures of most of the historic places within the district. By the time Friday came, Elizabeth knew the names of most of the famous monuments and buildings and their rough locations. George and Bernice never ceased to be amazed at how quickly Elizabeth adapted to things and how quickly she learned. It was another similarity between their Jennifer and Elizabeth.

Friday night they all checked into a very nice hotel in downtown Washington. The hotel, as always, was "top drawer," as George liked to say. After dropping off their overnight bags and freshening up, they left the hotel. George had called for a taxi to take them to a little Spanish restaurant in the northern part of the district.

"El Bordegon restaurant over on R street," he told the driver. Ten minutes later the taxi pulled up in front of the restaurant.

"What an interesting name for a restaurant. Does the name mean anything?" Elizabeth asked.

"Yes, the name El Bordegon is Spanish for 'wine cellar.' They were greeted at the entrance by the owner.

"I have not seen you for such a long time," Antonio Rivera said.

"Yes, we have been out of the country for two years," George replied. "I hope you have a nice table for us tonight."

"But of course!" replied Antonio, leading them down the stairs to the floor below.

The main dining room was not very large, but it had tables scattered around. In the right side corner, Elizabeth saw a small raised wooden platform, and she asked, "Is that for a band and entertainment? If it is, it is very small."

Antonio responded, "Not a band. Do you know flamenco dancing?"

"Truthfully, I have never seen it," she replied.

"You will tonight, honey," Bernice said. "And the food here is very good too. It might be best if George ordered for all of us."

"Oh, yes! I wouldn't know what to ask for."

George told their waiter, whose name was Paco, "First, we shall all have the *caldo gallego*, and then we shall have a paella ala Valenciana for the three of us. Oh, yes, and a bottle of your house light red wine … I can't remember the name."

"Yes, of course," replied Paco. "You mean the traditional *porron of wine*." A *porron* was a flask filled with wine that Antonio usually poured for each guest. Paco scurried off to place their order.

"We have plenty of time to enjoy this meal so do not rush your eating," George said.

A platter of tapas, a variety of bite-sized delicacies, was placed before them. Later the soup came—steaming hot—and Paco added a dash of ground pepper. It was delicious. Elizabeth fell in love with the bread sticks.

"Don't eat too many of those," cautioned Bernice, "or you won't be able to eat the main course, when it comes."

Paco brought a decanter of wine and poured each a glass, setting the decanter in an ice bucket. The paella arrived uncovered and took Elizabeth's breath away. Steaming hot from the oven, the top was covered with shrimp, mussels, bits of Spanish sausage, and a host of other tasty morsels. Paco served them all generous portions—making sure that everyone got some of all the ingredients—including the *langosta*, which had been added as an extra special treat.

Finally, Elizabeth said, "I surrender! It is so good, but I cannot eat any more."

They all laughed and sat back while their table was cleared and coffee was served. Antonio came to the table and said, "*Con su permisso*—sorry, with your permission—I have a special dessert for you."

With that, he snapped his fingers, and Paco brought out three little dishes that each contained a small *flan de caramelo*—a vanilla-flavored custard with a caramel sauce. Antonio poured warm liqueur over each flan and lit a match to set fire to the dessert. It was served, still flaming, to all three of them. The flame quickly died away, and they all tucked into the custard-like flan.

"Yummm, this is good," Elizabeth said.

Antonio beamed and moved off. An after-dinner liqueur followed, and then it was time for the show. A man with his guitar stepped onto the stage and gave a barrage of sound with his guitar strings to gather the attention of the audience. A flamenco dancer then entered the little stage. She wore a long red Spanish dress with large white polka dots with a black sash running over her shoulder to her left side. Her hair was piled high up in the traditional Spanish manner. The guitarist played, and the dancer stamped and danced while clapping her castanets to the rhythm of the music. The patrons joined in with clapping and shouting. The show lasted thirty minutes, and then it was time to leave. George paid the check, leaving, as always, a generous tip. A taxi had been called and was waiting for them as they left the restaurant.

The following day after breakfast with the Templetons, Elizabeth was left to her own devices and decided to look around. After viewing the Capitol and seeing the outside of the White House, she continued on up Pennsylvania Avenue to Foggy Bottom. Georgetown was a long way beyond, but Elizabeth decided to walk there. Strolling along, she noticed such a variety of restaurants and eating places. *Americans have a love affair with food,* she thought. *They eat so much!*

Thinking of food, she suddenly realized that she was getting a little hungry, but she didn't want to eat a big meal—*maybe a cup of tea or coffee and a cake,* she thought.

"Tell your future, my dear!" a voice called out to Elizabeth.

Turning, she saw an old gypsy woman sitting outside a little teahouse. Wanting to be considerate and courteous, Elizabeth she stopped to listen to the old gypsy woman.

"Come inside and let Madame Zelma tell your future," she repeated. Elizabeth hesitated.

"I will charge you only five dollars, she said.

Elizabeth smiled. *Why not?* she thought. *It might be fun!*

They sat down in the corner that Elizabeth could tell was reserved for Madame Zelma. Taking up a worn deck of tarot cards, the gypsy handed the deck to Elizabeth to shuffle. Next, she asked Elizabeth to cut the cards into three piles. Taking the first pile, Madame Zelma put cards down, face up, but Elizabeth noticed that she hardly even looked at the cards. Instead she was looking at the wall straight ahead and to Elizabeth's left side.

"I see a large body of water. I see that you came from across the sea," she said.

Elizabeth thought that wouldn't be too hard to figure out, because of her accent.

"I see a small town or city, very pretty with a river running through it. A bridge goes across the river and there is some mountains off to one side." After hesitating briefly, she continued, "On top of the mountain, I see something like an old castle."

Now, this description startled Elizabeth. It was a concise description of Heidelberg. Elizabeth acknowledged that this was near where she used to live. Going on, the gypsy said she saw Elizabeth traveling on a streetcar many times. And she saw her working with some kind of smelly solutions in a small shop. Elizabeth thought of her aunt's hairdresser salon. The gypsy revealed many small bits of information that Elizabeth had to admit were fairly accurate.

Moving on, the gypsy woman said, "I see some happiness many years before and then a great sorrow."

Elizabeth only nodded her head.

"Someone who loves you," Madame Zelma said. "He is gone for now, but you will meet again. He is searching for you, even now."

Elizabeth had enough and said, "No, that is not possible! I really don't want to hear any more of this." She began to gather up her things to go.

"Please! Let me go on," the gypsy woman said. "I see you living in a great house with servants. Are you rich? And I'm only charging you five dollars!"

Elizabeth reached into her purse, took out a ten-dollar bill, and gave it to Madame Zelma.

"It is only five," Madame Zelma said.

"That's alright," Elizabeth said. "I have to be going now." She rose to leave.

"Hold on, my dear," the old gypsy woman said. She reached into an old leather bag at her side and appeared to search for something. After a moment, she brought out a small, almost round stone that looked like it was a piece of a gemstone.

"I want to give you this jewel," she said. "It has special powers, and it will always bring you good luck and good fortune. Carry it with you always, for it is like a beacon."

Elizabeth didn't believe the old gypsy but, not wanting to offend her, she slipped the stone in her purse anyway. "Thank you," she said and started to leave.

"Remember," the gypsy called after her, "keep it with you always."

Elizabeth forgot about the stone, which settled in the bottom of her purse. Every time she started cleaning and tidying her purse, she came upon the crystal stone and remembered what the gypsy said about keeping it with her always. *What the heck*, she thought, and threw it back in the purse again.

CHAPTER 11

Three years passed by as Pat was kept in a sleeping state of grace. When he finally woke, the two men in white were at hand.

"Pat looks well," Ames said to Brewster.

Aware that he was very rested and refreshed, Pat found that when he concentrated, the more he remembered. His recall was crisp, accurate, and intense. Pat sensed that he had been asleep for some time, and he asked, "How long have I been asleep?"

"In earth terms, three years", replied Brewster, "but here it is but a short time."

Pat's thoughts concentrated on his concerns for Lily. *She was waiting for me and I let her down.* Pat recalled that Brewster had said they were only to have two arrivals and not three. He then asked Brewster if, as he suspected, his accident was not supposed to have happened, what could be done about it.

"There is a divine plan on the drawing board, so to speak," Brewster said, "but for the time being we will try to teach you a few things, and then when it is possible, all will be revealed to you."

"What happened to Westy and Dick?"

"If you're up to a visit, I will take you to see Dick Levans and, later, to see Westy Cragmore," Brewster said, taking Pat by the hand. Pat felt a little rush of air and then found himself at a patio with tables, chairs, and children gathered around watching someone working on something. As they approached, Pat realized that it was Dick Levans.

Dick looked up and, seeing Pat, sprang to his feet and rushed to hug him. "I see you're finally up and about! I came to see you a few times but you were still resting."

"What do you do here?" Pat asked.

"I've been busy creating some toys for some of the youngsters to play with," Dick said. "You sound like you got your batteries recharged. I'm sorry you had the accident with us, Pat. I understand that you weren't supposed to cash in your chips. I think something is going to be done."

"I was surprised that you didn't bail out and save yourself Dick?" Pat asked.

"I tried to bring the nose of the plane up and set it down, but it was too late."

Brewster interrupted, saying, "Would you like me to take you to see Westy now?"

It was Pat's cue to exit, which they did. Once again, the trip was instantaneous—a rush of air, and there they were. Upon seeing Pat, Westy rushed up to him and was immediately very apologetic that he'd caused the accident that took both Levans' and Pat's lives.

"It was all my fault. I knew I wasn't one hundred percent, but I was an old fool to think I could continue as if I were a young man. Please forgive me," he begged Pat.

Feeling sorry for Westy, Pat asked, "Was the accident bad for you, Westy?"

"I don't honestly know," he replied. "When I had that second heart attack, I went out like a spent light bulb. Next thing I remember is waking up on a cot with some tall fellow in white, leaning over me and asking how I felt. I knew right then and there I'd had it! Only, to be truthful, I was expecting I would be going somewhere toward the hot basement. I have had a lot to think about since I've been here, and some of it was good and some of it was bad. The hell of it—um, bad choice of words there—is, I can't do anything about those bad aspects of my life. I understand now that even the little things were important, and I could have done something about it, but didn't."

"What are you doing now?" Pat asked, to get Westy off his guilt trip.

"I have been talking with some master advisors about how I can help my two kids. Did you know I was married and had a family?" Not waiting for an answer, Westy continued, "I have two kids ... Well, they aren't kids anymore. My son Shawn is now eighteen years old, and he needs my help. Lisa, my daughter is sixteen years old. She is at a vulnerable age and is proving too much for her mother to handle. I want to reach them. Reach their minds if I can. The master advisors are teaching me how to project my thoughts in order to influence my kids, but everything has to be cleared by higher up." He looked upward.

"Gee," Pat said, "I thought that once you were a goner, you were gone for good." A thought sprang into Pat's head: *Maybe, just maybe.*

Brewster cleared his throat, and suddenly he was beside Pat.

"You sure do that thing of yours fast," observed Pat. "I'm glad you're here. I have a few questions to ask you."

"I know," replied Brewster. "In your case, it is a little different. Let me explain."

He grasped Pat's hand, and then they suddenly were in a round, domed building of white marble. He led Pat inside the building, where they saw men and women in little cubicles. Brewster said, "I would like you to meet someone, who was from India," and pointed to a young boy who looked about fifteen years old. "His name is Sunghi."

"What does he do here?" Pat asked. "What do these people do here?"

"This is called the Hall of Choice or opportunity, if you prefer. Here you can learn about the choices our brothers and sisters on the earth plane have in their journey through life. They can go left, or they can go right, they can go up, or they can go down, they can do something, or say something, or not. Every choice—whatever it is—has a direct impact on the course of one's direction through the maze we call life," explained Brewster.

"I think I understand," said Pat.

"I'm sure you do," Brewster replied. "Here, your mind is not cluttered with all the trials and tribulations one experiences on earth. We can see things more clearly and we can recognize what is important and what is not. There is one other important ingredient here. This building has several 'Regents' who have the authority to approve or disapprove influence—guidance, if you will—that can be used to nudge some people on earth in the right direction. Even those who are undeserving get a chance of two or more. We never give up on anyone.

Pat wanted to ask the question most on his mind. Brewster seemed to know instantly what that was and brought Pat to Sunghi.

Brewster said, switching his language to the Indian dialect most familiar to Sunghi, telling him that Pat had many questions as a new arrival.

Sunghi answered in English. "I received the thought that you were bringing this young man to see me."

"Don't let the young age fool you," said Brewster. "Sunghi may be young in earth years, but he is as wise as an old sage!"

Sunghi modestly bowed his head and said, "I have a lot of help!" He looked above briefly and then looked at Pat. "You want to ask me some questions?"

Without waiting for an answer he said, "I will show you a picture." He had Pat sit down and placed a Satin-like cloth over his head and asked him to relax. "What you see will move quickly, but you will recognize and understand its full impact, even later on", Sunghi advised.

Pat got a flash of Lily in a nurse's uniform, studying in a hospital. He saw her working in a chemistry lab, doing hair for nurses, and crying at night. Pat felt the sorrow also and wanted to reach out and comfort her.

Next he saw her in another place. He saw her with people, staying in the same house as they did and then traveling across the ocean to America. While watching some of the sequences, Pat experienced several spurts of emotion that he felt came from Lily. In a sequence when she was on the trolley, he felt a heart-wrenching pang and a longing to comfort her.

He saw that Lily looked well, but he also saw that she did not reflect an aura of happiness deep inside. The vision ended. Some tears streamed down Pats cheeks.

Sunghi pretended not to notice, and advised him, "Your reaction is quite normal, especially when two people really care for each other as you two did. You have felt her emotion, and that is good for the future."

Pat was a little confused at his remarks.

"What I mean to say," he went on, "is that if you can have that emotional response, and then it means that you can reasonably expect to send thoughts and feelings the other way. But that would only be permitted under certain situations. Yours, for example."

Pat was startled and perplexed. "How? What do you mean?"

"It is not my place to advise you on these matters. Brewster will guide you properly. Meanwhile, I invite you to visit me again, before you embark on another life experience."

Pat had noticed several animals that appeared to belong to some of the people in the room, some of which, on earth, were considered dangerous. He asked about them.

"Those few animals laying down next to those persons are their pets."

"You see, here we have no need for food, meat, water or any of the things that are needed on earth. All that substance we call 'material things.' After all, we are no longer material things but rather spiritual beings. Understand? So we have no need for food. Neither do these animals need to hunt for prey to eat. Their bellies are always full of manna, spiritual sustenance, so they are content and want to be close to their master."

The Keeper

"I have some questions for you, Brewster," Pat said later.

"I know, I know," Brewster said. "I wish that Sunghi hadn't said as much as he did because you are never going to give me any peace now!"

Brewster told Pat to hold onto his hand, and they left for another place where not too many visitors were permitted to go, he was told. Before Pat could say anything, he felt a slight rush of air, and suddenly they were in a beautiful garden with several pathways leading off in many directions. In the center was a small gazebo, and an elderly man who had been sitting there stood up and beckoned to them to come to him. Brewster greeted the elder and said how beautiful all the flowers were.

"It is always so refreshing to visit here," Brewster said.

"Thank you, Brewster." Turning to Pat, he said, "And greetings to you, young man."

He reached out to shake Pat's hand, and when their hands touched, Pat felt a surge of pleasant warmth and an extreme feeling of well-being envelope his whole body.

"I have been keenly interested in your situation and the developments since your arrival here," said the elderly gentleman.

Pat was forming the question in his mind. *I wonder who this man is?*

"Brewster, I believe that we have not been properly introduced," he said, apparently reading Pat's thoughts.

"I'm sorry, Your Eminence. I am always at a loss of words for the first few moments when I visit here," Brewster said with a somewhat embarrassed expression.

"That is quite a natural occurrence, so don't feel bad about it." Turning to Pat, he said, "I am called 'The Keeper.' A strange name, to be sure. I can't exactly recall how I got that title. It doesn't matter really. I love to garden, and I supervise all the growing of flowers you see in this realm. We just don't plant seeds and sprinkle water on them and watch them grow. The parent flowers are the crafted results of many persons creating the shape, delicate colors, and aroma of each flower. Each petal, seed, or leaf must be as perfect as we can get it. From the parent flower we take the seeds, and they are sown with the same loving care and attention. We call for and receive, whenever it is needed, a special radiation from an even higher realm. Sometimes we need that extra help when we are developing a new kind of flower and scent."

The Keeper reached down into the soil and removed a small spray of flowers growing from one main stem. He placed it into a small flowerpot with soil, put his hand over the top of the potted flowers, and handed it to Pat.

"I would like you to have these flowers as a token of your visit here," he said.

Pat took the flowers and was immediately aware of the rich fragrance of the flowers. It was almost intoxicating.

"Before you leave," said the Keeper, "I want you to know that we have a plan for you to return to the earth plane, but not right away. You must be patient, for we, who are responsible, must be certain that everything in this universe is as near to perfect as it is in our power to make it."

We are being dismissed, Pat thought.

"Let me assure you, Pat, that you shall return to the earth plane, and you shall have the opportunity— understand, the opportunity—to rejoin the one you care for the most. But that may be her choice, not yours. Do you understand? You cannot exercise your will over her. You will be a stranger, because we cannot create another Pat Duran. Instead, it will be a person who meets all the requisites and who will be in a position to otherwise be terminated as a result of a foolish war that is raging. We have plans that the shell of his being and part of his mental facilities and awareness will be infused and integrated with yours. Of necessity, you will have great difficulty recalling your past life and your interlude of a visit here. You will have the opportunity to press on with your life and make whatever progress you can. In this, we all wish you well." He pointed to the flowerpot in Pat's hand. "These flowers I gave you will have a calming and influential effect and will help to prepare you for that journey you must eventually make," he concluded.

Raising his hand above both Brewster's and Pat's heads, the Keeper asked a blessing for them, and Pat felt a wonderful, pleasurable warmth caress his whole being. Not only did it feel physically good, but Pat's mind felt content and at peace. Pat was not aware that Brewster had taken his hand, but in the next instant they were back at Pat's little chalet with the patio at the back.

"That was some experience," Pat said to Brewster.

"It is always a great privilege and experience when one is in the Keeper's presence. Consider yourself fortunate to have that experience so soon in your visit here."

Because of the Keeper's influence, Pat visited one of the sites in his realm where there were floral nurseries. He wandered in and wondered if someone would chase him away. A young woman approached Pat and said, "Welcome, Pat!"

"You know who I am?"

"Oh, yes. When you thought about visiting our flower nursery, your thoughts were instantly transmitted to us. It just took you a long time to get here," she ended with a laugh.

Pat took an instant liking to this young woman, who introduced herself as Celia.

"I know you have a wonderful plant that the Keeper presented to you. I hope you will bring it along so all the workers here may see it," she said.

"Sure," Pat said. "But don't you have all kinds of flowers here also?"

"We do, but I am sure that your plant will be perfect in all respects. We would like to compare it with what we grow, and with your permission we can extract a seed or two to create a better parent flower."

So it seemed natural to Pat to busy himself learning about flowers, their growth, nourishment, and so on. He was also surprised at the distinctive differences between his cherished plant that the Keeper gave him and those grown at the nursery. Pat named his plant "Eminence." When looking at and comparing the Keeper's plant to the other plants, he noticed that his was taller and had brighter colors, each petal perfect in size and uniform in shape. Even the blending of the color shades was perfect and uniform, tapering to the stems in perfectly coordinated groupings.

"Truly wonderful," gushed Celia.

Pat watched as the others carefully extracted a few seeds from within the tulip-shaped flower—except they were not tulips. This was a plant with several stems and a spray of eight blooming flowers. The intoxicatingly lovely scent never diminished or wore out, nor did the flowers ever wilt or sag.

When Pat marveled at this, Celia explained, "As long as you like the flowers, keep them, and admire their beauty and fragrance, the flower will continue to live and prosper. If you did not care for the flower, it would shrivel up and die."

"If you didn't like the fragrance, it too would go away and you would smell nothing," Dora said.

Pat visited the flower nursery every day and spent many enjoyable mornings or afternoons among the workers. He learned many things about how to care for flowers and about growing vegetables as well. He especially liked working in the orchards with the various fruit trees.

"How does pollination occur when you have no bees for the job?" he asked.

"We use a fine artist paintbrush," replied Claire, who devoted much of her time at the fruit orchard. "We can control the pollination in a precise and uniform manner, and we can blend in and create other strains of pollen to make a different variation of flowers and fruits."

"I've never seen that one before," he said, pointing to an exotic-looking flower.

"Well, that flowering plant has not made the trip to the world you left. It is a new plant that was developed here. Many things are created here, and sometimes they are passed on to the earth plane."

A question formed in Pat's mind. *I think I would be interested in learning about these plants and flowers.*

"You are welcome to come and join us here whenever you want or for as long as you want."

"Wow! You answered me before I even asked."

"We heard your thoughts. You don't even have to speak the words."

CHAPTER 12

In his present state, Pat was not aware of the movement of earth time. In fact, in terms of earth years, Pat had been a visitor for four and a half years. Pat had worked very hard creating a plant and was rewarded when the plant turned out better than he expected. The girls complemented him on his achievement, but Pat thought they were just being polite. His plant, he felt, just barely made the grade—it was nothing great. Nevertheless, he was quite proud of it and saved a lot of the seeds the plant produced. He decided for some reason that it should be given to that fellow Sunghi, whom he had not seen since his first visit to the Hall of Choice.

By just focusing his thoughts on where he wanted to be—a skill he'd learned from Brewster—he was able to instantly transport himself to places in a fraction of a second. Pat had also learned that there were places he could not go. He had thought about his visit to the Keeper, and he tried to project himself there but could not. He felt like a pinball in a machine going "Tilt … Tilt … Tilt."

Going to the Hall of Choice, however, was easy, and with just a though he found himself standing at the entrance. When he entered the building he did not see Sunghi and was a little disappointed. He turned to leave, and suddenly he saw him coming down the path.

"Greetings once again," called Sunghi as he advanced to Pat.

"I thought you were not here, and I was going to leave," explained Pat.

"No, no, that is alright! I received the thought that you were going to visit me, and I was on my way back here to receive you."

I hope I didn't call you away from something important," Pat said.

"No, nothing as important as your visit," he said with a smile.

Pat handed Sunghi the plant and said, "I have been working at creating a plant, and this is my very best effort so far. I wanted someone to have it, and I thought of you. I know it is not the best plant. I have seen so many that are much better."

Sunghi looked seriously at Pat. "No, you are wrong in that, my friend. This plant and its flowers are the creation of your efforts. You have created it—that is what is important. I thank you for this lovely present. I will take good care of it you can be sure," he said graciously.

He asked Pat if he would like to view the one he was concerned about. Funny enough, that had not been Pat's primary thought in visiting. However, since Sunghi brought it up, he was suddenly very keen to know and observe.

This time, Pat's level of awareness was extremely acute and accurate. He observed that Lily was no longer in Germany but in the United States. He saw that she was moderately happy and busy settling into her new environment. He also saw and recognized that Bernice Templeton was benefiting from Lily's influence and care. He noted that Lily now used Elizabeth as her first name. He sensed a harmony and accord between the Templetons and Elizabeth. Focusing in on Elizabeth, Pat observed that she was standing at a dresser and looking into an open box in the top drawer. She was holding a small gold ring in her hand—holding it on her pinky finger and rubbing it with her other hand. Pat received the thought message that Elizabeth had a passing memory of him. It was of a short duration, but the feeling was intense.

Pat willed his mind to focus on what he was thinking, and like an arrow, sent it to Elizabeth.

The message was *I will always love you!*

Pat didn't know whether or not his message got through to Elizabeth. She put the ring back into the box. Then she put the box away in the dresser and turned around. Pat saw a few tears run down Elizabeth's face. She dabbed the tears away with her hankie.

"She heard! My God, I think she heard." He turned to Sunghi. "Do you think she heard?"

"Yes, Pat, her mind picked up that thought. Holding the ring created the opportunity to join your minds. I want to show you something, and we will talk," Sunghi said. "Your visit here today had another purpose. I will show you."

Sunghi asked Pat to seat himself in a lounge chair next to him. He then asked Pat to close his eyes as he placed a satin-like cloth over Pat's eyes. He asked Pat to remain quiet and to focus his thoughts on what he was going to see, hear, and feel. Pat relaxed, and suddenly a figure of a young man came into view. He was in an Army uniform, and he had gold bars on his shoulder—a second lieutenant. The officer was next observed on a troop transport aircraft, crossing a big body of water. At first the weather felt warm and balmy, but then as the aircraft neared its destination, Pat felt the chill of cold weather and winter. The young officer was assigned many different duties and was always on the go. Pat could see that he was the type of person who could get along with anyone, and he could see that even though he was a second lieutenant, the enlisted men respected him.

Pat was aware that time in this theater of war was moving more quickly. The lieutenant and his driver were moving through a dangerous stretch of the road when the left front tire of the jeep hit a buried land mine. Both men were flung from the vehicle. The driver's neck was broken when he hit the rocks at the side of the road. The young officer was thrown to the other side and fell partially down the ravine, striking his head several times and injuring his spine. The North Koreans and their Chinese observer looked over their work and assumed that both men were dead. They searched the lieutenant's pockets and took away his wristwatch, leaving him for dead. He lay there, perfectly still, breathing and barely alive.

Snow was beginning to fall, and as Pat watched a patrol of Korean soldiers approached cautiously. They were ROK soldiers. Inspecting the two victims, and being careful in the event the bodies were booby-trapped, they discovered that the lieutenant was still breathing. The radio call went back to the command post, and others came with stretchers to carry him to an aid station. A flurry of sequences took place where the soldier was moved from a field hospital to a major hospital in Japan and then on to Walter Reed Army General hospital in the United States.

Sunghi said to Pat, "This man is Erik Neilsin. He is going to be moved, for some compelling reason, to another hospital. At the moment he is a neurological question mark problem. He has not regained consciousness, and there are no injuries that require surgery—just a great deal of trauma and, it is thought, a serious spinal injury. Extensive tests show that he is settling down to a more normal state. The medical staff feel that his condition is not life threatening. Because of his guardian's concern, a special request was sent to the Department of the Army requesting that Lieutenant Erik Neilsin be medically discharged. He will receive all the benefits due him, including veteran benefits and government-subsidized assistance while he is in a civilian hospital. Lieutenant Neilsin is also to be awarded the Purple Heart and the Korean Service medal along with his other service ribbons.

"He will be discharged from Walter Reed Army General Hospital and will be transferred to Johns Hopkins Hospital. He will remain in a comatose state—like suspended animation—until the time he will expire, and the hospital will go into a state of emergency to bring him back to life. This will happen fairly soon," he said, looking at Pat. "This is your new place of entry back to the earth plane. At that moment Erik Neilsin expires, you will be his replacement, and the medical team will bring you back. You will be, let's say, a 'walk in.'"

"What about this fellow Erik's life? Won't I be taking his life?" Pat asked.

"Not really," Sunghi replied. "You see, Erik would have been killed in that land mine explosion anyway. Through divine manipulation, his body is being made available to accommodate your situation. This has been a long time in evolving. You can, of course, refuse. If you do that, you must accept your present situation, and it will have no effect on the outcome of Erik Neilsin's life."

"What will I have to do?" Pat asked.

"You will do nothing. You will remember very little. You will recover, and you will have the opportunity for continuing your life on earth. That is all I can tell you," Sunghi said.

"Oh my God, I'm scared," Pat cried.

"Don't be afraid! You are not going to be alone. You're walking into, and replacing yourself with, Erik Neilsin's body. This is an integrated effort on the part of many from this realm. We are not going to cast you adrift in uncharted waters," explained Sunghi. "The Keeper has said, 'so it is written in the book of life, and so it shall be carried out!'

Pat returned to his realm residence, deep in thought.

Awaiting his arrival, Brewster said, "I came to cheer you up and to give you some encouragement. It isn't very often I get to send someone back. This time I'm going to help sending a soul back to Mother Earth instead of receiving one here."

Pat was not cheerful, and he expressed his concern about being able to meet his Lily or Elizabeth again.

"Pat, remember what the Keeper said. It will be a matter of free will. Every effort has been made to present the opportunity for a reunion, but that is no guarantee, because Elizabeth might meet some other person. She might meet you and reject you because she still thinks of Pat Duran, and she won't know who you are. For that matter," cautioned Brewster, "you probably will not know that you were ever Pat Duran. But I promise you that Ames and I will be around as much as possible to help 'tune in' the opportunities for you."

"Thanks, Brewster! I appreciate all your help. You have been a real friend and a great help in guiding me and giving me purpose and direction."

Brewster smiled. "We shall miss you, Pat, but remember, if you see us again, you'll know it is for keeps," he said jokingly.

Pat laughed. "Yeah, and the next time I won't be frightened out of my wits either." Getting serious once more, Pat asked Brewster, "When will this happen? Will I know ahead of time, so I can prepare mentally?"

"I can only tell you that it will be soon, perhaps in a few more days or a week. You will be rested, probably asleep for the equivalent of several days in readiness to be switched. It will be a peaceful transition. Nothing to be alarmed at. I will tell you that your project is directed by the Keeper himself."

This knowledge gave Pat the confidence he needed. Mentally, Pat sent a thought message, thanking the Keeper for his help and protection. Almost immediately, Pat felt a surge of well-being and calming within himself.

Brewster seemed to be aware of what was going on and suggested that Pat rest on his lounge chair. Pat went to the table and picked up a little blue and gold enamel metal box where he kept his seeds from the Keeper's plant. He had been storing some seeds for some time, hoping to plant them soon but not getting around to doing it. Pat had hoped to plant these seeds and start a small garden of his own.

Pat asked a favor of Brewster. "When I make the journey back, would you give my treasured plant to Claire and Celia at the flower gardens?"

Brewster agreed and reassured Pat that he would not forget. He again suggested that Pat stretch out on the recliner and rest. Pat, still holding his little metal box, stretched out and relaxed on the lounge chair. In that relaxed stage, he dozed off into a very deep and lasting sleep. Though Pat did not know it, the time was now right for him to become a "walk in" with a new identity as Erik Neilsin.

CHAPTER 13

The Neilsin Family

Lars Neilsin had a good reputation in Skien, Norway, as well as in Goteborg, Sweden, as a master designer and builder of boats. At the beginning of the century he had turned out his sixty-fifth sailing vessel. Lars had turned forty-eight years old when Brad Cavanaugh of North Carolina, a builder of racing boats, approached him. Cavanaugh had become interested in the boats that Lars had designed. They were not large sailing vessels, but they were very seaworthy. The economy in Norway at the turn of the century left much to be desired, and Lars Neilsin was restless to progress. He spent much of his free time designing new and different types of small boats. So when Brad Cavanaugh approached Lars and made him an offer to go to work in America and build boats there, Lars didn't hesitate.

Lars sold his boat-building business to his longtime friend, Lounk Haverson. Packing up all his drawings and personal affects Lars, his wife, and their three children set sail for New York in the spring of 1902.

Arriving in New York, Lars and his family were met by Heinz Dortmond, chief foreman for the Cavanaugh Boat yards in Wilmington. Heinz Dortmond was formerly a native of Cuxhaven in Germany. He spoke Norwegian and several other languages, so he was the logical choice to meet the Neilsins and escort them to North Carolina.

Lars spoke a little English, and his wife spoke none at all. The Neilsin children had learned some English in school before they left for America. Once in America, the children only spoke English, except at home with their parents. So it came to be that the three Neilsin children—Jennie, Clauson, and Krissten—were the English-speaking persons of the household. Jennie, the eldest, was fifteen when they arrived in America. Next was Clauson, who had just turned fourteen. Krissten was the baby of the family, who. soon after arrival, on her twelfth birthday, caught diphtheria. The fever and its cause were not properly diagnosed, and the local country doctor had not recognized the illness until it was too late to save Krissten. Clauson and Jennie were healthy, robust children, accustomed to hard work and long hours.

Clauson followed in his father's footsteps in the boat designing and building. Clauson had an attraction to mechanical things, so it was natural that with the arrival of steam engines and other mechanical inventions, he urged his father to think about building metal boats, powered by engines instead of sails.

After six years with Cavanaugh's Boat builders, Lars felt that old restlessness gnawing at him. The Neilsins were thrifty, and all the money saved from his business in Norway added to his other savings came to a tidy sum. Lars, along with Jennie and Clauson, nicknamed Claus, visited Norfolk, Hampton, and Newport News in Virginia. Lars fell in love with the area—it was his kind of place!

Lars had a boat design that on the outside was much the same as other vessels. It was in the "spine" of the structure where Lars had incorporated a technique he used for his small seaworthy Norwegian boats. *If it works for the small ones, why not for the big ones, too?* he thought. Armed with various drawings, Lars set out with his two English-speaking experts, Jennie and Claus, to visit the Pershing Boat Builders and others, whom he might interested. Lars had a list of those he considered the better builders, and he started at the top of his list. Pershing's barely gave him the time of day and brushed his visit off. Lars worked his way down the list, with little success. He had three more companies to go; the next was Apex Builders.

After waiting in the reception area for almost an hour, Lars was ready to give up and leave, but Jennie said, "No, we will wait."

The door of the large office opened, and they could hear a lot of loud talking from inside. At the door stood a man in his late twenties, with bronze-colored hair and a mustache to match. He blinked, seeing the three Neilsins sitting in the waiting room, and then looked over at the wall clock. It was past office hours, and the receptionist had already left.

"Who are you? What do you want?" he asked in an annoyed manner.

Jennie jumped to her feet and said, "We have been here for over an hour, waiting to see the owner of this business."

"Have you now?" he said, his voice softening, and for the first time really noticing the handsome young woman standing before him. "I am awfully sorry to keep you waiting. Did you have an appointment?"

"No, we did not have an appointment, but we did come a long way to see the owner," Jennie said with a slight smile at the corners of her mouth.

At twenty-one years of age, Jennie was a real Norwegian beauty. She was a very slim ship at her waist, with a full and imposing topsail. Karl Knutson, son of the owner, decided not to dismiss these visitors.

"One moment, please," he said and stepped back into the office.

Olaf Knutson and the two other partners were still very agitated with each other. Olaf had wanted to take the risk of building small, quick transports or cargo boats because, in his estimation, the world events seem to be leaning toward a war. If that happened, Knutson told them, boats would be needed—and plenty of them. The partners did not want to invest money, time, and effort into such a venture. Instead, they wanted to continue custom building for small, offshore vessels. Business was not good, and the company's profits were hard to earn.

"What is it?" Olaf asked his son, Karl, when he came back into the office.

"We have some visitors outside who have been waiting for quite a while. They said that they have come a long way," Karl said. "They sound like they are from the 'old country.'" He knew his father enjoyed talking to others from Norway.

"We can finish haggling on this some more tomorrow," Olaf said, dismissing the partners.

"As far as I am concerned, there is nothing further to talk about," Timothy Block, one of the partners said.

"If that's the way you feel about it, you can always pack it up, take your ten percent, and get the hell out of the business."

"I will do just that." Timothy then left.

"How about you?" Olaf asked Frank Marsh.

"I'll let you know," he replied, and he too left the office.

"Okay, let's have those visitors in here and get this over with. I haven't eaten since breakfast time and am hungry as a horse," Olaf complained.

When the three Neilsins were ushered into the office, Lars immediately scanned the room and the boat pictures on the wall. He noticed the name on the desk, Olaf Knutson, and was a little heartened. *Sounds like a fellow countryman*, he thought.

Jennie was the first to speak, introducing her father and brother to Mr. Knutson. "We are sorry to come without making an appointment," she explained. "We have come here from Wilmington in North Carolina. My father has been designing and building boats in Norway, and here in America, for a long time. My father has some new ideas for building the bigger metal boats. He wants to work with a big builder who might be interested."

"Can't he speak for himself?" an annoyed Olaf Knutson asked.

"My English is not so good!" ventured Lars.

Olaf Knutson knew he was talking to a fellow Norwegian, and although he had not spoken the language for years, he addressed Lars in his native language. Lars was immediately animated and got right to the point. At first Olaf Knutson was abrupt and wanted to end the conversation and get out to eat, but as he listened to Lars, he became curious and then more interested. *This fellow has some good ideas,* he thought, *and he thinks the way I do, also!*

Looking up at the clock, Olaf inwardly groaned. It was now nearly seven o'clock. He made a rapid decision.

"Hold on," he said. "My son and I have not eaten, and I'm sure you have not eaten either. Why don't you folks join us for a meal, and we can talk some more. There's a good Scandinavian restaurant near here called the Three Vikings." When Lars's face brightened at the name, Olaf bragged, "Their food is like in the old country."

They all agreed, though two of them appeared to be interested in more than just Scandinavian food—Jennie Neilsin and Karl Knutson.

At the restaurant, which had the big, long tables Scandinavians preferred for smorgasbord meals, the five of them sat at one of the big tables. Olaf said, "They have food off the menu, or you can take food from the smorgasbord."

Being tactful, Claus asked, "What do you recommend?"

"If you are hungry as I am, take the smorgasbord. There is plenty, and it is waiting to be eaten!"

Without any further hesitating, the five made for the table and loaded up their plates. The waiter brought a large pitcher of draft Three Towns beer.

"This is not Norwegian beer," Olaf said. "It is Swedish beer. And very good, considering it came from Sweden."

The five Norwegians laughed as they continued the centuries-long tradition of Norwegians and Swedes poking fun at each other.

The meal was satisfying, and Olaf and Lars made small talk about Norway, sailing, and boats. The chemistry between Olaf and Lars was good, but Karl had his attention diverted to the wholesome Jennie. Jennie's smile was like a beacon, drawing Karl into dangerous waters—but he was entering these uncharted waters willingly! Claus was amused, sitting back and listening to his father and Olaf and then switching back to observe Jennie and Karl. Claus recognized that Karl Knutson was already hooked. He had seen other young men vie for Jennie's attention. In the past, she had never really been interested in anyone—until this Karl. Claus could sense a current flowing between the two of them.

"And where are you staying?" asked Olaf.

"A hotel just outside Newport News, the Anchorage, I believe. Yes, the Anchorage," said Lars.

"Why don't we get together tomorrow then," suggested Olaf. "We don't need the youngsters, do we?"

"Only Claus," suggested Lars. "Claus is my right hand in designs, and he is a mechanical wonder. He can help fill in the details if I leave something out."

Turning to Jennie, Lars asked if she would mind being left to herself tomorrow.

"I can manage all right, but I think we might want to tell the hotel people how long we intend to stay."

"Listen, don't worry about Jennie. I can call on Jennie tomorrow and take her around to see Newport News and Hampton," volunteered Karl anxiously. Jennie tried to hide a blush, but she couldn't be more pleased.

"What time shall we come to Apex shipyard?" Lars asked.

"I am up early, have a coffee, and then off to the yard," Olaf said. "I have a breakfast meal around nine thirty. I just can't eat first thing after getting up."

"Neither can I," Lars said.

"Fine! Come just after eight. We will talk, drink coffee and have a breakfast together, and then talk some more," Olaf said.

With that they all got up to leave. Jennie and Karl were slow catching up with the others and lagged behind, walking next to each other. Lars didn't seem to notice, but Claus kept a watchful eye on his sister.

Several hours ran into days, and days ran into a week. Olaf and Lars were hammering out ideas that each of them had. Olaf liked Lars's plans for the reinforced and strong backbone for a metal ship. He also liked the idea of making compartments that could be sealed off. Many such pockets within a vessel could help keep a ship afloat in times of war or disaster at sea. Both Olaf and Lars agreed that a war of great magnitude could become a reality, and since it took a long time to build good boats, anything they built now could be highly in demand. The two other, ten-percent partners were not in agreement. Like Timothy Block, Frank Marsh lacked vision and intestinal fortitude, and he too decided that he no longer cared to maintain his interest in Apex Builders. Olaf said that he would buy back Marsh's ten-percent ownership of the company. Later, talking to his son Karl, Olaf said, "Well, there goes twenty percent of the business! Marsh and Block wanted out, and I made it easy for them."

"How are you going to pay them off?" Karl asked. "I know we have some money in savings and some money owed us from the offshore trawler sale. Will it be enough?"

"No, it won't," replied Olaf, "unless I can pay them part now—at least as much as they put in—then maybe the rest later."

Lars understood part of the conversation, and he interrupted, saying, "Olaf, I have saved money from selling my business in Norway, and I have put some money aside for the past six years, too. I understand that you own seventy percent of Apex and your son, Karl, ten percent. Will you let me in on the remaining twenty percent?"

Working out the details with pencil and paper, Olaf, satisfied that he'd considered all assets and savings, determined he would need at least forty thousand dollars to clear off both Tim Block and Frank Marsh and another twenty thousand to meet the minimum value of the shares. Consulting his little leather book, Lars said that he could provide forty thousand dollars in return for the twenty-percent share of the business.

"It will not be easy," cautioned Olaf. "We will be very short of ready cash to operate, but our credit is good. We have always paid what we owed, in good times and bad."

Lars then said, "Since I am to be a partner in the business, I will work very hard to make sure we make the best boats. Also, I will be able to put an extra ten thousand dollars in cash into our account as soon as everything is settled."

So it was that Lars and Olaf, along with their two sons, Karl and Claus, created a new Apex Builders. The reinforced "spine" concept along with the below-waterline compartments were new techniques in boatbuilding. Apex was a struggling, but successful, company—one ahead of its time.

Kaiser Wilhelm of Germany set the world in motion as he unleashed his war machine. Almost overnight, the demand for oceangoing vessels became critical. The American industrial machine slowly started gearing itself for the coming war, and although some politicians were saying, "We shall not get into it," others knew that it was only a matter of time. The United States entered into the Great War. Three months later, one of the seven new ocean vessels was launched down the slide at Apex Builders. Fitting of the vessel was carried out in port with advisors from the US Navy aboard to ensure their special needs were met.

Apex vessels were not the biggest in hauling tonnage, but they were extremely seaworthy and handled well. During the World War, Apex built eleven vessels of the same type. The company and its building yards expanded and grew. Apex became known for its quality workmanship and its on-time deliveries. Claus had been responsible for designing an extra gearing arrangement that later became known as "the sprint gear." This gearing system could be engaged when the engines were operating at near its full capacity, and it provided increased propeller revolutions with the same engine torque. Used for a short duration, it gave a vessel the capability "to sprint" out of harm's way of an incoming torpedo from a lurking U-boat. Later, this theory applied to automobiles became known as "overdrive."

Before the Great War ended, the Naval Department had commissioned Apex to design and build three ocean cutters—smaller than a destroyer, yet fast and capable to hunt submarines and operate close to shore, as escorting vessels. When the ships were halfway completed, the war ended and the US Navy cancelled their order for the three ships. However, work continued so that they reached the state where they could be launched and floated without the superstructure built.

The Navy paid Apex for the work that they'd performed up to that point. Large layoffs became necessary, and plans were made to convert the research and planning to peacetime endeavors. Later, in the spring of 1920, the Treasury Department needed offshore Cutters for the US Coast Guard, and they approached Apex. After inspecting the three completed boat shells, coordination got underway on redesigning the fittings for Coast Guard use. Apex was able to put two hundred workers back on the job, its future assured.

Karl Knutson never stood a chance and fell hopelessly in love with Jennie Neilsin. They were married eight months after Lars and Olaf joined forces. Karl and Jennie had three girls, naming the third girl Victoria to commemorate the armistice signed at the end of the war. Karl and Claus became close as brothers and later shared with the management and operation of Apex. Olaf and Lars retired. In 1937 they visited Norway together. Lars's wife had passed away a few years earlier, and Olaf's wife had died before Lars came to Apex. With little to hold them back, they toured Norway, and Lars was pleased to point out to Olaf some of the vessels he built that were still in use. Their visit started in Norway, and then they traveled to Sweden, Denmark, and Germany. Lars and Olaf left Germany for Great Britain and then headed back to America.

"It is not going to be a lasting peace. I swear, I can see it coming!" Olaf said.

"I have to agree," Lars said. "The Germans are going to start something again, for sure."

"We are getting too old for this, Lars."

"But we can't leave the kids in the lurch."

"We will serve on the board of the company and put our two cents in," volunteered Olaf, "… for as long as we can!"

Olaf and Lars advised the board of Apex that they should be ready for a major war that was "just around the corner." Clauson Neilsin and Karl Knutson had improved upon the old, but viable, reinforced spine. They had been involved in developing a low-draft, ocean-worthy craft of modest size that was intended for unloading cargo in places where there was limited docking facilities or piers. One of the target markets was South America. Heeding the old-timers' advice, Karl and Claus designed the shell that was the sturdy and seaworthy Apex trademark, and Claus set about designs to adapt this special low-draft vessel to unload its cargo without the aid of piers or dockage.

Would there be a market for such a vessel?

The answer came after the Germans invaded Poland and other countries fell under the Nazi onslaught.

It was evident that the world was headed once again toward a major conflict. Talking with naval personnel who were soliciting new, innovative ideas for a pending conflict, Apex presented their plan for a low-draft oceangoing vessel of sufficient size for limited cargo. The navy suggested that if the front of the vessel could open doors like in "Ali Baba and the Forty Thieves" —with an "Open Sesame!" equivalent that lowered a ramp in front—it would provide a useable landing craft for combat troops and their heavy equipment. Claus and Karl worked long hours and conducted many tests. The problem was water coming into the boat while it was pounding through ocean waves. The solution came in the most unexpected way.

Clauson, a late bloomer in life, had met Stella Bergen, an American girl of Swedish background, in the spring of 1925. They met in New York while visiting the Statue of Liberty. For both of them it was love at first sight. They were married two months later and settled down at Virginia Beach. Their son, Erik, was born on July 4, 1926. He was a healthy and robust baby Stella had not fared too well in her delivery of Erik, and the doctor told her that she would not be able to have any more children. Erik was a good child, as obedient and sensitive as he was talented. He was gifted in music and art and even some designing, but his interests were not as tied to the sea as his father and grandparents were.

However, even if the ocean wasn't his first love, as a child he did enjoy playing with model boats. One day, young Erik was playing with a homemade boat he had designed. The model he'd made was greatly out of proportion: the front of his model boat was much too high, and as Erik swished it through the water he made the front of the boat stick upward.

"Why do you have the front of your boat so high?" Claus asked his son.

Pausing to think of a good answer because he thought his father was going to criticize his boat, Erik offered, "If my boat is high up in front, the waves won't come in."

"Then how can you see where you are going?" asked Claus. "The front is too high, and you won't be able to see."

"Well, you see," Erik went on, "I haven't finished it yet. In the back, it will be high up, so the captain can see where he is going."

Claus laughed and started to walk off, but then the simplicity of what Erik said and the crude model gave him pause to think the idea through.

"Karl, can you slip over to my office right now? I think I found a solution. You see, if we raise the front of the boat—starting just underneath its front and build it high and sort of blunt—we could have hydraulic doors that open up and a ramp lower into the water in front of the vessel. It is a shallow-draft vessel now, but we can further enhance its ability to get closer to shore if the front of the boat is raised so as to have a planing effect. With the front high up, it will provide possible protection from ground fire and the normal ocean elements," suggested Claus.

"Yes, I see," replied Karl. "We can locate the vessel's bridge in the back. This will allow more cargo space, troop space, and space for vehicles and armor. The engines would also be in the rear. The extra weight in the rear will also help to keep the front up, but we must make sure it remains seaworthy and not porpoise up and turn over. That would never do."

Three design concepts were blue-printed, and the "Norsemen"—as the company's employees referred to Claus and Karl—presented the idea to naval coordinators, who later made minor recommendations as to tonnage, power, some turrets for gun emplacements and emergency equipment.

Two prototypes were authorized, and Apex was soon busy at the job. Lars Neilsin would have been very proud of the boys, had he lived long enough to see their finished product. As it turned out, Lars retired to bed early one night with a slight head cold. Sometime during the night his heart skipped and then stopped beating. It was a peaceful passing. Lars had lived a full and rewarding life. Olaf sorely missed his friend and constant companion of late. Lars was seven years younger than Olaf. Lars had been seventy-nine years old, just a few months shy of his eightieth birthday. Family and friends buried Lars in Virginia Beach on Monday, December 1, 1941.

The next Sunday, chilling news report flooded the airwaves—the Empire of Japan had attacked Pearl Harbor. The United States was in a state of war!

One of the requirements of the navy was for a suitable landing craft that could haul tanks, trucks, and field artillery as well as fighting men. The Apex ocean transport, modified for US Naval combat use, helped to satisfy that need. Apex as well as other companies produced this type of craft, and the Apex board made sound investments to protect the company's future.

Olaf Knutson lived to see the victory in Europe and later in the Pacific. Though quite old, he was still of good mind, and he enjoyed the celebration at the end of the war. Karl and Jennie brought the two girls and their newest baby daughter, Victoria, who was born on VE Day, to see Grandpa "Ollie." It was a happy evening for Olaf. That night, the Viking warrior vessel came and carried Olaf away. He passed away at the age of ninety-four.

Claus kept up with the ever-growing technology advances, especially after 1945. Fearing a recession, Claus invested his money in several segments of the market. A company that manufactured and leased their punched card equipment caught his attention. He decided to invest in the company and bought five thousand shares of International Business Machine. Claus knew that newer and better commercial aircraft would follow World War II, so he also invested in Boeing, Lockheed, and Grumman Aviation. Claus also did some speculative investing in future medicine and bought shares in a group that was working on developing a vaccine to combat diseases such as polio. Mechanically minded to start with, Claus watched with interest as IBM introduced newer and more advanced data processing machines and then the development of super calculators, which were the forerunners of the computer.

CHAPTER 14

Second Lieutenant Erik Neilsin

An exceptional student, Erik graduated from high school with honors at the age of eighteen. He received a scholarship to the University of Maryland, which he wanted so he would not be too far from home. Erik entered the ROTC and received his bachelor's degree in electrical engineering, although he really had no idea what he wanted to do with that knowledge.

Because of his ROTC achievements, Erik was commissioned in the US Infantry as a second lieutenant and sent to the Officers' Basic Course at Fort Benning, Georgia. He also completed Airborne training at Fort Benning and received an "Airborne Qualified" rating. Early in his senior year in ROTC, Erik asked to be sent to the Rangers School at Fort Benning. The request was approved, and he made it through the rigorous training and methods of survival. Following completion of the course and being awarded ranger qualification, Erik went on an eating binge to gain back the fifteen pounds of weight he lost. He was a lean fighting machine.

Near the completing his ROTC training in college, Erik requested he be assigned to the army infantry branch of service. Following his basic officer's training, which was a snap after Ranger School, Second Lieutenant Neilsin went car shopping. It was June 30, 1950, and he purchased a one-year-old 1949 Pontiac sedan and was now eager for his two-week leave back to Virginia Beach to see his relatives. A week before his leave, he received orders instructing him to report to Fort Lewis, Washington, for overseas processing. The word quickly circulated that the North Koreans had invaded South Korea on June 25.

"I guess I will be going to Korea," Erik told his father.

His leave at home gave him the opportunity to see all his cousins, Aunt Jennifer, and Uncle Karl. While on leave, Erik celebrated his twenty-fourth birthday on the Fourth of July. Erik was restless and displayed an optimism that he did not feel inside. The two weeks of leave passed very quickly. Erik turned the year-old Pontiac over to his father's care and asked if it could be stored at the yard while he was away.

"Sure thing, Erik. Have no fear—I will take care of it and keep it clean. I will probably have to drive it every now and then to make sure it's still working and that the battery keeps its charge."

"Sure, Dad! You drive it all you want."

Clauson drove his son to Norfolk Airport, where Erik would catch a flight to Atlanta and connect to a flight to the West Coast. Before leaving, his father cautioned Erik, "Be careful, Erik!"

"Don't worry, Father."

"That's easy to say but hard to do," his father replied.

After arriving at Fort Lewis, Washington, on July 15 and processing in, Erik noticed that the fort was busy processing troops to go to Japan and Korea. Fort Lewis, he also learned, was responsible for transporting priority material and supplies to Korea and Japan. After in-processing at Fort Lewis for his overseas movement, Erik received word that he had been assigned temporary duties to assist at the S-4 Logistics branch as a supply officer. This, of course, was contrary to Department of the Army procedures. Erik had assumed that upon his arrival at Fort Lewis he would be shipped to Korea. He could not understand why he was not being sent to Korea as a replacement officer.

The S-4 Logistics Officer, Lieutenant Colonel Ruppert R. Roberts, quietly referred to as "Old Triple R" by the junior officers, liked to run an orderly supply system. He was a stickler for exact numbers and everything in its proper order. He was an "all ducks in a row" person, for sure! Colonel Roberts didn't know what a shortcut was. He never had any time for doing anything quickly. "Haste *is waste!*" was his motto. He drove the junior officers crazy with numerous clichés.

At Fort Lewis headquarters, Colonel Roberts was held in high esteem as "a doer." Actually, had anyone checked, they would have found that Colonel Roberts's record for expediting was achieved by the large number of junior officers that he had side-tracked from going overseas and "conscripted" for temporary duty in Supply. His predecessor had six junior officers. Colonel Roberts had nineteen. Colonel Roberts was a young forty-two-year-old. He kept himself in tip-top shape working out at the gym and also doing some weight lifting. He had a great physique and was very proud of his solid build and his trim, waxed mustache. Colonel Roberts always had an eye out for a good-looking lady and a well-turned figure.

Second Lieutenant Dale Swan was his undoing, however. Screening the records of personnel due in for overseas replacements, he selected Lieutenant Dale Swan. Colonel Roberts never held up personnel more than six to eight months and always made sure he had a replacement for that officer before releasing them to go overseas.

"Second Lieutenant Dale E. Swan reporting as directed, sir," she said, rendering a proper and snappy salute.

Colonel Roberts's mouth dropped open in surprise. "I thought … that … the record said 'Dale E. Swan'," he managed to get out.

"Yes, sir. Dale Emma Swan, sir," she replied.

"Well, I'll be," Colonel Roberts said. Thinking fast, he added, "Yes, I've been thinking that I needed someone to assist me, take down notes and, well—sort of an aide. Just temporary duty, you understand."

Dale Emma Swan was a beauty. She stood about five feet four inches tall. She had lovely blue eyes, strawberry blonde hair, and a sprinkle of freckles. She had a slim waist and was perfectly proportioned. Lieutenant Swan had a cute, turned-up nose and a quick, contagious smile and fun disposition. Beside the good looks and model-like figure, Dale Swan was a very savvy girl who'd earned her spurs in Boston. She was street smart and recognized the signal flags going up in Colonel Roberts's eyes. Furthermore, Lieutenant Swan was not crazy about going overseas. As a matter of fact, she had recently decided that she was not crazy about the Army—roughing it in tents and facing all the elements of nature.

Japan would be an okay assignment, but Korea? That was something else. She wasn't terribly happy about her assignment to the supply activity at Fort Lewis, but it was only for a short duration, so she reckoned that would be all right. *Maybe I can get reassigned to Japan instead of Korea*, she thought.

Colonel Roberts had been married to Joanne Kylie for nine years. She was a minister's daughter and, as it turned out, was an absolute prude when it came to sex. If someone told an off-colored joke, she would hurry to the bathroom to wash her hands as if to ensure that it didn't rub off on her being. Joanne was a content wife and adapted somewhat to the life of an Army wife. Her redeeming qualities were that she was a good cook and housekeeper.

It irked Joanne Roberts that her husband's younger brother, Cliff, was in a mental institution for the criminally insane. Cliff Roberts adored his older brother, and Colonel Roberts made it a point to visit him several times each year and always sent him letters, cards, and a little money. Still, Joanne felt the stigma of this brother-in-law who'd murdered his own abusive father. Knowing this also made her worry that "bad genes" ran in the Roberts family.

Ruppert Roberts almost had to make an appointment to get amorous with Joanne in bed. Their relationship came to an abrupt end when one night Ruppert, in a fit of determination, prepared a sweet and refreshing drink that he laced with cherry liqueur and a shot of vodka.

"I prepared this cocktail for you my dear," he said. "A before-dinner cocktail. Very low alcohol content—just a pinch of cherry brandy for flavor."

"Umm, yes, that does taste good," she said.

"I prepared a little pitcher of it for later," sneered Ruppert, but Joanne missed the sneer. She swallowed her drink, and they sat down to eat.

"My, it's warm in here," she said, fanning herself, and gave a little giggle.

Following supper, Ruppert coaxed Joanne into the living room for a few more "fruit punch" drinks.

"Well maybe just one more."

After the third drink, Joanne Roberts was nearly bouncing off the walls, giggling and acting silly. Ruppert maneuvered Joanne into the bedroom and playfully pushed her onto the bed. Joanne was acting giddy and said, "Ohhh, the room is spinning around." Ruppert had her shoes and stockings off and started undoing her skirt.

"What are you doing, dear?" she asked him.

"It's bed time, my dear," he said, pulling Joanne's skirt off and tossing it on the floor. He unbuttoned her blouse, and that too made it to the floor. He started on the next layer of clothes—her underclothes. *Christ almighty,* he thought, *how much stuff does she have on?* Despite her apparent dowdiness, Joanne had a fairly good figure—under-utilized body, Ruppert always thought—which he started to fondle. Through the maze of her intoxication, the puritan strain in Joanne's character raised its ugly head.

"Ruppert Roberts," she demanded, pushing his hand away, "what do you think you are doing? Stop that!"

Joanne was very vulnerable at this point, and Ruppert pressed his advantage—savagely. All the pent-up desire from the times he wanted to make love but didn't manifested itself in these few moments. Without hesitation he entered her and worked her like a broncobuster breaking in a new pony. Joanne was muttering all kinds of sounds so that Ruppert couldn't tell whether it was in agony or ecstasy. He had a large appetite for lovemaking and was not about to settle for "a quickie." When he was through, he continued to fondle Joanne and, rising to the occasion once more, employed other techniques and positions to satisfy his sexual appetite. Eventually, though, Ruppert felt some remorse and apprehension. He wondered what his wife's reaction in the morning would be.

The following morning Joanne awoke, sick and hung over. Drinking her coffee in silence, she remembered what had happened the night before and closed her eyes. When Joanne opened her eyes she had made a decision. She left her husband, and a divorce followed shortly thereafter. Ever since, Ruppert had decided that he would "pay and play" or just play the field—discreetly, of course. He was a career officer and had to maintain his image.

Just the sight of Second Lieutenant Swan started the yearning within his loins. Colonel Roberts was working out a scheme to get close to Dale Swan and bed her good and proper. Swan he noted joked a lot and was very casual and friendly around him. There were a few instances when Roberts would accidentally rub a hand against her body. There was no pulling away or resistance. In fact, Roberts was greatly encouraged, and entertained the notion that Dale was interested in his advances. Actually, Dale could read Colonel Roberts like a book and allowed him a little rub here and touch there. The situation had its advantages. She could suggest little things, and Colonel Roberts was quick to agree to it.

Colonel Roberts began to spend much more time in his office and ignored most of the junior officers, sending them instructions by memoranda instead of by personal contact. After delivering several memos to some of her fellow officers, Dale had a coffee break with Erik Neilsin. They had become good friends, and although Erik admired Dale's good looks and tempting body, he never made any advances and called her "*little sister.*"

Dale was quick to notice that Erik was not like the other guys, and she felt very comfortable and relaxed when she was with him. Erik had another quality that Dale liked: he did not brag about himself or talk about anything personal. Several of the other junior officers assigned to be Triple R's supply men tried to "put the make" on her, but they soon found out that the colonel had designs on Lieutenant Swan—and that meant "*hands off.*"

Taking a daring step, Colonel Roberts had another CQ (Charge of Quarters) cot brought to the supply room in his outer office in case he wanted a short nap when working late. Dale duly noticed the cot, and her mind wrestled with the impending situation. She was not against having a little sex, but not with the colonel. . However, she decided to play it cool. *Here it comes,* she thought.

"Lieutenant, I need you to work with me a little later tonight," Roberts said. "I will need your help on some notes and references." Looking at his watch, Roberts added, "I've taken the liberty of ordering us some food. We can eat it right here."

Dale was agreeable and gave Colonel Roberts what she hoped was an encouraging smile. She did that so innocently and effectively that it was hard for Colonel Roberts to realize that it was she who was in control. The food was excellent, and included a bottle of wine. They ate the meal and drank all the wine. Dale, Colonel Roberts was pleased to note, drank most of the wine. They both smoked a cigarette, and Dale asked if it were all right if she made herself comfortable—seeing as they were working late and informally. Colonel Roberts couldn't agree more. Dale took off her shoes, picked up her pen and her tablet to take notes . Colonel Roberts nearly lost control of himself and was anxious to make advances to Dale.. An hour passed with little work being done. Dale glanced at her watch and decided to get away from Colonel Roberts as soon as possible. She planned to be over at the Officers' Club, as she was meeting Erik there for a drink or two and a dance.

Getting up, Dale turned, and Colonel Roberts suddenly wrapped his arms around her. He took hold of her and hungrily kissed her, crushing her toward him. *How clumsy he is,* thought Swan. *He's gonna do something stupid.* Hardly able to contain himself, Roberts tore at her clothes to undress her.

"Colonel, I don't care to play this game with you," she said, brushing the colonel's hands away. "I think it's time for me to go." She straightened her uniform, put her shoes back on and said, "Good night, sir," opened the door, and left.

Colonel Roberts started to say something, but she had already gone. Later, stopping by the Officers Club for a drink, Colonel Roberts heard that familiar laugh and, turning, spied Dale in the company of Second Lieutenant Neilsin. He stared a long time at the two of them and became very jealous. That night, Colonel Roberts wrote a letter to his brother Cliff telling him about Dale Swan and Erik Neilsin. It was his way of venting off steam and frustration.

The following day, still smarting with jealousy, Colonel Roberts accused Dale Swan of playing him up and teasing him along, and then getting him all hot and bothered and running out on him for a crummy Second Lieutenant. Tired of dealing with this pompous ass, she told him that he was trying to use his rank to force her into bed with him. Trying to feed her food and booze and then expecting her to pay the price by giving in to him. When she said this to Roberts, the deputy post commander was walking toward them and coming within earshot. Tears sprang into her eyes, and she cringed backward from Colonel Roberts.

Not knowing who was almost right behind him, Colonel Roberts said in a loud enough voice to be heard, "You're damned right I was pulling rank on you, Lieutenant!" His voice rose. "You were egging me on, and I'm going to get into your pants for a bit of ass one way or another. Your ass belongs to me!"

"Colonel!" the deputy post commander called.

Colonel Roberts turned and felt like fainting. Standing in back of him was Deputy Post Commander Brigadier General Theodore Sturmus. The general eyed Second Lieutenant Swan and ordered that she report to his office immediately and await his return.

"Yes, sir," she said. She saluted and marched off.

Turning to Colonel Roberts, General Sturmus said, "Colonel, you will report to me at my office at ten o'clock sharp today."

Colonel Roberts was weak at the knees.

After a discussion with Lieutenant Swan where she told him of Colonel Roberts's actions, the general dismissed her. Dale returned to duty with a promise that she would soon receive movement orders to her next assignment. By not pressing charges against the colonel, she saved the US Army from an embarrassing situation. Colonel Roberts was read the applicable portion of the Uniform Code of Military Justice, wherein an officer in the military service who violates those statutes would be subject to the penalties that a general court martial could bring. A court martial could result in loss of rank, dishonorable discharge, forfeiture of all pay and allowances, and prison time.

The alternative? The general suggested that if Colonel Roberts didn't want to face a court-martial, he should put in for retirement from the Army immediately.

Colonel Roberts had twenty years service and was eligible to retire, and he did just that. It was fifty days before Christmas when Colonel Roberts joined the civilian ranks. A lieutenant colonel recently from Japan replaced Roberts. He required a small staff of five junior officers, and all the "temporary duty" officers side-tracked by Colonel Roberts were soon on their way to the Far East.

Sitting at the kitchen table in his rented apartment, Roberts wrote a long letter to his brother Cliff explaining how he had been forced out of the army, telling him that Dale Swan and Erik Neilsin were the cause of his problems. He neglected to tell his brother the whole truth. He mailed the letter to Cliff and, as usual, included a twenty-dollar bill.

CHAPTER 15

Twenty-two passengers were permitted on the next cargo flight. Just before loading up, the last passenger hurried to the waiting line. It was Dale Swan. Erik was surprised; he'd thought Dale would somehow wangle a good, comfortable flight to the Far East. Instead, there she was, waving furiously to Erik. Even in her combat fatigue uniform, Dale E. Swan was a knockout. Everyone was watching her, and they all turned around to see to whom this cute dish was waving. In a normal reflex, Erik turned and looked in the same direction as the others. Dale made her way down to where Erik was in the rough line.

"Least you could do is wave back," she said, reaching up and pulling Erik's head down so she could kiss him on the cheek. A chorus of whistles started, and Erik could feel his face getting warm and reckoned that he was blushing. Nothing affected Dale; she just naturally gave her dazzling smile to everyone. She hauled her duffel bag and a flight bag up next to Erik's. None of those waiting had any qualms about Swan moving in front of them. Just looking at her face was a pleasure! She had that kind of wholesome, all-American "girl back home" look about her. When she talked, everyone went silent, listening to her voice.

"Dale," Erik said, "I thought you weren't going out on this flight. I figured you would get a commercial flight or something grand, not an old transport like we're gonna fly in."

"Well, I'll tell you how it is," Dale said with a chuckle. "I could have had another flight, a nice transport with only a few passengers. I was nearly booked on it but then found out that the crew wanted to cancel out all the other passengers but me, and I said, 'Uh-oh, this sounds like bad news at twenty-five thousand feet!' I told them, 'Forget it, fellows. I'm going on that flight there.' The co-pilot asked me why I wouldn't fly with them, and I told him that I was safer around twenty-one guys than flying in his wolfmobile."

Everyone within hearing range roared with laughter. Dale laughed and said, "Ain't that right, guys? There's safety in numbers."

"Okay, everybody, listen up," said the crew chief. "We have dual seats arranged on the left front side of the aircraft. Stow your gear in the large containers as you enter the aircraft. We will secure it before take-off, because we don't want baggage flying all over the place." Checking his manifest, he said, "When I call your name, sound off and climb aboard the aircraft." Looking at Dale, he asked, "What's your name, Lieutenant?"

"Dale Swan," she answered.

He checked off the last person on his manifest and then read the names from the top. Erik was number eighteen on the list and climbed aboard, stowed his duffel bag and B-4 bag in the container, and then walked toward the seating. Dale Swan was fending off other guys who wanted to sit next to her, and Erik heard what she told one persistent guy. "Listen, I'm saving this seat for my boyfriend, and he's Ranger-qualified," she said sweetly. "So if you don't get out of my face, you're gonna get your fuckin' ass kicked."

The poor guy's mouth dropped opened, and he moved on back.

"My God, Dale! What the hell did you tell him that for?" Erik said as he sat down next to her. "You keep doing that, and sooner or later someone is going to put me to the test, and I'll be fighting for my life, and you know I'm a peaceful guy. And what's with this 'he's my boyfriend' bit?"

"Psychology—it works all the time! No one is going to mess around on short notice, thinking some brute will be entering to bust him to pieces."

"Okay, everyone, make sure that your seat belts are securely fastened," announced the crew chief.

He then made the rounds to personally check each one. Walking back to the bulkhead, he picked up a mike and talked to the flight deck. The engine roar increased, and the lumbering aircraft started to taxi. In position for takeoff, they got the okay from the tower, and the aircraft started its takeoff roll.

Erik dozed off for a while and woke up when the crew chief brought hot coffee and handed out an in-flight dinner to each soldier. When Erik woke he found Dale's head on his shoulder. He could smell the faint aroma of her perfume. It was subtle, not overpowering. They tucked into their dinners. The boxes contained two sandwiches, fresh fruit, a chocolate candy bar, cookies, and a can of fruit juice. They both ate part of their food, saving the rest for later. It was a long flight, and because the lighting inside was poor, reading was out of the question. It was nearly nine thirty at night when they took off and dark already. It was really boring.

"Lieutenant." A hand shook Dale awake.

"Yeah, what is it?" Dale asked.

It was the flight engineer. "We can't ask everybody, but would you like to come up and see the flight deck?"

Dale looked at Erik, as if asking his permission. Erik moved his eyes, which said, *Go!* Dale was impressed with the large array of gauges, levers, and a radarscope going back and forth in front of them. Looking out, she could see the darkness up ahead getting lighter.

As if answering her thoughts, the pilot said, "We've crossed the

International Date Line into tomorrow. We just lost a day! What you're looking at is the coming of dawn in the orient."

Dale noticed that neither the pilot nor co-pilot had their hands on the controls.

"Does this fly by itself?" she asked.

"We're on automatic pilot," the captain said. "We can make all kinds of adjustments and still keep the plane on automatic. It makes for a smoother flight."

"Thanks for the view. I think I'll go back to my seat now," she said.

Erik had dozed off again. Dale got herself comfortable again, leaned against him, and she too drifted off to sleep.

Pusan

The aircraft arrived in the Far East on November 8th, 1950, touching down in Pusan on the southeastern coast of Korea. Everyone debarked and went through the customary military routine: *What's your name? Where are your orders? Got your shot record handy?* Then a table was set up with people from the Army Personnel branch. They took the military records and copies of PCS (Permanent Change of Station) orders.

"Lieutenants Swan and Neilsin," a man called out. "You will be assigned right here in Pusan. Corporal Davis, take these two officers over to Depot Supply."

Both Erik and Dale were too tired to argue or protest. All they wanted was a good hot shower, some decent food, and to sack out. After being assigned their own billets, they crashed. What seemed like the middle of the night was actually morning.

"Good morning, Loo-tan-nant-son."

A voice penetrated in Erik's ears. Opening his eyes, he saw a young Korean man bending over him. Suddenly becoming wide awake (an attribute of his Ranger training), Erik was ready to get up fighting.

Something in Erik's expression told the young Korean that this lieutenant didn't know he was the houseboy.

"My name Kim! I nummer one houseboy here," he said quickly and with a smile.

Yes, of course, thought Erik, it would be natural to hire local Koreans to clean the barrack quarters and do the odd jobs.

"Hiya, Kim," Erik responded. "Kim, what?" Kim looked at Erik with a blank expression. "I mean, what is your last name? Kim, what?

"Evbody call me Kim-Chi! Like good Korean food," he added.

Erik knew what the GIs used the term "Kim-chi" for, and it was not for a good Korean dish!

"I nummer one houseboy here. I do good woik. You be verra happy wif Kim. You betcha! You want coffee? Tea? Kim bring you. Yes?"

"Yeah, Kim. A cup of coffee would be number one," Erik replied.

He got out of bed and took stock of his little room in the officers' barracks. His duffel bag and B-4 bag were right where he'd dropped them when he entered his room, fell on the bed, and went fast asleep. Kim brought him a little wooden tray that had a mug of hot steaming coffee, a little bowl with lumped sugar cubes, and a small jug with milk in it.

"Thanks, Kim. Did you make the coffee?" Erik asked.

"No, me get from Offersers' Crub—cross ah street. I bring big pot—get beaucoup coffee—everbody happy wif Kim!"

Erik laughed and said, "Yes, you sound like number one houseboy!" Kim smiled broadly, showing a mouthful of white, overcrowded teeth.

Erik felt drugged and headed for a nice hot shower and more coffee. But first he had to do some unpacking. He found the shower room at the end of the barracks. There was four shower stalls. Erik turned on the water and cautiously tested the temperature. The hot water felt good and helped to relax his sore and tense body from the long, cramped flight. Drying off, he went back to his room and found that Kim was into his B-4 bag and was in process of putting his clothes on hangers and in the wardrobe closet.

Looking up as Erik entered, Kim said, "You need crows press, Kim do for you. You boots—Kim do number one spit shine—see you face, for sure!"

"Who pays you?" Erik asked.

"You do, Loo-tan-nant-son! You pay once mont—same as odder GI's," he said. "You not be sorry—I be nummer one house boy, for sure, you betcha!"

"Okay, Kim, but if you are not number one, I will get me another number one boy," Erik said.

Erik had been told that the only authorized uniform to be worn in this theater of operations was his combat fatigues and combat gear. Erik laid out his wrinkled fatigues and went to the latrine to shave and do the rest of his toiletries. Returning to his room, he found his fatigues on a hanger—they had been pressed and had a nice crease in them. Erik also noted that his jump boots were sporting a new shine. He was pleased to put on a fresh uniform, and that it was neatly pressed made him feel better. His fatigues had the stitched jump wings and ranger patch sewn on. Erik was proud of them because he'd earned them the hard way—by jumping out of fast moving planes at various altitudes in daylight and night. Ranger School had been even tougher. It was a longer course and it also included survival training—eating bugs, plants, and snakes. But that was behind him now. Here in Korea would be the real thing!

Erik reported to the Personnel Office as he had been directed. He did the "In Processing" required and was finished before lunchtime. He was told to report back at 1330 hours at Major Harmon's office for his next assignment. Erik left to find the mess hall and had to ask for directions before he found it. He entered, signed in, using his in-processing orders as he had been told, and walked down the aisle to get a metal food tray and silverware before heading for the chow line. Erik was very hungry for some solid food. The offerings for the day was "Salisbury Steak," the attendant said, but it was hamburger. The usual stuff followed—mashed potatoes, lima beans or string beans, gravy, and bread. Dessert was some kind of pudding that Erik decided to pass on; he helped himself to the fresh fruit instead. The mess hall was full, and Erik walked around looking for a place to sit down and eat his meal.

"Hey, soldier," a woman's voice hailed, "over here!" It was the familiar voice of Dale Swan.

"Hi, brat," Erik said affectionately and sat down next to the best-looking female in the place. "How's it going? Been through processing yet? I have to go back at thirteen-thirty for my assignment."

"I've already in-processed and got my assignment. Guess what. I am supposed to be photo intelligence analyst. Where do you think I've been assigned? Goddamned Supply! I will probably be the lieutenant in charge of linen, pillows, and mattresses," she snorted.

"It could be worse," Erik said. "Don't get caught sleeping on the job!"

"Oh, isn't he funny. What a clever boy we have here! You just wait until you need clean sheets and a pillowcase," she said. "I'll tell you, 'So sorry, GI, you number ten … you go wash, come back next week!'"

Erik said, "I take it you have a Korean house boy … or rather house girl?"

Mimicking her housemaid, Dale said, "She velly old mama-san—maybe hunered years!"

"You do that well," Erik said. "Better watch it—it could be catching!"

They finished their lunch and left the mess hall.

"Where did they put you last night—which barracks?" Dale asked.

"Don't know the barracks number," he said, "but it's the one across from the Officers' Club. Where did they put you?"

"Barrack number T-281. Can't miss it! The sign above the door says 'Women Only. Off Limits to Male Personnel.' Like I said, you can't miss it. It's right next door to the chapel. Anyway, see you later. Oh, by the way, I'm in room number eight on the ground floor," Dale said.

With that, Erik went to Personnel to get his job assignment. He expected to get orders to head north and probably to command a platoon.

"Major Harmon will see you now, Lieutenant," the sergeant at the desk said.

Erik knocked on the door and heard "Come in."

Looking up from his desk, Major Harmon said, "Hello, Lieutenant. Have a seat. I see your last assignment was as a supply officer at Fort Lewis."

"Yes, but that was a temporary thing. I was supposed to be going to Korea as an infantry replacement. A colonel at Fort Lewis had me side-lined for temporary duty in Supply. I was only there for nearly five months then released to come over here."

"Be that as it may, you are going to be assigned to our Supply Depot, and I may also have to assign you an additional duty as the Post Exchange Officer." The major could see that Erik was tight jawed and not thrilled with his assignment.

Erik asked, "Will this be another temporary assignment, sir, and then I'll be sent to a combat unit?"

"I couldn't say just now. It depends on what replacements we get. Let me say this, Lieutenant. Consider yourself lucky. Going up to the front lines is not a picnic. You grow up fast up there!"

Erik nodded but said nothing. The major gave him a printed form that had the hours, location, and who he was to report to at 1500 hours.

Erik left and sought out the location of his new assignment. Two NCOs (Non-Commissioned Officers) were arguing with three Korean workers when Erik entered the supply compound.

"What's going on here?" he asked.

One of the NCOs came to attention as Erik approached them; the other just stared at Erik with a contemptuous look on his face. Erik repeated himself, getting a little agitated in the process. "I asked you, what is going on here?"

"Ah, well ... these guys are supposed to be working," replied the NCO at attention. "We found them in the warehouse cooking up food on their burner and stinking up the whole place."

The older, surly NCO, a technical sergeant, finally said, "We wuz readin 'em the riot act! This one," he said, pointing to an old Korean who looked like he was in his seventies, "was warned about this before. I'm gonna kick his ass off the post!" Looking at Erik and sneering, he added, "and I don't give a shit if some shave-tail second Louie agrees with that or not."

Erik eyes narrowed at the remark and the body language of the technical sergeant, recognizing the challenge to his position.

"I would hold off doing anything, if I were you," advised Erik. "Tell these people to get back to work, and it can be dealt with later."

The sergeant bristled and glared at Erik. He was a big, burly man and not accustomed to backing off for anyone—let alone a wet-nosed second lieutenant. The sergeant caught the glint in Erik's eyes, and he did not see fear there. In fact, he saw a look that said, *Don't screw with me!* His eyes shifted to the patches on Erik's jacket, and he saw that Erik was both Airborne- and Ranger-qualified. Licking his chops and mentally counting his blessings, he changed his whole attitude and said, "Yes, sir!" Turning to the Koreans, he ordered them back to work.

"One other thing, Sergeant," Erik added. "This second lieutenant"—he pointed to himself—"may not have as many years in the Army as you do, and he may have a great deal to learn about supply, but I can assure you, he knows how to fight and kick ass. Are you reading me, Sergeant?"

The response was immediate. "Yes, sir, Lieutenant!"

Continuing, Erik said, "I hope there won't be a next time that I find you insubordinate, Sergeant, because it would not go well for you!"

With that, Erik turned and went into the office nearby.

Entering the supply office, Erik announced himself to the corporal busy working at his desk.

"Hi, Lieutenant. Captain Humberson is over at the colonel's office, and he should be coming right back here in a few minutes. How about a cup of coffee? I just made a fresh pot."

"Sure! Thanks," Erik said. He took a seat and sipped his coffee. "Ummm, this is good coffee! You make this yourself?"

"Yes, sir, I get the coffee beans … heat them up and then put them in the old grinder. I do it fresh, and the coffee smells good and tastes good too."

"Boy, you sure are resourceful," Erik noted.

Erik asked the corporal about the type of supply work going on and what the procedures were. Corporal Kevin Spence, Erik noticed, was not a kid, maybe in his late twenties. Corporal Spence gave Erik a verbal summary of the present operation. Erik was very impressed with Spence's ability to concisely express himself.

"Are you Regular Army?"

"No, sir. I'm a draftee. I have about six months to go, and then homeward bound," he replied.

"What did you do in civilian life?" Erik asked.

"I ran a small garden equipment and supply place. Did some engine repair work and sold new equipment. I don't think I'll get back into that though." He added, "I sold my half of the business to my partner when I got drafted, so I don't have anything like that to get back into."

The door opened, and Captain Clyde Humberson entered.

"I'm back, Spence." Then, noticing Erik, he said, "Hello there. Just get in, did you?" He extended his hand. "I'm Clyde Humberson. Welcome aboard! Come on into my office," he said, leading the way for Erik. "I saw your personnel file. You worked Supply at Fort Lewis for a while, but I see that you're Infantry, and I've seen all your other qualifications. Don't tell me that Colonel Roberts waylaid you—same as half a dozen others?"

"Yes, sir, he sure did."

"Well here's the deal," Humberson said. "We are the major supply receiving depot for our guys. We get the material off planes from the CONUS and Japan. We also get most large items by surface transportation. Our big job is getting stuff sorted out, documented, and shipped to where it is needed." Raising his hands in the air, as if talking to the Almighty, he added, "But not necessarily in that order! We try to get it sorted out and shipped—then we wrestle with the paperwork. We have a big problem with stealing around here. We need a lot of Korean labor, and we don't have enough military personnel to operate the material handling equipment—forklifts, tugs, and such."

"What will be my job here?" Erik asked.

"I have three other officers beside yourself. I got a new lieutenant this morning, a WAC."

That would be Dale, Erik thought.

"Buddy Sloan has his crew and handles the incoming munitions and priority stuff from the cargo planes. Richie Meyers handles the dockyard crew and knows all the ins and outs. He also speaks Korean—a big help to me, he is!"

Humberson appeared lost in thought for a moment, but then he recovered and said, "Oh yeah! The new WAC is going to handle and coordinate the paperwork—something I need help with—and you, I hope," he added, putting his hands together in prayer while Erik just looked at him, "will be my expeditor for getting everything on its way in country. This is going to be something a bit different. Before, everybody was trying to do everything, and I had people duplicating shipments and screwing up the works. I only had two people beside myself then."

"Are there written procedures or guidelines?" Erik asked.

"Well, sort of," replied Humberson. "We have some old SOPs, but they won't work now because we are twenty times busier. The rest of the supply depot is handling fuel, munitions, heavy weapons, aircraft spares, and rations. Let me tell you that rations are A-One priority! Some of it is perishable, but it's all subject to pilfering if you turn your back on the Koreans working here, and we got thanksgiving frozen turkeys to get out to all food services"

Captain Humberson spent the rest of the afternoon filling in Erik. Erik found his new boss to be a very likeable and flexible fellow. Anything to get the job done was his motto. Suppertime came around quickly, and Erik went back to his room to freshen up. He then stopped by the APO to see if any of his mail had caught up with him. Erik had not had any mail since Colonel Roberts had his assignment temporarily diverted. The overworked postal clerk rolled his eyes when Erik started to explain his situation. Suddenly the clerk's face lit up.

"You were at Fort Lewis? Got pulled from your overseas shipment? One of Roberts's supply people?"

Erik nodded to all three questions. The postal clerk went to a box on a shelf. Sorting through bundles of mail, he asked, "What's your last name? How do you spell it? Ah-ha!" Pulling out a bundle fastened with a rubber band, the postal clerk returned to Erik in triumph. "Second Lieutenant Erik Neilsin?" he asked.

"Yeah … All right!" Erik shouted as he took the bundle of mail. "Thanks a lot!"

Following a quick supper, Erik retreated back to his room to sort through his mail. There were seventeen letters—six from his father, three from Aunt Jennifer, a couple from Erik's friends from ROTC School and Ranger School, three official-looking envelopes, and the rest Erik considered junk mail. He arranged his letters by the mailing date and started to read through his dad's letters. Erik's father continually cautioned him to be careful and not get hurt. In the last letter, Erik's dad said that he had not heard from him in a long time and that he should write—if only a few lines. Also, Erik noted, for the first time his dad mentioned that he had not been feeling well lately. Erik wrote a quick letter to his dad telling him briefly how he had been diverted in his assignment and that he was fine. He also asked what was wrong and said that his father should take the time to see a doctor.

The three official-looking envelopes were from the company lawyers. One letter informed Erik that in accordance with his father's wish, he would receive forty-nine percent of his father's share in Apex Builders, Inc. The second letter was to inform him that his father had set up a trust for Erik since he was in the service and in a war zone. Erik learned that the trust contained some stock shares, money, and some other assets. The third envelope informed Erik of the accounts that had been set up for him by his father and other information that he just skimmed through.

There was a knock on the door. It startled Erik because it interrupted the quiet. The knock came again, and Erik went to the door. Glancing at his watch he saw that it was ten-thirty. When he opened the door, there stood Dale Swan.

"Hiya, Erik! Want some company?"

Not really, he thought, but he said, "Sure! Come on in. I guess nobody is going to say anything if you're visiting. Hey, look at the pile of mail I had waiting for me at the post office."

Dale glanced at it. "I checked also," she said. "I got my last bank statement, a notice from the finance company saying that if I didn't make my last payment they would repossess my car, a whole pile of catalogs, and my *Reader's Digest* book. So what else is new?"

"I met our boss, Captain Humberson, this afternoon," Erik said. "He seems like a good guy. He said he had a new lieutenant WAC officer who would be heading up the paper trail. I figured that was you."

"Yeah, it is a lot of paperwork. Most of it's old, but I have some ideas that I can put to work since I'm to have a pretty free hand with my job." She then asked, "Anything here to drink?"

"I only have a can of beer left," Erik apologized.

"That's okay. I figured that you hadn't had a chance to locate the booze yet, so I brought something over." She pulled out a quart jar that contained ice, a couple of slices of lime, and tonic water. "Gin and tonic," she said. "The best I could do was this glass jar. They had boiled eggs in it, and I talked them into giving me the jar."

"Over at the O Club?" asked Erik, guessing that the Officers' Club would have been one of the first places Dale checked out.

"Yep. I'm one of thirteen girls at Pusan, I think. I had to get out of the club. I could feel all those eyes eating me up."

She removed her fatigue blouse, and Erik had to admit that she looked great with her olive-drab T-shirt. Erik produced two coffee mugs, and Dale filled each one.

"Here's to the new job," she toasted.

Erik felt tired, but a few sips of the gin and tonic gave him a pick-up. "Boy, Dale, this is good!"

The drinks were nice and cold, and it was warm and dry in the barracks. The drinks hit the spot.

"Gee, you don't have much of a room here," observed Dale. She sat on Erik's bed and bounced up and down a few times. "Well, at least you have a good bed. Your mattress is better than the one I have," she said.

"Well, maybe you should move in here," Erik joked.

"Hmmmm, I'll give that some thought. Anything to eat?"

"Now, there I can help with something," Erik said. Getting up, he went to his wall locker, brought out a small box, and out of it produced a package of crackers, a can of boned chicken, and a jar of cheese spread. They spread out the crackers on a paper towel, and with two teaspoons they spread the cheese and ate little chunks of chicken, washing it down with the rest of the gin and tonics. Finishing, Dale gave an unceremonious belch and then offered a "Pardon."

Running out of small talk, Erik glanced at his watch and was surprised to see it was already eleven thirty.

"Well, old girl," he said to Dale, "want to call it a day?"

"Sure, why not," she replied.

Dale got up and stretched that stretch of hers, giving the impression that she was going to burst the fabric on her olive drab T-shirt. Dale put her arms around Erik's neck and said to him, mischief dancing in her eyes, "I have to ask you a question, Erik. How come you've never made a pass at me? You know I like you, and I know you like me, but you always hold back … how come?" Not waiting for an answer, she continued, "Do you find me attractive or does the uniform turn you off?"

"Holy cow!" cried Erik. "Boy, you are really giving me the third degree! For the record, I think you are more than attractive. You have a great 'weapons system'"—he wiggled his eyebrows comically as he eyed her body—"and what's more, you have a sharp brain, and you're quick witted. You even have a great sense of humor. Does that make me sound like a fan club member?"

"Thanks! A girl likes to hear all those things, and I appreciate the comments about my brain. Most guys think all I've got is what they see between my waist and my shoulders. But you didn't answer my question."

"You mean, how come I've never made a pass at you?"

"Yeah! That makes me feel like I'm deficient in some way."

"Dale, I've watched you in action! It's a pleasure just to look at you, and I have always enjoyed our friendship. I never wanted to be like the other guys and have you think all I was interested in was a shot of leg."

Dale was silent for a few minutes as if deep in thought. She looked up into Erik's face, her arms still around his neck.

"You're a good guy, Erik, and I like you. Like you a lot! I am not interested in a love affair with you," she explained, "but I value your friendship and the close companionship we seem to share. I have been asking myself the question of whether or not you and I could have this type of friendly relationship without romantic entanglement, and still satisfy our physical desires."

Where is this going? Erik wondered.

"Why are you telling me this, Dale?"

"'Cause, I want you to make love to me now," she said without any pretension.

She then reached Erik's lips with her own and kissed him long and tenderly. Erik felt an immediate response, and with Dale's body pressed against his T-shirt, he felt sure that her breasts were burning holes in his undershirt. Erik felt a little awkward but kissed Dale with equal passion—the level of desire increasing. Dale turned off one light, moved to Erik's bed, and slipped out of her clothes. She looked a little funny, but desirable, standing there with an olive-drab T-shirt and white frilly briefs. Pulling back the covers of Erik's bed, she jumped inside.

"Come to Mama," she murmured.

It was four in the morning, and something had wakened Erik. He was suddenly aware that Dale was no longer in bed with him. She was nowhere in the room. *She must have gone back to her billet*, he thought. *That's just as well—I'd have a time of explaining her presence in my room all night.* He drifted back to sleep, and his alarm woke him at 0600 hours. Erik forced himself to get out of bed. He sat on the bed for a few minutes, reflecting on the previous night. *Boy, she was great!* Despite the fact that he had been tired, making love with Dale helped him to release all the tension he had the past few days. *Perhaps it was the same for her!*

A knock sounded on his door, and the door opened.

"Morning, Loo-tan-nant-son! Kim bring you hot coffee. Okay?" Kim had a mug of steaming coffee for Erik.

"Thanks, Kim! Just what I need."

"You got crows for Kim to wash, you put on bed, Kim do ever tink."

"Okay. I'm going to take a shower," Erik said and left.

Arriving at his place of duty, Erik jumped right into his new job. He reviewed the supply requests and an updated roster on the location of the units that requested the supplies. He checked the roster for a few days before and noticed that the units had moved. He cranked the handle on the field telephone, and Captain Humberson's cheerful voice answered.

"Neilsin here. Got a few questions. How do we know where the units are that get these supplies? I just checked three rosters for the past ten days, and the unit changed location three times. How am I going to get them supplied?"

"Look for the rear command post location," Captain Humberson suggested. "They won't be far from that point, and that is where we leave the supplies. I suggest that your men ship to the stationary units first. The others take more of your time."

Erik and three of his assigned men screened the supply lists, matching up the stationary units by distance. Erik was glad to find that the supply request list had already been pulled and the list marked with the supplies pulled. Those not filled were marked as "killed" from the list. They were not handling back orders—it was fill or kill!

Several six-by-six trucks were loaded up, and the three men assigned to each truck were dispatched. Two men rode in the cab while the third rode shotgun in the rear of the truck. That man was armed with a selective automatic .30-caliber M-1 carbine that allowed him to choose between single rounds or automatic bursts—like a machine gun—and was also armed with a Colt .45 automatic pistol as a sidearm. The trucks were dispatched, and Erik turned his attention to the other shipments that were much closer to the thirty-eighth parallel.

A few hectic days passed, and he had not seen Dale. They had both been working twelve- to fourteen-hour shifts. Erik came through the mess hall line with his food tray and was looking for a place to sit when he noticed a hand waving at him. He drifted over to a smiling Dale. He sat beside her and noticed that she looked tired.

"You look tired. Are you okay?"

"Yeah! Tomorrow is Thanksgiving and the mess hall is advertising real turkey."

"Yeah! Just long hours and frustration," she said,"but I'm looking forward to eat some turkey."

"You know, in thirty days it's going to be Christmas. We have to do something about that!"

"Like what?" Erik asked.

"Well, you're the only family I have—sort of," she ended lamely. "I just love Christmas time—but not alone and somewhere far from home."

Erik reached out and touched Dale's hand. "I'll have to see about getting us a little tree. You try to get something to put on the tree. We'll plan for a little celebration, if you like."

Deep in thought, Dale then said, "You have to get me a present. I'll get you one too. Nothing expensive. Nothing from Saks Fifth Avenue. I don't expect too much."

"I'm sure Saks is out," chuckled Erik. "I'll see what I can manage. Where are we going to put a tree, and where are we going to celebrate our Christmas?"

"Let's make it my room," she suggested.

"I thought your billets were off-limits to all male personnel. Isn't it going to be a bit hard for me to enter your barracks?"

"Oh, I forgot to tell you. I have a new room. It's on the ground floor, and it is one of two rooms in the barracks that has an outside door. It is usually well secured from outside entry, but I'll make an exception in your case," she said, smiling.

Twenty-two days of fifteen hours work completed the current shipments to all the units before Christmas. Erik was exhausted. The weather had turned bitter cold. The news in the North had not been good. The North Koreans had pushed south into Seoul, occupying the capital. The South Koreans, with American help, reentered Seoul, but then the Chinese entered to aid the North Koreans, and once again Seoul was threatened. Refugees were fleeing south. The North Koreans with help from the Chinese "volunteers" then recaptured Seoul. Everyone was getting jittery and concerned. The enemy was moving South toward Pusan. Suwon, Yojo, and Kangnung were threatened. Thousands of South Korean refugees were fleeing to Pusan, which was heavily armed and had a strong military force.

The American Seventh Division launched a counteroffensive and tried to hold off the southern advance of the Red Army. The Air Force was dropping around sixty thousand tons of bombs on the North Koreans. All said and done, Christmas Day was going to be cold and fraught with worry about the enemy reaching Pusan.

Erik had found a roll of mechanics' wire and showed his houseboy, Kim, how to take green tissue paper, cut it into small rolls, and then wrap it around the mechanics wire. Erik took a broken wood broom handle and drilled holes in it. He fashioned a tree stand out of a coffee can filled with rocks. Kim placed a wrapped wire into each hole, making little branches for a green tree. Little by little the tree took shape, with the branches getting smaller as they reached the top. When Kim and Erik finished they stepped back to view their handiwork.

"Not bad, at all," Erik said to Kim. The tree was about four feet high, and the branches were a bit fragile, but at least it looked somewhat like a small, skinny Christmas tree. Erik carried the tree over to the back door of Dale's room and kicked at the door.

"Who's there?" he heard Dale call.

"It's me," he yelled back. "Open the goddamned door. I'm freezing out here."

It took Dale a minute to unlatch everything and open the door. Erik, nearly turning blue with the cold, brought the little tree inside.

"There's your Christmas tree," he said. "Special ordered from Spokane."

"Oh, Erik, it's lovely," cried Dale, giving Erik a hug. "Erik, your face is freezing cold! Come stand by the stove."

Dale had a roaring fire going in the little pot-bellied stove. In a few minutes Erik had thawed out and found it was getting so hot he was now beginning to sweat. He stripped off his field jacket and sweater and felt more comfortable.

"Well, where are the tree decorations?" he asked.

Dale brought out a little bag in which she had saved aluminum caps from large bottles. Some were silver, some red, and some blue. She had fastened a bobby pin to each cap, bending the pin into a small hook. They put the caps on their little tree. Next, Dale brought out long strings of popcorn threaded onto sewing thread. She had three strings of popcorn—each about four feet long. They wound the popcorn strings around the tree like a regular garland. Dale finished off the tree with little thin strips of aluminum foil she'd cut up. "Got the foil over at the club kitchen," she said.

Erik was impressed with how nice their little tree looked. It was December 23, and tomorrow was going to be another busy day.

"I have to get going," Erik said to Dale. "I have to go shopping for your present." He laughed as he put his sweater and field jacket back on.

"Remember," Dale said, "don't spend too much on my present." She gave Erik a nice, long kiss. "Thanks for the lovely tree, Erik. You are a true, brave Viking! Watch how you go—it's snowing and blowing hard," she warned.

Erik had told Kim that he had to get a Christmas present for Dale Swan. Kim had been talking about a cricket cage, and he now presented Erik with a tiny wooden cage about eight inches square, with a little swing-open door. Erik had an idea. He gave Kim a package of cigarettes as a present and he then pursued his idea. He tore a wad of cotton from the roll, which he used for spit-shining his shoes, Erik wet the wad and molded it into a bird-like shape. He made two legs out of toothpicks and stuck them into the bottom of his bird form. Taking his pen, he drew a wing on each side and then a pair of eyes up front. He took another piece of toothpick—the sharp, pointed end—and cut it off and shaved it to a sharp point. He placed it into the head to simulate the bird's beak. He then slipped a piece of mechanics' wire around the toothpick legs and fashioned a perch, attaching it to the inside top of the cage. Now it looked like a miniature bird in a miniature birdcage. He then took one of his business cards, cut it in half, and printed "Korean Kanary" on the back.

Erik checked the post office and found to his delight that he had a package from home. It was from his Aunt and Uncle Knutson. Erik opened the parcel and was overjoyed to see its contents: a package of twenty Lipton tea bags, a box of sugar cubes, a package of homemade Christmas cookies, a foil-wrapped small Italian salami, and several cans of fruit salad, peaches, and pineapple. It also contained a box of saltine crackers and several cans of sardines, tuna, and chicken, and last, a box of Fanny Farmers butternut crunch. It was a timely blessing, thought Erik. He was set to throw the box in the corner when he felt something roll in it. Checking a little further, he found a small, five-ounce bottle of Norwegian Aquavit. He sorted out his dresser drawers, searching for more tissue paper, but he had used it all for the Christmas tree. Erik had saved two empty cigar boxes that he now used to put his Christmas goodies in. At the end of the day, he headed for the mess hall. As usual, Dale was there before he was. The meal was a little extra special that evening. The cook even made some chocolate pudding. The meat loaf was also a bit different; it was loaded with Spam and lots of gravy, but if you were hungry enough, it tasted just fine.

"Well, tonight's Christmas Eve," Erik observed. "Do we celebrate Christmas tonight or tomorrow night?" he asked.

"We have to work tomorrow, even if it's Christmas Day." Watching Erik's face, flushed with excitement, Dale responded with anticipation. "What are you up to," she squealed at Erik.

Other people sitting in the mess hall looked over at the two of them, wondering what that was all about.

"I'll be over around eight tonight, if that's okay?" Erik asked. "I have to pick up your present and other things—and I'm not going to reveal anything further."

Dale was all smiles when she left the mess hall with Erik. Captain Humberson was just coming into the mess hall and, seeing them both, he stopped for a quick chat.

"Erik," he said, "there's a big push going on north of Taejon. We have a convoy of trucks bringing supplies of food and cold weather gear for Seventh Division troops nearby. I got a report that the trucks have not arrived yet. They should have been there yesterday."

"How many trucks did we send out?" Erik asked, trying to remember.

"This convoy is composed of twelve six-by-sixes and three semi-trailers," Captain Humberson said. "There are at least fifty armed personnel in that convoy. They are somewhere in those mountains," he said, pointing to the map he had in his hand, "and so it's hard trying to reach them by radio—beside this weather is number ten. If we don't hear something by tomorrow, I'm going to have you take a quick run up there with a jeep to see what's going on. You are combat-trained and the logical choice. I hate to lay that on you, but I have little choice in the matter."

"I understand," Erik said, "but before I head out anywhere, I want some of that good cold-weather gear we recently got from the States. I want one of those arctic parkas and the heavy waterproof trousers too."

"You got it!" Humberson said as he turned to enter the mess hall. Pausing for a moment, he added "Merry Christmas, you two!"

"Same to you, Captain. Good night!"

Eight o'clock came, and Erik rushed over to Dale's billets loaded with his Christmas goodies and Dale's present. Dale was ready and on the lookout for him. When she saw him crossing the compound road, she hurried to open the side door. Hearing footsteps approaching, she swung the door open for Erik.

"Merry Christmas, little sister!" Erik greeted Dale. Dale gave Erik a big kiss and pulled him over to their little Christmas tree. Under the tree was a pint of Scotch whiskey, a wedge of wrapped cheese, some crackers, and also a small wrapped present with a small card saying "Merry Xmas, brother ... Sis."

Erik started to unload his things but kept her present behind his back so she couldn't see it. "First of all," he said, "close your eyes and don't open them until I get set. Your present was too big to wrap, and I want to make sure it's okay."

Dale was squirming with excitement. "Oh, hurry up. I can hardly wait to see what you brought me," she squealed.

Erik examined the little bird cage and the bird inside. Everything was intact.

"Okay, you can open your eyes now." He presented the gift to Dale, saying, "Merry Christmas!"

Dale looked at the tiny birdcage and the handmade cotton bird and screamed her delight. "Oh, Erik, you sweetie! It is simply lovely. How did you ever manage this?" she said in wonderment.

"Well, they didn't have what I wanted in Sears, and Montgomery Ward was out, so I shopped at the Birdland of Pusan and bought the last Korean Kanary."

"Oh, it is really very clever, and the cage is really something else," she said.

Erik opened up his cigar boxes and produced the Christmas cookies, tinned meats and fish, Aquavit, and the other things. Between them, they had quite a nice Christmas spread. There was a knock on the door, and Dale opened the door to two of the other women living in the billet. They did not appear to be surprised to see Erik there with Dale. They entered, and Dale closed the door and made the introductions.

"This is Mary Louise, Red Cross," she said, "and this is Sue Vandermeir. She's medical."

Everyone wished each other a Merry Christmas.

"What a lovely tree," Sue said.

"I have a terrible cold. Isn't that cough medicine under the tree?" Mary Louise asked, eyeing the scotch.

"I have some ice cubes for the scotch." Dale opened the door and brought in a small pan that had cracked pieces of ice in it. "I stuck the pan out there an hour ago, and the water froze fine. My little hammer did the rest."

Sue and Mary Louise had brought their own glasses, and everyone had a healthy scotch on the rocks. Erik broke out the salami, cheese, and crackers. He opened a can of Norwegian sardines, and they all nibbled away and recounted previous Christmas holidays. Among the four of them, they finished the pint of scotch and most of the snacks. Mary Louise got up, thanked Dale and Erik for a lovely Christmas Eve, and announced she was heading for the sack.

Sue Vandermeir also got to her feet, somewhat unsteadily, and said, "I guess I'll head for home too." Looking at Erik, who'd risen to his feet when the two girls were going to leave, Sue said, "I am going to kiss your Erik." And with that announcement she went over to Erik and gave him a kiss full on the lips. "Don't say you never got anything from the Medical Corps."

It was past midnight, and Erik held Dale and wished her a Merry Christmas again.

"Should I be heading back now?" Erik asked.

"Only if you want to," Dale said, smiling. "You know you haven't even opened up my present to you."

"Gee, I'm sorry! When the other two girls came in, I just forgot," offered Erik while opening his package. Inside was a small medallion made of pewter. It was a Saint Christopher medal, and it was attached to a thin chain. Erik gave Dale a questioning look and said, "Dale, this must be your own personal medallion, I don't feel you should give it to me as a present."

"Hush now," Dale admonished Erik. "I had two of these, and I wanted you to have one, especially since you may be going to go 'up country' in a few days. And right now, I have another present for you." She gave him a mischievous look. Dale opened the stove, shoveled in some more coke, and then closed the damper with only a slight opening.

"There! Now we won't freeze later on." She slipped out of her jumpsuit and slid under the covers, waiting for Erik to join her. The stove emitted just enough light, once their eyes adjusted to the darkness. Dale whispered in Erik's ear, "Thank you for making our Christmas special! It was more than I expected."

Dale took the initiative and was aggressive in their lovemaking. It was both tender and sweetly satisfying, and they were both soon lost in a deep sleep.

Morning came too soon, and Dale's alarm woke them up at 0630 hours. Erik quickly got into his clothing, gave Dale a kiss, and was off to his own barracks. The morning was frigid, and Erik could feel the hair inside his nostril freeze. He entered his room and got ready to shower. Kim was there in a few minutes with his mug of fresh, hot coffee. Washed, shaved, and dressed, Erik headed for the mess hall and met Dale heading there also. They enjoyed a powdered scrambled eggs breakfast with French toast and syrup, washed down with coffee. They departed, heading for their own duties. Erik was busy with truck assignments with his NCOs when Captain Humberson came in and caught Erik's eye.

"Hi, Captain … Merry Christmas!"

"Same to you, Erik. I've got some bad news, I'm afraid." He paused briefly and then said, "No, it's not what you're thinking. I received word that you are to be transferred to Seventh Division as a qualified infantry platoon officer. They have been taking a real pounding, and the Seventh is critically short of officer replacements."

Erik knew his expression was grim. "What are the details?" he asked. "How much time do I have before I have to be there?"

"Don't rightly know," Captain Humberson said. "They are going to send down a jeep to pick you up in a day or two. I sure hate to lose you, Erik. You have been a great help to me and our operation here."

Erik was lost in deep thought. He quickly considered his situation and decided to put some things aside that he felt he could not take with him. He would have to travel with his combat gear and no extras.

That evening, Erik knocked on Dale's door, bringing over many of the things he would not take with him. Dale answered the door.

"You back for seconds, so soon?" she asked, grinning, but seeing Erik's strained expression, she quickly became very concerned. "What is it, Erik?"

"I've been reassigned to the Seventh Infantry Division. I'll probably leave here later today or tomorrow. A driver is coming to pick me up."

"Oh Christ. No!" Dale cried and held Erik in a tight embrace.

"It's okay, Dale. Please don't act like that. This is what I've been trained for. They're short of combat officers, and I'm needed there."

"Do you have the Saint Christopher I gave you?" Dale asked. Erik opened his fatigue shirt, and Dale saw the medallion around his neck.

"I want to leave some things for you," Erik said. "I can't take all this extra stuff with me, but they are items you can use. Also, I'd like you to do me a favor. I have some legal stuff here in this envelope. I want to send it to this law firm and the other to my dad in Virginia. I don't think I'll get a chance to mail it. Would you mail it for me?"

"Sure, Erik, you don't have to ask!" A little shudder passed over her. "Erik, you probably won't get a chance to write much, but even if it's just a card saying 'Hi. I am okay, Erik', will you promise to send it to me, so I know you're all right?"

"Sure I will," Erik promised. "You take good care of yourself, little sister. Maybe next Christmas," he said, "we'll get a better tree!"

Dale was choked up and just hugged Erik. "You better take care of yourself," she said, choking back the tears, "else I won't invite you for Christmas again."

Corporal Spence interrupted them. "Hey, Lieutenant!" he called out.

"There's a driver here from Seventh Division to pick you up. Says he's in a hurry to get back. He's over at your barracks waiting on you."

"Okay, Spence, I'm on my way!" Erik hugged Dale and turned to leave.

"Hey, Lieutenant," Spence yelled at Erik. "Good luck and keep your powder dry!"

Erik grinned and headed for his barracks. He had packed all his gear, so he was ready to roll. They stopped for Erik to pick up his records and then headed north in the jeep.

"Where exactly are we going?" Erik asked the driver.

"Headquarters for the Third Battalion, Twenty-Third Infantry Regiment," the driver said.

"I'm Erik Neilsin. What's your name, soldier?"

"Jorge Rivera, with a 'J,'" he replied. "Everybody spells it wrong, and nobody pronounces my name right either!" He snorted.

"I know what you mean. I get about four different spellings for my name."

They drove in silence for a while, neither one talking. It was too cold, and the jeep offered little heat. Erik checked his weapon and worked the slide of his M-1 carbine to insure that it was not frozen. He checked the clip and then put it back into his weapon. It took a good three hours to reach the Third Battalion headquarters because of the ice and drifting snow on the roads.

"This way, Lieutenant," Jorge Rivera directed, leading Erik into a covered entrance.

It was a field mess tent, and they both made a beeline for the hot coffee. Ten minutes later, Erik reported to Lieutenant Colonel Tate Greenwald, Battalion Commander.

"Stand easy, Lieutenant! Made the trip okay?"

"Yes, sir. Pretty cold and slippery on the way up here," volunteered Erik.

The colonel just nodded his head. "I am sending you over to Baker Company—Captain French's company. He's a West Pointer and a good soldier. Follow his lead, and you'll do well." Dismissing Erik, the colonel added, "Good luck over there, Neilsin. We need a few more good officers."

"Thank you, sir." Erik saluted and then left to find Baker Company.

CHAPTER 16

"I'm trying to locate the company commander, Captain French," Erik said to the soldier typing at a desk.

"The captain is checking out the platoons. Should be back pretty soon. He's been gone over an hour," the clerk said. "Sir? Are you Lieutenant Nelson? We're supposed to be getting a new lieutenant soon," he asked.

"Neil*sin*," Erik said, emphasizing the pronunciation. He then spelled it out and said, "Neilsin! Not Nelson! Okay?"

The clerk checked a paper on his desk and nodded. "Could be, sir. I thought Headquarters said Nelson—sorry!"

"That's okay, happens all the time. Just don't want to wind up with someone else's paycheck or vice versa."

Erik went over to the command organizational chart and looked at Baker Company. There were four platoons. Platoons One and Three had officers in charge. Platoon Two had a master sergeant leading it, and Platoon Four had a technical sergeant in charge. Each platoon had three squads. There usually were twelve men to each squad with a NCO in charge.

An officer entered the field tent and tossed his helmet on the cot next to the desk before plopping into the chair.

"Captain, this is Lieutenant Erik Neilsin. He arrived just a few minutes ago," the clerk announced.

A weary looking captain rose to his feet and went to Erik with an outstretched hand. Erik saluted and took Captain French's hand.

"Louis French," he said to Erik. "Glad to have you with us." Without any further preamble, Captain French continued. "I saw the brief of your records. You've had jump school, and you passed Ranger School at Benning." It was a statement and not a question. "That's good. That means you've been through some of the roughest training the Army has to offer. Out here you need it! I'm giving you Number Three Platoon, and I'm leaving 'Frosty'—Tech Sergeant Michael Frost—with you as your assistant platoon leader. He's as good as any platoon leader I have. You also have a platoon sergeant. Sergeant Frost took over the position of Third Platoon leader when we were shorthanded. He's a good man, and you can learn a lot from him. If there is a need elsewhere and I feel that you can handle it okay without him, I may pull Frosty back here in reserve."

"I'm sure glad to finally get to an infantry unit. For a while there, I thought the Army was going to make me a permanent supply officer."

"I know what you mean," Captain French said. "There are a lot of units in the rear echelons with empty slots being filled with combat-trained soldiers that should be out here with us. Our regimental commander is looking into that situation. Division Headquarters was supposed to have some additional S-2 photo intelligence personnel. Regiment was promised the use of one of these personnel who arrived in Korea and then disappeared," he confided.

Erik bit his tongue, thinking of Dale Swan and the fact that she was a photo intelligence officer and probably destined to complement a Headquarters S-2 section. *Ah, what the hell*, thought Erik. *Dale is trained for that job, and lives may depend on her being assigned where she belongs.*

"Captain, a moment please?" Erik asked. "There is a Second Lieutenant Dale E. Swan in Pusan at the same supply depot I was at. The lieutenant is a she. She is also trained in photo intelligence, and she is sharp. We served together at Fort Lewis and again in Pusan. We were both diverted from our assignments at Lewis and Pusan."

Captain French studied Erik's face for a minute. Then he picked up the field phone and cranked the knob. "Niagara Three," Captain French said. "Would you put me through to Apple Patch, Third Regiment? Thanks, I'll hold ... Apple Patch? This is Niagara. Can you put me through to Apple Six, Colonel Servando? Yeah, I know, but this could be important. I have some information he would want to know."

Captain French drummed his fingers on the small desk while he waited. "Yes! Apple Six? Niagara Three here, Baker Company. Sir, weren't you looking for some inbound S-2 personnel? Right! And a photo intelligence analyst? Right, I thought so. Sir, I have a newly assigned officer here who says that both he and this Second Lieutenant Dale Swan, a photo analyst, were sidetracked into Depot Supply in Pusan. By the way, this person is a she. My guy said that she's sharp. Thought you'd like to know. Yes, sir, you're welcome, sir!" Captain French hung up the field phone.

"Thanks, Neilsin. I think we just made the colonel's day. I hope he has a place for females at regiment." Getting up, Captain French said, "Let's go meet your men."

Third Platoon

The acting platoon leader, Technical Sergeant Michael Frost, heard the jeep coming down the road and observed the two officers approaching. The jeep pulled up beside the tent, and the officers got out.

"Sergeant Frost, Lieutenant Erik Neilsin. Lieutenant Neilsin is the new Third Platoon leader," Captain French announced. "Frosty, I want you to stay with the platoon as assistant platoon leader and help Lieutenant Neilsin get settled in. Do you have any problem with that?"

"No, sir," Sergeant Frost replied. "Be glad to have someone else making the decisions!"

"Hello, Sergeant," Erik said, extending his hand. "Mind if I call you Frosty also?"

"Not at all. It will avoid a lot of confusion."

Captain French said, "Get the lieutenant a place to bunk and settled ASAP." Turning to Erik, he said, "Come up to Baker Company after chow—say around seven. I want you to meet the other platoon leaders. We will have some patrols going out tonight from First Platoon. I want to get you filled in on everything as soon as possible."

Not waiting for an answer, Captain French said, "I'll see you at seven. Frosty, you be there too," and he left.

"Let's get you bunked down, Lieutenant," Frosty said, leading the way through a row of tents.

Sergeant Frost introduced Erik to the men of the Third Platoon. Erik shook all their hands, studied their faces, and tried to remember all their names. Erik had a small room in the cabin-like tent. The floor was wood sections; the walls and top were canvas, and there was a little pot bellied stove whose chimney went through the canvas roof. It had a round hole of metal with the look of asbestos around it.

"We try not to let the fire go out," Frosty was saying. "We have one man whose job it is to make the rounds and fuel up the field heaters."

Erik met the other platoon leaders and was briefed on the evening's scouting mission and the company's military objectives for the next few days. The following day, Erik and Frosty were summoned by the captain. Looking at his wall map, the captain pointed to numbered sections on the map.

"We got word that there may be some Reds up in this area. From the description, sounded like some Chinese with them. This is Hill 413," he said, pointing with his ruler. "Over here is a frozen stream running through that gully, and over here is Hill 416. I want Third Platoon to feel out the left side of Hill 413 with one squad and have another squad work the right side of Hill 416. I want a coordinated scouting of both hills. Ten minutes later, I want the remaining squad to flush down the middle. With a deployment like that," he explained, "you reduce the chance of being ambushed."

"Any idea how many gooks were spotted, Captain?" Frosty asked.

"No. I had the impression that it looked like a scouting patrol, maybe eight to ten Reds." Looking at his watch, Captain French said, "I make it 0945 hours. See that you get in position by 1045. Frosty, radio me when Third

Platoon is in position. I will have First and Second Platoons in position in back of you, just in case."

"Yes, sir!" both men answered.

"Okay, Frosty, let's move out and get ready to move into position," Erik ordered.

All three squads moved silently to their designated locations, and Frosty heard three clicks of the radio to signify that First Squad was in position. Almost immediately, four more clicks were heard on the radio.

"Okay," Frosty said, "it's a go!"

He clicked his radio twice and then looked at his watch. Erik followed suit and saw the time on his watch. When the big hand reached ten minutes, Frosty and Erik rose to their feet and signaled Second Squad to move forward. Erik was studying the terrain and looking for footprints. Suddenly he froze. Frosty saw him stop, and he stopped also. Just ahead of him, the snow looked like it was slightly packed down. There were no footprints, but Erik saw what he thought might be snow brushed over to hide tracks. Erik pointed to the spot, and Frosty hand-signaled the squad to be alert and check ahead of them. Reaching the spot, Erik removed his trench knife and gently probed around the smooth spot. Nothing there... Nothing here... then *clink*. Metal. He worked his knife further back and eventually around the metal object. Carefully he scraped away the snow to reveal a land mine. Frosty removed a short red cloth patch from his pocket, a small wire strand through it, and attached it to the mine.

The squad, moving cautiously, uncovered three more mines. They had been laid out in a diamond shape about thirty feet apart at the sides and about sixty feet from the front and back. Troops running into this small field at night could get into serious trouble. Moving forward, the squad lead scout gave a circling motion with his hand, indicating they should assemble there. The squad moved up to his lead position. Crouching down, they looked over the snow mound and saw a group of twelve soldiers busy burying more land mines. From their position, Erik felt they could take out at least seven or eight of the North Koreans. The trees prevented them from getting clear shots at the other five.

Erik raised his eyebrows at Frosty—a question on what to do! Frosty looked at his watch and shook his head but pointed to the radio. Erik tapped the send button twice to let the other squads know that Second Squad, coming down the middle, had the gooks in sight. The taps also signaled that all squads should converge on the middle.

Second Squad held their position silently. Erik was glad that they were wearing white parkas. The two Chinese soldiers with the North Koreans kept looking about nervously. *He's got good instincts,* thought Erik. Suddenly all the Reds jumped up, startled, looking to their left side. One of First Squad's men had slipped in the snow, and the North Koreans heard him. Erik took aim at one of the Chinese and fired. The rest of the squad opened fire and caught seven of the enemy by surprise. The five remaining soldiers turned toward their fallen comrades just at the moment the right side of the hill opened fire and dropped the remaining five soldiers. It was the Second Squad.

Frosty supervised the digging up of the other mines and marked them for disposal. Erik searched the pockets of the Chinese soldier who appeared to be an officer. He found what seemed to be a map of the land mines that the Koreans had set up. The other soldiers did not have anything that appeared to be significant. Erik cut off a patch from the Chinese officer's jacket. He removed the officer's quilted gray cap. Inside he discovered another map, which showed the whole of Korea. The map had bold light green lines traced down to Seoul and beyond to the south. To the north, the line traced right up to the Yalu River and into Manchuria. It appeared to be the Chinese supply route.

Returning to the company, after radio contact, Erik and Frosty went to Baker Company HQ to brief Captain French. Looking over the captured documents, French said, "This looks like some good stuff! I'll get this up to Battalion to forward to Regiment. Something that the Air Force can do," he surmised.

"Here's something else of possible interest," Erik said, taking the Chinese soldier's shoulder patch out of his pocket. "The Chinese guy had this patch on—I didn't know what outfit that signified."

Captain French examined the patch and said, "I don't recognize it either. We'll send this up the G-2 at Headquarters also."

Erik stepped away to help himself to a cup of coffee. He observed the captain talking with Sergeant Frost. When he returned, Captain French said, "Erik, Frosty gave you high marks. Says you're real savvy. Picking up on that minefield was important. Aside from your patrol stepping on a mine in broad daylight, I would have had a patrol going out that way and probably had half of them blown apart." He then looked at Frosty. "You'd better pass the word to the other platoon leaders, Frosty," Captain French ordered. "Tell them to check inside the hats of the Koreans and especially any Chinese!"

"Good idea as a reminder," Frosty said. "Our platoon leaders have been told to search for information, but I'll remind them again."

A few days later Captain French called Erik to inform him that the map he'd taken from the Chinese soldier was the supply route and infiltration route for the Chinese into North Korea. "Remember that patch you took off that guy's jacket? Well, G-2 says it is a patch from the Sixty-Sixth Corps of the Red Chinese Army. G-2 didn't have anything on the Sixty-Sixth Corps, so this was important information. The intelligence people are really buzzing now."

During the following three weeks Erik went on numerous patrols with his platoon. His men soon had confidence in Erik as a smart leader. Captain French told Erik that he wanted Frosty back at the company now that Erik was settled in. In the short time Erik had been with Third Platoon, he and Frosty had become good friends.

One night all the company platoons were called into action and directed to move up into an area called Chochiwon, north of Kongju. Captain French briefed his platoon leaders, saying, "Third Battalion will be pushing north, up the right side toward Ch'ongju and fanning out to the west toward Ch'onan, while the battalion's main thrust goes to take the Umsong rail point. Part of the battalion will spearhead east toward Chungju—another rail point. Our mission is to make sure that the North Koreans do not move west and do an end run around our flank and come up behind us. We will take and deploy machine guns, BARs, and bazookas. I want our light mortars, too. Divarty will be in a 'stand ready' mode to support our needs. We will have an FO assigned to Third Platoon to spot and call the shots if we need them," Captain French explained.

"It is important that you all have your maps and all able to coordinate information on any movements or actions under way. One thing more. This is Sergeant Andy Knor, who was sent down as our FO, and he will be our link for calling in artillery. Pack up and be ready to move out by twelve hundred hours today. Questions?" When nobody responded, he said, "Okay, let's do it!

Baker Company moved out to their appointed destination. All the men were armed with ARs and .30-caliber M-1 Garand rifles. They all carried extra field rations, as it might be a while before they ate in a mess tent again. A squad from Fourth Platoon, with their heavy weapons, was attached to Third Platoon's operation. They were equipped with two .30-caliber air-cooled machine guns and two 60-mm mortars.

Arriving at the staging area, the company split up into platoon elements and moved out to their assigned positions. It was getting dark as Third Platoon formed into three columns, with Erik leading Second Squad up the middle and flanked by the other two squads. The area that Erik's platoon was assigned to required that they entrench themselves in the vicinity of Chochiwon. Frequently checking his map and compass, Erik reckoned that they were very near their objective. He halted the platoon. Erik called in his squad leaders to discuss the situation.

"There is a hill with cover over to the left," he said, pointing. "See it? You take Number One Squad up there and dig in. I want a machine gun set up in that rocky area on the high ground," he said, again pointing. "Spread out the men, Sergeant."

"Yes, sir!"

One of the machine guns was set up in a rocky elevated point overlooking the frozen stream. The other machine gun was placed on another ridge, which would allow good crossfire. Two mortar teams were positioned on other high points, with a squad spread out to provide cover for the mortar teams. The remaining soldiers quickly headed for the thick cover and dug in. Turning to Second Squad, Erik took them further to the right onto another small hill. It was about five hundred yards from the other position.

"Find some rocks and brush that provide good cover." The squad leader left to spread his soldiers out in defensive positions.

"I'm going up ahead with this squad. I will try to get into a position up there," Erik said, pointing to another ridge about a thousand yards ahead. "I'll be able to see what's going on, and between the three squads we'll be able to bring a triangle of fire to bear on any troops trying to sneak through our position."

Pausing for a moment of thought, Erik told the forward observer to stick close to him. "I want each squad to set up trip flares. If they come through here tonight, we might not see them in the dark. Pass the word to the other squad leaders, Frosty."

Erik moved out. Looking out over the ravine in front of them, he saw the frozen stream that looked almost like a trail, winding through their position. "I want trip flares set up there, there, and there!" he directed. "Chuck", one of the squad sergeants!"

"Yes, sir?"

"I want you to rig a few grenades with trip wires in those small areas where someone might slip through."

After an hour and a half of preparation, the triangular defensive position was wired with trip flares and grenades. All they had to do now was wait and keep alert. It was late in the night when Erik and his men heard the faint noise of firing. It sounded a fair distance away. Keeping his voice low, Erik got on the walkie-talkie and gave his squads a "heads up."

"Did you hear that firing in the distance?" Erik asked. Two clicks sounded, meaning Yes.

"It sounds like the main part of the battalion or regiment are engaging someone—most likely on the right flank. We might see some gooks coming our way from this left side, trying to get around the main assault battalion. Keep on your toes, everyone!"

Two more sets of clicks came through on the radio.

Erik turned to Andy Knor, the FO, who had tuned his radio to Division Artillery, code name: "Beefsteak."

"Andy, we going to be ready with artillery if we need it?" he asked.

By way of an answer, the FO spoke into his mike. "Beefsteak One, this is Sierra Four."

A pause and then the earphone came alive with a voice. "Roger, Sierra Four. Beefsteak One, reading you loud and clear. Do you want to place an order?"

"That's a negative, Beefsteak," Andy responded. "Just letting you know we're in place at coordinates whiskey one zero zero, tango two-twenty."

"That's a roger, Sierra Four. Out."

It was past two in the morning. Erik had been dozing while his squad leader and some of the men manned their posts. A hand touched Erik's arm, and he was instantly awake and alert.

"What is it?" he hissed quietly.

The squad leader said nothing but pointed up ahead. Erik strained his eyes but could not see anything. His ears, however, picked up the sounds of branches snapping. The noise, slight as it was, sounded like the movement of several soldiers. Someone was heading their way.

Erik picked up the radio and hit the "talk" button three times. *Click, click, click.* Erik got two sets of clicks back. Everyone was alert and ready.

Andy Knor put on his radio headset and spoke quietly but distinctly over the radio. "Beefsteak One, this is Sierra Four. I have a menu order for sector whiskey nine zero, tango four-twenty. I say again—whiskey nine zero, tango four-twenty. Hold the order! I say again, hold the order!"

A voice came back repeating the map reference positions. A menu order meant that Andy was ready to ask for some rounds to come in for effect, but only on his command.

Erik passed the word to his squad leaders by radio and heard the two-click acknowledgements. Two North Korean soldiers could be seen moving slowly forward, looking left and right as they came. Erik whispered, "Scouts! Let them pass. Hold fire—pass the word."

The scouts moved forward and passed beneath Erik's position. Up ahead and not moving as quietly were two columns of soldiers heading through the ravine. Erik estimated at least a company-sized unit. Suddenly one of the two scouts that had passed Erik's position tripped a flare. Both scouts were downed with a few rounds.

"Beefsteak One, Sierra Four. Fire for effect," the FO ordered.

Just then a grenade went off to the left side. First Squad had opened fire on yet a third column heading their way, which had set off the grenade. A whistling sounded briefly, followed by *Whomp! Whomp! Whomp! Whomp!* as the area in back of the advancing soldiers exploded.

"Beefsteak, Sierra! Bring that forward two notches," ordered the FO. Now the incoming rounds from the battery of heavy artillery pounded the fields and ravine in front of Erik's position. The machine gunners were now firing from their positions, catching the North Koreans in a deadly crossfire. The mortar teams were targeting soldiers on their flanked positions. Erik saw to his surprise that there were many more soldiers breaching his right-side position.

"Beefsteak, Sierra! Correct and give me maximum on positions whiskey ninety-nine, tango three-twenty," the FO ordered, asking for shelling from north to south this time.

The incoming rounds were falling fast and close. Erik could feel the heat from some of the explosions. "Keep your heads down," Erik cautioned. "Fragments go a long way!"

Erik heard a yell from his left side and, turning, saw that a small group of North Koreans had breached his left flank position. Firing his pistol as he ran toward them, he cut down two right in front of him and rolled when he saw a third taking aim at him. Erik was back on his feet quickly and upon the gook. Too close for firing, Erik shoved the Korean's rifle to one side and swung his fist in a downward chopping motion into the soldier's throat, crushing the larynx. The soldier grabbed for his throat, trying to breathe, and Erik fired his pistol at point-blank range. Erik and his men engaged in hand-to-hand fighting while the incoming barrage continued.

A bugle sounded, and whatever enemy soldiers were still alive began running back from the way they came.

"Beefsteak One, Sierra Four. Cease fire! I say again, Cease fire!"

"Great job, Andy! Tell Beefsteak there's dead gooks all over here," Erik said. "Better pass on the word to your other beefsteaks in the northern sector that there is a large number of gooks heading back north. I estimate a couple of hundred."

"That's a roger, Sierra. We copy."

After hearing the acknowledgment of Andy Knor's message, Erik tuned the radio to the company's radio frequency. "Niagara Three, this is Coffee Two." Erik repeated the call several times before Captain French's voice answered.

"Coffee Two, Niagara Three. Go ahead," he said.

"We've had about two hundred that we dropped here, and about another couple of hundred turned around and are heading back north. We brought in Divarty that was very effective. I have three in my squad wounded, and I don't know yet about the other squads. I haven't had a report yet."

"Good going, Coffee Two! We got three more hours till daylight. I want you to reposition and dig in. Keep me posted."

Daylight came. Third Platoon had suffered two killed and five injured in the night's action. Fortunately, the five injured soldiers did not have serious wounds, and the squad leaders saw to their men and patched them up with sulfur powder and dressings. The action lasted two more days before the North Koreans retreated to the north, back toward Seoul. Erik received orders for the platoon to go back to the rear company position. Erik and his men were very tired, cold, and hungry.

Erik had not noticed at the time, but he had suffered several minor flesh wounds from a grazing bullet or two. In the heat of battle he had only felt a hot sting, which had quickly passed.

"Better get that seen to, Lieutenant," a medic said to Erik.

Erik entered the field dressing station where two medics were busy patching up slightly injured soldiers. The more serious cases were sent to the rear and to one of the MASH units, most likely near Pusan.

"Be with you in a minute, Lieutenant," the medical corpsman said.

Erik sat down and closed his eyes for just a second. He snapped awake when a medical corpsman waved an ammonia capsule under his nose and only then realized that he'd slid off the stool onto the floor.

"You gave me a scare," the medic said.

"I'm okay, just tired." Erik managed to get out. The corpsman started checking Erik's injuries and got Erik's fatigue blouse off. There was dried, caked blood at the back of Erik's left shoulder. The wound had come from a fragment of artillery. Erik had lost some blood, and the combination of that plus lack of sleep, excitement, and poor food all made for one tired soldier. The medic applied a sterile cleaning agent to Erik's shoulder and, now seeing the wound, said, "You've got some metal fragments in there, and you need a doctor to take them out. Aside from that, it doesn't look too bad. I want you to lay down there." And before Erik could protest further, the corpsman gave him a shot of something, and Erik dropped off to sleep.

"Tag this one for non-critical surgery," the corpsman said to one of the medical team.

When Erik came to, he was in a MASH hospital unit. A nurse in coverall-type fatigues came by and said, "How you doing, Lieutenant? You've been asleep for over sixteen hours!"

Erik tried to raise himself up on his elbows, and a sharp pain shot across his left shoulder.

"Yikes!" Erik yelled.

"Stay put or you'll pull those sutures," she said. "You had a piece of jagged metal the size of a nickel in that shoulder," she said, handing Erik a small wax paper cup with the cleaned-up piece of shrapnel in it.

"That's it?" asked Erik. "Thanks, I'll put it in my trophy case," he joked.

"Are you hungry, Lieutenant?" she asked.

"God, am I ever!" he replied. "I could eat a horse!"

"We don't allow horses in here," she said, "but I'll get you something to eat." Returning ten minutes later, she brought a metal food tray with bread, meat, and potatoes.

"I think I'll make this into a sandwich for you so you can eat it better." She forked the meat onto a slice of bread, spread a little mashed potato on top, and then put the other slice of bread over it. "It's a little sloppy," she said, "but I think it will be easier for you to manage."

Erik agreed. He wolfed down the sandwich and turning on his side was able to use his fork to eat the rest of the potatoes. The nurse handed Erik a cup with a flexible straw so he was able to drink hot coffee. Erik finished his meal and was surprised to learn that he had some visitors. Captain French and Frosty came in.

"How ya doing, Lieutenant?" Frosty inquired.

"Glad to see you awake and eating," Captain French said. "I thought I was losing another officer. How come you didn't report that you were wounded?"

"Honest, Captain, I didn't think I had anything serious till the corpsman got to me. How did things go? The battle, I mean?"

"It was a good offensive. Do you know what the body count was in your sector?" Mike French asked.

"I reckon about hundred to two hundred," Erik guessed.

"We received a report that three hundred forty-seven North Koreans and three Chinese were among the dead. We recovered twenty-seven wounded as well. I have debriefing reports from your squad leaders, and I talked to your men. I learned how you came to their aid when they got overrun. According to your men, you took out four gooks and secured the position on the high ground. The artillery spotting was on the money as well. You all did a good job, Erik. The company is proud of you!"

Erik felt a little embarrassed.

"Colonel Servando was particularly pleased that your platoon tore up at least three North Korean companies of soldiers and turned them north again. He said you shouldn't be a second lieutenant!" Reaching into his field jacket pocket, Captain French brought out a pair of silver bars. "These silver bars were mine when I made First," he said. "I'd be pleased to have you wear them. You're First Lieutenant Neilsin now."

He laid the two silver bars on the table next to Erik's bed.

"The doctor says you'll be out of here by the end of the week. We will see you back at the company then. Okay?"

"Sure thing, Skipper," Erik replied.

As Captain French and Frosty got up to go, the captain said, "Oh yeah! Almost forgot! Colonel Servando says he's now got the best-looking photo intelligence analyst in the Army on loan from Division and working for his S-2. And what's more, she's smart! One thing more," French added. "When she saw your name on the casualty list, she was burning up the phone to find out how you were doing. She told the colonel, 'He's like my brother!' Colonel says S-2 has had a lot of business and visitors since Lieutenant Swan arrived. Boy, she must sure be something to look at!" Chuckling aloud, Captain French and Frosty left.

When Erik returned to duty, Captain French said that he would use him for "light duty" for a week or two, to aid the healing process. "I have some paperwork that has to go up to Battalion and another dispatch for Regimental. Care to take a ride?"

Erik perked up, noting the gleam in Captain French's eye. Erik thought, *I'll get to see Dale! Hot damn!*

"Remember Rivera here?" asked Captain French.

Erik recognized the driver who'd brought him up from Pusan. "Jorge Rivera, right? Jorge, spelled with a J!"

"Yeah, that's right. You remembered!" the smiling soldier said.

"Rivera will drive you up there and bring you back," Captain French announced. You should get going before 0900 hours so you can get back before dark."

Erik made sure he was clean-shaved and found some aftershave to pat on his face—it stung!

They left in an open jeep with only a top on. It was cold, but the weather was fairly clear, and the snow was packed down. Both Erik and the driver were warmly dressed as they started on their two-hour drive to Battalion.

In time for lunch with Dale, perhaps, thought Erik.

Erik kept his eyes scanning along the snow-covered ridge as their jeep moved along the road. As they rounded a slight curve, the jeep slowed down. There was a steep ravine on the side of the hill. The left front tire of the jeep hit a land mine, and a loud explosion tossed the jeep over, flinging Erik partly down the ravine and smashing him against some trees. The brunt of the explosion tore Jorge Rivera's body apart. The jeep burst into flames, and the gas tank underneath the seat ignited and exploded. Erik was knocked out, and Rivera was dead.

Coming out of the woods from their place of hiding, three North Koreans checked the driver and then went down the ravine to check Erik, who was lying in an awkward position that suggested his body was all smashed up. The shoulder wound on Erik's shoulder had burst open, and the blood from his shoulder dripped onto his face and neck. The soldiers took Erik for being dead and went through his pockets and removed his wristwatch. They left quickly because the burning Jeep was sending up a smoke signal. Five hours later, a ROK patrol came upon the smoldering jeep and the dead driver.

Looking down the ravine they spotted the silver bars of a lieutenant who they were surprised to find was still alive. They called on their radio for an American field ambulance. Erik was rushed to the field hospital and then further evacuated to Pusan.

Erik had not regained consciousness, and the medical work performed was only superficial—redoing the sutures to Erik's shoulder and treating the badly bruised body. Fearing severe head injuries, Erik was air evacuated to Japan to the general hospital there. He was placed on IV fluids, and his vital signs were closely monitored, as was a possible change in his condition. When three weeks passed with no change, he was transferred to a medical vessel returning wounded to the United States and then placed in Walter Reed General Hospital for further treatment and observation.

The surgical team that examined Erik could find no reason to surgically correct any problems. It was felt that he was suffering from acute trauma to his entire nervous system, which might be complicated, his injuries not yet diagnosed. Nothing was yet evident to confirm any diagnosis. Erik's vital signs were good, so he was kept on IVs for medication and nourishment. For all practical purposes, Erik was still in a deep coma. Even though Erik was deeply comatose, he did show occasional automatic responses. He was breathing normally and occasionally eye movement was detected, indicating that the lower brainstem, which controls these responses, was still functioning.

Unknown to Erik, his father had suffered a heart attack and was hospitalized. While he was recuperating, he suffered two strokes. The first was mild; the second stroke took his life. Erik's father had set up a trust and set legal wheels into motion for Erik's future with the contingency that if Erik were killed in the Korean War, and then the trust would go to Jennifer and her children. The executor in charge of these matters was the attorney for Erik's father and Apex Builders and was a close personal friend to the Neilsins and Knutsons. So it came as no surprise to the Knutson family members that the attorney would be monitoring Erik's treatment at Walter Reed General Hospital.

Talking with the head of the neurological department about Erik's condition, Conrad Flemming was advised by the doctor that it was quite possible that Erik could remain in a deep coma for years. The encouraging aspect was that Erik's vital signs were within normal limits and he needed no assistance to breathe. He would occasionally cough, even yawn and blink, with indications of roving eye movement.

"He could wake out of the coma, just like that," the doctor said, snapping his fingers, "or he could remain that way for a while, and then perhaps there might be a deterioration that would affect the lower brain. If that occurred, and then it would be likely that he would lose the brain stem function, which we could not reverse."

Conrad was silent and thoughtful for a long time.

Dr. Sanford cleared his throat and said, "You know, if Erik was my son and I thought there was a chance that he could pull through this, I would want to have therapy on his arms and legs so that atrophy—shrinkage of muscular tissue—didn't occur from the long periods of being immobilized."

"What kind of therapy is Erik getting now?" Conrad asked.

"None has been started that I'm aware," he replied.

Conrad came to a decision. "I have been in touch with the hospital's administration and talked with the people at Army Headquarters. I was told that Walter Reed Hospital would grant Erik a one hundred percent medical discharge. I have placed all of Erik's back Army pay as a first lieutenant into the trust set up for him. Did you know that Erik was awarded the Bronze Star for heroism and the Purple Heart?"

"Yes, we know about the medals," the doctor acknowledged.

"Doctor, what I am thinking is that Erik would be eligible for veteran's benefits that would cover a great part of any hospitalization. I would like to get Erik discharged and place him in private care over at Johns Hopkins. The trust will provide whatever additional funds are needed for a private or semi-private room for Erik. I want to set up some sort of therapy program to keep his body healthy."

"I think I can help you in one respect," Dr. Sanford said. "There is not much more we can do for Erik now in his present state. I will write a recommendation for a medical discharge for Erik if you agree with that decision."

"Fine," said Conrad. "Let's do it!"

CHAPTER 17

The Templetons were true to their word. Elizabeth still found it hard to credit her good fortune. She had learned how to drive a car and make her way around Baltimore and the District of Columbia. Elizabeth gave her car a name, as had Max in Germany. She called her car *Kampfwagen*, which was German for "chariot." She later shortened the name to "K-Wagon" and then simply "Wagon."

Elizabeth sat for her final written examinations and passed with flying colors. Next she was evaluated by the hospital board for her nursing skills. Elizabeth had decided not to pursue being an OR nurse, as the staff was frequently on call at all hours, especially very early hours in the morning. Elizabeth would have at least a one-hour drive, which would allow her little time to care for Bernice.

Elizabeth was admitted to the nursing staff at Johns Hopkins Hospital and was assigned to rotations in the orthopedic, pediatrics, and surgical recovery wards. At this point, Elizabeth was a "floater nurse." She was a good nurse, and she had developed good nursing skills. She established a very good rapport with women, children, and senior adult patients, and of course, the young men loved her!

In the first eight months, Elizabeth's varied duties took her to many areas of the hospital. With long hours and extra duties and then a long drive home, Elizabeth caught herself falling asleep at the wheel of her car in the early hours one morning. She recovered just in time to prevent driving off the road, and she opened the window so fresh, cold air could rush into the car. Finally arriving safely home, she went to bed and was disturbed with herself for being lax. She was thankful that she would be off work for the next three days!

The sun was shining very brightly when Elizabeth woke to discover she had slept right through the morning and past lunchtime. She showered, tidied up her room, and went downstairs. Bernice was out on the back patio, and Elizabeth could hear her talking to someone. Bernice heard Elizabeth approach and called out to her to join them on the patio. The visitor was George Templeton's cousin, Ralph, whom Elizabeth had seen and talked with on several occasions. However, she had never tried to use George Templeton's relationship with Ralph to better her situation at the hospital.

"Why, hello there, Elizabeth," Ralph said, rising as she approached.

"Please don't get up!" she implored him. "Hello, Mrs. Templeton," Elizabeth said. She always used a formal title when visitors were present, despite Mrs. Templeton insisting that she call her Bernice.

"We are having coffee. Would you like to join us?" Bernice asked.

"I'll have coffee and some of those cookies, if you don't mind," she replied, helping herself.

"My dear, you haven't eaten, have you?" Bernice asked. "I didn't hear you come in from work. You must have been late."

"I think early would be more like it," Elizabeth said. "I had to take over part of my replacement's shift because she was delayed getting to the hospital. I got home around three thirty in the morning."

"Did you just get up, honey?" Bernice asked.

"Uh huh!" acknowledged Elizabeth. "I nearly fell asleep at the wheel coming home this morning," Elizabeth blurted out. "It really scared me!"

Ralph Templeton said, "Elizabeth, I know of a certain situation, perhaps a nice opportunity for you if you are interested."

"Yes, dear. Ralph was only just telling me about it!" Bernice added.

"Well," continued Ralph, "you really don't have to take on the amount of work you are presently doing. We have a very special situation coming up at Johns Hopkins. The trustee for a wounded Korean veteran has requested a private room for his ward, who is to be medically discharged from Walter Reed and transferred over to Johns Hopkins." Ralph paused.

"This poor fellow, a lieutenant, was involved in an explosion with a land mine and has been in a coma for over a year. His vital signs are good and functioning well. There are times, I'm told, that he almost wakes up. The trustee, Mr. Flemming, wants to set up a private personal nurse who can take charge of the lad, and, we hope, help him recover. The pay would be very good and would be paid by the trustee and not the hospital. In this instance," Ralph Templeton said, "you would be actually working for the patient."

"When is all this going to come about?" Elizabeth asked.

"Erik Neilsin is expected to be discharged next Friday, and then he be will brought over Friday afternoon. You know the vacant room next to the ICU?" he asked.

"Yes, I know the room you mean."

"We will get that room ready for Lieutenant Neilsin. I have had discussions with the Physical Therapy Department; they will follow up on the doctors' recommendations from Walter Reed Hospital."

"There you are, Miss Elizabeth," Martha said, carrying a tray of hot food out to the patio. "I know you haven't had a bite to eat since you got home and certainly not since you got up." In a scolding tone, she added, "Now, you just sit down there and eat, miss! I don't want you missing meals. You are skinny enough as it is." Everyone laughed.

"Well, what do you think, Elizabeth?" asked Ralph. "Are you interested in taking the position?"

Elizabeth looked at Bernice, who was nodding her head.

"What about the hospital and my other assignments?"

"I'll see to that," Ralph said. "I will arrange for you to do light 'help-out duty' with the ICU, and you will be close at hand for your patient Erik. Of course, you will be paid by the hospital for working ICU in addition to the salary that Mr. Flemming has agreed to pay. Mr. Flemming was insistent that the nurse be top notch and a caring person. In my opinion," Ralph said, "that describes you!"

"That sounds like a very attractive offer, indeed," Elizabeth said. "I trust that I will not have to work late hours and early morning hours?"

"I shouldn't think so," Ralph said. "It is normally during the daylight hours that the hospital staff is so busy. Your being there at the that time relieves staff and provides the level of care that Mr. Flemming desires for Erik."

Elizabeth had a few days off hospital work to rest and relax. The weather had turned warmer, and the first days of summer were not far off. Elizabeth took Bernice out for a drive and stopped at a point overlooking the Pretty Boy Reservoir, which was not too far from Four Winds. Bernice liked to be near the water and enjoyed coming up to the reservoir.

"You know something, Elizabeth," Bernice said, "I am feeling so much better now, both physically and mentally. I told you about Jennifer and Jimmy." She hesitated. "Well, you have made a big difference in my life and George's too! It's not just because you have been such a great help as a nurse, but something else … Something that I feel inside—that you care! The icing on the cake is that you also resemble Jennifer in a lot of ways." Elizabeth reached over and took her hand as Bernice continued. "And that has helped George and me to face up to the loss of the children and face the realities that life must go on!"

As always, Elizabeth felt great empathy for Bernice and George. They were such good people, and how they loved their children!

"Well, I think we should be going back home now," suggested Elizabeth.

"Oh, all right," agreed Bernice, looking at her watch. "I didn't realize that it was this late."

When they entered the house, Martha came to Elizabeth and said, "A message came for you, Miss Elizabeth. Ralph Templeton, it was. Said for you to plan on starting with your new patient this coming Monday. He thought you should come over in the morning to make sure everything is prepared. The patient will be transferred to Johns Hopkins in the afternoon."

"Thanks, Martha, I think I will go up to my room for a while and look at some of my school notes. Would you like me to help out with anything before dinner?" she asked Bernice.

"No, you go ahead, honey."

After a few minutes, the intercom in Elizabeth's room buzzed, and Bernice said, "Elizabeth, there is a letter in the mail for you from a law firm, and it has the name Mr. Conrad Flemming on it."

"Okay, Bernice. I'll be down in a few minutes."

Elizabeth joined Bernice on the patio and examined the official-looking envelope. The return address showed the law firm's name: "Flemming, Lichfield & Barton, Attorneys at Law." Elizabeth opened the letter from Mr. Conrad Flemming, Esquire, and read:

Dear Miss Feldmann,

On behalf of my ward, Erik Neilsin, I would like this opportunity to thank you for accepting the position of caring for him under these unusual conditions. I have coordinated most of the details with Mr. Ralph Templeton, Johns Hopkins Hospital, and he has assured me that you have been briefed on the level of care Erik requires. I am insistent that he be afforded every chance of recovery. That means that he must be given the level of therapy to prevent any muscular atrophy.

It was agreed that you would attend Erik during the peak, daylight hours of the hospital, Monday through Friday, and as changing physical conditions might require. I have agreed with Mr. Templeton that I have authorized double pay. I hope that you will find that sum acceptable. And, should any other expenses be incurred, the trust will pay for them.

One last thing, and it is important: I am counting on you to be the "eyes and ears" for Erik and the advocate who will watch out for him. In the busy atmosphere at Johns Hopkins, Erik could be overlooked in his treatment, or have a medical emergency, if no one had an eye on him.

Should you have any questions or need to contact me you will find, waiting for you at the hospital, a manila folder that contains detailed instructions and other useful information you might require. That includes being able to contact me, day or night.

Yours very truly,
Conrad L. Flemming

Elizabeth read the letter again and said nothing, handing it over to Bernice Templeton to read.

"It sounds like a very responsible undertaking, Elizabeth! And the money is not too bad either."

"Yes!" replied Elizabeth. "It is good pay. I hope that my services will be worth it."

"Now there you go, deprecating yourself again! You are a good nurse. You are a very caring person, and you're very efficient and alert. You are the best one for the job!" Bernice said emphatically.

"Of course, you might be a wee little bit biased?" suggested Elizabeth.

"Of course, my dear! My confidence in you is higher than this house."

"It is a wonder my head doesn't get so big and fall off." Elizabeth smiled. "I wonder what I will be able to do for my patient," she said, worrying already.

"You'll have medical guidance and a therapist, and you'll have to make sure that your patient Erik receives the care and attention he needs. I'm sure you will do just fine," Bernice concluded.

Elizabeth was in the habit of telling Bernice all the events of her work days at the hospital. Bernice was always very interested in anything Elizabeth said or did. It was nice for Elizabeth, too, since she not only had a sounding board for complaining, but also someone to get things off her chest.

Elizabeth woke up before her clock alarm. She switched off the alarm so that it wouldn't go off. Today she would start on this new nursing adventure, but first, a nice hot shower! Elizabeth dried herself off and checked out her figure in the full-length mirror. *I'm not skinny like Martha says*, she thought, looking at herself critically. Looking at her face in the mirror, Elizabeth noticed some lines forming around her mouth and at the corner of her eyes. *I am getting older*, she thought. *Oh well*, she said to herself. *I must get going!*

Elizabeth checked her handbag, looking for a lip balm she had in her bag. She picked up a round object and held the old gypsy's "good luck gemstone" in her hand. She had forgotten about the gypsy's stone, and as she held it, she thought that the stone suddenly felt very warm … or had she imagined it? She dropped it back in her handbag. *I have to get ready to leave soon*, she thought. After gathering up her things, Elizabeth went downstairs, and she had a thought.

"I'm going to pass up breakfast, Martha," she called out. "Just a cup of coffee, please! I'll be right back. I want to see Queenie." She then went out the back to the caretakers' cottage. Queenie was outside tending her flock—her flower garden.

"Mornin', darlin," Queenie said, as Elizabeth approached.

"Queenie, I would like to ask a favor."

"Sure, Miss Elizabeth! What is it?"

"I have a new patient, and I was wondering if I could have some of your nice flowers to take to the hospital for his room. He won't have very much there, and even though he might not know it, the room would look nice."

"Sure thing, Miss Elizabeth. I'll just get my shears and make you up a little spray of flowers. Shouldn't take me but a few minutes. Flowers, we have plenty of … and they are so nice right now."

"I'm just going to have a cup of coffee, and then I must be off."

"Don't worry, you go have your coffee, and I'll be along in a shake of a lamb's tail with the flowers." A short while later Queenie brought a beautiful spray of flowers to Elizabeth.

"You're an angel Queenie. Thanks!" She dashed to her car and was off to the hospital and her new patient.

The hospital room was rather sterile and bare, lacking warmth and color. Elizabeth checked for cleanliness, since the room was not used frequently. She detected the smell of tobacco; someone had been smoking in this room not too long ago. She opened the window to let in fresh air. Checking the small bathroom, she found cigarette ashes on the floor, and the bathroom smelled of cigarette smoke too. She put on the exhaust fan and left the door open. Elizabeth went into ICU and saw Fran Collier, a nurse she had worked with several times before.

"Fran," she asked, "I need some deodorant spray. Someone's been smoking in the special patient room, and I have the patient coming today. The room smells of cigarettes."

"Hold on a minute," Fran said and left then returned with a can of Lysol deodorant spray. "Will this do?"

"Yes, thanks," Elizabeth said and left.

She cleaned the room; the Lysol spray left the room with a clean, fresh smell. She found a vase and arranged Queenie's flowers in them. The vase was barely large enough for the big bouquet of flowers. The flowers emitted a nice, fragrant aroma, and Elizabeth was pleased. Elizabeth left the room and went down to the cafeteria. It was nearly ten o'clock, and she was hungry, "Two eggs, over easy … bacon, hash browns, toast, and coffee, please," Elizabeth said as she sat down at the counter.

She noticed two of the hospital orderlies sitting in a corner booth, watching her. Bart, the dark-haired one, often tried to start up a conversation with her, trying to get friendly. Elizabeth was cordial enough but was not interested in anyone, not even after so long a time. Right now her work and life with the Templetons were her main focus. The two orderlies got up to leave, and as they walked by Bart was waiting for Elizabeth to look up so he could strike up a conversation. Elizabeth never gave him a chance or a glance, just concentrated on the plate in front of her; she thought he probably got the message.

Elizabeth helped out ICU for the remainder of the morning. ICU had a heart monitor go off, and there was a rush to get the patient breathing again and stabilize the heart. Thankfully, the patient made it. Before she knew it, it was one thirty, and the telephone at the ICU counter rang.

"Hey, Elizabeth, they're bringing a patient up to your floor now. Patient is Neilsin. Erik Neilsin," the receptionist said.

Elizabeth met the orderlies at the elevator and directed them to the proper room. The orderlies transferred Erik from the gurney into his bed. Elizabeth arranged the patient and placed pillows to insure his comfort. Elizabeth took his pulse and temperature and recorded it on his new chart. Next she took his blood pressure, pleased to see that it was normal. Temperature was also normal; the pulse was slow but strong. Elizabeth started a head-to-toe examination of her patient, looking for and noting a few bedsores. She also noticed how thin his legs and arms were. His breathing was normal. Elizabeth had the apparatus and medical supplies on hand for continuing Erik's IVs. He had been transferred with the IV needle in place, and it was time to attach a new medication bag and connect it to the IV.

Three hospital specialists came to examine Erik and checked his chart. Dr. Frederick said, "I am familiar with this patient's case. You call me if there are any changes in his condition."

"Yes, Doctor," Elizabeth replied. She ordered some vitamin E oil, which was good for the skin. Starting with his arms and shoulders she gently massaged the oil into his skin, which was pale and very dry.

In the following few days, Conrad Flemming came by twice. Elizabeth thought he seemed to be a very caring person. On the third day, he said, "His skin is looking a little better, don't you think?"

"Yes, I think so too," replied Elizabeth. "The vitamin E oil is good, but I would like to go with warm castor oil packs."

"Castor oil? Isn't that a laxative?"

"Well, yes, it is, if you take it internally," she said, "but I am talking about using it externally. I think it has better healing qualities than vitamin E oil."

"I never heard of such a thing before," Conrad said.

"Castor oil is nothing new," Elizabeth continued. "People who have used it call it the *Palma Christi*—Palm of Christ—because of its healing properties."

"Miss Feldmann, if it will help Erik in any way, you have my blessing. Do it!" Conrad remarked.

And Elizabeth did every chance she could. It was not an easy task because she had to move Erik many times during a day, just to get to other parts of his back, shoulders, legs, and arms, as well as his torso. For this reason, she set out to do his castor oil packs on Tuesdays and Thursdays. She decided to go in on Saturday morning to complete a three-times-a-week regimen for Erik. Conrad approved her plan, so the treatment continued.

Specialists in physical therapy and occupational therapy, a fairly new kind of therapy, visited daily to evaluate and work on improving the movement of Erik's limbs. Frequent repositioning of Erik's body was recommended to prevent muscular and joint contracture.

While making his usual rounds of patients, Dr. Pierce was checking Erik's reflexes when Erik experienced some muscular spasms. The doctor and Elizabeth were startled, caught unaware. Erik started to have some minor convulsions. The doctor asked Elizabeth to alert ICU to stand by for anything.

"I don't like these new symptoms," he stated.

An ICU nurse and an attendant came into the room and brought a respirator and the cardiac resuscitator kit with them. EKG monitoring was attached to Erik, and the beeps, monitor, and tapes were showing a very erratic heartbeat. Suddenly the screen went from up and down beats to a steady line, and the medical team jumped into action, sounding the code for cardiac arrest. Within a few seconds another doctor and other nurses were at hand.

"What have we got?" Dr. Kaufmann asked.

"Just started with a few leg spasms and then convulsions and then cardiac arrest."

They hooked up oxygen to Erik and started CPR. Erik had stopped breathing and had no pulse.

"Is the clock running?" asked the surgeon.

"Yes, doctor," one of the nurses replied. "We have one minute and passing thirty-two seconds. We are only a few seconds off time."

"I think we have a ventricular fibrillation problem here! Let's go with defibrillation," Dr. Kaufmann ordered. Placing the electrical pads on Erik's chest, he yelled, "Clear!"

The doctor pressed the switch, and Erik's body jumped as the electrical charge passed through his body. The monitor remained constant. No heart activity was being shown.

"Clear," he shouted again.

Erik received the second electrical charge. Suddenly the monitor restarted with a *beep* and then a more steady *beep ... beep ... beep*. The monitor was showing a good heart beat, and the tape readout, tracking the heart, resumed a normal pulse.

"We got him back!" Dr. Kaufmann said. "We don't have to move him into an ICU bed," he said, "but I want regular, around-the-clock monitoring."

"Doctor, I will be with him until I know he has stabilized," Elizabeth said.

"That's fine, Elizabeth," he said. "That will help out ICU."

No one noticed the two men in the white linen suits who stood off to one side, watching what was going on. They were not visible to mortals; they were not of this world.

Elizabeth's nerves were a little on edge with Erik's emergency. She picked up the telephone to call Conrad.

"I'm sorry," the receptionist said. "Mr. Flemming is away from the office at the moment. Can I give him a message?"

"Yes, please tell him that Nurse Elizabeth Feldmann called from the hospital and that it is urgent that he call me back."

Sensing the urgency in Elizabeth's voice, the receptionist asked, "Is this an emergency concerning Erik Neilsin?"

"Yes, it is. He suffered a cardiac arrest, and we lost him for about four minutes," she replied. "He is stabilized now and under ICU monitoring. I am staying with him for the time being until I know the danger is past."

"I will try to get a hold of Mr. Flemming," the receptionist said and cut the connection.

Fifteen minutes later the telephone rang. It was Conrad. Elizabeth gave him a concise summary of what had happened and when. "He has been fine since then," she said. "His vital signs are all good. His color is good." Pausing and looking at Erik's face, she saw a flickering of his eyelashes.

"Mr. Flemming!" she said, excited. "His eyelashes just flickered. This has never happened before!"

"I'll be right over," Flemming said and hung up.

Elizabeth wrote on Erik's chart, noting the eyelash movements. Elizabeth noticed that Erik's right hand was clutched in a fist. She had not seen that before. Going to the other side of the bed, she took Erik's hand and tried to open his fist. His hand was tightly closed, and Elizabeth had to pry the hand open. In the palm of Erik's right hand was a pretty little blue and gold metal box.

How strange, she thought. *Where did that come from? I never saw it before.*

Elizabeth removed the little box and placed it in the nightstand drawer with Erik's few personal effects, which included a Saint Christopher medal on a chain. Conrad entered the room and approached the bed to look at Erik.

"How's he doing?" he asked.

"No changes," she said. "He is still doing fine."

They both watched the monitor jumping to the pulsating of Erik's heart.

Elizabeth took his blood pressure and noticed that it had increased slightly, closer to a more normal reading. She made the notation on the medical chart. Taking Erik's pulse she noticed that it was stronger and a little faster. Elizabeth checked Erik's pulse again, fifteen minutes later.

The pulse was stronger and a little faster! *Surely this is a good sign,* she thought.

"What do you think, Elizabeth?" Conrad asked.

"I'm no doctor, but I think that whatever caused the heart fibrillation seems to be gone and now Erik seems to be reversing. He is getting stronger, and I don't know why."

It was seven o'clock in the evening, and Elizabeth stifled a yawn.

"How long have you been working?" Conrad asked.

"Oh, since about eight this morning. I wanted to be on hand when the doctor and therapist made their rounds."

Conrad looked at Erik again and then said, "I think the other ICU nurses can take over for now, Elizabeth. You are tired—you've had a full and hair-raising day, and I doubt you've had anything to eat since lunch time."

Elizabeth just gave a tired smile.

"I thought so," surmised Conrad. "Come on, young lady, you and I are going to have a nice supper together."

"Thank you, but first I must call the Templetons, so they do not worry about me. They would expect me to be home by now."

"Templeton?" Conrad Flemming asked. "You mean Ralph Templeton?"

"No, George and Bernice Templeton. They live at Four Winds—their home is in Hereford."

"I know of a George Templeton," Conrad said, "Works for the State Department or something. The family is extremely wealthy, I believe."

Elizabeth didn't say anything, but Conrad pressed for an answer. "Is that the Templetons you are referring to?"

"Yes," Elizabeth replied quietly.

"Well, I'll be a son of a gun! George Templeton!"

They left the hospital and walked to Conrad's car. It appeared to be a foreign car.

"This is not an American car, is it?" Elizabeth asked.

"No, British. It's a Mark IV Jaguar sedan." Conrad held the passenger door open for Elizabeth, and she sat down onto plush soft leather seats. He drove to a small restaurant in a very nice residential neighborhood and stopped at the curb of the Chez Gustav. Elizabeth observed the restaurant's valet rush to open the car doors.

"Good evening, Mr. Flemming," he said, taking the keys to the car. As they entered the Chez Gustav, the valet whisked the car away for parking. Obviously, Conrad was well known at this restaurant.

"Good evening, Mr. Flemming," the maître d' greeted them.

He immediately escorted them to a charming and elegant booth. Conrad asked Elizabeth if she would like a cocktail before dinner. Knowing she was going to have to drive home and she was already tired, Elizabeth said, "May I have a glass of dry sherry?"

"Good choice!" Conrad said. "What kind of food do you like?"

"I will eat almost anything," Elizabeth said, sipping her sherry. "I did not realize just how hungry I am. Perhaps that is why I feel so tired!"

"In that case," Conrad said, "allow me to order for us both. We will start with shrimp cocktail. Then a cup of your turtle soup. We will have a Delmonico steak, some mushrooms and onions, and"—looking at Elizabeth—"baked potato?"

Elizabeth nodded.

The waiter asked, "How would you like your steak cooked, madame?"

"Medium rare, please."

Mr. Flemming ordered a small bottle of Blue Nun Liebfraumilch. The turtle soup arrived piping hot, and the waiter served a ladle of sherry into each cup of soup. The entire meal was excellent, and Elizabeth ate every morsel.

"How about dessert?"

"Oh, no, thank you! I couldn't eat another thing," Elizabeth said, "but I would like a cup of coffee, please."

With the meal finished, Conrad asked Elizabeth if she would mind if he lit his pipe. She had no objections, and Conrad filled his pipe and lit it, tamping the ashes down and settling down to a few good puffs before he spoke.

"Elizabeth, I would like you to know that I am very pleased with all you are doing for Erik as his nurse. I couldn't have found anyone else who has given one hundred percent in care and attention ".

"That is what you are paying me for," she said.

"True, true, but you give more. I can feel it. It's not just a job for you—it's like a sacred mission."

"I take my nursing responsibilities seriously," Elizabeth attested. "I hope I am not acting so reverent in my daily work."

"Absolutely not. I hope you are not taking offense," Conrad was quick to interject. "I just wanted you to know that I care very much for this Neilsin boy, and I wanted the best care for him. I find that excellence in you," he concluded.

"I am truly very flattered," Elizabeth said.

Conrad told Elizabeth about the Neilsin and the Knutson families and the boatbuilding.

"It is a very sad thing," Mr. Flemming observed. "Erik is the last of the Neilsins. Both his mother and father have passed away. His father died while Erik was in the war in Korea. I don't think he even knows that his father is gone. Of course, he has his Aunt Jennie and some cousins."

Mr. Flemming brought Elizabeth back to the hospital so she could get her car. It was late, and after thanking Mr. Flemming for a lovely meal, she set off to drive home. It was nearly eleven thirty when she pulled into the driveway. Entering the house, she saw George and Bernice in the living room having a nightcap.

"Ahoy there, Clara Barton!" George called out.

"I hope I didn't keep you up waiting for me," Elizabeth said.

"No, my dear," Bernice said. "What was this big thing that happened today?" Elizabeth told them the highlights and her expectations and Conrad Flemming's dinner invitation.

"That was sensible," George Templeton said. "And, also, thanks for calling to let us know you were going out. We would have worried about you. Care for a nightcap?"

"No thanks, just a good night's rest." Getting up, she said good night and went to her room.

Elizabeth took off her clothes and set out some clothes for the next day. She thought that she might pack a small bag of "extras" just in case her patient's condition changed and she had to stay on a longer tour of her job. Finally, Elizabeth emptied her purse; she threw away some empty mint packs, and there again was that gemstone the old gypsy had given her.

Why do I keep that damn thing? she thought and decided to throw it away. Elizabeth picked it up and held it in the palm of her hand for just a moment.

Am I feeling warmth coming from that stone? she wondered. She shifted the gemstone to her other hand, and she again thought, *This stone feels warmer than ever before. Oh, I am so tired.* The stone dropped from her hand, bounced off the top of her dresser into the open drawer. Elizabeth reached to retrieve the stone. It had fallen into her little jewelry box. Elizabeth had opened the box looking for a pair of earrings to wear the next day. The stone landed on top of a ring—a small gold wedding band. She picked up the stone with one hand and the ring in the other hand.

What happened next startled Elizabeth; she had no explanation for it. She felt a warm, exciting current shoot from her left hand to her right hand. She also felt her heart quicken its beat, and she found herself short of breath. *I am tired and overwrought*, she thought, *and I had better get to bed*. She placed the stone back into her purse and the ring back into her jewelry box and went to bed.

CHAPTER 18

Dr. Kaufmann examined Erik thoroughly when he made his rounds. He read Elizabeth's nurse's notes on the patient's chart and rechecked all the vital signs. Very unusual and uncharacteristic of this type of case, he thought. Erik's pulse was stronger and the heart rate a bit faster. Taking Erik's blood pressure, the doctor noted the systolic pressure was now at ninety over a diastolic pressure of sixty-eight. *You couldn't ask for a better blood pressure,* he thought. The doctor, with Elizabeth's help, tested Erik's reflexes. Earlier, they had not gotten any response. Taking his small reflex hammer Dr. Kaufmann tapped Erik's knee. There was a slight jerking movement—very slight, to be sure, but nevertheless a movement. Dr. Kaufmann was getting a little excited and tested further. The other knee did not respond to the tap. The doctor took the teaspoon from Elizabeth's coffee cup and ran the handle across Erik's stomach. The stomach muscles contracted!

"Boy! We're getting good response," the excited doctor said.

More tests were done, but there were no more startling responses. Other doctors visited and consulted amongst themselves.

"Body tone is good."

"Color is good."

"Muscular tissue is weak, but that is to be expected."

"Let's do a complete work up. Blood, chest X-ray, ECG, EEG—the whole works."

Elizabeth asked about the X-rays. "Have X-ray bring up the portable unit, and we'll get a bedside film," Dr. Kaufmann said. All the tests seem to point in the direction that the body and its intricate systems were gradually returning to a more normal state. Elizabeth continued with her massaging of Erik's hands, arms, and legs using the vitamin E oils. Elizabeth was going to write something on Erik's chart and could not find her pen.

Darn it, she thought, *I must have left it on the ICU desk.* She reached in her purse for a little pen she carried there. As her fingers closed around the barrel of the pen, they also took hold of the small gemstone. Elizabeth pulled them both from her purse. She took the pen and slipped the gemstone into the pocket of her uniform. She entered the data on Erik's chart. She reached into her pocket again and took out the gemstone, looking at it. Again, it felt very warm. As Elizabeth looked at it, she thought her eyes were playing tricks on her. The stone seemed to be glowing slightly. Just then the telephone rang. Elizabeth put the gemstone on the nightstand next to Erik's bed.

"Hello, Elizabeth!" It was Conrad. "How is Erik today?"

Elizabeth briefed him on the doctor's examinations and some of the positive results to Erik's sensory testing. Elizabeth turned to look at Erik as she was talking to Conrad. She gasped and nearly dropped the telephone.

"Elizabeth! What is it?" shouted Flemming. "Elizabeth, answer me!"

Elizabeth was speechless and unable to respond. Erik's eyes were open, and he was looking right at her. Finally, Elizabeth quickly said to Conrad, "He's got his eyes open, and he's looking at me—got to go!" and hung up.

She reached for Erik's hand and held it in hers.

She pushed the buzzer on the bed, requesting assistance. One of the ICU nurses popped her head in the door and asked, "Need something?"

"Yes! Get Dr. Kaufmann—the patient has opened his eyes," she said. "Oh, have someone bring me sterile pads and some boric acid solution, will you?

Elizabeth was bathing Erik's eyes with the solution when Dr. Kaufmann rushed into the room. Erik did not blink his eyes and just seemed to stare. Dr. Kaufmann checked Erik's eyes with his light and talked to him. Erik made no effort to talk, nor did he give any sign of comprehension. Suddenly he closed his eyes and gave a sigh. Twenty minutes later a disheveled and excited Conrad dashed into the room.

"Got here as fast as I could," he panted. "Just creamed the front end of a taxi cab as I was rushing to get here."

"Calm down," the doctor told him. "He closed his eyes. We are going to have to go slow and have some patience."

"Yes, of course, you're right," Conrad acknowledged.

Elizabeth and Dr. Kaufmann briefed an elated Conrad Flemming.

"You should go home now, Elizabeth," encouraged the night nurse from ICU. "We'll take good care of your young man until you get back tomorrow."

Checking her wristwatch, Elizabeth realized that it had gotten late. "Sure thing, Nancy."

Taking a last look at Erik and satisfied that he was okay, Elizabeth gathered up her things and left to drive home. As soon as she arrived home Elizabeth told Bernice and George all about her day's experience.

"It sounds so very exciting," Bernice said.

Elizabeth was concerned and bothered that of late she had not been very attentive about keeping up Bernice's castor oil packs and checking on Bernice's health.

"Don't you worry, darling," Bernice said. "I am feeling much better and stronger with every passing day. Matter of fact, day after tomorrow, I have a checkup scheduled at Hopkins. It is the 'two-year evaluation' checkup."

Elizabeth checked her own notes and said, "Do you want me to go with you?"

"No, dear," Bernice replied, "but while I am there at the hospital, we can do lunch together after my appointment and we can brief each other. Okay?"

"It sounds like a plan!" Elizabeth said, imitating Queenie's saying.

Elizabeth bathed Erik and was massaging his wrist and hand with the special lotion. She was looking at his hand as she was rubbing in the vitamin E cream when Erik's opened hand closed over hers. Looking up she saw Erik had his eyes open, and this time she saw his pupils move. She saw awareness in his expression that had not been there before. She smiled at Erik and took the water pitcher and poured a small amount of water into the glass. Taking a tongue depressor, she wrapped it with some gauze, dipped it into the water, and passed it around Erik's lips and into his mouth. Erik tried to swallow, but Elizabeth saw he was having difficulty. She quickly ran into ICU and took a few flexible straws and asked one of the other nurses for some iced water and other liquids. Returning, she elevated Erik's bed to an upright position, put a flexible straw into a partly filled glass of water, and put the straw to his mouth.

"If you can understand me, Erik," she said, "take small sips of this water."

It took Erik a few minutes to work his lips and sip the few ounces of water. Elizabeth kept giving Erik more fluids a little at a time and then waiting for a while.

"Can you talk to me?" she asked.

Erik's lips parted ever so slightly, but no sound came. Elizabeth could see in Erik's eyes that he was trying to say something, but he seemed too weak to make the effort.

"Don't worry, Erik," she said. "We will do it a little bit at a time. We need to get some real nourishment into your system soon."

Little by little, Erik tolerated more fluids and finally managed to say "thanks!" to Elizabeth. Elizabeth was thrilled with that and told Erik so. His eyes seemed to say more than the words he could speak. Elizabeth reached out to hold Erik's other hand, which he held closed into a fist. She gently pried open his hand and, to her surprise, saw her gemstone. For a moment she was at a loss for words. *Where did he get that gemstone,* she thought, and then she suddenly remembered that yesterday she had lain it on the stand next to Erik's bed.

It seemed that Erik wanted to form a word, that he had something to say. Elizabeth, sensing his inner struggle, put her fingers to his lips, and said, "Wait! All in good time."

Elizabeth had warm broth frequently brought up from food services. She had talked to the dietician. She asked for a concentrated broth, explaining Erik's condition. After testing the broth's temperature, she placed a flex straw in the broth, and Erik slowly sipped all of it. He was propped up and resting after taking the broth, when he suddenly emitted a fairly loud belch. The belch must have cleared his pipes, so to speak, for Erik again said "Thank you" to Elizabeth.

She asked, "Do you know your name?"

There was a pause, and he formed an "Err" sound then "Errrick!"

In the next few days, Erik continued taking broths and light foods. A dentist was asked to check Erik and was pleased that his teeth and gums were in a fairly healthy state. Erik was not yet strong enough to get out of bed, but Elizabeth arranged the bed so that she could turn him onto his stomach and use the castor oil packs on his back. The skin on Erik's back needed attention in the area of his shrapnel scars and burn-like scars just above his waist. Erik managed to say that the pads felt good on his back. Within two weeks more, Erik was referred to in the hospital as the "Miracle Man." Elizabeth talked to Erik whenever she was with him and while she was massaging lotions on his body. Erik would frequently lapse into sleep and wake thirty or so minutes later.

Elizabeth came back into Erik's room and found that he had dozed off again. She retrieved the gypsy's gemstone from the nightstand and returned it to her purse. Opening the nightstand drawer, she saw the little blue and gold metal box that she had removed from Erik's grip. She had forgotten about it. Picking up the little box, Elizabeth examined it to find how to open it. She could not see any clip or catch to open it. Shaking it, she heard something in the box. She put the box back into the nightstand drawer. Elizabeth turned and saw Erik stirring. She wanted to refill the water pitcher and started to leave to get fresh water.

Seeing Elizabeth moving toward the door, Erik called out, "Lily!"

Elizabeth was surprised and turned in confusion to Erik. "What did you call me?"

Erik just looked at Elizabeth and said, "I thought you were going away!" He did not give Elizabeth any explanation for calling her Lily.

"I will return in just a minute with fresh ice water. Why did you call me Lily?" she prodded Erik.

"I don't know," he said. "It just came out!"

Elizabeth reluctantly let the coincidence pass. Answering the telephone, she heard the cheerful voice of Conrad calling for an update on Erik's progress.

"That is just splendid!" he said. "Every day that passes is more encouraging than the last."

"Yes, that is true enough," agreed Elizabeth. "I am hoping to get Erik strong enough to spend some time in a wheelchair. I think that a little sunshine and fresh air would do him a lot of good."

"I am inclined to agree with you. I'm sure the doctors would also agree," Conrad said.

Dr. Kaufmann and the PT escort came to Erik's room to transfer Erik onto the gurney for a trip to the PT facility. Dr. Kaufmann asked Elizabeth to join them. With help from the PTs, they placed Erik onto a special countertop. It was a scale that showed his weight was only one hundred and twenty-two pounds. His height, build, and military records all indicated Erik should be at least one hundred and seventy-five pounds.

Erik was placed in a special chair and hoisted into a warm whirlpool tank. He acknowledged that it felt good all over, especially to get up off his back. The therapy lasted only fifteen minutes, and Dr. Kaufmann prescribed daily visits for the baths. Erik was getting much stronger and was able to tolerate some solid foods. A barrage of various vitamins and minerals—vitamins C, E, and B-12 and calcium and magnesium concentrates—and high-calorie fluids were supplementing Erik's diet.

Elizabeth brought a wheelchair to Erik's room and, with the help of two orderlies, transferred Erik into the chair. Elizabeth arranged soft cushions at Erik's back and bottom. She helped Erik into a bathrobe and placed warm socks and slippers on his feet. She covered Erik with a blanket, and they were off.

"Where are we going?" Erik asked. Elizabeth could see that Erik was excited about doing something that was different. She was also excited that he was talking more, and all his comments were coherent.

"We are going to go outside on the hospital grounds. It is a beautiful day—sunny and warm. I think that you will like it."

The sun was very bright, causing Erik to squint. The sun was also quite warm, and Elizabeth sought a place under a shade tree where they could enjoy the fresh air and Erik not get sunburned. His skin was far too sensitive to tolerate a heavy dose of sunshine. This was something that would have to be approached little by little. Elizabeth left Erik for a minute and returned with two ice cream cups and spoons. Erik had not tasted ice cream for well over three years. His taste buds were reacting to the sweet, smooth taste of the dessert.

The following day was another such day, and Elizabeth took Erik out again. This time, she brought Erik a chocolate malt, making sure it was blended smooth without globs of ice cream, so that Erik could sip it through a straw.

"That was really good! I can't remember the last time I had something like that," he said.

One afternoon while out on the hospital grounds enjoying the good weather, Erik nodded off to sleep. Elizabeth had brought some nursing magazines to browse through. She was reading an article on temporary memory lapses in surgical patients. Erik woke up and saw Elizabeth sitting next to him reading the magazine.

He said, "You're not wearing your ring!"

Elizabeth, startled, turned to Erik, who she saw was now awake.

"What ring are you talking about, Erik?" she asked.

"The ring … the gold band," he replied.

Elizabeth just stared at Erik. For a few seconds, Elizabeth felt uneasiness and a prickling of the hair at the nape of her neck. Elizabeth showed both her hands to Erik. She did not have a ring on any of her fingers. The only ring that she ever had or wore was the gold wedding band that Pat Duran gave her for her birthday.

"See, I do not have any ring! Where did you get the idea that I had a ring—a gold band ring?"

Erik looked embarrassed. He always had that look when he blurted out something and then either could not recall why he said something or remember any details of it. "I don't know, I don't know. I thought I saw your hand with a gold band on your finger. I guess I must have had a dream," he said, lamely, and closed his eyes as if to shut out his frustration.

That night, at home, standing in front of her dresser, Elizabeth was deep in thought, reflecting on Erik, looking in her jewelry box, and thinking about the past. She picked up the gold wedding band and read the engraved name "Pat" inside the ring. Elizabeth felt a pang of sadness and of longing that she knew could never be recaptured. She also felt a little resentment that Erik's comments could penetrate her shell of protection against the hurt of losing Pat.

But it is not Erik's fault. That poor fellow is like a leaf floating in a fast-moving river. I must try to help and not find fault, she thought.

Erik had another complete and comprehensive physical examination. He had gained more weight and was now at one hundred and forty-five pounds. His muscle tone had greatly improved because of the therapy and exercise sessions. Erik was getting stronger and was able to take short walks with Elizabeth, though he frequently needed to rest during the walks.

CHAPTER 19

In four days, it would be the Fourth of July—a national holiday and also Erik's birthday. Elizabeth mentioned this to Bernice and George Templeton.

"I have an idea, Elizabeth," Bernice suggested. "Why don't you invite Erik to come visit with us on this weekend? His birthday and the Fourth are on Friday, and we can show him a grand time as well as the fireworks at Gunpowder Falls."

"That's a great idea!" George chirped in. "We have plenty of room around here, and we can help with any chores you may have with Erik," he added.

"Oh, thank you—I will ask Erik. You are both such wonderful people!" Elizabeth said. "You have never met Erik, yet you will open your home to him!"

"He's one of our servicemen who fought for his country, and that in itself is enough," George said, "But we know so much about him from your daily updates at the hospital that we already feel we know him."

The following day, Elizabeth talked with Conrad and mentioned her plan to ask Erik to the Templeton home for the weekend, his birthday and the Fourth of July fireworks display.

"I think that is a very fine gesture from the Templetons," Mr. Flemming said. "There are some legal matters that I must discuss with Erik very soon. He has not ever mentioned his father or asked about any relatives?"

"No, he hasn't," Elizabeth replied.

"This weekend might be a good time to talk to Erik and maybe break some of the news to him. What do you think?"

"I have a thought," Elizabeth said, "Give me a few moments, and I'll call you right back."

"George Templeton here!" the cheerful voice announced.

"It is Elizabeth. I have a question for you."

She explained about her conversation with Conrad Flemming.

"Why, by all means, invite Mr. Flemming to Four Winds also," he graciously offered. Elizabeth called Conrad Flemming and extended the Templetons' weekend invitation to him. "This way you will have plenty of opportunities to talk to Erik, and if something goes wrong health-wise, I will be on hand."

She heard Mr. Flemming muttering about packing a bag and what he should or should not bring with him.

"Mr. Flemming," she said, "don't make a big fuss about all this. The

Templetons are very nice, down-to-earth people, and you will be very welcome there. Bring some casual clothes and be prepared to enjoy yourself."

Erik was excited about leaving the hospital on Friday afternoon for the entire long weekend. Conrad Flemming was a big help in deciding about Erik's clothing needs.

"He can't go in his pajamas and bathrobe," Elizabeth pointed out. Erik was so thin that any clothing he had now would most likely not fit later on. Money was not a problem, in any case.

"I'm not a good shopper," Conrad admitted. "Why don't we get Erik's measurements, and then we'll shop together for them?" he suggested.

"You're not a married man, are you, Mr. Flemming?" Elizabeth asked.

"No, I was always too busy and never got around to it. Say, why don't you stop calling me Mr. Flemming and just call me Conrad," he implored. They obtained a measuring tape and started measuring Erik, who protested that his modesty was being violated.

"Why are you saying that?" Elizabeth asked, when they wanted to measure his inseam for trousers.

"I'm not covered up," an embarrassed Erik claimed.

"Listen, Lieutenant," Elizabeth said in exasperation, "I have bathed you from head to toe, changed your bed with you in it, not to mention applying lotion all over your body. Now you are going to tell me that you are afraid I am going to see your behind?"

Conrad roared with laughter while Erik shrank back on the bed and submitted quietly until they finished all their measurements. Seeing the expression on Erik's face, Elizabeth felt sorry for him and that she had been so harsh.

"We will be back in a short while," she said, and she and Conrad left on a shopping spree.

Conrad wanted to go to a tailor for fitted clothes, but Elizabeth vetoed that in favor of Sears. They bought him two pairs of slacks with adjustable tabs on the sides (allowing for two inch or more spread). The shirts were easier. Shoulder sizes with tapered body cut. "Athletic cut, is what you want," the sales clerk advised. They got Erik six sport shirts, underwear, socks and T-shirts. Elizabeth was concerned about Erik getting a chill. She insisted on a matching V-neck sweater. They moved on to the shoe department.

"Let's go for something we know will be comfortable," Conrad said.

They chose a pair of soft leather loafers and a pair of canvas deck shoes.

"Don't forget—he needs a belt for his trousers," Conrad remembered. Their shopping was complete, and as they started to leave the store, Elizabeth stopped at the men's shaving and lotion counter.

"I will need your help here," Elizabeth said to Conrad. They bought a shaving kit for Erik, after-shave lotion, and deodorant stick and body cologne.

"Better throw in a new toothbrush, also," Elizabeth added.

They returned to find Erik sitting up in bed watching for them anxiously. Elizabeth left the room while Conrad helped Erik sort out his new clothes and helped him to get dressed to go out.

Erik enjoyed the drive out to the Templetons' house. Elizabeth drove her Ford, and Conrad followed in his Mark IV Jaguar. Elizabeth pulled up near the garage area, leaving space for Conrad near the front entranceway. Chester came out to greet Conrad, taking his bag and leading him into the house.

Elizabeth waved and yelled, "We'll be along in a moment!"

Erik was trying to carry his own small suitcase, but Elizabeth would not allow it. He started to protest, but Elizabeth cut him off quickly, saying, "Erik Neilsin, I am responsible for your safety and welfare. If I say no I mean NO!" she said, "Understand?"

"Yes, sir, madam!" Erik said, snapping a salute to a smiling Elizabeth. They walked slowly to the front entrance and up the few stairs to the front door. Martha was at the front door with a vase of fresh flowers.

"Hello, Miss Elizabeth," she said, and all of a sudden she saw Erik, made a gasping sound, and dropped the vase on the floor. The vase smashed, and water and flowers went everywhere.

"Oh my God! Look at what I've gone and done," she cried. Martha was very upset, and Elizabeth tried to help her.

Penny came rushing over to her mother with a pail and mop and the dustpan to help clean up. She looked up at Erik, and she too uttered a gasp, but she recovered quickly, saying, "He looks a lot like Jimmy."

The rest of the household was on hand to greet Conrad and Erik. Seeing Erik was another shock for every member of the household. After a few embarrassing moments and much shyness on Erik's part, the family settled down.

Regaining her composure, Bernice went into the library and brought out a huge photo album. She said that an explanation for all of their surprise was due. Bernice withdrew two eight-by-ten photographs of Jennifer and Jimmy standing near the doorway with the new "Four Winds" sign in the background. The other photograph was of Jimmy looking very serious in a staged pose. Even for Elizabeth, it was a bit of a shock. Erik looked like an older Jimmy. Looking at the photo of the two children, Elizabeth could see a similarity between herself and Jennifer. Queenie was muttering to herself and walking around making the signs of the cross every time she crossed Erik's path.

"For God's sake, Queenie, cut that out," George called after her.

Bill said, "It's all right, guv'nor, the old Queen has had a bit of a shock. Same as when our Elizabeth here, first came. She'll be over it shortly."

Conrad settled in nicely with the Templetons and the household staff. Erik was feeling a little tense. His long duration in a coma had a decided effect on his memory recall. He had difficulty remembering details of his childhood and growing up. His recollection of his military training was somewhat vague also. This worried Conrad. While Erik was friendly and cordial with Conrad, he seemed somewhat distant.

Elizabeth didn't quite know whether to pamper Erik or try to let him adapt to his present surroundings—and cope. Erik seemed to be keenly interested in Queenie's garden, and when he wanted to go into the garden, Elizabeth let him. Queenie was at the entrance of her cottage and saw Erik walking in the garden, showing interest in her flowers. If anything won Queenie over quickly, it was Erik's interest in her flowers. Over her initial shock of seeing Erik and his likeness to the deceased Jimmy Templeton, Queenie approached him.

"Well, how do you like my little garden?" she asked.

"It is a nice little garden," Erik replied. "I think that your snapdragons would do better planted away from the pine trees."

"Is that so?" Queenie bristled. She was not used to having anyone tell her how to plant or manage a garden. "Why do you say that?" she asked.

"Well, the pine tree needles, when they fall to earth, get into the soil, and they are highly acidic. Snapdragons like nonacidic soil," he said. "They will also grow bigger with more sunlight."

Queenie didn't argue with Erik on that. She seemed to remember reading something about pine needles and soil and its effect on other plant growth. She couldn't remember the article, but what Erik said jogged her memory.

Elizabeth took her guests around the Four Winds estate. Erik was very interested in the vineyards and fruit trees. Elizabeth was impressed with his knowledge on the fruit and pollination.

"Erik, where did you learn so much about growing things?" Conrad asked. "I thought that you were an electrical engineering major in school."

Erik did not answer right away. He seemed deep in thought.

"I'm not sure exactly," he said, "but when I saw the trees and gardens, I just sort of remembered some things about gardening."

A bell rang back at the house. Turning, Elizabeth said, "If you are hungry, what you just heard is the dinner bell. That's Martha's way to let all of us know that she is ready to serve food."

"I could eat a horse right now," Conrad said.

They headed back to the house by a different direction, past the hen house and other maintenance buildings.

"They have their own poultry and plenty of fresh eggs," Elizabeth said. They entered the house by the rear patio door.

"They certainly have a nice place," both Conrad and Erik said.

Chester greeted them as they came onto the patio. "We have arranged a buffet, and we will use the main dining room for seating," he said. "If you would like to freshen up, the rest rooms are over there," directing Conrad and Erik.

The buffet was set up with hot steaming trays, heated to keep the food warm. They worked their way through the buffet line and found several steamed vegetables, baked potatoes as well as roasted new potatoes. The next pan held fresh spinach cooked with olive oil and garlic. Following were compartments for lobster with broccoli florets, baked chicken, and a standing rib of beef that Chester carved. George did the wine honors, opening one wine for the appetizers and another to complement the dinner. Martha had also made fresh dinner rolls that were served warm. Bernice announced that they would have coffee and dessert out on the terrace after a short interval, to allow the food to settle. It was an abundant and delicious meal.

Conrad sat with Erik after dinner and talked with him at great length about what had happened after he left for Korea. He asked Erik if he remembered getting the letters from Conrad on certain legal matters. Erik said he sort of remembered the letters but had trouble recalling the details. Conrad went over all the details and told Erik that his father had passed away while Erik was in a coma.

"Your father, I believe, knew that his health was failing and he wanted to make sure that he didn't leave any loose ends with regard to your future and eventual return from the war."

Erik did remember the boat building business and his Aunt Jennie and cousins.

"I guess I will have to get a job real soon," Erik said. "I must have some back pay from the military," he surmised.

"Yes, you do! A considerable amount, I must say. Besides that, you need not worry about money, because your father left you a trust fund, which has been accumulating interest and dividends for some time."

Erik thought for a few minutes then said, "It would be nice to have a car. I think I would like that," he said.

"Well, Erik, you know you do have almost a brand new 1949 Pontiac sedan that you bought used and like new, just before you went away to Korea. Your dad took care of it for you. He had it cleaned every few months and then would run the car for an hour or so. The car is as good as the first day you bought it! If you want a newer car—get one, but I would advise that you keep the Pontiac as a collector's car. Someday, in the not too distant future, a car like that and in that condition, will be worth a lot of money."

It took Conrad three long discussions for Erik to learn most of the details about his inheritance and financial situation. Erik was told that he had stock in IBM and other investments that his father bought and transferred over to Erik.

"It comes to a tidy sum," Conrad said.

Erik somehow brushed off that information, assuming that it represented a couple of thousand dollars. In fact, the original stock holdings for IBM, five thousand shares, had split several times, and he now owned over twenty thousand shares currently valued at $300 per share. Erik was not counting money in his head, and showed little interests. While Conrad was talking to him, Erik was watching Elizabeth.

Hmmm, thought Conrad.

Apex Builders, Inc., had built many types of landing craft for the government. While current building was slow, the demand for replacement parts and refitting, became a major business for the company. The company itself was worth over $250 million.

Yes, thought Conrad, *you don't realize what your father left you or what the value is.*

Conrad decided to keep much of this information confidential since he could see Erik's interest in Elizabeth was obvious. George approached Conrad and asked if he was comfortable and being attended to.

"Indeed, indeed," he said. Looking at Elizabeth, Conrad said, "I like that girl! She is rather special, I think. There is nothing pretentious about her and she is a straight-shooter, if I'm any judge of character."

"Yes, she is." George said. "By the way, I just happened to think of something. Bernice and I are planning to fly out to the West Coast next week, and we wanted to take Elizabeth because her folks are near San Francisco. But she is tending to Erik, and we didn't want to interfere with his treatment and care that she is responsible for. My thought is, do you see anything wrong with my bringing Erik along? Elizabeth could still watch out for him, and they could both enjoy the trip. We are planning to visit San Francisco and then take a hop over to Las Vegas for them to see the Grand Canyon. What do you think?"

"I don't see why not. One thing though, I will have to get Erik out to do some more shopping, or rather get Elizabeth out with us. She is a good shopper, has good taste, and has good color coordination."

CHAPTER 20

George and Bernice talked to Elizabeth first to inform her of their idea for the coming trip.

"What do you think?" Bernice asked Elizabeth.

"I think that would be really wonderful. What a surprise for my parents to see me there. By the way, Bernice, you never did tell me how your physical examination went at the hospital the other day. Remember, you were going to come over and tell me and we were going to have lunch together."

"Oh, I am sorry, dear. The exam report was excellent, and I am clean as a whistle! I was just so happy about the good news that I dashed home to tell George, and I forgot all about our arrangement. Then Erik popped out of his coma and you were all tied up, so I didn't bother to tell you anything."

"Oh, Bernice, I am so happy for you! Does that mean that I am no longer needed here, and I should be looking for someplace to live?"

"Good heavens, no!" Bernice gave Elizabeth a bear hug. "Having the two of you around—you and Erik—it's like having our Jennifer and Jimmy with us," she confessed in a whisper. "Believe me, the last thing in the world I want is for you to leave us!"

Elizabeth had suspected that the Templetons wanted her for more than the nursing aspects, especially when she learned about her resemblance to Jennifer Templeton.

Imagine that Erik bears a close resemblance to Jimmy, she thought. *Can this be mere coincidence?* Elizabeth felt that her mind was getting cluttered with many things she did not understand.

It was starting to get dark and the Templetons called everyone together and announced that they would take three cars up to Gunpowder Falls to watch the firework display at nine o'clock. The travel distance to Gunpowder Falls was about fifteen minutes. Chester brought the pickup truck and unloaded enough lawn chairs for everyone to sit. Next he brought out a little folding table and set up with a cooler, wax paper drink glasses, and two tubs—one with potato chips, the other with pretzels.

"There! I think we are all set now," he announced.

Elizabeth sat next to Erik, and as the sky darkened, a slight breeze blew toward them. Elizabeth felt the chill from the cool breeze and gave an involuntary shiver. Erik noticed and put his arm around Elizabeth's shoulder. She stiffened when his arm went around her, and then relaxed, realizing that he was trying to keep her warm. Erik's casual arm around her shoulders did bring some warmth to her. She leaned further back and Erik encircled her shoulders with his other arm.

"I've got you now, so don't try to escape," he said jokingly.

She just smiled. *I don't really mind*, she thought.

Loud speakers boomed out with a heralding of music. Then the fireworks started, building up and increasing in the type and volume of rockets, flares and boomers. Nearing its conclusion, the speakers blared out Sousa's "Stars and Stripes Forever," with the tempo of fireworks exploding and the star bursts reached its climax and ended with the conclusion of the music. It was a well-executed firework display.

Elizabeth noticed that Erik had his lips close to her neck and brushing his lips on her. Elizabeth worked free of Erik's grip and stood up. They all returned to the Templeton home, and hot coffee and snacks were served.

Elizabeth was excited and pleased at the opportunity to visit San Francisco and see her sister and parents. Erik was a bit reluctant at first to accept Bernice's invitation until he knew that Elizabeth would accompany them on the trip. Elizabeth checked with the hospital doctors in charge of Erik's case. They were pleased with the progress that Erik was making. He was not only putting on weight and getting stronger, but also his improving state of mind. He was adjusting very well to recuperation. George arranged for their flight out of Baltimore's Friendship Airport.

The flight to the West Coast would be on the new Pan American Boeing 707. The jet-powered aircraft would fly to the West Coast in five and half-hours. When they boarded, Erik and Elizabeth had two seats on the right side of the first-class cabin while Bernice and George were across the aisle from them. After the aircraft had reached its cruising altitude and drinks had been served, Erik nodded off to sleep. *He seems to do that quite often,* Elizabeth observed. *Erik has not built up any reserve stamina and gets tired quickly*, she thought. When food was served, Elizabeth asked if Erik's could be served later. She did not want to disturb his sleep. Elizabeth propped a pillow next to her shoulder for Erik's head to rest against. She took the blanket and tucked it around Erik so that he would be warm.

A movie was put on, and Elizabeth watched it while hearing through the headset. When the movie ended, she had to go to the toilet so she gently pushed Erik to his left side so she could get up. Erik stirred when he was moved. Elizabeth got up and was starting to walk away when Erik awoke and called "Lily! Lily!"

Elizabeth looked at Erik and saw that he was not quite fully awake.

"Erik, what did you say?"

"Where are you going?" he asked.

"No, I mean what did you call me?"

Erik looked puzzled. "Elizabeth … I think."

Elizabeth turned and went to the toilet in a very disturbed state. She had never said anything to Erik about being called Lily and not even to the Templetons. Now this was twice that Erik called her Lily. It was very disturbing, something that she could not understand.

After picking up their luggage, George hired a limousine to take them all into San Francisco to their hotel. Naturally, the hotel was rated at least five stars. The Templetons had arranged for a very elegant suite with three bedrooms—each with its own bathroom with the Living room in the center of the suite. The suite had a closet and a small kitchenette. Their suite was on the fifteenth floor and Erik was checking out the view of the city.

A thought crossed Elizabeth's mind, and she asked, "What is it like to jump out of an airplane with a parachute?"

Elizabeth was startled by the look of horror that momentarily flashed across Erik's face. She could see that Erik seemed to be agitated by her question. She thought that it was an innocent enough question—seeing that Erik had qualified for airborne and had made many jumps by parachute.

"I … I wouldn't jump again. I don't like parachutes. You can't get out," he stammered.

Elizabeth could not fathom why Erik was going on this way, so she ended the conversation by saying, "I'm going to shower and freshen up for supper," and left the room. It was still afternoon when Elizabeth showered and laid down for a short nap. She was awakened by a knock on her door.

"Are you up, Elizabeth?" Bernice called.

"Just a minute," Elizabeth replied and went to the door and opened it. "I just had a little nap."

"We are planning to go out to eat very shortly. Do you like seafood?" Bernice asked.

"You know I will eat just about anything," Elizabeth responded. "I have showered already, so I just have to put on a little makeup and arrange my hair. What time do you want to leave? What is the plan?"

"George has arranged for a limousine service. They will take us down to Fisherman's Wharf, where I hear the food is outstanding. When you go to see your folks tomorrow, you can have the limousine drop you off and call to pick you up again. Okay?"

"That would really be nice. It sounds like a great plan," she said, imitating Bernice.

Elizabeth slipped on a light blue floral print dress that had a matching long scarf, which could be worn over the shoulders. Elizabeth could wear her hair up or down. Tonight she chose to let her hair down and combed it out into soft waves.

Opening her jewelry box, she selected a pair of earrings and found that she had put the gemstone that the gypsy woman had given her in the box. The stone was resting on her gold band. Elizabeth picked up the stone tentatively, expecting to feel the stone get warm. It did not! Holding the stone in her right hand, she then reached into her box with her left hand and picked up the wedding band that Pat Duran had given her. There was no change in the stone's temperature. Instead she felt a faint vibration coming from the ring and the stone at the same time. It was like two sets of vibrations were reaching out to each other at some point in Elizabeth's body. Startled, she dropped both of the articles back into the jewelry box. She picked up the stone again. Nothing happened. She decided to place the stone back in her purse. Elizabeth puzzled over the gemstone and the strange happenings when she picked up the ring and stone at the same time.

When I get back, I think I'll look up that gypsy woman, she thought. *I need some answers!*

Fisherman's Wharf offered the finest in all kinds of food, but the best in fresh fish and other seafood. The scenery at the Crown and Anchor seafood restaurant, looking out to San Francisco Bay, was an artist's dream.

"What a fine painting this scene would make," Elizabeth said.

The food, when it came, was a medley of tasty seafood hors d'oeuvres, followed by baked red snapper, California fried potatoes, and a mixed fresh salad. George selected a South African hock wine to complement the meal. Coffee, a dessert, and an after-dinner liqueur completed the excellent meal.

Bernice was talking to her husband about their plans for the next few days.

"Elizabeth will see to Erik, and she is going to take him with her to see her family in Santa Rosa, just north of San Francisco."

"Have you been in touch with your family yet?" George asked.

"Yes, I did call, and I talked to my mother. I told her that I would come to see her and the family tomorrow. I explained that I had Erik with me. I wrote to my sister a few weeks ago telling her about my work at the hospital and also about my looking after Erik."

"We will have the driver take you there in the limousine. When you're ready to head back, call the hotel and if we are not here just leave a message and tell us what you are doing and when you'll be coming back."

"I expect that they will want me to stay longer than just a one day visit," Elizabeth said "but I don't know how much room they have. We may have to go into a hotel, if that's the case."

George was already reaching for his billfold, but Elizabeth cut him off. "I have plenty of cash with me. If we need to go into a hotel, I can handle it all right."

"Very well then. Be sure to keep us posted, so we won't worry," he said.

Elizabeth explained their planned visit to her sister's house to see her and her mother and father. Erik was very content with whatever arrangements she was making. Elizabeth stopped at the florist shop in the hotel to buy a lovely floral bouquet for her mother. She was surprised when Erik stopped her selection and asked the florist to make a bouquet from several other flowers. When his choices were arranged in the bouquet, Elizabeth was impressed and so was the florist.

The limousine was at the front entrance waiting for them. They climbed in and Elizabeth asked the driver to stop at a wine shop so she could select some wine to bring also.

"I know just the place and it's on our way too," the driver said.

Twenty minutes later they stopped at a wine and liquor store and Elizabeth went inside to pick up some wine. George Templeton's taste in wine was evidently rubbing off on Elizabeth as she selected a fine French wine—a sauterne, and also a Rhinewine (from the homeland). Satisfied, she got back into the car and they were off to Santa Rosa.

"Nine-oh-four, Cumberland Road, right?" asked the driver. "This is it, then."

The house did not appear to be big or high, but it was longer from front to back.

"I will wait to make sure this is the right place," the driver said.

Elizabeth rang the doorbell and waited. Then she rang the doorbell again, this time for a longer duration. She heard some yelling and a scampering of feet heading for the front door. The door swung open and a much grown Heidi leaped at Elizabeth and gave her a bear hug. Before Elizabeth and Erik could take two steps forward the family members surrounded them. They gathered their overnight bags just in case and went in. The driver waved goodbye and left for the return trip back to San Francisco.

Elizabeth was pleased at how well her mother and father looked. Older, to be sure, but healthy.

"So, Papa," she asked, "how do you like living in America?"

Mr. Feldmann just smiled at Elizabeth.

"Your papa doesn't hear very good now," her mother said. "His hearing was starting to go bad before we left Heidelberg. Now, he doesn't hear much. We have to yell."

Elizabeth looked at her father, patted his arm, and gave him a big hug and a kiss on the cheek.

"Where are Frank and Hilda?"

"They are out and they will be coming back very soon," squealed Heidi, Hilda and Frank's daughter.

"*Ja, und einen,*" Heidi said, interrupting.

"In English, Oma. Say it in English."

"*Ja, und* a surprise is she coming *mit,*" Elizabeth's mother said.

Elizabeth gave her mother the flowers and another hug and kiss. "What a pretty little house."

Taking Elizabeth by the hand, Heidi was set to pull her Aunt Elizabeth along with her.

"Hold on a moment!"

Elizabeth introduced Erik to her mother and father and then to Heidi. Giving in to the insistent tug on her hand from Heidi, she said, "I will have to go with her and see the rest of the house, or else this arm is going to be longer than the other one."

The house was narrow, but much longer. An unusual shape and order of rooms. The house had a main passageway from the front, almost to the back, with rooms branching off to one side. At the back of the house there was an addition that opened up into something like a conservatory. The abundance of windows permitted a lot of sunshine, and the room was very warm. The upper part of the windows were open to allow the hot air to escape. Elizabeth could see Hilda had some healthy-looking plants growing here.

Returning to the rest of the house, she and Erik joined her parents in the dining room where coffee had been laid out for them. Elizabeth asked Erik if he would be offended if she conversed with her mother in German.

Erik said, "Go ahead!"

Heidi had her eye on Erik and decided that she liked him and that being the case, he was accepted. She took him by his hand and dragged him off to the back of the house and outside to show him that they were growing their little vineyard.

There was a big commotion in the house and Heidi, with Erik in tow, brought him back inside. Elizabeth's sister and brother-in-law had returned. Elizabeth was in for a big surprise. Her Aunt Marie was there and Elizabeth screamed her surprise and rushed to kiss and hug her aunt.

"When did you get here? Why didn't you tell me?" she asked, turning to her sister.

"When you said you were coming, I thought it would be a nice surprise. Tante Marie has been here for a week already."

Everyone stared at Erik when he entered the room with Heidi. Heidi introduced him, "This is Erik."

"A little skinny, but nice," her aunt said to Elizabeth in German, adding, "He doesn't speak German, does he?"

"If he did, you would already be in trouble," Elizabeth said.

They all laughed. Erik felt a little embarrassed and awkward. Elizabeth took his hand and said, "My aunt thinks that you look nice," was all she said.

Erik was sure that there was more to it but didn't comment.

A fine lunch was set out for everyone. Elizabeth brought out the wine that she had bought and the whole family ate, drank and reminisced. Aunt Marie was the life of the party and after several glasses of wine, she was her old self—full of fun and laughter.

"So, you handsome fellow," she addressed Erik. "What do you do?"

Erik answered very simply, "I do whatever she tells me to do," he said, pointing to Elizabeth. Everyone roared with laughter.

"Elizabeth quickly explained in German that Erik was an injured lieutenant and was in her charge, even now. Marie eased up a bit and went to Erik and put her arm into his and said, "Erik can you sing?"

"Not very well. I haven't sung for a long time, I think."

"Come sing me a little song," Marie coaxed Erik.

Erik stammered and was not sure how to handle the situation. Elizabeth was about to step in and tell the aunt to quit, when Erik started to sing.

"There ain't nobody here but us chickens. There ain't nobody here at all, so point that gun …" Erik's voice trailed off at the expression of the faces looking at him.

"*Gott am Himmel*!" Marie exclaimed.

It was a moment of shock for them all.

"Erik? Where did you learn that song? Why did you start to sing that song?" Elizabeth cried.

"I, I don't know, it just came out! I don't even know the song," he said lamely.

Mrs. Feldmann made the sign of the cross and for a full minute everyone just stared at Erik and no one said anything more. It was a truly awkward moment for everyone, especially for Elizabeth and Erik. Even as shocked as she was, Elizabeth felt she should protect Erik from … *from what?*

I don't understand what is going on myself, she thought. Erik stood up and left the room, walking to the back of the house and went outside into the conservatory and out to the garden and vineyards.

Elizabeth's family was chattering back and forth in German about the song Erik sang.

"It is a sign from over there!" Aunt Marie said, pointing to the sky.

"Nonsense," Elizabeth's sister Hilda said. "A coincidence … he heard it on the radio," she offered as an explanation.

"I haven't heard that song for a long time," little Heidi said.

"Your American boyfriend sang it all the time. I remember him singing it. It was the only time I ever heard it until now," Heidi said.

Frank, who had been silent until now said, "That song was popular back in 1947! It was a hit that year, and then we didn't hear it anymore. I don't think he heard it on the radio lately. I just don't know what to make of it."

"I think I should go to Erik," Elizabeth said and went to find him.

She found him standing in the midst of the grape vineyards. He was staring away in the distance as if deep in thought. Gently she touched his arm and asked, "Erik, are you all right?"

Erik did not answer or seem to acknowledge her presence. Elizabeth shook Erik's arm, getting his attention.

"Erik, answer me! Are you all right?"

"Yes," he answered and turned away from Elizabeth. "I think that I am a problem for everyone. I just don't seem to be able to remember everything. Sometimes I think that I am dreaming, and I can't tell what is real or what was from a dream."

Elizabeth felt so bad for Erik and realized that he was going through a bad time.

"Don't worry about it, Erik! The doctors told me that you would have lapses in memory and that you might also suddenly recall things from way back in your mind."

Erik shrugged his shoulders and didn't say anything else. Erik was quiet for the remaining time of their visit. Hilda wanted Elizabeth to stay over for another day, but Elizabeth felt that the incident with Erik singing had dampened the happy atmosphere because it brought the acute memory of Pat back to the family. Aunt Marie was feeling very bad at teasing Erik and perhaps causing this incident to come about. She was an extremely superstitious person, and she was sure that she was ' tempting the gods'.

"No, we will be going back to San Francisco this evening," Elizabeth said.

"We have hotel accommodations there so we can come and go as we please. I am concerned about Erik. He is very upset and confused. I am responsible to make sure that he does not come to any danger, including mental problems," she offered as an explanation.

"He is awfully thin, isn't he?" asked Marie.

"Well, he is now around a hundred fifty-five pounds. He gained four pounds this past week," Elizabeth said. "He is about fifteen pounds under his normal weight now. We have been feeding him with good food and plenty of vitamins, and he is getting back to his regular weight."

Elizabeth was going to call for a taxi, but Frank said he would drive them back to San Francisco in his car. It was seven thirty in the evening when they left. When they arrived back at the hotel, they went upstairs to the suite and Erik told Elizabeth that he was going to go to bed and get some sleep, that he was tired.

He does look tired, she thought! She sensed that Erik was not happy and was still feeling awkward and somewhat abused. It was still quite early so she got out her book and read awhile. At ten-thirty the Templetons arrived back at the suite.

"Ah ha, there you are!" Bernice announced.

"Where is Erik?"

"I think he is asleep. I will check on him in a little while before I go to sleep."

Bernice asked about Elizabeth and Erik's day. Elizabeth didn't offer too many details, but said Erik was tired out. Awaking the next morning, Erik was up early and dressed in his shorts and T-shirt and left the suite. Elizabeth was not aware that Erik had left and did not make that discovery until she knocked on his door to wake him up. Getting no answer, she opened the door to an empty room. She started to feel a little panic, rushed out of the suite and took the elevator down to the lobby. She appeared little frantic as she looked out the front of the hotel and canvassed the whole area.

"Can I help you, miss?" the hotel concierge asked.

"Yes! I am looking for Erik Neilsin, who is with us in our suite. He left earlier, and we don't know where he might have gone."

"I think I know the gentleman. I saw someone earlier dressed in shorts and T-shirt. He is probably in our workout and conditioning gym. See that door over there," he said pointing.

She thanked him and rushed over to look. She did not see Erik in the gym and went up to the clerk at the desk.

"Would you know if Erik Neilsin has been in the gym this morning?"

"Yes. He's still here. He worked out with the weights and other exercises then showered. I believe he is in the pool doing some lap swimming."

Elizabeth checked and saw the lone swimmer doing the sidestroke. It was Erik.

"Excuse me, soldier," she asked, "are you getting hungry?"

Erik smiled at her and Elizabeth knew right away that everything was okay again.

"I understand that you were doing some very strenuous exercises. I don't want you to do too much too soon. Doctor's orders. Why don't you and I explore San Francisco today," Elizabeth suggested. "We will spend the whole day seeing all the sights. There are streetcars that run all the way down the hill, like you see on television! We can also go and see the big bridge. What's the name?"

"You mean the Golden Gate Bridge?"

"That's the one! I read that you can see a prison out in the middle of the water."

Erik was amused at Elizabeth working herself up with excitement at the prospects of playing the tourist. They told Bernice and George what they were up to and left. Armed with maps and sightseeing brochures that the concierge had provided, they set off on their San Francisco adventure. First they took a bus to the bus station and looked for the sightseeing tour buses. The tour buses were there in the bus terminal and the new tourists had a choice of five different trips. They chose the ride that went to the Golden Gate Bridge and views of Alcatraz. Elizabeth was busy taking photographs. As they were waiting for the return trip back into the city, two playful squirrels were scampering around them looking for tidbits of food being handed out. Erik had some crackerjack popcorn and threw a few pieces to the squirrels. He really started something then.

The little critters came right up to them and cautiously approached the extended hand with the crackerjack. Quick as a flash, the squirrel grabbed the kernel from Erik's hand and retreated a short distance away to eat it and then it was back for more. Before Erik knew it, he was out of squirrel food and the squirrels deserted him for other prospects.

Getting off the bus before it returned to the bus depot, Erik and Elizabeth went into a small snack place to get something to eat. It was called Chock Full of Nuts. They did serve other food besides hot dogs and coffee. They both wolfed down a sandwich and had a bowl of tomato soup and a cup of coffee. Then they were off again! Elizabeth asked a passing couple where she might find the streetcar that goes all the way down the hill—like on TV. The couple laughed.

"You're close by. Go three blocks over and you will see the trolley tracks."

Erik looked up and down the street and he thought he could see a sign that might mean that it was a trolley stop. They walked over, and sure enough, it was a streetcar stop. They waited for about ten minutes and saw the streetcar approaching. Elizabeth waved and the streetcar stopped and they got on board.

It was a long slow ride and the *clockity clock clockity clock* sound got to Erik and he nodded off in a nap. Elizabeth noted that he was tired from all the running around. She felt a little guilty that she felt fine and Erik was still recovering his strength and stamina. Erik's head was leaning toward Elizabeth so she moved a little closer. Now his head rested on her shoulder.

Fifteen minutes later the streetcar reached the bottom of the hill and gave a lurch as it stopped.

Erik immediately woke and was looking across and above at the writing on the wall of the streetcar.

"Nicht auf den Boden Spucken!" he uttered to Elizabeth's amazement.

"Erik, what did you say? You do not speak German. Where did you learn that phrase?" Erik had that awkward look on his face again.

"I read it, up there," he said, pointing to the words printed there.

The words, Elizabeth saw, read "Hold onto the straps while the car is in motion."

Elizabeth didn't know what to say. She was at a loss for words and felt panic building up inside her. "Come, let us get off here!" she directed.

The streetcar moved off and Elizabeth felt her knees shaking a bit. She looked at Erik's face. He had sort of a lost look in his expression. There was a little park rest area close by and they sat down on the bench. Elizabeth felt a strong emotional tug, bringing her close to tears. That phrase! That was Pat Duran's favorite saying on the streetcar. She reached into her purse for her hankie and felt the gemstone. It was extremely hot! This time, there was no doubt about it! The stone was warmer than ever. She looked at the stone in her purse and she was sure that it had grown lighter in color.

She quickly said a prayer in German. One that she knew as a small girl, asking for protection and guidance. Erik reached over and took Elizabeth's limp hand and brought her hand up to his face and kissed the palm of her hand. It was like a mini electric shock—or was she just startled? Elizabeth's eyes were moist and she felt that she would surely start crying like a little girl. *I must keep emotions under control* she thought, and quickly stood up.

"Let's go!" she ordered.

Returning to the hotel, they both freshened up and Elizabeth, still unsettled, resolved that when they got back home she was going to find that old gypsy woman and ask questions about the gemstone. There was a knock on her door and George said, "We are going to dine out tonight and tomorrow we will fly to Las Vegas for a few days."

"What is in Las Vegas?" Elizabeth asked.

"They are starting to have gambling casinos and live entertainment there. It may become the major attraction in that area, the same as Reno. There is a great plane ride that takes you over Boulder dam and Lake Mead. It's something different."

"Okay! I am just getting myself ready now," Elizabeth said. Already dressed, hair done up and make up applied, Elizabeth stepped out of her room. Erik was dressed in coat and tie and he looked like he put on some more weight, she thought. Glancing once again at Erik, she thought, *he looks rather handsome, all dressed up!* Bernice and George came out of their room and Bernice said, "Look, George! Don't they make a handsome couple?"

George thought the same thing, but decided not to add fuel to a fire that Bernice might be trying to kindle. The evening went well. Erik ate his biggest meal yet, and Elizabeth wondered where he was putting all that food.

The flight to Las Vegas lasted only two hours. The twin-engine Convair touched down at eleven o'clock in the morning. Elizabeth was amazed to see slot machines all over the airport. People waiting for their flights were depositing coins and pulling the handle—non-stop. George chuckled and had to urge Elizabeth on as she stopped to watch people playing the slot machines.

"This is a gambling town," George said. "You will see those one-armed bandits all over!"

They took a taxi to the hotel. George had rented one of the VIP master suites near the top of the hotel. The suite had three bedrooms, a wet bar, two bathrooms, a dining room and a large living room.

"I don't usually recommend it," George said, "but I have taken the liberty of having the house provide us with some playing ammunition," he said with a laugh and produced several stacks of large round chips that were imprinted with the hotel name and the number ten.

"These chips are ten-dollar chips," Bernice said. "You can use them anywhere in the hotel. You can change them into smaller amounts plus you can get special coins for the various slot machines!"

Erik and Elizabeth each were given a stack of chips, which they placed in a "Sands" plastic tub.

"There are fifty chips for each of you!" George said. "The drinks are on the house, so you won't be paying for them. There is a floor show on at nine tonight. I made reservations for the four of us. Dinner will be at seven—Okay?"

"That sounds great," Erik said. "Mr. Templeton, you are paying for all these things for us. I think I should pay my fair share so you don't have to carry these expenses."

"That's quite all right, Erik. I appreciate the offer, but Bernice and I enjoy seeing our money put to good use. Seeing you kids having fun is a tonic for us."

Elizabeth laughed. "I gave up trying to help with the expenses long ago," she told Erik. "They are just generous people with their wealth, I'm told. C'mon, Erik! It's two in the afternoon and we have at least four hours to see the casino and all the games."

"I think you need an awful lot of luck with these games," Erik said. "And

I think that I will change these chips into the smallest amounts, because it will go fast enough."

Elizabeth thought that made sense so she did the same. Now her plastic tub was full of chips in smaller denominations. Elizabeth wet her lips and was surprised that they felt chapped. *It must be very dry climate here*, she thought. She reached into her purse for her lipstick and touched up her lips. Putting the lipstick away, she felt the gemstone.

This is supposed to be a lucky stone, she thought. On impulse, she brought the gemstone out of her purse and dropped it in with her chips for luck. Elizabeth moved up to a roulette table and watched as people were placing chips all over the board. The croupier's assistant was watching Elizabeth and asked if she knew how the game worked. She shook her head. He explained about the betting, the amounts and the odds (which she still did not understand), but she got an idea on the columns, numbers and groups. The minimum bet, she was told, was five dollars in chips. The croupier asked for some of her chips and he counted them out and gave her twenty of the five dollar chips. She still had plenty of chips left. She waited for the next chance to play. She placed one bet in the middle of the block of four numbers seven, eight, ten, and twelve; then she also placed a bet on number eight.

"No more bets!" the croupier cried.

Everyone watched as the wheel turned and the little ball went around the wheel in the opposite direction until it fell into a slot.

"Black—Number Eight," he said.

He cleared the table, except for Elizabeth's bet and pushed over thirty-five chips and then another eight chips. In that one round of play, Elizabeth won two hundred and fifteen dollars.

"Place your bets please!"

Elizabeth placed three chips on the edge of number fifteen, and five chips on the three through thirty-six row. The wheel spun and the ball was released. The ball starting to fall and then bounced back up and then down again— landing in number fifteen. She won thirty-five chips for number fifteen and another ten chips for the winning row. That amounted to $215. Elizabeth was really enjoying this. She played twice and won twice! *This is easy*, she thought. She reached out to place her bet, and one of her chips fell out and rolled to the middle of the table onto number twenty-three. The croupier went to retrieve the chip for Elizabeth, but she told him it was okay leave it there. She handed the croupier four more to add to that number.

"No more bets!" he called. The wheel spun round and the click as the croupier released the ball in the opposite direction. It landed. "Odd, red, number twenty-three," he announced.

Elizabeth heard a loud murmur from the other players as she received another stack of chips—$175. She asked the croupier if he could change them into bigger amounts, which he did so she did not have so many chips in her tub.

"I want to try something else," she said.

Feeling generous and in the style of George Templeton, she gave a ten-dollar chip to the croupier and moved off.

Elizabeth found Erik at the slot machine, playing twenty-five-cent slugs.

"How are you doing, Erik?"

"Not so good. I put in around twenty and win three or five back."

Elizabeth sat down next to him. He put in another coin, and she said, "Let me pull the handle for you."

Pulling down hard, she then held the lever down and at the last minute let go. *Clomp, clomp, clomp*—Three yellow bells! Coins started to come out of the machine—eighteen of them!

"That's my first big win," Erik said. He played six more coins and nothing came up. Elizabeth picked up one of Erik's coins and put it into the slot and cranked the handle. *Clomp, clomp, clomp.* Elizabeth was disappointed when three black bars appeared, but then the machine started pumping out coins and a bell rang. An attendant came over, verified the jackpot, and gave Erik four hundred dollars in chips. He asked Erik to clear the jackpot. Erik pulled another coin through.

"Wow! You have the lucky touch," Erik said, very excited.

"Let's see some other things," Elizabeth said.

"By the way, did you win anything? I saw you at the big roulette table."

"As a matter of fact, I did," and she showed Erik her tub, which had a pile of twenty-five dollar chips on top. "I don't know how much is there. I only played three times," she said.

"You hit once in three tries? Boy, that is pretty good," Erik said.

"Oh no!" she said. "I played three times and won three times."

They approached a table where a bunch of very excited gamblers were throwing dice. They watched for a little while and decided that they were not interested in it. Erik put some more coins into the slot machines while Elizabeth walked around the casino. She stopped at one station where they had an electronic wheel that was about eight feet high. The wheel had ninety-nine numbers with eight "No Win" spaces spread amongst the numbers.

The man was talking to a group of people and saying, "Place a bet on a number. If it comes up you win five hundred dollars and a one-week trip to Hawaii, all expenses paid. That includes airfare, hotel and meals. C'mon, give it a try, it's only twenty-five dollars. How about you, young lady?" he asked Elizabeth.

"Okay," she said, reaching into her tub for four twenty dollar chips and got a five dollar chip back. "I'll take three numbers—number fifty-seven, number twenty-one, and number fifty-six." All three numbers, with a space in between, were next to each other.

"That's the way to go, little lady," he said.

"Okay, who's next?" he asked.

The numbers were starting to fill up.

"Okay—here we go!"

He pressed the button and the light started rotating around the wheel, lighting up each number as it passed it. The light turned several times around and was now slowing up. It slowly passed Elizabeth's three numbers and started to jump from one number to the next as it slowly … very slowly came around and stopped on number twenty-one.

"The lady is the winner!" he announced. He gave her a five-hundred dollar chip and asked her name, giving her a special token to take to the cashier's window. At the window, the cashier congratulated Elizabeth on her win.

"I need your full name and address and your signature down here," the clerk said. She then gave Elizabeth a special packet of things, which included a certificate for an American Airline Hawaiian trip for two, hotel vouchers and other items.

Elizabeth retrieved Erik who was working his way down the row of slot machines. When she reached him, he was down to two hundred dollars worth of chips. She took one of his coins and put the coin into a machine across from Erik. She pulled down the handle, releasing it slowly. *Thump. thump, clomp.* Two sets of cherries. Five coins came out. One more time, she pulled the handle. *Thump, thump, clomp!* Three oranges. Out came ten coins. One more time! She pulled the handle. *Thump, thump, clomp!* Three bells and eighteen coins came out. Erik stopped playing and watched what Elizabeth was doing.

"One more coin," she said, pulling down the handle and holding it down—not letting the handle go up on its own. *Clunk, clunk,* and *clunk*! "JACKPOT!" Coins dumped out and the bell started to ring! The attendant verified the jackpot and paid Elizabeth four hundred dollars in chips. Looking at her watch, she saw that it was nearly six o'clock.

"Let's cash these in now and go upstairs to get ready for dinner. I am getting hungry, how about you?"

"My throat is awfully dry," he said. "I am hungry, too!"

They stopped one of the girls serving drinks, and Erik had a beer and Elizabeth a gin and tonic.

"I have never seen you drink a beer before," she said.

Arriving back in their suite, Elizabeth showed Bernice and George their winnings. Elizabeth had over five thousand dollars—plus the all-expenses-paid trip to Hawaii. With Elizabeth's good luck and her Midas touch, Erik won eight hundred dollars.

"I'd say that was a pretty good day's work," George commented.

They all dressed up and went to dinner at the Sands. George asked for one of the best tables, close to the runway where the entertaining artists would be. George told the usher that he made reservations for four.

"The name?"

"Grant," he said and slipped a fifty-dollar bill into the usher's hand. Elizabeth asked Bernice why George said his name was Grant. Bernice chuckled and told her that President Grant's image was on the fifty dollar bill that George gave the usher.

"Yes, sir! Right this way, Mr. Grant." He then led them to the best table in the house. The music was great and a little loud for where they were seated, however when the entertainers performed, they had the best view of all.

"Ladies and gentlemen! The hotel is happy to present the greatest show in Vegas …Please welcome Freddie Calaro!" The applause was deafening. He sang several popular ballads including "Young at Heart." Elizabeth was thrilled at seeing this top celebrity in person on stage. The audience gave a thundering round of applause and brought him out for an encore. It was late when the floorshow ended.

"How about a nightcap before we retire?" George asked.

Everyone agreed, and they went into one of the special lounge areas in the Sands. Elizabeth asked for a coffee and had a cognac with it. Erik decided on a draft beer, while Bernice fancied a brandy Alexander.

"I'll have a Remy Martin and soda!" George said.

"What is your agenda for tomorrow?" Bernice asked Elizabeth.

"We are going to take the bus down to the small airport. They have planes that take people up over the Grand Canyon and Hoover Dam."

"That sounds like a good idea! You'll like it! George and I have flown over it several times and it is always a thrill," Bernice said.

After breakfast, Erik and Elizabeth set out to take the short trip down to the small tourist airport. The bus pulled up next to a small building. There were five single engine aircraft parked there.

Erik was getting extremely nervous and a bit anxious.

"Are you sure you want to fly in one of those things?"

"Sure! What's wrong?" asked Elizabeth.

She bought two tickets and went out to the aircraft that was boarding two passengers. There were three vacant seats. Elizabeth sat in the second row of seats, behind the pilot. Erik climbed up and sat up front next to the pilot.

Elizabeth could see that Erik was looking rather anxious. The pilot toggled a switch, pulled a lever out and the propeller started to turn and then the engine caught in a sputter and then roared. Without any hesitation the aircraft started to taxi down the rough hard ground toward the end of the earthen runway. The pilot was telling them, as they flew, that they would climb to several thousand feet and keep climbing to cross over one particular high point and then over the grand canyon.

"We are passing over the Hoover Dam," he pointed out, "and the large body of water you see is Lake Mead."

The view was awesome. Elizabeth noticed that Erik kept looking behind them. "What's the matter, Erik?" she asked. "Why do you keep looking behind you?"

"Just seeing if there was another aircraft behind us."

The pilot laughed and said, "We are pretty much alone up here. No one would be flying that close to us."

Still Erik kept looking behind every so often. It was very distracting and Elizabeth noted that he did this at least five times. The pilot, Elizabeth noticed, was starting to look behind also, as if to double check on what Erik was looking for. When the trip was over and they touched back down at the dirt airstrip, the pilot was glad to get rid of the passengers.

This guy gives me the creeps, he thought.

Elizabeth was thinking about the series of events surrounding Erik. She thought about the unusual happenings with the gemstone and the startling things that Erik had uttered—*calling her Lily twice before.* Thinking about it, Elizabeth felt the hair on the back of her neck tingle.

What can I be thinking of? I must not allow myself to become confused about all these things. Still, she wanted very much to re-visit the gypsy woman in Georgetown. There are many unanswered and confusing questions that need to be sorted out. She and Erik returned to the Sands for lunch. Erik learned that the Sands had a spa and other facilities for massage and steam bath. He returned to his room and changed into his trunks, bathrobe and slippers then went to the spa.

Elizabeth wanted to browse through the many shops to check out the clothing. She checked her purse and realized that she had a very tidy sum of money and thought to treat herself to some new things. Something caught Elizabeth's eye in a jewelry store that featured other artifacts beside jewelry. What piqued her interest was a small-framed picture of unusual composition. It was a picture of two cherub angels hovering around a woman. The picture and figures were composed of small bits of colored glass, instead of paint. She learned that this artistic technique was very unique and that the picture, once blended with the varying bits of colored glass, was then fired in a kiln where the glass fused together in one piece. The picture was at least one inch thick, and required a special frame. Special eye-fasteners had been fused into the back of the unusual picture. It was only a twelve-by-fourteen-inch picture, and the price was $3,500.

Elizabeth looked at the picture and what she interpreted was that the two "angels" could be two children … (*Jennifer and Jimmy? Or Elizabeth and Erik?*) The woman—Bernice!

"I'll take it!," she told the clerk. "I want it for a gift to a special person. Could you please gift wrap it and put it into another wrapping so that it doesn't get broken?"

The return trip back to Baltimore was by way of Chicago. When they did arrive back at Friendship Airport, it was already getting dark. Everyone was tired. Chester was waiting for them when they arrived and they all piled into the car and were soon back at Four Winds. Elizabeth contacted Conrad to let him know that they had returned.

"Splendid! I would like to come by in the morning to take Erik with me for the day," he said. "I have a lot of legal stuff that needs to be sorted out with Erik, and tomorrow seems as good a time as any."

"Fine," Elizabeth said. "I need to go to Georgetown, and this is a good opportunity to do it."

Returning to her room, she took out her jewelry box and put the gemstone back in the box. A strange thing happened. All the other jewelry items seemed to be repelled by the gemstone, and formed a circle away from the stone … all of the jewelry except one—the gold wedding band. Elizabeth felt the hair on her neck standing on edge. The ring was slowly moving on its own toward the gemstone. It stopped when it reached the stone. Still watching in awe, she noticed that the gemstone changed from its dark color to a bright yellow green.

A little frightened, she quickly closed the cover of the jewelry box and pushed the dresser drawer shut.

It was a long time before she could close her eyes and fall asleep. As she finally drifted off to sleep, Elizabeth, in her dream, saw herself walking down a path. Someone was coming up the path toward her. She strained her eyes to see who it was.

The man looked familiar. As they drew closer to each other, Elizabeth recognized with a start that it was Pat Duran! Unable to contain herself, she ran to him and opened her arms to gather him close to herself. Suddenly his face changed just as she reached him. It was not Pat Duran's face. It was Erik's. Elizabeth woke up terribly shaken. She went downstairs to the kitchen and heated a cup of milk. Feeling a bit better, she chastised herself for being such a ninny and a foolish girl. She went back to her bedroom and in a few minutes was fast asleep. When she awakened, Elizabeth found that it was already nine a.m. She had intended to be up much earlier. She showered and got into a casual outfit, did her make-up and went down to catch a bite to eat. Bernice was out on the terrace. Elizabeth joined her.

"What are you doing, Bernice?" she asked.

Bernice had two big waffle irons going and was making a pile of waffles.

"Come, have some waffles," she said. "I'm getting this down pat now. Martha and I are having a contest on producing the best looking waffles." Elizabeth wolfed down two waffles and a couple of pieces of bacon. She enjoyed all of that with an excellent cup of coffee.

"I am going into Georgetown," she announced. "Can I get anything for you?" she asked.

"No, darling. You go right ahead. Watch out for the traffic. If you're later than four o'clock, you know how bad the traffic gets," she cautioned.

"I know," Elizabeth said, and then she brought out the gift she had purchased in Las Vegas. "Bernice, I saw this in Las Vegas and it struck me as being very special. I would like you and George to have it."

"Why, thank you, my dear. You really shouldn't have got us anything." Opening the box and then the gift wrapping, Bernice caught her breath at the weight of the framed picture. "It is beautiful," she said. "And so unusual too! "Does it have a name?"

"Yes," Elizabeth said. "Twice Blessed."

Elizabeth left Bernice holding the picture and noted the tears on her cheeks.

"I'll see you later," she said, she did not want to embarrass Bernice. Elizabeth backed the car out and headed for Washington DC and Georgetown.

CHAPTER 21

Madame Zelma

It was difficult to find a place to park her car in Georgetown in the late morning. After driving in and around the back streets Elizabeth spotted a small parking lot and pulled in. She had a little trouble remembering where that little teahouse was located. She remembered that it was on the west side of the street and on the main drag. Elizabeth checked all the shops, little snack bars and restaurants as she headed up the avenue. Suddenly, she spotted the little teahouse. Entering, Elizabeth looked around but did not see the old gypsy woman.

The waitress looked at Elizabeth and asked, "Lady, are you going to sit down so I can serve you?"

"Oh, I'm awfully sorry," Elizabeth said. "I was looking for the old gypsy lady that used to be here."

"She's not here anymore. She was only here for a couple of weeks, and then she left," the waitress replied.

"Where can I find her?" Elizabeth asked.

"Beats me! I just work here, I don't keep track of people that drift in and out of here." The waitress could see that Elizabeth was really upset, so she called out, "Hey, Lou!" to the man behind the small counter. "The old gypsy—what's her name? Where did she go?" the waitress asked.

"The old gypsy? Oh yeah, Madame Zelma. Not sure ... I think she's uptown somewhere around T Street across the river," he answered.

Elizabeth asked for directions and thanked the waitress and the man behind the counter.

Elizabeth realized that she was holding her breath in anticipation. Her sense of urgency was now great. She had to find the gypsy woman! She went back to the parking lot, got in her car and turned north, down a main street to cross the bridge into the District. Driving down R Street, she thought that it looked familiar. As she drove east, she noticed the Spanish restaurant, the El Bordegon, across the street. When she reached the next corner, she turned left and looked for T Street. She pulled into a parking garage and figured that she was close enough to seek out the gypsy on foot. It turned out to be more difficult than she hoped for.

She walked up one side of the street and then down the other side. It was past one thirty in the afternoon and her stomach was growling in protest. Two waffles and a piece of bacon can only go so far!

She needed to stop for a bite to eat and entered a place that had many people already seated. She was quickly seated and a waiter came to take her order. The service was fast and the food hot and tasty. Elizabeth asked the waiter if he knew of an old gypsy woman around this neighborhood called Madame Zelma.

"Naw, I never heard of her," he replied, and walked off.

Finishing her lunch, Elizabeth left to hunt some more. A taxi was just dropping off a fare. She saw that the cab driver was sort of dark skinned. Maybe Lebanese, she thought. On impulse, she called out to the driver.

"Taxi! Do you know of a gypsy woman around here called Madame Zelma?"

Using one of George Templeton's tactics, she held out a five-dollar bill.

"Madame Zelma? Sure! She lives a long ways from here," the driver said, laughing. "Right around the corner. "Hop in!" Taking the five dollars, he said, "I won't put the meter on cause it's just around the corner."

He pulled up in front of a small row of houses with many steps leading to the first floor.

Elizabeth looked up, and the cab driver said, "No, down there," pointing to the basement apartment.

"Are you sure?"

"Yeah, sure I'm sure. That's where she lives!"

Elizabeth gave him another five dollars.

She had to walk down five steps to the doorway underneath the main stairway to the house. The front door was open but the screen door was closed. Elizabeth could hear some music in the background and not seeing any bell, she called out.

"Hello ... hello! Madame Zelma, are you there?"

She heard the sounds of feet shuffling and Madame Zelma came to the screen door. "Yes! What do you want?"

"Madame Zelma, I need to talk to you," Elizabeth implored.

"What's this all about?" Madame Zelma asked suspiciously.

"Oh, I spent the whole morning looking for you. You told me some things when I went to the little tea house ... and you gave me a small stone," she said.

Madame Zelma seemed to remember then. "I sort of remember you, but I don't know how I can help you. Come in, child, come in!" she invited.

She led Elizabeth into a small sitting room that had a strong smell of incense. Madame Zelma raised her hand to silence Elizabeth who was about to talk. She fussed with a kettle and teapot and returned to sit at the little table with a teapot and two cups and saucers. She poured tea for them both.

"Take sugar and fresh lemon," she said. When you stir it, let it sit for a minute. There's tea in here, not tea bags."

The tea was strong and tasty with the tang of lemon.

"And now," Madame Zelma said, "What did you want to ask me?"

"You gave me this stone," Elizabeth said, holding the gemstone out. "Some very strange things have been happening. I sometimes think I am losing my mind."

Madame Zelma looked at the gemstone, but she didn't pick it up. "I don't get much business, I have my Social Security and so few people passing through," she murmured.

Catching the inference, Elizabeth took out a twenty-dollar bill and gave it to Madame Zelma. "For the tea," she said.

Madame Zelma smiled and slowly rocked back and forth in her chair with her eyes half closed. "Drink your tea," she told Elizabeth.

When Elizabeth put her cup down, the gypsy woman took the cup and started to read the leaves.

"So, what kind of strange things have been happening to you?" she asked.

Elizabeth told her about the gemstone getting warm in her hand and that the colors changed and that the gemstone sent a sort of sensation from one arm to the other when she was holding her ring. "You also told me something that upset me and I didn't believe you. I'm not sure I believe any of this," she qualified, "but I have to admit, these things are beyond my understanding! Can you help me?" she asked.

"I will tell you something, my dear, if you'll believe this old gypsy woman. The stone that you have there came from Spain. It was one of many such stones that my father and my mother passed on to me. If the stone is given away, it can carry a spell with it. It can be a good spell or it can be a bad spell. Whenever I see the sign, I know I am to give away one of these stones. I can never take the stone back or touch it again. The stone is yours and yours alone to keep," she explained.

Looking at the tea leaves in Elizabeth's cup, the gypsy woman said, "The man you lost has come back!"

Elizabeth started to speak and protest, but Madame Zelma held up her hand, and continued.

"You do not understand, so I will have to explain. The person who you lost should not have gone away. It was not to be. To be sure, he is back, but the picture is different. Inside he is part of the same person, mixed with the other."

Elizabeth had a really confused look on her face.

"Look, my dear, I will be blunt. Your man is back, but in a different body! You are already getting the signs of recognition and remembrance. It was not an easy thing for him to return. He has to find himself again and to adjust to this new situation. If you cared that much for him, as he must have cared for you, and then you will do everything in your power to help him fully return. But, remember this! It can never be exactly the same. There are some things that have been removed and some things from the new body that cannot be taken away. This is something very rare!" the gypsy said.

Elizabeth's mind was numb and all the mental gears came to a profound halt.

"Do you have your ring with you?" the gypsy asked. Elizabeth nodded. "Give me the ring," and taking the ring the gypsy held the ring in her hand and rubbed her fingers on the gold band.

"Yes! I will tell you for sure! Accept what I tell you as the truth. No one will believe you! Even the lost one will not know everything that you know. He will retain all the important things necessary. The greatest of all, will be his love for you! Trust in that love! Know that it can and did survive, and with the help of the spell from the stone, all these strange and wonderful things can come about. Another thing," the gypsy said. "When all the leaves have settled and you two are joined, keep the stone safe and secure, for it is the link between the past and present. The future will be where you both take it," she concluded.

Elizabeth was digesting all that Madame Zelma said, and the tears started to stream down her cheeks.

"There, there. It's all right," Madame Zelma said. "Go in peace and go with confidence."

Elizabeth took the stone and placed it back in her purse and then after thanking Madame Zelma again, she left.

Elizabeth had many things to think about on her drive home. All of a sudden, all of the little things—the German words in the streetcar, Erik calling her Lily, his singing that silly chicken song, and asking about her ring. They were all making sense now. But it just was not the same. Erik was good looking and handsome, now that he was putting on more weight. The strange happenings with the stone and the ring—all these things were mind boggling.

I will have to sort this out in my mind, she thought.

Elizabeth was not paying attention to her driving. Her mind was elsewhere and she did not see the intersection "yield" sign, as she approached. Too late, her car shot into the middle of the intersection and a truck carrying vegetables ran into the right side of her car. The force of the truck slid the car across the road and into an embankment.

The ambulance backed into the emergency entrance, and Elizabeth was transferred to a gurney and wheeled into the emergency room.

"I don't know how she came through that wreck without more evident injuries," the paramedic said. "We had to cut part of the door away to get her out. Oh, yeah—here's her handbag." He handed it to the nurse in the emergency ward. A state trooper checked the handbag and found Elizabeth's wallet and address and then picked up the phone.

"Mr. Templeton," Martha called. "It's the police—there's been an accident!"

George grabbed the phone. "Hello, this is George Templeton. Who am I speaking to?" he asked.

"This is Trooper Jeff Roberts," he said, "We have an identification for a young lady by the name of Elizabeth Feldmann. Does she live at this address?"

"Yes, she is sort of a ward of my wife and I. She's a nurse at Johns Hopkins. What has happened?"

"Car accident at an intersection. The car she was driving was totaled, and she might have a concussion. You'll have to talk to the doctor about that," the officer said.

"Where is she—what hospital?"

"Johns Hopkins—Emergency Room!"

"I'll be right there," George said.

"Mr. Templeton," the officer asked, "the registration is in your name. Is this your vehicle?"

"Yes," answered George, "it is one of our vehicles."

Bernice and the whole household were in a high state of anxiety.

"I think it's all right," George told them. "The trooper said he thought it might only be a concussion. Bernice and I will drive over to the hospital."

A car pulled up at the front door as the Templetons were getting ready to leave. It was Erik and Conrad. Chester opened the door for them.

"What's up?" Conrad asked straight away, seeing the expressions on everyone faces.

"There's been an accident. ... Elizabeth ... the hospital called," Bernice managed to get out.

"Oh my God! Is she hurt bad?" Conrad asked.

"We don't know how serious yet. They said the doctor thinks it's a concussion. We were leaving for the hospital just as you pulled up," George said.

"I'm going with you," Erik said, visibly shaken.

"I'll go also, but I will drive my own car," Conrad said.

Both cars made it to the hospital in record time. Everyone identified themselves to the nurse on the Emergency Ward; she directed them to a small waiting room on the ward. A doctor approached them in the waiting room.

"I'm Dr. Packard," he said. "I understand that the patient is staying with you folks.

"Yes! How's she doing, Doctor?" George Templeton asked.

"She took a nasty smack on the head. The X-ray doesn't show any fractures, however she has a mild concussion.

"Is she conscious?" Erik asked.

"Yes, she did come to but she is still kind of groggy. She's been asking for Erik. Is that you?" he asked Erik.

"Yes, I'm Erik," he said. His throat was so dry he found it hard to talk.

Continuing, the doctor said, "I'm going to keep her in the hospital for a few days. I understand she is on the nursing staff here. I didn't recognize her right away," he said. "We'll take good care of her." The doctor kept looking at Erik and finally asked, "Aren't you the lieutenant miracle man who was in here for a while?"

"Yes, he's the one!" Conrad said. He handed the doctor his card and said, "Please see that she gets the attention she needs. She is a special person, and we want to insure that she is well looked after."

George also gave the doctor his card, saying that Elizabeth was to have a private room and made the same emphasis on care. The doctor knew that these were influential people and that Templeton—*Yes! That's it! His cousin is bigwig at this hospital*, the doctor remembered.

They were permitted to visit Elizabeth for only a few moments. Bernice was near to tears and George's face was white, reflecting his anxiety. This accident was too reminiscent of the accident in which their two children were lost. They held Elizabeth's hand and smiled lovingly at her. Elizabeth managed to say a few words. "I'm so sorry about the accident and breaking up the car. I am so much trouble for you," she said, the tears formed at the corner of her eyes and rolled down her cheeks.

"Oh no! Don't say that, dear," Bernice said. "The car is nothing! You are the one that is important, and you are no trouble to us." Changing the subject, Bernice said, "Look who's here," giving Erik's arm a tug forward.

Erik looked at Elizabeth and reached down and hugged her gently and whispered to her. "I love you. I won't leave you," he kept saying over and over to Elizabeth. She could feel Erik's warm wet tears dripping down on her. Still in a daze, but her mind functioning, she reached up and stroked Erik's head and said "Don't worry, everything will be okay. I know you won't leave me."

Conrad finally had to pull Erik up and away from Elizabeth.

"You planning to camp there?" he asked.

They could all see Erik's eyes were filled with tears. George and Bernice squeezed each other's hands. They knew that something was blossoming. As they were all leaving the hospital, Conrad said goodnight and assured them that he would check on Elizabeth first thing in the morning.

The following morning Elizabeth woke with a terrible headache, and she asked the nurse on duty if she could have something for the aching. She also asked about her handbag. The nurse said that Elizabeth's handbag had been placed in a large sealed envelope and went to get it for her. Opening it, Elizabeth took out her makeup and her comb and tidied herself up. Again reaching into her bag, she brought out the gemstone and held it in her hand. As she lay there reflecting about the previous day events leading up to the accident, she imagined she was lying on a beach, just at the water's edge, and every time the water washed up to her, she could feel the headache draining away as the water receded.

She was not aware how long she experienced this sensation. The fact is, that when she realized it, all the pain was gone. Only a matter of one hour had gone by.

Elizabeth found her mind was sharp and no longer hazy. She reflected on what Erik had whispered to her and was surprised that she accepted it. She closed her eyes and tried to think of Pat Duran. She remembered the dream she had—seeing Pat coming toward her and then all of a sudden the face changed to Erik.

The doctor made his morning rounds; the neurological specialist also checked Elizabeth out.

"Well, Lizzie," he said, "you're on the receiving side today!"

He checked her eyes, nose, and mouth. Then felt her skull and neck and did some sensory tests. "I checked all the X-rays, and you look okay. No hairline fractures. You're a very lucky lady."

"Yes, I know. I feel a lot better now and hungry too," she added with a smile.

"Now, that's a good sign," the doctor said. "Okay! Eat a light diet then later on you can go for the heavier stuff."

"A cup of coffee first, please!" Elizabeth asked.

She had the coffee, and a light breakfast. Feeling much better, she decided to get out of bed to shower and freshen up. Getting up, she felt no dizziness and informed the nurse that she was going to shower. Elizabeth reached for the telephone and called Four Winds. Martha answered the phone and was very excited to hear Elizabeth's voice.

"Mrs. Templeton! Mrs. Templeton!" she cried. "It's Miss Elizabeth, she's on the phone!"

"Christ Almighty, Martha! You scared me half to death. I thought it was bad news." Bernice snatched the phone from Martha. "How are you doing this morning, dear?"

"I feel a little sore, but all right. I do need some of my clothes and underthings."

"Don't worry dear, I'll pick out something for you and we'll get it down to you this morning."

"Erik dear! Be a sweetheart, I want you to take some things down to the Hospital for Elizabeth. Chester will drive you down there."

Erik had been away from the States too long and no longer had a valid driver's license. He would have to take a complete driver's test and be medically certified that he was physically fit to drive. Chester dropped Erik off at the hospital and told him that he would be doing some shopping and errands for Miss Bernice.

"I'll come back here around three this afternoon, if that's all right with you, Erik?"

"Sure, that will be swell. Thanks, Chester!"

Erik checked with the receptionist telling her he would be visiting Elizabeth Feldmann. He had spent enough time in the hospital to know his way around. Erik went to the hospital gift shop to purchase flowers for Elizabeth.

"I see that you have some yellow roses. I would like a dozen of them please." Armed with the flowers, he made his way upstairs to visit Elizabeth.

He tapped lightly on the door. When he heard Elizabeth say "come in" he eagerly went in with his bouquet. Elizabeth was in her robe, sitting up in bed, reading one of her professional magazines. She greeted Erik first. "Hello, Erik."

Suddenly, Erik was at a loss for words. He again experienced dryness in his throat as he tried to speak. "Lil...Elizabeth," he said, "how are you today? I brought these flowers for you."

Erik busied himself arranging the roses in a vase and filled it with water. Elizabeth watched him and said nothing. Erik walked back to the bedside stand and placed the flower arrangement there. He stared at Elizabeth with such an intense and searching look, that Elizabeth felt like he was actually looking through her. Erik reached out for her hand and bent over to kiss Elizabeth. It was a gentle and tender kiss, tentative, like he was trespassing and unsure of himself.

"Oh, Erik," she said. "Can you know all that's happened? Can you tell me all that you remember? Talk to me," she coaxed.

"Elizabeth, I want to call you Lily. I'm not sure why. It just seems natural. When you had the accident, I nearly went out of my mind. I knew, I felt there is something special between you and me. I wanted to discover what it is, but I didn't want to lose you," Erik rambled on.

There was an atmosphere of electricity around them, almost tangible. Elizabeth could feel it; she and Erik were intently looking at each other.

She opened her arms in a gathering motion, and Erik went to embrace her. Elizabeth felt a sensation of a vibration pass between them *(or was it her imagination?)*. Erik loosened his embrace and lifted his face to Elizabeth. Their lips met, tenderly at first, and then both of them felt the other's response and their kiss became more passionate.

"I love you," Erik said. "I don't want to lose you again."

Elizabeth understood Erik's subconscious fears, but still found it hard to rationalize that the two—Erik and Pat—could be one. They were still locked in an embrace when the nurse popped her head in the door.

"Oops! Hope I'm not interrupting anything," she chuckled.

Elizabeth was a little embarrassed, and she and Erik disengaged from their embrace.

"Erik, I have to get up and change my clothes. You did bring my clothes, didn't you?"

Erik brought the small suitcase up onto the bed for Elizabeth. "I will go down to the coffee shop while you change."

"Okay! I will give the coffee shop a call when I am dressed, and you can come back up."

It was forty-five minutes later when the lady behind the coffee shop counter answered the telephone and asked Erik if he was expecting a call from Elizabeth.

"Yes, I am," he stated. "Well, she said for you to come up."

Erik paid for his coffee and headed back upstairs. When Erik reached the room, Dr. Quimby was just leaving Elizabeth's room. He recognized Erik and asked, "Are you taking care of Miss Feldmann now?"

He chuckled and walked off—not waiting for an answer. Erik gave Elizabeth that inquiring look of his.

"Dr. Quimby is discharging me today and said I can leave but he wants me back next week for a checkup." Picking up her small suitcase, Elizabeth announced, "I'm ready to go!"

Erik checked his wristwatch and saw that it was 2:30. Chester was expected to come back to the hospital around three o'clock. They left the hospital and walked out to the parking lot where they were greeted by a honking horn. Chester was a little early and had parked in the lot. Seconds later Chester pulled up in front of them and jumped out to put Elizabeth's suitcase in the trunk.

"How are you, Elizabeth? I'm sure glad to see you up and about. Have they discharged you from the hospital?"

"Yes, thank you, Chester! I have to go back next week for a checkup, otherwise I'm free to go."

Chester drove them back to Four Winds, and the household was delighted that Elizabeth was back home. Conrad was also there, having coffee and chatting with Bernice Templeton.

"I need to have a word or two with Erik," he announced, taking Erik off to one side. "Erik, I have been getting some things in order for your consideration. You know your father's home in Virginia Beach is being well maintained, but it is still unoccupied. Have you decided where you want to live yet?"

"I really haven't given it much thought," Erik said. "Maybe I should visit Virginia Beach and check things out. Like you told me the other day, I have to start putting my life back in order. There are still some things that are hazy in my mind and I want to try to catch up with everything."

"I think that would be a wise decision for now," advised Conrad.

"There are also some legal considerations regarding Apex Builders, you know. If you decide to get into the business—fine! If you do not want to do that, you have two other options. First you could sell your inherited shares of the business, or you could retain your shares as a non-participating shareholder and keep it as an investment."

"Conrad, will I have enough of my military pay to see me through for a while?" Erik asked.

Conrad snorted. "Erik, I can tell that you haven't been listening to me. If you didn't want to work for the rest of your life you would have enough money in savings, securities and stock investments to see you through."

"I am that wealthy?"

Astounded, Conrad said, "Of course! Have you ever heard of IBM?"

"The name sounds familiar," Erik said.

"Well I can tell you this," Conrad continued. "Your dad bought five thousand shares of IBM stock back in 1945 or 1946. That stock has increased in value several times over and has split at least twice since then - maybe more. Last time I checked it was around four hundred dollars a share. Let's see that would make the stock worth around ... twelve million dollars!"

Erik was speechless. Conrad continued, "Your other stocks—all held in trust for you—are probably worth one or two million more. Your share of ownership of Apex Builders, I value at around five million dollars! Yes, I'd say you could be quite comfortable for many years to come!"

Erik made arrangements with Conrad to visit Virginia Beach and to look into the business and the other trust holdings. Flemming used the telephone and called his law firm associates to set certain things in motion. Erik asked Conrad to go with him and brief him as they traveled. Conrad agreed, and they made an announcement to the Templetons and Elizabeth.

"Erik and I are going to be leaving today for Virginia Beach to handle certain business matters. These are things that have to be taken care of, and now seems the right time to take care of some details, plus get him his driver's license," Conrad said.

Elizabeth wasn't sure whether she was relieved or apprehensive about Erik leaving. These past few days had been hectic and confusing. *I still need time to sort things out in my mind*, she thought.

The Templetons seemed a bit distraught that Erik would be leaving, but were quick to remind him that he was expected to come back soon and be a guest at Four Winds. Conrad addressed Elizabeth and told her that her services for Erik would terminate today, and that he was very pleased with all she did for Erik.

"I will be settling up with you in the next few days."

"But I have already been paid," Elizabeth protested.

"In accordance with our agreement, you should receive a two week notice. Since I am not giving you notice until now, you will have two weeks salary, plus a bonus for a job well done!" Conrad concluded.

Two days later Elizabeth received a check for her two weeks salary, plus a bonus check of ten thousand dollars. Erik had departed for Virginia Beach and other points south. The Templetons were sorry to see him leave. If anything, Elizabeth, now free of responsibility for Erik's well being, was able to relax and put the puzzling questions about Erik and Pat to one side.

CHAPTER 22

The Past

Erik had found it hard to leave Elizabeth. It was even harder for him to put into words exactly how he felt. He was not even sure about that himself. All he knew was that, without thinking, he would say things that he did not understand himself. The only thing he was sure of was that he felt such a strong attachment to Elizabeth. Moreover, he told her that he loved her among other things that brought tears to her eyes. Yes, he needed time to sort out his thinking and get his life back on track.

The house in Virginia Beach was as he remembered it. He went upstairs to what the family had referred to as the lookout because it had a big skylight and large windows—almost like an artist studio,

Erik's father made the room into a navy man's den. A big telescope was mounted on a tripod, exactly as Erik remembered. He looked through the telescope and saw the ships at anchor. Moving the telescope to the left, he was able to see the dockside and the eastern shores of Virginia Beach. He remembered the many hours he spent as a boy tinkering around in this room. Erik felt a little ashamed that he had little interest in the sea and shipbuilding, or for that matter, in electronics.

Conrad picked Erik up and they drove out to Apex Builders. Erik's two cousins worked at Apex. Jennie's husband Karl owned half of the business. The other half, Erik had inherited from his father, Clauson Neilsin. Erik met with his Uncle Karl and the general manager. He also went around to say hello to the shop foremen and other top yard management people. He knew most of them on a first name basis and knew that they had always given Apex Builders their best in loyalty and job performance. Erik had been talking with Conrad about the business and learned that many of the employees, especially those in top management, were apprehensive about what would happen to the business if Erik should decide to sell out to someone alien to the business. Over lunch with his Uncle Karl and Conrad, Erik brought up what he had in mind.

"Uncle Karl, I know that there are many of the top supervisors who were here when you and dad took over running the company. I don't want to do anything that would hurt the company, but I do have some ideas about what I would like to do," he said. "Here's my plan. I would like to give ten percent of my shares in Apex Builders to Aunt Jennie. This would give you absolute control over Apex. Next, I would like to give five percent of my shares to our general manager, and one percent each to our next top supervisors. I will keep the balance of shares for myself, but I would decline to be an active participant in the business or be a director. Would you agree with that?" Erik asked.

"Erik, I don't know what to say." Karl said. "I appreciate you wanting to give my Jennie ten percent of your shares. One percent would be sufficient, if that's what you wanted to do."

"No! Ten percent," Erik insisted. "This way you have something for the kids without sacrificing your control of the business. The others deserve something, which I think my father would have done anyway."

"Yes, I think that would be greatly appreciated and it would even help the business grow more. That is a very generous gesture on your part, Erik," Uncle Karl said.

"So be it!" Erik said.

After lunch, Karl and Erik called a special short meeting with the general manager and Apex's key supervisors. Erik informed them about the shares and ownership that he was going to pass over to them.

Karl thought it was the appropriate time to open his special safe (that grandfather had) and removed a bottle of Norwegian Aquavit, which he chilled in some ice from the fridge. Several small wax paper cups were produced and filled. Karl lifted his cup and asked for a toast, "Here's to continued growth with loyal and devoted friends!"

Work for the remainder of the day was not possible. Erik talked with his father's old friends and tried to answer their questions about his experiences in Korea, jumping out of airplanes and military training. Erik found that he did not really want to discuss things about the military, and the old friends sensed not to ask anymore.

"That was a fine thing you did," Conrad later told Erik. "You did not throw money away, instead, you invested in the future of Apex Builders."

"I have been thinking about the house in Virginia Beach. It's a great house and I have nice memories from there, but I really don't want to live there," he said. "Does that sound as bad to you as it does to me?"

"I think I understand, Erik," he said, "but if you don't want to live there—fine! But I wouldn't dispose of it. I would keep it. Virginia Beach is a growing community and property that has exposure to the beach and water, such as your house, is worth a lot of money and will be worth even more later on. I would suggest that you put the property into the hands of a reputable real estate agent and lease the property. I know a real good man in Virginia Beach, and I think that you would be surprised at how quickly you would lease that house and the price it will fetch," he said.

"That sounds like a good plan," Erik said. "Let's do it!"

Conrad made a few calls and set the wheels into motion. Erik decided to have most of the furnishings put into temporary storage.

"I want to move to the countryside," he said. "I would like to buy some property suitable for growing things—maybe even some orchards, and certainly flowers and plants."

Conrad raised an eyebrow at this.

Erik had to sit down for his drivers written test and then take the actual driving test, along with a handful of sixteen and seventeen year old youths. He actually felt like an old man among all those kids. Erik passed his test and contacted Conrad about his funds. Conrad took Erik to the bank and he acquired a checkbook and was issued an American Express credit card, which he had applied for.

"You have a balance of twenty five thousand dollars in this checking account," Conrad advised. "This other checking account is special because it draws upon your invested savings. In this account the total is fifty thousand dollars." Conrad handed Erik fifteen government paychecks receipts for money deposited in another savings bank.

"I think that should hold you for a while," Conrad said.

They had Erik's 1949 Pontiac serviced, and Erik decided not to take it, but left it in storage. The August summer was hot and Erik fancied a convertible of some kind, and went shopping for a suitable car. He knew he could have a more expensive car, but he fancied a Studebaker convertible It didn't take long to get it ready, licensed and ready to roll. Erik was off, scouting for the property he had in mind.

Conrad found a pile of mail waiting for him when he returned back to work. His law partners had been very busy not only with their own clients, but also covering some of the standing accounts that Conrad normally handled. Conrad sifted through his mail, sorting out five piles of various categories. He paused at an envelope postmarked Fort Belvoir, VA. Curious, he put the envelope to one side and finished sorting out the rest. Coming back to the Fort Belvoir envelope, he slit open the envelope:

>Captain Dale E. Swan, US Army
>Post Office Box 134
>Fort Belvoir, Virginia

11 August 1953

Mr. C. Flemming—Attorney
Flemming, Lichfield & Barton
1527 Lombard Avenue, N.E.
Baltimore, Maryland 21096

Dear Mr. Flemming,

I have taken the liberty of writing to you as you may have personal knowledge of a fellow Army officer, Erik Neilsin. I served with Lieutenant Neilsin in Korea and learned that he had been wounded and medically evacuated. I checked with medical staff while I was in Korea and was informed that Lieutenant Neilsin was transferred to an Army General Hospital in Japan. I was not able to locate the hospital or find out the condition of Erik Neilsin.

Before leaving Pusan to join the Seventh Infantry Division, Lieutenant Neilsin gave me some of his letters to mail as he had to leave immediately. I did write down your name and address because it looked like legal stuff—just in case Erik's mail got lost. After my tour in Korea, I returned to the U.S. with an assignment at Camp Carson, Colorado. I was later transferred to Fort Belvoir (where I am now). I met someone who is knowledgeable about the Army's medical procedures, etc. I learned the name and location of the General Hospital near Tokyo where Erik was sent. I learned that Erik had been transferred back to the States, and later he was sent some place in the East.

I am assuming that you might be doing some legal work for Lieutenant Neilsin and that you might know of him being wounded, whether or not he has recovered and his present whereabouts. At this point, I am grasping at straws. The Army, I'm afraid, does not give out much information unless you are family.

I hope that you might have the information I am looking for. If so, I would be very grateful to know how Erik is doing and where he is. He may be overseas again for all I know, or on some assignment out West.

Yours Truly,
Dale E. Swan

Conrad silently contemplated the letter from this Captain Dale E. Swan. He wondered what her connection might be with Erik. *Obviously, she knows a good deal about Erik—although Erik has never mentioned anything about this officer friend of his*, he thought. Conrad decided that he wouldn't ignore the letter, as Captain Swan seemed quite concerned. Since Erik was driving all over the countryside, he decided to call Fort Belvoir, Virginia.

"Yes, Operator! A listing for Captain Dale, middle initial E, Swan—like the bird or ballet," he said.

"What was that again?" he said, jotting down the telephone number. "Thank you!"

A thought occurred to him. *Why do I think this is a woman?*

He dialed the telephone number, and the phone rang and rang. Looking at his watch, Conrad rationalized that Captain Swan was probably at her job. Conrad stopped what he was doing. *Why did I think it was a woman?* he asked himself, the thought nagging him. Dale Swan could be a male and not a female. Looking at the letter again, he noted the handwriting and said to himself that this was a female's handwriting. He picked up the letter and sniffed at it. He detected a slightly sweet scent.

"Yep! It's got to be a woman!" he muttered to himself.

Conrad worked his way through all the mail he had sorted out. Some of it went into the trash can. Before he knew it, it was after five o'clock.

Gloria, his secretary, poked her head in the door and said, "I'm outta here, and going home! You need anything before I leave?"

"No, Gloria, I'm fine. You go on home."

He reached over and picked up the letter from Captain Swan and read it again, and then reaching for the phone, he dialed the number again. A female voice answered on the third ring.

"Captain Swan here," the voice said.

"Good evening, Captain Swan. My name is Conrad Flemming, and I am with the law firm you sent a letter of inquiry concerning the former First Lieutenant Neilsin."

Conrad noticed the change in the woman's voice.

"Oh, yes! You said the former Lieutenant," she countered. "What exactly does that mean?" Is he out of the service or … He's not dead, is he?"

"No! I'm sorry if I gave you that impression. Erik was medically discharged after a very long state in a coma. He is up and about and trying to get himself situated back in society."

"Great!" the voice said with enthusiasm. "Where is he then?" she asked.

"I really couldn't say at the moment," Conrad hedged.

"I mean, what's his current address perhaps his telephone number, for starters?" Dale asked.

"Well, I'm afraid I have to strike out on both counts, at the moment. Erik is on the road and he doesn't have a current address where he has hung his hat. The same goes for a telephone number. I expect him to call me fairly soon. When he does call I would be happy to give him your message and have him contact you," Conrad offered.

There was some hesitation, then, "Okay! Oh, by the way, is he in Maryland or the Virginia area?"

"Yes! Actually he is out house or land hunting. I will see that he gets the message to contact you. Have a good weekend," Conrad said and hung up.

CHAPTER 23

New Real Estate

Erik reviewed his clipboard of adverts and leads for property being offered for sale. He was leaning toward land away from the salt water. He drove westward through Virginia and stopped at a small country restaurant in Rustburg, Virginia. Scoffing down his lunch and gulping a large glass of milk, he looked out at the local scenery and liked what he saw. Finishing his lunch, he asked where the local real estate place was.

"Right down the street on the right side you'll see Hardell's Insurance and Realty."

He walked down the street and spotted the small Insurance and Realty sign in the window and he entered. Gladys Neidecker worked part time for Ed Hardell, and it was her day to work.

"Can I help you?" she asked.

"I'm looking for a piece of property suitable for a home and good soil for growing things," Erik said.

Gladys perked up. "Just a moment and I'll get Mr. Hardell."

She went into the small office, and Erik heard the exchange of muttering voices. Finally Ed Hardell came out to greet Erik.

"Hello there, young fellow! How can I be of service to you?"

Erik explained what he was looking for in general terms.

"I want to have some acreage—enough to build a house and grow some flowers and vegetables."

"Just how many acres are you interested in?" Ed Hardell asked. "The old Lambert farm has plenty of acreage. The old house and barn are condemned and near falling down. The land was last farmed about four years ago—and nothing since then," he said, sizing up Erik. Ed thought, *This young fellow is probably on a shoestring budget. Maybe the old Lambert farm would suit his needs.*

"How many acres is the Lambert farm? Does it have water—a well, or what?" Erik asked.

"The farm is around a hundred and fifty acres. It has two wells that I know of. Can't be too sure about the rest," he allowed.

"Can we go take a look at it?" Erik asked.

"Don't you want to know the price first?" Ed Hardell asked. Erik looked at him and raised an eyebrow in a "*how much?* look.

Ed thought quickly and padded the figure. "It's five hundred an acre," he said, watching Erik for reaction.

"How much?" Erik asked. *Wow*, he thought. *I thought he was going to say twice that amount!*

Ed recovered quickly, lest he loses a potential sale. "But," he went on, smoothly, "I do believe that the price is negotiable. Maybe around two-fifty an acre," he amended. "Why don't we go look at the property," he said, taking Erik by the arm and out the door.

The old Lambert farm was just that. It was old. It was worn out. The old farmhouse and barn were nearly falling down. Nature was reclaiming the property, as the weeds and brush were everywhere. It was hard to define the contours of the land. They approached the farmhouse and Mr. Hardell suggested that they not go into the farmhouse, because it was condemned and not safe. Erik looked in the old barn and found a small hand trowel on the floor. Walking out into what should be the field, he started to dig up some of the brush and weeds with the trowel and held some of the soil in his hand. The soil was somewhat damp and a dark rich brown.

You could grow just about anything in this soil, he thought. He looked at the old wells and walked the length of the acreage. The property was sort of a thick L shape. The bottom of the L doglegged to the right. He noted that a small stream ran through the property, probably coming from the hills in the distance, he thought.

Erik asked for all the details to be written down, as it was recorded.

"Is the property free of all liens?"

"Yep! Old Man Lambert never owed anyone a cent, leastwise up until he died," Ed Hardell allowed.

"I'll have to get back to you," Erik said. "I am very interested in the property because of its size and the quality of the soil. I will give you a retainer, pending any formal arrangements, should I decide to take it," he said.

"I'll give you two hundred dollars to keep my option for one month. If I don't buy, the money's yours. If I do buy, the money is yours anyway. Deal?" he asked.

"Yes, sir—it's a deal!" Ed Hardell replied, sticking out his hand.

"Oh, one other thing before we conclude our deal," Erik asked. "Can this property be used for any purpose I choose, or is there some local ordinance that says that it can only be used for farming?"

"I don't know of any ordinance in the county that would say what you can or can't do with the property," Ed Hardell said.

"Okay, we have a deal!" Erik said. "I will get back in touch with you." Erik got into his car and drove off.

Conrad's phone rang, and his secretary announced that Erik Neilsin was on the line.

"Hello, my wandering boy! Where the hell are you?" Conrad asked.

"I'm on my way back up to Four Winds to see Elizabeth."

Conrad noticed the excitement in his voice. Continuing Erik said, "Conrad, I'm going to ask Elizabeth to marry me," he blurted out. "I also found some nice property. It's an old deserted and rundown farm, but the land is good and it has water. I would like you to help me on this. I never bought property like this before."

"Sure. No problem," Conrad responded. "Where is this property?"

"A little town in Virginia that goes by the name of Rustburg. I want to take everything down and have the land leveled and cleared. I will have enough money to do that, wont I?"

"Just how much is this property?"

"Five hundred an acre was the asking price, and when I must have looked astonished, asking the price again, he dropped the price to two-fifty an acre." Erik laughed.

"How large a property is this—how many acres?"

"Roughly, around a hundred and fifty acres. I gave a two-hundred-dollar retainer to hold things for one month. Did I do right?" he asked.

"Good grief! A two-hundred-dollar retainer? I should hope to tell you that it's a good deal! Normally, one has to cough up at least five thousand dollars or five percent. So, yes, you did well!" Conrad barked. "So, tell me, you say you're going to ask Elizabeth to marry you?"

"Yeah! I've been thinking about her ever since I left Four Winds and I feel I have to be with her."

"Ahhh." Conrad paused. "Erik? I had a letter the other day, and I called someone who is interested in getting in touch with you."

"Oh, yeah! Who was it?"

"A captain. Let's see … oh, yes. Her name is Dale Swan." There was a long silence, and Conrad asked, "Erik? You still there?"

"Yes. Dale Swan. Dale Swan. Captain Dale Swan …Captain? Dale Swan! Well, for God's sake! Sure, I remember her! We were overseas in the same place. I went north, and she was still in the south. I think we were good friends," Erik said somewhat hesitatingly.

He was trying to remember details, but his memory was confused with a lot of details before the war injuries.

"I told this Captain Swan that I would pass on her message to you as soon as I heard from you. I understand she is stationed at Fort Belvoir in Virginia. I didn't say too much about you since I wasn't sure if you and she had anything going between you," Conrad managed.

Erik put the matter on hold. He had written down the telephone number that Dale Swan gave to Conrad. He felt a little disturbed about her call but could not figure out why.

I'll call later, he thought.

Erik turned the car into the estate's long roadway up to Four Winds. He blew the horn a couple of good blasts as he pulled up at the front of the house. Penny Somers came crashing out of the front door and ran to Erik and gave him a kiss on the cheek and a bear hug.

"Wow, that's some reception!" He laughed. "Is everyone at home?" he asked.

"No! Mr. Templeton is away, but Miss Bernice is out on the back patio with Elizabeth," then added: "We were wondering what happened to you. You just up and left and not a word," Penny scolded him.

Somewhat embarrassed, Erik realized that while he had been wrapped up with his thoughts, he had failed to call or communicate with Elizabeth or the Templetons. "Gee, I'm sorry Penny. I really feel bad, but I had so many things that I had to do and think about."

Erik went through the house onto the back patio. Both Elizabeth and Bernice had heard the car and seen it coming up the winding road, so they knew it was Erik. Elizabeth's heart beat faster but she didn't want to appear anxious or even happy to see Erik. She was, in fact, rather annoyed that after his making the "I love you" overtures to her, he left at the first chance and did not bother to call her for over a week.

"Erik, how nice to see you again," Bernice greeted him, somewhat formally and cool. "Look who's here!" she said to Elizabeth.

"Hello, Erik! How are you?" Elizabeth inquired.

Erik immediately sensed the coolness, and he looked at Elizabeth's eyes, but she looked down.

"Listen, I'm sorry I left so quickly. ... and I didn't call. So many things I had to do and check on. Conrad had so much to show me. Time ran on!" Erik offered lamely.

All of his excitement was being dashed by the coolness of these two women—one of whom he loved.

"That's okay, Erik," Elizabeth offered. "You don't have to tell us anything about what you are doing or where you are going!"

Erik felt frustrated and guilty. He was at a loss for further words, and was feeling rejected; he turned and asked Elizabeth how she was feeling after the accident. The response was polite but still cool.

"I guess I am intruding," Erik finally said, and turned to leave. "I did want to thank you all for helping me. ... get better ... the trip and all," he managed to get out. Erik's throat felt dry and it was hard for him to continue talking. "Elizabeth, I wanted to," Erik ended.

He turned and started to leave the room. Almost simultaneously, both Bernice and Elizabeth realized that Erik was about to leave. They could see he was having a difficult time, and they sensed it was time to become more cordial. Elizabeth saw the expression of pain in Erik's eyes. She knew that expression. She had said many times that the eyes are the windows of the soul. When you see pain—whether it is physical or mental, it is pain and the eyes reflect that condition. Elizabeth quickly got up and went to Erik.

"Erik," she called to him, "where do you think you're going?"

That confused look was evident on Erik's face again!

"I thought you wanted me to leave," Erik managed to get out.

"No, not really. I am mad at you for not calling me. I … we, were all worried about you," she said. "Come." She took Erik's hand. "Let's walk in the garden."

They walked for a few minutes in silence and then Erik said, "I found some land that I like and I am going to buy it and build our house on it," he announced. Elizabeth had momentarily missed the "our house" part of what Erik said.

"Where is this land you are going to buy?" she asked. And then she suddenly realized that Erik had said "and build our house."

"Our house?" she asked.

"Yes, Elizabeth. Our house! I want to marry you. I have missed you so much in just one week. You have been on my mind constantly and I had so many other things I had to do, it made my head spin," he blurted out. Elizabeth had stopped and her face reflected her surprise.

"You are asking me to marry you?"

"Yes! I love you and I want you to be my wife. I have loved you since that first day," he said, "when I gave you the wedding ring for your birthday," Erik said casually, without thinking.

"What? What did you say?

Elizabeth looked into Erik's eyes and remembered the gypsy woman's words about Pat. Elizabeth also recalled the dream she had of Pat, coming toward her open arms, only to find the face changed to Erik's. Erik persisted, "Will you marry me, Elizabeth?"

Inside, within her, a voice screamed, *Yes!*

"This is so sudden for me, Erik. Do you want my answer right this instant, or will after dinner be soon enough?" she asked, laughing.

Elizabeth and Bernice were in deep private conversation.

"I am not surprised," Bernice was saying, "The first time I laid eyes on him, I said to George, what if he and Elizabeth hit it off."

"He wants an answer right away," she explained to Bernice.

"So! What's the problem?" Bernice asked. "You know you two are like bread and butter. You go together!"

Elizabeth's face looked very serious. She asked Bernice if she could tell her something very confidential. Bernice agreed, and they excused themselves and went up to Elizabeth's room.

"I don't know where to begin," she said.

Bernice said, "Start at the beginning!"

Bernice knew about Pat Duran being killed in the aircraft accident. She also knew that they were very fond of each other too. Elizabeth explained about their intimate relationship and the wedding bands. She went to her dresser drawer, opened it and took out her small jewelry box. She took out the gold wedding band to show to Bernice. The inside of the band was engraved with the name "Pat." Elizabeth then went on to explain about the gypsy in Georgetown and explained about the gemstone. Elizabeth removed the gemstone and held it in her hand. She closed her hand around the stone and could feel the stone getting warmer and warmer, at though it were emitting energy and heat. Opening her hand, she showed the stone to Bernice, but cautioned her not to touch it. "Instead, touch the palm of my hand," she said, removing the stone to her other hand.

"My God! Your hand is hot to touch," Bernice exclaimed in surprise.

"Yes! Strange things have happened with this gemstone. I was thinking just the other day that when we were in Las Vegas, I put the gemstone in with my chips at the casino, and I won almost every time," she said. "I thought it was just pure luck. Now, I'm not so sure." She then told Bernice what the gypsy woman had said when she gave her the stone, and also what the gypsy woman said when she went back to see her.

"I was on my way home, with so much on my mind … that's when I had that accident," she finished.

Bernice made the observation that the state trooper had said it was a miracle that Elizabeth had gotten out of that wreck in one piece. "They had to cut away the vehicle to get you out and all you had was a concussion!"

As they were sitting on the bed talking, Elizabeth had the wedding band and the gemstone in her hand. She felt a buzzing vibration and looked down on her hand and was astonished to see the wedding band move on its own onto the second finger of her left hand. It happened in just a second. More importantly, Bernice also saw it happen. Elizabeth started to ask Bernice if she had seen it, but Bernice cut her off.

"I saw it happen with my own eyes!" she said.

"I'll tell you frankly, Elizabeth, I believe that there are many things that happen in this world and in our lives that defy logic or satisfactory explanations. I for one, have believed for a long time, that someone or something over there," she said pointing upward, "is watching out for us and nudging us this way and that way. I don't know what to tell you about Erik and Pat. I think that you have to know by how you feel inside. No one can do that but you."

The Templetons were noted for their grand patio cook outs. That night was no exception. Chester manned the barbecue pit, and Martha served the steaks and chicken. Everyone helped themselves to the small trolley of vegetables, salad, and hot rolls.

"You doing some for yourselves?" asked Bernice.

"Yes, ma'am! Just as soon as you all are taken care of, I'm doing a steak for Penny and me. Martha wants a chicken breast," Chester said.

As they were ready to tuck in to their dinner, Chester brought out a bottle of Blue Nun, Liebfraumilch—a premier German Rhine wine—and then retired to eat his own dinner. George was pressing Erik for the details of the property in Rustburg, Virginia.

"Why Rustburg?" he asked.

"Finding a large enough parcel of land with the right terrain and good soil is not easy to come by," Erik advised.

"Why so much land? Are you planning on becoming a farmer?" he asked jokingly.

"No, not farming! I have a yearning to start planting some flowers and perhaps some vineyards. Of course, I will want to build …" He paused, looking at Elizabeth, and then continued, "… a house to live in."

The look did not go unnoticed by anyone. George looked from Erik to Elizabeth and then over to Bernice, who had that "plotting" look on her face. Finally, Bernice couldn't contain herself.

"Elizabeth! Are you going to keep us all in suspense or what?" she asked.

Elizabeth actually blushed and looked at Erik. She felt a rush of emotion, and before she could do anything about it, the tears came gushing like Niagara Falls. She got up and rushed over to Erik and threw herself into his arms.

Erik held her for a long while and gazed at the faces around them. Everyone was smiling. All was well in the world, he thought.

Elizabeth finally composed herself and stood up facing everyone with a tearful, but smiling face and announced, "Erik has asked me to marry him, and I guess I have just said yes."

"Bravo!" yelled George.

Bernice followed with a rebel yell, "Yeehaw!"

Before the evening ended, everyone—the Cranfields, the Somers, the

Templetons, and the newly engaged couple—put some dents in the wine inventory, killing off several bottles of champagne that were hastily iced for the occasion.

Elizabeth woke the following morning with a headache and thought that her tongue had grown a fuzz. *I've got a hangover,* she thought. It was her first. A hot shower helped some, but not a lot. She managed to make it downstairs and into the kitchen. Martha took one look at her and started to laugh.

"Here, Miss Liz," she said, handing Elizabeth a cup of steaming fresh coffee.

"This coffee is going like wildfire this morning," Martha said. Queenie came into the kitchen from the back door.

"Here, you put a drop or two of this in your coffee," she said and without waiting, spiked Elizabeth's coffee with some Burkes Old Irish whiskey.

Elizabeth gulped a few sips and found that the spiked coffee did the job, indeed.

"Thanks, Queenie! My head felt like it was ready to come off."

"I'm not surprised. If you're gonna drink, you drink the right stuff. Either good ole Irish whiskey, or a nice Guinness stout," she said with a twinkle in her eye.

Elizabeth refilled her cup with more coffee and went out on the back patio where she saw the rest of the hungover group. Actually George was in pretty good shape. It was Bernice and Erik who were a bit subdued. Martha came out on the patio and looked at everyone.

"I don't suppose anyone would care for some breakfast?" she asked. Everyone looked a little sheepish. George said, "I think I will have some breakfast, Martha."

"Some kippers, two fried eggs, toast and some more coffee will suit me fine!"

Bernice blanched. "A British breakfast? Kippers, no less! How utterly disgusting. Martha, I'll just have some dry whole wheat toast and more coffee," she said.

Martha looked at Erik.

"Could you scramble a couple of eggs for me and put it on toast?" he asked.

"Sure thing! Be back in a jiffy," she said and left them to bathe in the morning sun.

The telephone rang, and Penny took the call. "It's Mr. Flemming for Erik," she announced.

Erik excused himself to answer the phone.

"Morning, Erik. How's it going? Did you pop the question?"

"Yes, I did, but she had me going for a while!" he replied.

"Any date set?" Conrad asked.

"Nope! I just want to make sure it's yes before I go any further."

Conrad changed the subject. "Erik, I just got another call from Dale Swan. I told her that you had called in and that you were on the road at the time, and that you had the number to call her."

"Oh, hell! I was intending to give her a call when I got to Four Winds," Erik said.

"Is that a wise thing to do, Erik?" Conrad asked. "I mean, is this captain just a casual friend or something more?"

Erik declined to answer and said nothing. "I will give her a call later today," he said.

"Anything you say, Erik, I just wanted to keep you posted and help avoid any land mines."

Erik flinched. "Bad choice of words," he said to Conrad.

"Yeah, that was kind of thoughtless of me," Conrad said. "Anyway, do keep in touch. I will be going over the deeds and records for the Lambert place, and I'll need you to sign some papers."

Erik rejoined everyone on the back patio. Elizabeth looked at Erik and asked, "Any problems?"

"No. Conrad said I had a telephone call and also that he would be looking into the legal details for this property I'm interested in buying."

"Yes, come and tell us what your plans are, young man!" Bernice demanded.

"Which plans?" Erik asked.

"Marriage, of course, you silly goose!" Bernice scolded.

Elizabeth interrupted. "We haven't discussed any details yet. The only thing we know for certain is not to get smashed on champagne!"

Everyone had a good chuckle at that remark. Erik looked at Elizabeth and she interpreted his look as saying *Let's take a walk*.

"I am going to pick some flowers from the garden," Elizabeth said, rising up from her lawn chair.

Erik was quick to move to her side and accompany her.

"Oh, I'll go with you too," piped up Penny.

"I don't think so, Penny!" Bernice said. "Maybe some other time."

Penny looked a little put out, and Bernice called her over to whisper in her ear. "They want to be alone, dear," she said.

Suddenly Penny understood and gave an understanding little giggle.

Erik and Elizabeth walked through the garden and out to the back of the grounds to the apple and pear orchard. An old park bench was situated at the entranceway to the orchard. The Templetons had several benches scattered around the property, especially at the scenic locations. They sat down and Erik took Elizabeth in his arms and kissed her forehead, her cheeks and finally rested his lips on hers. The kiss was electrifying to Elizabeth. She could feel the once dormant currents stirring within her.

"Erik, dear," she said, "we have no plans. What do you want to do?"

"Naturally, I want us to be married. I want to buy that land and build a house on it for us," he said. "I don't know how long we can wait. It will take time to decide on what kind of house we want, and all the arrangements that go along with it."

"If we wait for all that, we may be talking about a long engagement," Elizabeth said chuckling.

"No! I can't wait that long," Erik confessed. "I don't know why, but I feel like I have been waiting for years for us to get married."

Elizabeth just stared at him, understanding the situation and knowing that it was Pat Duran speaking from his heart. *Poor Erik*, she thought. *He doesn't know all of the details. Should I tell him, or should I just keep silent?* She decided that by just knowing, she could control the situation.

It is like loving two men at once, she thought. "When would you like to get married then?" she asked Erik.

"How about tomorrow?"

"That is out of the question," she cried. "We just can't elope! We have new friends. You have relatives and friends who will want to share that special day, and besides, I have family in California who will want to come to our wedding."

"Okay, okay, I give in! You did ask me when," Erik said.

"I will have to save up for the wedding, for a reception, and oh my goodness—there are so many things to think about," Elizabeth said, now starting to get into a panic.

Erik kissed her, and she stopped talking. He could feel her body relax as he held her close.

"I think we should plan to get married just after Easter, in the spring." Elizabeth was thinking about when she and Pat first met. It had been on Easter Sunday.

"That would be okay, too," agreed Erik. "It would give me time to get the land developed. I would have to find a temporary place for us to live while the house is being built."

"We have time for that too," Elizabeth noted. "Let's go back to the house to tell Bernice."

It was easy for Erik to see how excited she had become making a plan for a spring wedding.

"What do you mean, you have to save up to pay for your wedding?" Bernice bellowed. We'll have the wedding here at Four Winds! I can see it now," she said, her arms waving all over the place. "We'll convert the game room into the wedding site. That will give us plenty of space for lots and lots of seats. We'll set up an altar, and Queenie can supply all the flowers. Oh, it will be just grand!"

His eyes looked upward as George muttered his reluctant approval with the comment, "She's off and running!"

The rest of the day was a whirlwind. George and Erik stood by while the women talked about this and that, without so much as a glance at the men. Now Queenie and Martha, Penny included, were into the frenzy. Bill Cranfield came to the door and tilted his head to them both with a "come here" nod.

"I've seen this before, guv'nor, and so have you," Bill said to George. "Right now, them women don't know we exist. I have a remedy for this," he said and led them to his shed and brought out three fishing rods, with reels attached.

"I know a lovely spot or two, not far from here, where it is restful and the fish are plentiful," he announced.

Bill produced the tackle box and a fresh supply of worms from the garden. The three of them set off for a few hours of peace and with hope for a nibble or two from some hungry trout. Bill led them to a stream and they walked along the upward path to a small pond. The pond had an abundance of shade trees along its banks, and the three men spread out and cast upon the waters with their garden worms. Bill was the first to get a nibble and said "Hello! Who's calling?"

Suddenly he lifted the tip of his rod, and the line stiffened, indicating a fish on the line. Bill played him nicely and was rewarded with a fourteen-inch rainbow trout. That set Erik and George off in earnest. George felt the nibble on his worm and had to force himself to let the fish take some more of his worm before setting the hook.

"Now!" he said and set the hook.

The pole nearly bent into a circle and the reel protested loudly as the line stripped off. George finally adjusted the drag on the reel and took out a little slack in the line, the fish jumped a foot out of the water. It was a big one.

"Whee, look at that bugger go!" Bill yelled. "Don't lose him."

Erik was watching George and let the tip of his pole point toward the water. He wasn't paying attention to his own line, but suddenly he felt the rod jerk in his hand and realized that he had a fish on also. Erik's fish also made several leaps and splashes as he reeled it in. And so the rest of the afternoon went by. It was nearly four in the afternoon and they had caught thirteen fine rainbow trout. The smallest was twelve inches and the rest fourteen or more inches. They headed back to Four Winds and Bill took the fish and said he would clean them up, ready for their evening meal.

The three men returned to Four Winds with their catch. Martha Somers conceded that if Bill cleaned the fish thoroughly, she would prepare trout almondine for the evening meal.

"Well now!" George asked, "Have you women decided on the fate of this poor girl and her wedding plans?"

Elizabeth, George observed, had a dazed smile on her face and he wondered if she were off in the land of imagination. Bernice was the first to respond.

"Of course. We have a wonderful plan. The wedding will be the week following next Easter. We will have it on Saturday, here at Four Winds. We will fix up the big game room and use it for the wedding ceremony. If the weather is really nice, we can open the French doors to make it more airy. Queenie said that she will take care of the flowers and also suggested some of her potted plants for decoration."

George rolled his eyes upward and muttered about the other details. Bernice paused for a deep breath and kept talking.

"The reception will be a piece of cake. We can handle up to eighty people in here," she said, spreading out her arms. "Chester will handle the parking for all our guests. Oh, yes! We will keep five of the spare guestrooms ready. At least four or maybe all five of them will be used for Elizabeth's family in San Francisco and other guests."

Getting back to reality and into the conversation, Elizabeth took Erik's arm and said to him, "I have to plan things out. Look for a wedding dress, invitations, and you will have to make up a list of names of people to invite too."

"My list will be fairly small," Erik said, "mostly my aunt and uncle and their kids and of course, Conrad, who is like an uncle to me."

"Oh, speaking of Conrad, he called while you lot were out messing with those smelly fish," Bernice said. "He wanted to remind you about a call to Fort Belvoir."

Erik nodded and said he would take care of the matter. Elizabeth and Erik disappeared for a short walk around the house, and Elizabeth told Erik that Bernice insisted that the wedding be held at Four Winds and that she wanted to handle most of the details.

"Is that okay with you?" she asked.

"Sure! I don't mind, actually. I love it here at Four Winds, which is why I went out looking for a nice parcel of land," Erik said.

"Can you really afford to buy that land and build a house?" Elizabeth asked. "I can keep working and help you with the expenses," she volunteered.

Erik reached out and drew her close and hugged her tightly. "There will be no need for that, my love," he said. "While I was away, Conrad brought me up to date on my financial situation. It is almost scary."

"Thanks to my dad, I have a nice tidy sum of money and good sources of income, enough to last a very long time. But, I intend to work and maybe we can decide on doing something together besides making babies," he said with a naughty smile on his face.

Penny called out to them that supper was on the table.

"Come and get it!" she hollered.

Following a refreshing supper, dessert, and coffee, Erik announced to everyone that he would be gone for a few days but would call Elizabeth every day while he was away.

"Promise and cross my heart!" he said!

Erik drove back to Baltimore. He stopped at a phone booth to call Conrad, who had invited him to spend the night at his bachelor pad. Erik accepted the invitation and minutes later pulled up at Flemming's apartment.

"Did you remember to call?"

Erik's shaking his head cut off Conrad. "I'll call from here, if that's all right with you?" he asked.

The telephone rang four times, and Erik was just about to hang up when a female voice answered, "Captain Swan!"

"Captain Dale Swan?" Erik asked.

Dale caught her breath as she recognized Erik's voice. "Erik! Is that you?" Not waiting for a reply, she went on, "Christ! I thought you bought the farm. It sure took you long enough to answer my calls and messages."

"I'm awfully sorry. I was kind of out of things for a very long time," Erik explained. "Two years evaporated from my life. I was almost a vegetable—in a coma," he went on.

"You don't have to give me all the gory details," Dale said. "Your attorney, what's his name? Flemming—yeah—Conrad Flemming. He gave me a running commentary on your long sleep and resurrection."

"He's really a very nice guy," Erik responded. "If it hadn't been for him, I would have never made it out of the hospital, so I'm told."

"Poor Erik! God! What a shock I had when I took a call from your company commander saying he wanted to talk to you when you arrived at Battalion HQ. You never showed up! After a couple of hours, HQ asked for some ROK scouts to check out the route to our headquarters. They found you and got you to an aid station. They evacuated you back to Pusan. I didn't find out about this until that evening and called your outfit and passed on the word. The driver was killed outright! You're lucky you made it," Dale said. Changing the subject, she asked, "Where are you?"

"I'm at Conrad's place in Baltimore. I just got here. I did get your message earlier, but this was my first real chance to call and chat."

"First chance to chat?" Dale said, sounding a bit miffed.

"Let me explain," Erik pleaded. "Ever since I recovered and came across something new, like your phone call, I had to try to remember details … like who you are … where we were overseas, and things like that. Driving around, I had time to think and time to try to remember details. Little by little some things came back to me."

"Listen, Erik, I'm sorry! I didn't mean to come on like a pissed-off girlfriend. I really worried about you and not knowing the full details about your health situation, it had me frustrated. After all," she said with a chuckle, "I'm still your little sister, ain't I?" Erik cleared his throat—his memory coming back more rapidly now.

"What's the matter?" Dale asked. "Cat got your tongue?"

"Ahh, a little awkward to recall some things," Erik said. "I am heading out to Virginia to look at some property tomorrow," he said. "Maybe we could do lunch or supper. Do you have any plans?"

"No plans. Supper would be great! Have you ever been to Fort Belvoir?"

"No. I know where it is, but I never visited the installation," he responded.

"They have a nice O Club here, and the food is pretty good. Why not here?"

Erik was interested to revisit a military post again. It was a long time since he'd been in an officer's club or, for that matter, around a military post.

Conrad couldn't help overhearing some of Erik's telephone conversation with Dale.

"So you're going to see her tomorrow?"

"Yeah, for supper at the Officer's Club at Fort Belvoir. I plan on driving down to see about the property. Where are we on it, anyway?" he asked Conrad.

"I have all the papers ready and a certified bank check for the purchase, and another for some tax matters. I sent a five-thousand-dollar retainer. If you are going down tomorrow, I'll call down there, and you can drop by and complete the deal. Since there will be no mortgage to deal with or any financing, it will be a fairly straight deal. I have included a check for filing the deed with the county. All the other details I can take care of afterward," Conrad advised. "Now! How about a drink?"

"Think I'll just have a beer, if it's all the same with you," he told Conrad.

Conrad sipped his scotch and soda then asked, "Do you really find it hard to remember details from your past?"

"When it is something that was before my injury, yes. When you first mentioned Dale Swan to me, my mind registered that I knew the name, but I had trouble putting a face to that name until much later on. Then it started to come back to me, a trickle at a time."

"Do you remember her now?" Conrad asked.

The blush on Erik's face told Conrad the answer to that question.

The following day, Erik set off early for his trip back to the old Lambert farm in Rustburg, Virginia. He arrived midmorning, in time to join Ed Hardell for a coffee and sweet roll and then on to the local attorney's office to close the purchase.

"Yeah, your Mr. Flemming sent all the paperwork down, and I guess all we need is the check and closing costs," Ed Hardell said as they entered the lawyers' office.

The purchase and transactions took about forty minutes, and Erik was on his way. Arriving at the old Lambert farm, he was heartened to see pieces of heavy equipment on the property.

The Hammersmith Contractor's Company is on the ball, thought Erik. Lloyd Hammersmith got out of his pickup truck to greet Erik.

"Been waiting long?" Erik asked.

"Nope! Only got here about ten minutes ago."

Erik brought out a rough plan on paper, which he unrolled. "I want to save the water source, which probably will have to be capped off. Then I want the old farmhouse and the barn leveled and hauled to a dump. I want major mowing done so I can see what's hiding underneath all that growth."

"I already told my guys pretty much the same, as you told me when we talked. One thing before we start," he said. "I said I would give you a rough quote, and I would require some deposit."

"Sure! I understand," Erik said and brought out a bank-certified check for five thousand dollars. The check was made out to "Hammersmith Contracting."

Lloyd Hammersmith was impressed. He took the check and took a deep breath and then bellowed to his men, "Okay, let's go!"

He started barking out orders. The first order was to take care of the water and then the heavy equipment started to roll. A large Caterpillar front-end loader with a huge bucket in the front approached the farmhouse; it never hesitated as it knocked down the front quarter of the building. In ten minutes the farmhouse was rubble. A ten-wheeler truck rolled up and the front-end loader started scooping the debris into the waiting trucks. Erik left them to it, and drove off to meet his architect.

James Claudier was a designer and architect of some renown. He was far from inexpensive and he had been reluctant to consider working for Erik until Conrad called him. Conrad had told Erik, "Jim Claudier, in my opinion, is one of the best architects in the business today. He will not only design what you want and how you want it, but you can be sure that he will be out on the site inspecting the builders work and material."

Following a crisp business lunch with Jim Claudier, they had a detailed meeting. Erik liked Jim straight away. Claudier also liked Erik, and was pleased to learn that he would have a pretty free hand and would not have to cut corners on necessary expense. Further, he could tell that Erik had good taste, and the best situation would be to make a layout of the land and situate a house and some of the other things before actually deciding on a design for the house itself.

"For that," he said, "we will need to have your future wife here to learn what features and what type of house you agree on."

"That sounds like a good plan," Erik said. "I will get back to you soon. I have the contractors at the site now, leveling and getting rid of the old stuff. I'm having them mow, cut brush down and then when I have a chance to see the land I'll take pictures and we will talk some more. Okay?"

When he arrived back at the site, the men were taking a break and drinking coffee from their thermos flasks. Erik was pleased to see all the buildings gone and most of the debris.

"Hi, Mr. Neilsin!" he was greeted. "We're just about ready to start running some mowing equipment through that jungle," he said with a laugh.

Lloyd had three units ready to start cutting. Two were tractors fitted with long sickle mowing blades. The third unit was a tractor pulling a series of mowers, which Lloyd called "a gang mower." It took nearly two hours for the sickle mowers to cut back most of the tall grass. The gang mowers followed behind, trimming the growth down even further. Erik and Lloyd walked out into the cut area. Erik could see that underneath was good farm soil.

"Lloyd, I would like to have most of this cut stuff gathered up and piled ... over there," he said, pointing to an area off to the side. "I will set up that location like a giant compost heap and then I'd like to have a grader come in and level the ground off."

"I can have it done, easy enough," he said, "but we are talking a good three days work,"

"Whatever it takes," Erik said, "just do a good job. I'll leave you to it." And with that he left for his supper date.

CHAPTER 24

Old Friends

As he approached the main gate at Fort Belvoir, the sight of the MPs at the gate stirred Erik's memory of his military career and his experiences. He had a few flashbacks of Jump School ... then a flash of Ranger training. He was stopped at the gate and advised that he would have to obtain a temporary post permit in order to enter Fort Belvoir.

"What is the nature of your business here, sir?" inquired the desk sergeant.

"I'm meeting Captain Dale E. Swan—at her invitation—and going to the Officers Club," Erik stated.

The desk sergeant checked a list of personnel and made a telephone call—obviously talking to Dale. "Yes, ma'am ... certainly ... I understand ... right away."

The desk sergeant quickly filled out the permit and had Erik sign the slip of paper. "Captain Swan asked that you stay put, Lieutenant Neilsin. She is on her way to escort you personally." Almost apologetically, he stated. "I didn't know you were a first lieutenant ... sorry!"

"No problem, Sergeant, I was medically discharged, and I'm no longer on active duty. I am a civilian now," he offered.

He heard a horn blowing and looking out the doorway, Erik saw Dale heading his way on the double. If Dale was good looking a few years back, she was now a dazzling beauty, and all heads turned and watched her approach the Visitors Section where Erik was waiting. Without hesitation Dale threw her arms around Erik and planted a long and hard kiss on his lips. In the background a wolf whistle sounded, but Erik paid no attention to it.

"Welcome home, soldier," Dale whispered in his ear.

Dale had reserved a table for them at the Officers Club, and following a few cocktails and a lot of verbal back-tracking, both Dale and Erik brought things up to date.

"So tell me, what have you been up to?" she inquired.

"Well, you know as much as I do from your conversation with Conrad, that is, up to the point when I was still 'out of it,'" he said. "Since then, I've undergone all kinds of therapy and trying to build myself up with food and exercise. I am almost back up to my regular weight, and I am feeling much better. I should tell you that my nurse, that Conrad appointed to look after me, is very close to me."

"How close?" asked Dale.

Erik cleared his throat—he was getting that dried throat feeling again. "I've asked Elizabeth to marry me. I guess that's pretty close," he said.

There was a long pause before Dale spoke. "That's okay! You're still my big brother, aren't you?"

"Of course Dale," he answered. "We've been through a lot together and you brought sunshine at a time when there was nothing but snow and freezing cold."

Dale gave Erik's arm a squeeze and said. "I still have my little bird cage. It has traveled with me all this time. I even saved the tree, but it fell to pieces in my hold baggage when it was shipped to the States."

The rest of the evening was mostly small talk. Erik felt a bit awkward about where their relationship stood. Dale seemed to sense that Erik was a bit ill at ease.

"Let's get out of here," she said when they finished their supper. Erik wanted to pay, but Dale laughed. "This was my invite, and you're on my home turf."

Dale drove to the BOQ (Bachelor Officer Quarters) where she lived and invited Erik in. Erik was very nervous and showed it.

"Erik Neilsin! What ails you, boy? I am not going to devour you and spirit you away. Are you afraid of me?" she asked.

"Well ... I, well you see, I feel a little confused, and I don't want you to be mad at me. I really do love Elizabeth, and I also care very much for you, but I don't want to be tempted to something foolish," he said.

"That's okay, Erik. I understand and I appreciate your honesty. You were always straight with me, and I really did look upon you as a special kind of brother. Well, almost always as a brother," she said with a mischievous smile on her face.

Dale took a bottle from her little Japanese bar, and they enjoyed a few drinks and talked of old times in Washington State and then their duty at Pusan. Looking at his watch, Erik saw it was getting late and thought that he'd better get going. Dale gave him another one of her looks and offered, "Well, I hate to see you have to drive so late at night. You could stay here until morning," she said, testing Erik.

"That is tempting," Erik said "but I have a really busy schedule myself. I will probably go back to the farm at Rustburg, stay overnight there, and check on things before heading back to Baltimore. That would be better."

"I hope that this is not going to be the end of our friendship." Dale asked, "You will invite me to meet your Elizabeth and even to your wedding, wont you?"

"Sure I will. Matter of fact, I would like you to meet Conrad Fleming and the Templetons. If I call you and invite you, will you come?"

Dale gave assurances she would, and they parted at her quarters' door, but not before she gave Erik a long and loving kiss.

"This is from your sister," she said. "I don't expect you to love me, but I don't want you to forget me either."

Erik was glad to get moving. He had felt that stirring in his loins, and distance now offered safety. He recalled a saying that 'a stiff pecker has no conscience', and he was glad to have resisted the temptation to stay with Dale Swan.

Erik stopped at a motel that looked halfway decent, and checked in for a nights stay. He picked up the phone and called Four Winds. It was nearly eleven p.m. Bernice answered the telephone.

"Hello, Mrs. Templeton. Sorry to call so late, but I was on the road and had to pull into a motel for tonight and wanted to call Elizabeth."

"She just went upstairs, not five minutes ago. Let me shout to her."

Erik could hear her speaking on the intercom.

"Hello," a breathless Elizabeth answered.

"Hello, my love," he said. "I'm checking in as I promised. Sorry that I'm calling so late. How are you, sweetheart?"

"I'm fine, now that you called," she said. "Where is my Viking wanderer?"

"I'm not far from Rustburg. I will be down there in the morning to see how things are going, and then I will be heading back to Baltimore to see Conrad and, if it's okay, I would like to come to Four Winds and you," he said.

There was a brief pause as he heard Elizabeth's muffled question to Bernice.

"Bernice said you are welcome anytime and you don't have to ask, Just come!"

"I hear you loud and clear," Erik said. "Please convey my thanks to Bernice."

Erik arrived at the site just before noontime and he was pleased to note that the land was quite level and a big grader was just about finished leveling the land. Erik was equally glad to see Jim Claudier taking measurements with a surveyor's instrument.

Looking up, he saw Erik and said, "Glad you are here. I have been working on some ideas and now that I have finished checking the farm, I would like to sit down with you and Elizabeth and start working up some preliminary plans. I plan to be in Baltimore the day after tomorrow for a few days. Do you think it would be possible to get you two together there?"

"That would be really great," exclaimed Erik. "I have your number, Jim, and I will be at Four Winds tomorrow afternoon or early evening and I will call you. Would you mind coming out to Four Winds?"

"Not at all, as long as I get you two together. We should plan on at least three or four hours, if that is all right."

"I see no problem there. I will call you after seven p.m. if that is a good time?" Erik suggested.

They agreed on the time, and Erik headed back to Baltimore. He stopped to call Conrad and told him that he was heading in and needed a few minutes with him before heading for Four Winds.

Arriving, Conrad was all questions.

"Did you see Dale Swan?" Erik nodded.

"Well? For Christ sake, don't keep me in suspense. What happened?"

"Not what you think." Erik smirked. "We talked about old times, the Army, Korea, and my recovery. We are good friends and she was like a kid sister and she looks at me like a brother," Erik said, but he didn't think Conrad was convinced.

"Does she know you're getting married?" Conrad asked.

"Yes, of course! I also said I would invite her to the wedding but, before all that, to meet you, the Templetons, and of course Elizabeth."

Conrad eyed Erik carefully and saw that he was serious and he read the honesty in that statement.

"I think that meeting this Dale Swan might prove interesting," he said, adding. "She has a lovely voice."

"That isn't all that's lovely," Erik teased.

Conrad raised an eyebrow.

Erik pulled into the back driveway at Four Winds and found Elizabeth on the porch waiting for him. She had seen his car approaching and went out to meet him. The next five minutes were very quiet and neither Erik or Elizabeth uttered a word. Penny observed from an upstairs window that they kissed at least seven times. They finally entered the house, and Martha asked Erik if he had eaten.

"Yes, I have, thank you, Martha. But I wouldn't say no to a cup of coffee and one of your blueberry muffins."

Martha scurried off to fill the request, muttering, "The blueberry muffins gets them all the time."

Bernice entered the patio where Elizabeth and Erik were coiled on the couch like a pair of snakes.

"Behold, he cometh!" she said.

"Evening, Bernice!"

"Have you eaten, dear boy?"

"Martha already beat you to it." Elizabeth chuckled. "Erik's having a coffee and some blueberry muffins."

"From the lipstick on his face, I would say he already had dessert," Bernice teased.

Erik told them about the progress on the property and meeting Jim Claudier and that he would be coming to Four Winds the following day, to get Erik and Elizabeth's ideas on for the house to be built.

Bernice was happy to see this young couple so happy in making their plans. She pretended to be interested in a magazine she was reading but she managed a peek or two at them as they talked and teased each other. *How much they remind me of Jennifer and Jimmy,* she thought. These two gave both Bernice and George a joy in sharing their time at Four Winds. In Bernice's mind, they were her "kids" … sort of!

Erik remembered to call Jim Claudier at seven p.m. and invited him to Four Winds at ten o'clock the next morning. At Bernice's suggestion, they could work for two hours then take a break for lunch and another few hours afterward. Jim Claudier readily agreed. The architect was punctual and drove up to the house just a few minutes before ten. Erik greeted him and brought him out to the back patio where a pot of fresh coffee and some of Martha's pastries beckoned as a midmorning snack. Claudier had his arms full of rolled up paper and several binders of reference material that he spread out on the table where they were to work.

Erik introduced Elizabeth and Bernice to Jim Claudier and they tucked into the coffee and pastries. Jim Claudier commented on the design of Four Winds and said that he liked some of its features. He and Bernice talked for a short while and then without further ado, he said, "Well, why don't we take a look at the land layout and then my suggestions as to where the house should be located and the other units.

He spread out one of the large rolls of paper that identified the whole property, noting the roadway leading to the property and a series of small dash marks where the house and greenhouse would be located. The drawing also had areas marked out for outdoor planting.

"This is an overall, pre-building layout of the land you folks just purchased," he said. "I have indicated the location where I think that the house should be, with a functional driveway to serve the dwelling area and a branching off driveway to the greenhouse—or more than one if you want—and access to the fields. I also marked out an adjoining small building for storing related equipment I assume you will need. And last, space for storage within that building that I might call the utility shed."

"Erik, are you sure that you want to have all those buildings and things?" asked Elizabeth. "I think all that will be very expensive, don't you think?"

Jim Claudier gave a questioning look toward Erik, who responded, "Why don't we wait and see all the details? I want to have this done right, and I am not too concerned about the cost. I'm sure that Jim will see that we get what we want and good value for our money." He returned the questioning look to Jim Claudier.

Satisfied, the architect pressed on and produced the next rolled-up paper. It was the outline of the house with just a small amount of landscape shown. The house shown was spread out, and it was obvious that it was a ranch-type house.

"This is not the actual house I am suggesting. I put that in so that we had a starting point," he said. "What I would like to do is show you pictures and plans of some of the houses that I designed and supervised during their construction. There are also other houses, designed by some very good architects. You may see some features in a few of these houses that you would like incorporated into you own house. We will also design those things you would like to see in your home. I will then put all these features together—perhaps in two or three different house designs and we will sit down again and hammer out the likes and dislikes until we get what you think you would like. Last, I will prepare drawings of the layout and scale drawings of the house as it will stand."

Elizabeth looked a little bewildered, and, for that matter, so did Bernice. Erik seemed amused and obviously very excited.

"I like your game plan."

They spent over two hours picking out houses and features they liked. Bernice had to bite her tongue a few times, forcing herself to remember that this was not her house they were building. During a patio lunch they all discussed things and features they liked in a house. Bernice could not contain herself from asking one question: "What about a nursery or some children's rooms?"

Elizabeth looked a little startled, and it was plain to all that she had not even thought about that aspect or for that matter, neither did Erik.

Jim Claudier said that his ideas encompassed several other rooms that could easily serve for children and guests. That seemed to satisfy the anxious looks going around the table.

It was several hours later when they finished with a basic plan and some choice house designs. Taking Erik aside, Jim Claudier felt Erik out on what he thought his operating budget should be.

"Jim, I want a quality home, a very functional set up for the greenhouse, and good landscaping. I am prepared to pay for that kind of quality house and facilities. In terms of how much. I don't know. But you can use a seven-hundred-thousand-dollar figure, more or less, as a starting point. I have the money sitting in savings that will adequately cover what we want and then some," he said.

Satisfied, Jim Claudier said, "That is good! When I don't have to cut corners I can assure you that you will get value and quality in what you want. Knowing that I can go for good material and design that can save money. I will handle the purchasing of materials, and I always select builders I have dealt with before. I know the kind of work they do and they also know that I demand very high standards."

Satisfied, he left and promised to get started right away on the whole project. One of the key points at the initial stage, Jim Claudier said, was to direct the present construction crew in the preliminary landscaping and to work out all the details for water and sewerage lines and such.

After supper, Elizabeth and Erik took the car and drove out to the lake area to be by themselves. They picked a comfortable secluded spot to watch the sunset and the lake. Since it was not a weekend, the lake area was deserted and they felt they were alone. Erik brought a large plaid blanket and a couple of pillows, plus a small cooler with a few beers and some snacks. Elizabeth joined Erik with a beer and they talked about their future plans.

Elizabeth leaned back into Erik's arms as they lay, propped up with the two pillows. She could feel his heart beating like an engine, *thump, thump, thump.* Erik's hand reached around Elizabeth and he gently caressed her shoulders and then moved down to her breast. For some reason, which Elizabeth could not explain, she stiffened involuntarily. Erik immediately noted the response and his hand retreated.

"Anything wrong?" he asked.

"Oh Erik, I'm sorry. I am not sure why I reacted so," she said. "You know that I once had a relationship, and since then I never was interested in anyone else. I often repelled any advances made by others and I never had a boyfriend since then, except for you. You are special to me in more ways then you could possibly understand," she said, her voice trailing off.

Erik knew a little about Elizabeth's boyfriend of long ago, but he never gave it a second thought. Elizabeth sensed that she should not dampen Erik's affection. She turned and reached his head and pulled his head down to her and kissed him gently but firmly. Erik felt the stirring within himself and his kisses intensified, sending a message of insistence to Elizabeth. Caution was put aside and Elizabeth responded. It was as if a dam of water was suddenly released, after being held inactive for a long time. Erik embraced Elizabeth and they feverishly sought each other's lips again. Elizabeth could no longer deny Erik's or her own desire, which erupted like a kettle reaching the boiling point. Locked in a rhythm of love making, their passion took over and both reached a climax together. Time stood still, and Elizabeth felt a great sense of relief that was replaced with a secure feeling of contentment and love.

It was dark when they returned to Four Winds, and fortunately the household was occupied with other things, so Erik and Elizabeth lounged on the patio together and before they knew it they fell asleep. Martha shook them both awake and told them it was after eleven o'clock and unless they were planning to stay up all night, they might want to turn in.

"You're right, Martha," Elizabeth acknowledged. "It has been a long day, and I know that we are tired."

"There you two are," Bernice said as she walked through to the patio.

"We fell asleep on the patio, and Martha told us it was bedtime," Elizabeth said with a chuckle.

Erik excused himself for a moment and left the room. Elizabeth made a decision and she said to Bernice, "Bernice, I want to ask you something. Advice, I guess."

"What is it, my dear?"

"Erik and I are engaged and much in love. I know our wedding day is seven months away, but would you object …" She hesitated.

"Elizabeth," Bernice said, with a knowing look on her face, "you and Erik are not children, and you know what you are doing. I know it must be hard for you both to be under the same roof—so near, and yet just far enough away. If I understand what you would like to say, I would ask that lad to join you." She gave Elizabeth a wink.

"You would have already been married before now if it had not been for the house and grand wedding plans," Bernice said. "The fact that I know about Pat and Erik, and this strange relationship … well, I feel that you both need to have that closeness together. Why not now?" she concluded.

Elizabeth hugged Bernice. "You are so understanding. I will fetch Erik and spirit him away," she said, smiling.

Erik had gone to his room, showered, and was getting ready to retire for the night when he heard a tap on his door. Slipping on a robe he opened the door to find Elizabeth there.

"I just stopped by to invite you to my pad," she said.

It was nearly nine o'clock in the morning before either of them stirred. Elizabeth was already awake and was studying the wound scars on Erik's body. She had not looked very hard before when he was her patient.

"What happened here?" she asked, touching a scar on Erik's side.

"That was some artillery fragment I picked up in Korea," he replied.

Looking at his legs and other side, she noticed some other small thin, long scars. "And these?" she asked.

"I believe those are where I was grazed by some bullets."

Elizabeth kissed each scar—as if to make them better. "My poor Erik," she said. "I am so lucky to have you."

"No, it's the other way around," Erik said. "I'm the lucky one because I have you!"

On that mutual happy note they both enjoyed a shower together, exploring each other as they bathed. Finally it was ten-thirty before they made it downstairs for a bite to eat. After breakfast Erik excused himself and went over to Queenie to confer with her and "talk shop" about gardening.

Erik talked with Conrad on the phone and brought him up to date on their meeting with the architect Jim Claudier and the progress with the property.

"I would like you to take a break and come with me to go over some legal matters," Conrad suggested. "That is, if you can pull yourself away from Elizabeth and Four Winds."

A week had passed and Erik received a call from Jim Claudier informing him that the basic landscape work was completed and that Erik might want to bring Elizabeth out to the site and see the land for herself.

"That is a great idea, Jim, and long overdue. I will bring Elizabeth, and we could be there just after lunchtime."

"Fine! I'll see you there sometime around one or one-thirty," and he hung up.

Elizabeth was excited to see the property, and she enjoyed the drive to Virginia. They stopped for lunch at a fast food place and Elizabeth chastised Erik for his craving for "junk food."

"I have to eat this stuff once in a while. My body needs the fat," he said, and ducked as Elizabeth attempted to give him a gentle swat.

They arrived at the site and Erik was impressed with the lay of the land. No longer was there coarse grass and weeds. The ground was smooth and level and here and there he noticed that areas were marked out with ground pegs connected with string to denote each structure area.

"That must be the site for the house," Erik said, pointing to the large area marked out. Almost on cue, Jim Claudier drove up in a four-wheel drive truck. Calling them over, he said, "I want to show you something in the truck."

He slid out a panel of plywood on which a model of a house was placed and had material on it that looked like grass. It was like looking at the completed site from a thousand feet up.

"Jim," Elizabeth exclaimed, "it looks beautiful!"

"I'm glad you like it. Of course it is only a beginning model. I will use this same board and arrange some other houses on it," and proceeded to remove the house, which was clipped on. He then replaced it with another type of house model. Both Erik and Elizabeth were impressed. He removed that house also, and replaced it with a third house, and seeing it, it took their breath away!

"Oh, that is lovely. It's so grand, so elegant, such a lovely looking house," Elizabeth cooed.

Erik was equally impressed and guessed that Jim Claudier had saved the best for last.

"Jim, I am impressed beyond words. I think you know which one we are leaning toward," Erik said.

Jim laughed and said, "I am just as excited as you two are when I worked up this house design. It's an original, you know. I created this just for you. There is no other home like it! Once I started, I couldn't stop until I finished it. Everything flowed just right," he said.

He brought out the plans for the three models, but the first two received only a cursory glance. The third set of plans was set up with four overlays.

"This is what the roof looks like," he said, and then turned the top overlay like a page in a book. "This is what the second floor would look like." Turning the next page, he said, "This is the ground floor level, and this is the full basement plan."

"I like it," Erik said. "What about you, Elizabeth?"

"Oh, darling, it is just lovely. I don't know what to say. Can we afford it?" she asked again.

"Honey, you are a real worrier!" Turning to Jim Claudier, Erik asked, "What kind of a price tag are we looking at, Jim?"

"I estimate the house at around eight-fifty to nine hundred thousand."

"What?" Elizabeth started to say.

"Around eight hundred and fifty thousand to nine hundred thousand for the house, greenhouse and utilities, and so on. The major work for the utilities, sewerage and the works, added to the landscaping—brings my estimate to roughly, a little over nine hundred thousand, plus or minus fifteen thousand."

Continuing on, Jim pointed out that depending upon the appliances and required maintenance equipment, added to the projected cost, it would most likely exceed the nine hundred thousand mark, so he calculated another fifteen thousand dollars to cover everything else.

"Jim, this is a go!" Erik said.

"Okay. Fine! I would like you to set up a special account that Conrad can do for you. I would like you to transfer at least five hundred thousand dollars into that account that I am authorized to draw from to acquire the materials and take care of work underway. When more is needed, I will give you advance notice. I know you want it done ASAP and this will help speed things along," he said.

CHAPTER 25

Summer slipped by, and the leaves on the trees were starting to change into autumn colors. Elizabeth returned to part-time nursing to fill in and help the hospital. With the approaching holidays, the incidence of accidents increased and many hospitals experienced a major load of patients. It was necessary for Elizabeth to not only work part-time during the week, but sometimes to fill in for another nurse on a weekend.

Erik made frequent trips to the farm to check on the progress of the new house construction. He met often with the architect, Jim Claudier. They went over minor details and planed out the greenhouse Erik wanted. With the foundations laid and the framework well underway, the house was already showing signs of a custom built, grand house. Erik had been busy taking soil samples for analysis and obtained gardening reference books. He wanted to insure that he would be prepared with the right kind of soil.

The Templetons made several "hush-hush trips" overseas, on special shopping trips. On one of their trips they invited Elizabeth to go with them and took her to a special fashion house where she viewed wedding gowns. One particular wedding gown took her breath away and when she learned the price, she paled.

"The important thing is," Bernice said, "do you like it?"

"Of course, it is beautiful," Elizabeth said, "but it is too expensive for the likes of me!"

Bernice insisted that Elizabeth try on the gown, and after a little pressure from Bernice and George, she agreed. Just prior to viewing the wedding gowns, Bernice took Elizabeth to a beauty salon where she and Elizabeth had their hair done, a facial treatment and all the nice things a woman gets with a day of beauty. After Elizabeth put on the wedding gown, the attendants fussed over her until everything was perfect.

Elizabeth made her grand entrance in front of Bernice and George and the full-length mirrors. The manager handed Elizabeth an artificial bouquet to hold as she viewed herself in the full-length, wrap-around mirrors. She was the picture of a beautiful bride, and although Elizabeth knew the whole wedding outfit was beyond her reach, she was impressed.

"We'll take it!" Bernice said over Elizabeth's protests.

Elizabeth was numb and could hardly speak. It truly was the most beautiful wedding gown she had ever seen in her life and now it was to be hers! It took three days, after returning, for her life to get back to normal.

"Now, we must keep all this a secret and not let Erik see your wedding dress," Bernice said.

Thanksgiving was just around the corner and holiday preparations were underway at Four Winds. Bernice and George decided that it would be a good time to invite Elizabeth's parents for a visit and make plans for the wedding. Elizabeth called her sister and learned that her father's health was not good and that he was getting very feeble and she wondered if he would be up for all the activity of the wedding. The Templetons graciously sent the invitation for her parents to join them for Thanksgiving, and included first-class tickets for the flight to Baltimore.

Two days before Thanksgiving, Elizabeth's parents arrived and were met at the airport by the Templetons and Elizabeth. It was a tearful reunion for Elizabeth and her mother. Elizabeth's father was calm and just smiled, saying very little. Elizabeth felt a tug at her heart, seeing her father. He had really aged and seemed to be in a state of his own, not really aware of what was going on around him.

The Thanksgiving dinner was, in the tradition of the Templetons, magnificent. Bernice and George couldn't do enough for Elizabeth's parents. Mrs. Feldmann's English was limited, and she frequently spoke in German to Elizabeth. George spoke fluent German, and that was well received by Elizabeth's mother, who was feeling a little left out.

A few days after the holiday, the Feldmanns returned to San Francisco, and George called to make sure that Elizabeth's sister met the airplane for her parents' return.

The weather reports were forecasting colder weather the coming week plus a threat of snow—the first of the winter. Erik and Elizabeth drove to their almost completed home in Virginia to check on things. She had not been there since they laid the foundation and started the framework. Elizabeth was impressed with the size of the house and its big rooms. The foyer had a marble-like floor that was covered with runners to protect the floor from scratches by the craftsman at work. Hanging in the center of the foyer was a beautifully centered chandelier. Winding stairs led to the floor above. The steps were of matching marble, but partially covered with stair carpeting.

The kitchen was laid out and finished except for the appliances, which had been special ordered. Jim Claudier was on hand and joined them on their tour around the house.

"I took the liberty of ordering a special electric cooking unit. It is a professional model that has two ovens and six cooking points and grill on top. The firm of Coppersmith, Ltd., is making a special unit to go over the cooking area and it will have a very strong exhaust system."

The back view from the screened and covered patio took in a brace of newly planted three-year old trees. Just to the right of the trees, a pathway led to the greenhouse. The landscaping was expertly planted with mature trees and scrubs, and the house was almost ready for the finishing touches.

They spent several more hours looking in and out and around the house and, finally after a break for a snack that Jim had arranged, Jim took them to see the utility building.

"Careful attention to details here," he explained.

Erik saw that there was enough space, and that in one section that had a closed door, on opening the door, revealed a complete diesel electrical generating system.

"If you ever lose power, and especially for the greenhouse, you will be able to generate your own power," he said. "See this box over here?" He pointed to a box on the wall. "This is an automatic switching device! If your power goes out, in one or two seconds the generator will start up and the switching device will switch off the power main and send the generated power to the house and greenhouse. It's a powerful unit and it should be adequate for all your needs."

Erik noted that several pathway lamp posts were in place and led from the house to the greenhouse. It was something he had not considered, but was pleased that Jim saw the need for it, and had them installed. It was soon dark and Jim turned on a switch to all the lights that came on, giving them an idea of the adequacy of the lighting.

"Oh, one other thing. I have had motion sensors installed. When you approach the house the outside lights will automatically turn on," Jim pointed out.

It was a nice trip for Erik and Elizabeth, and they talked all the way back to Four Winds. It was late when they returned and everyone had retired except for Chester making the rounds and seeing the doors were locked and lights switched off. He stopped by to inquire if they wanted anything to eat and said that his wife, Martha had made up a few sandwiches of turkey and ham and that there was hot chocolate in the thermos for them, if they wanted it.

"Thanks, Chester! Thank Martha for us. It was thoughtful of her to do that," Elizabeth said.

"I'll say goodnight then," Chester said and made his was to bed.

Elizabeth and Erik sat on the rear patio, ate the sandwiches, and enjoyed the hot chocolate. It was late, but they were still too excited to go off to sleep, so they talked for a little while and soon they were yawning.

"I guess we should turn in now," Erik announced. "Let's go, honey!"

The following day at ten in the morning, Martha called Elizabeth to say that she had a long-distance call. It was Elizabeth's sister.

It was not good news, she said. "Father passed away in his sleep last night. When Mother went to wake him she found that he was cold and had died."

Elizabeth and Erik flew to San Francisco for the funeral and services. It was a sad gathering, but Mrs. Feldmann took it all in her stride, coping with losing him.

"He was getting weaker and failing," her mother told them. She said she knew his time was short but had hoped he would be all right for *Weihnachten*—the Christmas holidays.

Erik and Elizabeth flew back to Baltimore. Erik mentioned that with her father's passing, Elizabeth would have to have someone to "give the bride away." Elizabeth thought about it—but not too long.

"I will ask George to give me away," she said. "He is my choice—he and Bernice have been like parents to me."

When Elizabeth approached George and asked him, he said that he would be delighted to give her away and would consider it an honor. That settled that part of the plans for the wedding, and Elizabeth and Erik worked on a wedding invitation list of guests.

George suggested a pre-Christmas party for the closest friends, and invited Erik's aunt and family down also. The invitations were sent to them, as well as Conrad. Erik hesitated for a moment and asked about inviting Dale Swan. He explained that she was a fellow officer and like a sister. Elizabeth didn't hesitate in saying "Sure!" and Erik was somewhat relieved at not having to explain more.

George announced during lunch that he had a few notes for Erik and also calls from Conrad and Dale to say they would be pleased to attend. For those out-of-town guests, the rooms were readied for this weekend affair.

Following lunch the telephone rang. It was Conrad Flemming, and he sounded agitated. "I need to talk to Erik right away."

"Hi, Conrad. What's up?" Erik asked.

"Erik, I just opened some mail from the Veterans Administration. It was forwarded to me from the Johns Hopkins Administration office. It seems that someone in the military has questioned your being discharged from the US Army for medical reasons. It goes on to say that they think you are trying to pull the wool over the US Army and that you evaded further military service, using the hospital stay as an excuse."

That took the wind out of Erik's sail. "I don't understand. You probably know more about my condition at the time I was medically discharged than I do."

"That's true, and I will make the initial reply and also talk to some people I know in the Pentagon," Conrad said. "Meanwhile I will make a copy of this letter and send it to you. You should get it in tomorrow's mail."

Erik was frowning as he walked back to join the others.

"What's the matter, Erik?" Elizabeth asked, seeing the serious look on his face.

"I'm not sure I understand," he said.

"Conrad says he is sending a copy of an official Army letter that questions my being medically discharged or something like that."

Bernice perked up and offered that George was the one to talk to as he dealt with the State Department and other brass all the time.

The next day Erik received the letter in question and read the letter twice:

Department of the Army
Military Personnel Division
Fort Belvoir, Virginia

14 December 1953

Subject: Medical Discharge Inquiry—First Lt. Erik Neilsin

To: First Lieutenant Erik Neilsin
C/O Mr. Conrad Flemming, Attorney
Baltimore, MD

Dear Mr. Flemming,

An inquiry has been initiated by the Veterans Administration, reference VA # 27403.7, dated 9 November 1953, concerning the unusual circumstances leading to the medical discharge of First Lieutenant Erik Neilsin. Preliminary investigation reveals that subject officer was officially medically discharged while a patient at Walter Reed Hospital due to a diagnosis that his condition was of a permanent nature, thereby eliminating him from further military service or from completing his length of military service commitment.

A review by the VA records Division reveals that subject officer has recovered from his injuries and was medically restored to a state that would appear to require a reversal of the full medical discharge and restoration of First Lieutenant Neilsin to active military duty.

This division is assisting the Veterans Administration Branch in providing official notice to First Lieutenant Neilsin to report to the nearest VA Hospital for complete physical evaluation.

As a legal representative of Lieutenant Neilsin during his term of medical treatment and subsequent discharge, it is requested that Lieutenant Neilsin contact the VA Hospital Special Examination unit for scheduling the above requested physical examination.

Please acknowledge receipt of this correspondence and advise when Lieutenant Neilsin will contact the above unit. Upon receipt of your acknowledgement, we shall forward that information to the VA Specialist who is the point of contact for coordination between the US Army and Veterans Administration Services. Mr. R. R. Roberts' branch is responsible for initiating and handling this action.

S/ Eugene S. Vergio,
Major, US Army
Adjutant General

cc: R. R. Roberts, VAS Br.
VA Services—Records

CHAPTER 26

Conrad talked to Erik and decided to contact the VA Branch in Washington. First he sent an acknowledgement letter to Fort Belvoir and then contacted the Veterans Administration headquarters and asked to speak to the Assistant Director of Veteran Affairs. Lloyd Matthews, from the Director's office, talked with Conrad and said that he had only scant information regarding the unusual case of Lieutenant Neilsin, but that the POC, Mr. R. R. Roberts, was the "driving force" behind this inquiry.

"We are not usually involved in these matters, which for the most part," he advised, "is handled by the VA hospital."

Conrad thanked him for the information and decided to call Mr. Roberts at the Special Branch and find out what this was all about. What Conrad experienced when he called and talked to Mr. Roberts was a hot-tempered and mean-spirited person who was not very cooperative. In fact, Roberts was rude and terse with Conrad, and Conrad, bristling from that call, had the urge to go down to that office. He wanted to meet this person face to face and then knock him on his butt. Instead, wisdom and experience prevailed and, having dealt with senior medical personnel and some military brass, Conrad contacted Dr. Sidney Perkins, Senior Staff at the VA Hospital in Washington.

Dr. Perkins was not immediately available, the secretary announced, and said she would be happy to confirm an appointment for Conrad to meet with Dr. Perkins. A date and time was set for the next day at 1100.

Conrad was ten minutes early for his appointment and was asked to wait in the reception lounge. He saw an organization chart on the wall and was studying all the many sections and branches of the Veteran Administration.

"Dr. Perkins will see you now," announced the receptionist.

Conrad was ushered into Dr. Perkins' office.

"Hello, Conrad," Sidney Perkins said, rising from his chair to shake hands. "I haven't seen you for several years! How's the law practice these days?" he asked.

"Hello, Sidney. I see you are putting on some weight. It must be tough on an old rooster like you cooped up behind a desk!"

"Who are you calling an old rooster, you upstart! Are you still single and chasing women in one of your sports cars?"

"Yeah, I'm still single but chasing skirts was never my strong suit. The sports cars … well that is another story," he allowed.

"What can I do for you? I know you didn't come down here to rattle my cage with insults so you must want something for a client. Shoot!" he said.

Conrad explained the details concerning Erik's service and battlefield injuries sustained in Korea and brought Dr. Perkins through the recovery of Erik, up to the present time. Last, he then mentioned the strange inquiry that no one seemed to understand, also the unusual circumstances surrounding it. Conrad told Perkins about his conversation with Mr. R. R. Roberts, Special Branch, Point of Contact.

"I don't know this Roberts guy personally, but I know something about him," Dr. Perkins said.

"He is a retired Army lieutenant colonel. He had just over twenty years' service and retired from the Army at Fort Lewis in Washington. Grapevine has it he was told to put in his papers or face a general (General Courts-martial). The VA really didn't want him, but Roberts had some qualifications plus his veteran credit and he got a position with the VA. He has been an occasional pain in the ass and seems to enjoy singling out some cases to try to make a name for himself."

"He was going to earn a smack in the mouth from me," Conrad said, recalling Roberts' rude and discourteous manner.

"From what you tell me, it sounds like a pure and simple medical case that was compounded by the lengthy comatose state. I'll tell you what, I will ask for this fellow's full medical records. What's his name again?" he asked.

"First Lieutenant Erik Neilsin." Conrad also gave him the VA reference number.

"Okay, let me check it out. I will also send a memo to the POC that I will do a preliminary review of the case. This will get Roberts off your back for a while until I can see what's what," he said.

"Thanks, Sidney, I appreciate it. Erik Neilsin is a great young man who has been through an ordeal. He is lucky that he made it this far, and he certainly doesn't deserve this kind of treatment from the Army or the VA. You know a good part of his enlistment was spent in the hospital," Conrad said. "Now! How about lunch? Doctors do eat, don't they? Or are you on a diet?"

"You haven't changed a bit, Conrad. I am going to call your bluff. I have never got a meal out of you yet. The best I can recall was a lousy cup of coffee from a vending machine. It was so bad I poured it into my secretary's flowerpot and she was pissed when her geranium nosed-dived and died. I know of a good restaurant a short way from here but it's going to cost you," he said.

"You mean that hamburger joint around the corner?" Conrad responded.

"If this place serves hamburgers, it will still cost you! Let's go, I'm starved and tired of hospital cafeteria food."

Chez Allegro was somewhat crowded when Dr. Perkins and Conrad entered. The maître d' asked if they had reservations for lunch—which of course they didn't.

"It will be around a thirty-minute wait, I'm afraid," he said. Sidney Perkins glanced at his watch and shook his head.

Conrad then intervened and handed the maître d' a twenty-dollar bill and said, "The doctor has a busy schedule, and we are needing our time, so why don't you see if you can arrange to find us a table pretty soon."

"I'll see what I can do," he said, taking the twenty. He walked over to a table and pulled off a 'reserved' sign and said, "I just found a table, gentlemen. Right this way!"

The waiter came and asked if they cared for a cocktail before lunch.

"I'll have a Bloody Mary," Sidney Perkins ordered.

"Sounds good! Make that two of them, and we would like to order now also," he said.

They ordered an appetizer of mussels with the house specialty sauce, followed by a pasta dish. Dessert and coffee followed. Sidney Perkins inquired if a liqueur with the coffee was in order.

"Sure," Conrad said, "but I hope you are not operating on anyone this afternoon!"

"No fear—the closest I get to a knife now is at the dinner table."

They had a good chuckle over that. Glancing at his watch, Dr. Perkins said that he had to get back, as it was a busy day. They parted at the restaurant, and Dr. Perkins said he would be in touch soon.

"Oh yeah, Conrad, thanks for the lunch. You must do this more often," Perkins said.

"You're welcome, you quack! Now go back to work and try not to kill anybody."

Conrad drove back to his law firm office and upon entering his secretary said, "A young lady is in the waiting room to see you. She just stopped by and I told her you were expected back but I wasn't sure what time you would return. She said she'd wait a short while and then leave. Her name is Dale Swan!"

Conrad walked into the waiting room and saw a very attractive strawberry blonde woman with lovely blue eyes. She was dressed in a casual outfit but was tastefully attractive at the same time. She looked up from the magazine she was reading.

"Hi! I'm Conrad Flemming! We have talked on the phone and now I have the pleasure in meeting you in person," he said.

Conrad noted her appraising look; her manner was calm and assured.

"Ah yes, Mr. Flemming! I just happened to be in this part of town and I remembered that your address was close by. I've heard Erik Neilsin mention your name many times and it sounds like he doesn't take a step without checking with you first."

"Would you like to come into my office?" Conrad invited. "Coffee?" he asked.

"Yes, that would be nice," she said. Conrad nodded to the receptionist, who had stopped her typing to watch the two of them. She scurried off to bring the coffee. She was back in a minute with a tray holding two cups, cream and sugar.

After the sugar and cream ritual, Conrad cleared his throat and asked, "What brings you to my office, Miss Swan … or should I address you as Captain Swan?"

"I received an invitation from Mr. and Mrs. Templeton to attend a weekend party next week. The note that came with it said that Erik and Elizabeth asked that I be invited along with other close friends, and mentioned your name."

"Yes, that's right! Are you going up to Four Winds then?" Conrad asked.

"Actually I have had mixed feelings. I don't know the Templetons or Elizabeth. Only Erik. I guess I might feel a little awkward or intrusive if I accepted the invitation." Dale Swan suddenly smiled, and Conrad wondered why. His look asked the question.

"I thought you would be some old jurist with gray hair and a beard, or something," Dale said, smiling. "But you look a lot younger than I would have expected you to be."

"I'll take that as a compliment then! I take it that your visit here is to ask me about Erik, Elizabeth, and the Templetons?" he asked.

"Yes, I guess that's about it. I know that you have been like a guardian to Erik. He trusts you, so I guess I do too. Erik is my closest friend, like a brother to me. If he was not engaged to someone else, I think I would be after him. He is a very comfortable person to be with," she said, her voice trailing off.

Conrad watched Dale closely, and what he saw, he liked. He felt that warm feeling creeping up inside him.

"Let me tell you then," he said. "You should accept the invitation to Four Winds. You will like the company, and you will certainly enjoy the visit. It is the Templetons' wish that out-of-town guests stay for the weekend. They have plenty of room. The place is a mansion, and I would be happy to be your escort," he added hopefully.

"That sounds like an invitation I shouldn't pass up. However, I don't expect you to drive to Fort Belvoir to pick me up," Dale said. "Where and when shall we meet? I could drive to Baltimore next Friday and follow you to Four Winds, if you like."

They made their arrangements for the next week, and that settled, Dale asked about Erik and how his house was coming along.

"I haven't seen or heard from him since we had dinner at Fort Belvoir," she said.

"Yes the house is almost completely finished. They have done a really nice job on it. The wedding is planned for just after Easter. Matter of fact, I hope that the damn Army ... Excuse me," Conrad apologized.

"That's okay. Say what you want. I have at least three days out of the week that I say things even worse than that," Dale allowed.

"Can you imagine that with all that Erik has been through—the injuries, the extended coma and touch and go, that some civilian in the Veteran Administration network decides to give him a hard time and is trying to cause all kinds of problems for Erik," Conrad said.

"That really sounds stupid! Hells bells, he nearly gave up his life and lost a couple of years of his youth to boot," she said. "That's just what you would expect from a PFC."

"PFC?" Conrad asked.

"Sorry," she responded. "Poor Fucking Civilian!"

"Actually, he's a retired Army light colonel. I'm told he likes to give everybody a hard time. He has a nickname. Let me see what was it! Oh yeah! Triple R or something like that."

"Triple R? Crap! It's not Ruppert R. Roberts, is it?" she asked.

"Yeah that could be his name. He is referred to as R. R. Roberts. Do you know this guy?" Conrad asked.

"Oh yeah, I know him, and so does Erik!" Dale then gave Conrad a quick rundown on Triple R Roberts—the Fort Lewis lover boy.

"This is an interesting bit of information I had not anticipated," Conrad said thoughtfully. "Dale, that information can be very useful and so might you, if you wouldn't mind a little confrontation."

Conrad looked at his watch and saw that it was almost five o'clock. They had been talking for over an hour and a half. Conrad made up his mind and said, "What are your plans for this evening? I trust that you are going to have to eat soon. Why not join me for dinner. I have a very nice place in mind," he offered.

"Actually, I have no plans for this evening. I had no place in mind for this weekend and drove to D.C. and then to Baltimore, so ... Yes! Dinner this evening would be nice."

"I have a few items I need to check with my secretary and associates, and then we can leave—all right?"

Dale gave Conrad the yes nod, flipped open her handbag, and pulled out her compact to check her lipstick.

Conrad checked with his secretary and told her he was leaving a little early to take Miss Swan to dinner.

"I noticed you couldn't take your eyes off her," snorted Conrad's secretary, Gloria. Gloria had been with the law firm forever it seemed, and she was not shy with such comments to her boss.

"I think that lady has been around the block a few times Conrad," she said. "You may think you're in control, but watch out! I think she is warming up to you—but I can't for the life of me think why?"

"You're a big help, Gloria! You're just jealous," he teased. "Besides, she knows this guy in the VA that's giving our client a hard time. Also, for your information, she is also an officer in the Army who served with our Erik in Korea and at Fort Lewis."

"By the way," Gloria said joking, "Maybe you should stop by the drug store and pick up something ... just in case."

"I think I am capable of handling the unexpected," Conrad countered. Mustering up the most disgusted expression for her benefit, he left saying, "You women! If you can't have me, you won't let anyone else have a go!"

He ducked as Gloria almost scored a hit with an eraser she threw.

"Ready to go?" he asked Dale. Once outside, he asked, "Where is your car?"

"Just over there," she said pointing to a blue four-door Studebaker Commander. The car was clean and shiny and appeared to be well looked after. Conrad had respect for people who took good care of their cars.

"You and Erik have something in common! He bought a Studebaker convertible."

"I know, I saw it when he drove to Fort Belvoir!"

"Why not follow me to my place? You can park your car where it will be secure and we will go to dinner in my car."

With that, Conrad jumped into his Mark IV Jaguar sedan and led the way to his apartment complex. Dale parked inside the grounds where a caretaker was on duty. She climbed into the Jaguar and Conrad drove off to his favorite eating-place. Dale was admiring the old Jaguar sedan. She could smell the genuine leather seats and noted the polished wood dashboards and all the high tech instruments. Conrad handled the car smoothly, shifting gears at the right speeds without any jerky movements.

Arriving at the Chez Gustav—a small French restaurant that Conrad patronized often. They were greeted by the parking valet, who opened the door for Dale.

"Good evening, Mr. Flemming!" Getting behind the wheel, the valet drove the car to the restaurant's parking area.

Upon entering the restaurant, they were greeted by the maître d' and without hesitation, escorted to a reserved table. A waiter took their cocktail order. Dale was impressed as everyone addressed Conrad Flemming by name and obviously with a lot of respect.

They ordered different French meals. Dale started with escargot, broiled with butter and garlic, and then the soup, but passed up the salad for the main entree. They finished a leisurely meal with coffee and a brandy. Both passed on the rich creamy desserts. Their conversation was casual and friendly. The chemistry between them was good and both felt comfortable with each other. After a second coffee and French brandy, it was time to go.

It was not yet nine o'clock and Conrad asked Dale if she had driven around this area before. She said that she hadn't. Conrad pointed the car east (Dale read the compass on the dashboard). They then drove south direction toward Annapolis, but before going that far, Conrad turned east and drove down to the water at the small town of Arnold. There were not too many houses along the shores and occasionally, when in the area, Conrad would drive down there for the view.

It was ten-thirty by the time they headed back to Conrad's apartment. Being the gentleman that he was, Conrad invited Dale in for a drink and more conversation.

"What can I offer you to drink?" he asked.

"I'll have a Black Russian," she said. "You know—vodka, Kailua, ice, and stir."

"Excellent choice! I'll make one for each of us!"

Conrad put on his stereo system, playing soothing selections of mood music, while Dale strolled around the apartment looking at different pictures, knick-knacks and things Conrad had displayed. She noted photographs of some people—a man and a boy. Another of the man and the boy, but the boy was older. It was Erik Neilsin. Conrad explained that he was the attorney for the Neilsins and the boat building enterprise.

Dale asked about some of the people in one photograph. Conrad joined her and looked over her shoulder and explained that they were members of the company when Erik's father was still alive. Conrad was very close to Dale and she was aware of his closeness. She could feel the heat from his breath. She turned quickly and she was practically in Conrad's arms. He closed his arms around her and leaned forward to kiss her lips. Dale put her head back slightly to accept Conrad's kiss. They both felt that stirring and after the third kiss Dale looked at her watch and said, "It's after midnight."

Conrad felt a great disappointment, and tried not to show it. "Yeah! It is getting on …" he said, his voice trailing off.

"Of course tomorrow is Saturday so it's a no work day for me."

"For me also," Dale replied.

"I'll have to get to my car," she said and opened the door and left.

Conrad was getting ready to say goodbye and kiss her again. He was standing at the open door not sure what he should or should not do. He heard footsteps coming back upstairs and then saw that it was Dale, carrying an overnight bag. She entered the apartment, placed her bag on the floor and turned to Conrad.

"You look like you thought I wasn't coming back."

"Well … I—" was all Conrad managed to get out. Dale silenced any further excuses by sealing his mouth with her lips. Her body felt firm, yet soft against Conrad. Dale broke off the embrace and kiss, disappearing with her bag to the bathroom. Conrad took the empty glasses to the sink and washed them. Returning to the living room, he glanced at the bathroom door that was open and the light was out. He walked into his bedroom and when his eyes adjusted to the dimness, he realized with pleasure that Dale was in his bed.

The quietness of the night was only disturbed with occasional moans and sighs. When the pleasures of those moments subsided, they both fell asleep. Conrad's eyes opened briefly; the clock was chiming four a.m. He shifted his position in bed and was satisfied to feel the warm and firm figure lying in bed with him. He dozed off to sleep only to awaken again later. It was six o'clock now. He realized that something woke him and then felt the closeness of Dale's breath on his neck and then a kiss. It was only a few seconds before he felt his body responding. This time their lovemaking lasted longer and was unhurried and very satisfying. They both drifted off to sleep again.

The telephone started ringing at nine o'clock, and Conrad had to force himself to the edge of the bed and answer the call.

"Hello," his tired voice answered. "Conrad here."

A cheery voice boomed out, "Good morning, Conrad! I hope I'm not disturbing you." It was Erik.

"As a matter of fact … Oh, never mind! You know it's Saturday. Why are you calling at this ungodly hour?"

"I just thought you might not have any plans today. Elizabeth and I were thinking about taking a run up to the farm to check on the house. It's almost completed and the appliances are being installed. Do you want to join us today?"

"Ah. … As a matter of fact, I'm kind of tied up with other plans this morning, aside from the fact that I just got out of bed. Have they put a phone in at the farm yet?"

"Yeah, that is supposed to be put in today. At least one of the phones!"

"Why don't you give me a call after you get there, and I'll see if I can make the drive."

Dale was listening with interest to Conrad's conversation and interrupted, saying "Is that Erik you're talking to? I'll bet he's asking you to drive to the house that's being built. Ask Erik if you can bring along 'his' friend. I wouldn't mind seeing what Erik has been up to, and besides, I haven't met Elizabeth yet."

"Err, Erik? I'm expecting a friend of yours—Dale Swan—to drop by. Do you want me there for business or just to see the house?" he asked, giving Erik a potential out.

There was a muffled sound of voices on the other end before Erik answered. "Sure, bring her out! It will be a good opportunity for Elizabeth to meet Dale. Maybe we can do supper somewhere this evening."

"Okay, I'll check with Dale, and if she's agreeable, we'll drive up, but it won't be until after lunch time. What is your new telephone number anyhow?"

Conrad hung the phone up and rolled out of bed. He headed for the kitchen to put on the coffee maker. He started for the shower and saw that Dale was propped up on both pillows watching his movements.

"I put the coffee on," he said. "I'm going to hit the shower," and he disappeared in the bathroom.

Dale heard the shower going, got out of bed and headed for the kitchen. She located all the makings for a breakfast, noting that this apartment was strictly a single man's abode. She found some food going bad in the refrigerator and tossed it in the garbage. The bread she found was too stale for toasting. She settled for the eggs and bacon, saw a tomato that was not too far gone. She opened the freezer compartment and found bread stashed in little freezer packages—each with four slices. She brought one out and put on the oven to thaw out the bread slices.

Conrad came out of the bathroom and smelled bacon frying. He entered the kitchen, where Dale had set the table for two, and had breakfast almost ready to serve.

"Now this is a real treat for me," Conrad said. "I usually do something quick or go out for a breakfast. You know how it is for us single guys!"

"I chucked out some of the stuff going bad in your fridge, unless you were saving it for kim-chi."

"No! Thank you. That is fine. I really have to clean out that thing one of these days. I have a cleaning lady who comes on Monday, and she usually sorts things out for me," Conrad said lamely.

They sat down for breakfast. The eggs were just right, the bacon crisp enough; he sampled the fried tomato. "Umm, that tastes good. I never thought a tomato would taste good fried," he said.

"I put a little seasoning and garlic powder on them. I'm glad you like it! I don't get much of a chance to cook for someone beside myself."

They tackled the kitchen cleanup together and made short work of it. Dale then headed for her own shower. Conrad was rather pleased with himself and the fact that this lovely creature was here with him. The thought gave him a sense of emptiness for all his years as a bachelor and never really having anyone of his own to care for or have someone care for him.

"A penny for your thoughts," Dale said, seeing the serious expression on Conrad's face.

"Oh, nothing really! I was just thinking how nice this weekend has turned out. Come Monday, it's back to work for me, and more of the same grind. How about you, Dale?"

"I have ten days leave with no real plan to go by. I have put in six years in the US Army and have had a few lousy assignments. Fort Belvoir is really an engineering place. Now that there is no war, I have to be content with a lot of garbage jobs, unless I'm willing to climb into bed with some superior. I had enough of that with Triple R Roberts," she said. "I came to Baltimore to check on some business prospects. I put some money away during my six years in the Army, and I thought I might get the hell out of the service and start a business of my own. I even thought of becoming a private detective or some kind of investigative work."

"My, that's interesting! We shall have to explore those ideas some more," Conrad said. "About this guy—Ruppert Roberts. You'll have to tell me all about this ex-colonel while we are driving over to Erik's farm."

It was almost noon before Dale and Conrad left for the drive to Virginia. Dale gave Conrad a complete rundown on "Triple R" and his demise as a colonel—forced to put in his retirement papers or face Army courts-martial. They stopped for lunch at Ziggie's Barbecued Rib Shack, but did not linger, eager to get going.

Erik and Elizabeth had gone through the house a dozen times—not that anything was wrong, but because they were thrilled with everything. The kitchen had a huge cooking range with six cooking points and two large ovens. There was also a double-wall oven because Elizabeth had told Jim Claudier that she did a lot of baking. Erik was satisfied with the house and focused his attention on the greenhouse. It was a very big greenhouse for a private home.

"Why such a big garden house?" Elizabeth asked. "How large is it?"

"Honey, it's a greenhouse, not a garden house! How big? It is twenty-four feet wide and seventy-two feet long. In the center, it is sixteen feet high and that tapers down to eight feet on each side. It has its own water supply, heating system and the proper lighting. I will put in some work tables and whatever else I need to grow flowers and plants."

Elizabeth smiled at Erik and said, "You really amaze me with your talents. Can you really make a living from this?" she asked. Erik could see the old doubts creeping into her thoughts.

"Don't worry, it will all work out. Trust me!"

The sound of a car horn brought the couple out of the greenhouse. It was Conrad, and he had a very good-looking woman with him. They went to meet their first visitors. Conrad did the introductions. "Elizabeth, this young lady is Captain Dale Swan. She's not wearing an Army uniform, but nevertheless she is a captain in the Army."

Elizabeth extended her hand to Dale and was outwardly pleasant. She felt a little uncomfortable with this person, this captain who had been in Korea with Erik. Dale Swan was very feminine, pretty and seemed very self assured. *This will bear watching,* she thought to herself.

"Hello, Dale. Hi, Conrad." Erik greeted them and led them into the house.

"Let me show you around!" Together they all made the rounds of all the rooms then out to the greenhouse area.

Conrad was impressed and said so. "Erik, you have a splendid place here. I think that Jim Claudier really enjoyed creating this place for you!"

"Yes! We are very satisfied with his design and his supervision to see that everything was done right. He charged me a good fee for his work, but I think it's worth it." After a two-hour tour of the house and grounds, Erik asked, "Anybody hungry? Elizabeth and I are starving!"

"By all means! I know of a really nice place to dine, not too far from here," Conrad volunteered. Taking Dale by the arm, he led her back to his car. Erik and Elizabeth locked up the house and got into their car and followed Conrad. Conrad was true to his word and led them to a small inn that had an alpine look and atmosphere. The inn also offered bed and breakfast. The dining area was small and cozy with Swiss decor. The innkeeper showed them to a table, and lit the candle, which was fitted into an old wine bottle. Conrad ordered a bottle of Moselle wine that was brought to the table in a wine bucket to attain the right degree of chilling.

Since Conrad had been at the inn before, he did the honors of ordering for all. An appetizer of small mountain trout was followed by a German type salad and dressing. The meal was Viennese roast veal, complemented with young asparagus and potatoes with butter and parsley. Dessert and coffee followed, and of course, a glass of cognac. After another coffee and cognac, Elizabeth commented that it was getting late and she did not fancy a long drive back, especially since they had all had quite a few drinks.

Conrad gave Dale a quick glance and was sure her expression said, *Let's stay.*

"We can stay here if you like. It is rather quaint but clean, and the breakfast they serve is very good too," Conrad stated. Both Erik and Elizabeth nodded their okay.

"Let me go check to make sure that there is room at the inn." Returning, Conrad said, "Yes they have accommodations, and I took the liberty of making the arrangements." That decided, they switched to cocktails and after a while the restaurant was preparing to close for the evening. The innkeeper showed them to their rooms, and Erik raised his eyebrows at Conrad when Dale and he entered the same room. Catching Erik's look, Conrad winked his eye as he entered the room with Dale.

Erik and Elizabeth were wakened by the sounds of movement below and looking at the clock radio, saw it was nearly nine a.m. Showered, and changed into their jump suits they went downstairs to the dining area and found Dale and Conrad having coffee on the terrace.

"Ah, there you are, my sleeping beauties," Conrad said. "I was beginning to wonder if I was going to have to roust you out of bed."

"I slept like a tree," Elizabeth volunteered and they all laughed.

"You mean you slept like a log, is how the expression goes," Conrad laughed.

"Tree, log? Who cares. I had a good rest."

The breakfast, when it came, filled the plate. It was an omelet with German sausage, mushrooms, tomatoes and a variety of herbs—all in together and completely round in shape. Hot homemade breakfast rolls, a platter of Danish pastry rings completed the spread, and lots of coffee. Elizabeth jokingly complained that whenever they were out eating with Conrad it was like an eating marathon. Dale agreed, saying, "I think I've put on a couple of pounds in just three meals with him."

Erik was watching Conrad and thought that he had never seen him so happy and relaxed. He knew that Dale could fire up any male and wondered if there was a lasting future for them both—together. Elizabeth also came to a similar conclusion that Dale and Conrad had something going for them, and the uneasiness she felt when she first met Dale faded away.

It was time to return to Four Winds. Erik and Elizabeth reminded Dale and Conrad about the next weekend party, said goodbye and headed back to Maryland. Conrad gave Dale a questioning look and she returned his look with an "I don't care" shrug of her shoulders.

"I have a suggestion," he said, "If you don't mind the drive. I would like to take you down to see the shipyards where the Neilsins built their boats. It's a nice drive and it would be interesting for you. There are some great eating places too."

"You should have been an Army planner. You seem to have knack for improvising," Dale said.

Conrad chuckled and added, "Plus some ulterior motives," his eyes sparkling.

It was a pleasant day and not too cool for April as they drove to Newport News. The shipyard had a skeleton crew of workers on a Sunday. Conrad opened the gate for Dale and they both entered the shipyard. The watchman on duty recognized Conrad and waved to him.

"Nobody in the office today," he called.

"Yeah, I know. We're just going to have a look around, okay?"

"Sure. Go ahead, Mr. Flemming."

Dale was amazed at how big the boats looked when they were out of water. "You say that Erik's father owned this shipyard."

"Yep! Both he and Olaf's son. Erik has no interest in the boat building business. His training in college was electrical engineering. I was surprised to see him wanting to get into agriculture," Conrad said.

"I can tell you from experience that he can fabricate a Christmas tree out of nothing much!" Dale commented.

"That you'll have to explain to me," Conrad responded. Dale told him about Christmas in Korea, before Erik left for a combat unit.

They left the shipyard and headed for Virginia Beach where they stopped off for a late lunch. Following a casual lunch and lots of conversation, Dale thought to herself that she really liked Conrad very much. *True, he is a bit older than I am, but I feel very comfortable and safe with him!*

"I think we should start back to Baltimore. We can freshen up at my place, go out to dinner and who knows," he ended, his voice trailing off. Dale didn't answer; she just nodded her head and smiled. Whenever Dale smiled like that, Conrad felt a tugging on his heartstrings.

Arriving at Conrad's apartment, he asked Dale how she was fixed for her clothing, eyeing her overnight bag.

"Oh, I have another bag in the trunk of my car," she said as she went over to her car and pulled out a Pullman size suitcase.

Conrad hurried over to carry her bag up to his apartment. Dale showered, dressed, and did her make-up. She finally relinquished the bathroom so that Conrad could freshen up also. Conrad thought it would be nice if their relationship could continue as it had for the past few days. A startling thought entered his mind: he found instead of panic, he could enjoy spending a lifetime with someone like Dale.

When Conrad had finished his dressing he found Dale had prepared a drink for both of them.

"I hope you don't mind my helping myself," she said. "I made a couple of gin and tonics."

"That's fine, I like one every now and then," he said.

Finishing their drinks, they departed to drive to Chez Gustav, Conrad's favorite restaurant. Another drink, followed by an appetizer, and they settle into a leisurely dinner. Dale, Conrad noticed, had a good appetite and enjoyed her food. Again, that thought crossed his mind. *I would like to have her in my life permanently!*

Returning to the apartment, they talked about the past days' events over a few cocktails.

"Tell me about your plans to leave the Army," he asked.

"Well, in two months time I either reenlist or finish my six years and get out of the army. Everything is on the fence right now. I had planned to scout around and check the business potential before I made any kind of decision."

"You had mentioned something about investigations and starting your own business," Conrad pressed.

"I'm not sure exactly! I have a solid background in the intelligence field, and I have other complementary skills that I thought would be helpful, even a minor in law."

Conrad was very thoughtful for a few minutes and questioned Dale about her background in law. He found that while she was somewhat knowledgeable, her law background was a bit thin.

"Dale," he said, "I am entertaining an idea that might interest you. Before I go further, let me ask you what you think about this. Sinking your teeth into a split job. First, learning to become a paralegal plus working as a private investigator—not as a private eye, but as an investigator for a law firm?"

Dale was silent for several minutes and then asked, "What do you have in mind?"

"My law firm could use a paralegal, and we also hire independent investigators to work for the firm to gather various kinds of information that we might need to settle a claim or for defense of a client," he responded.

"Are you offering me a job?"

"At this point, I'm just thinking out loud. Would you be interested in this kind of work?"

"To be truthful, I would be interested in the investigative stuff, but I have my doubts about having the skills as a paralegal, and wouldn't want to get stuck in a filing clerk job," she said.

"When I said paralegal, I was referring to a more than casual knowledge in a law practice. As an investigator, you would be extremely valuable with skills and knowledge of the finer points of law, such as knowing what you are looking for and determining what is important to the law firm," Conrad said thoughtfully.

He could see that Dale was struggling with that and was at a loss for providing an answer.

"No need to answer right now," he said, "Just give it some thought and we can talk about it later on if you're interested."

Dale seemed a little bothered, she was thinking out loud now: If she got out of the army and went to work for Conrad's Law firm, he would be her boss. She wondered what impact that would have on their present relationship.

"You have a valid point there," he said.

"Why don't we just sleep on it for now," he said with a smile—the conversation taking a lighter turn.

God! I think I'm in love with this girl, he thought. Conrad took the empty glasses to the kitchen sink and returned to the bedroom to find Dale already settled in for the night.

Monday morning, Conrad was the first to wake up, and he quietly looked at Dale asleep beside him. She looked beautiful. No "Ugh in the morning" looks but clear and lovely features. He slipped out of bed and made his way to the shower and returned to the kitchen to make coffee. Conrad was deep in thought. In slightly less than a week she would be returning from her ten-day leave. The thought of her not being around was gnawing away at him.

"Hell," he muttered as he checked the refrigerator, "I didn't get any food in! He smelled the milk container, and it didn't smell sour.

He had two eggs left and after inspecting the cupboard, found some pancake mix. Hunting through the bottom of the cabinet, he found some pancake syrup. Dale awoke to the smell of fresh coffee and heard the clatter in the kitchen. Conrad peeked around the corner and saw that she was awake and brought her a cup of coffee.

"Pancakes okay?" he asked. "It's the best I can do for now. I didn't get a chance to restock my eating supplies."

"Pancakes will do just fine! I'll get up now and shower, if you don't mind," as she shuffled across the bedroom in his pajama top.

Breakfast out of the way, they both were deep in thought as they sipped more coffee. Conrad seemed to arrive at a decision. "Dale, I would like to say something, but I don't want you to say anything until I finish. Okay?"

Dale nodded, wondering at the frown on Conrad's face and curious about his seriousness.

"Dale, I know that we have known each other for only a short time," he paused and then went on, "I find that I am extremely fond of you and I hope that it is mutual between us!"

"Dale!" another pause, "I know this is sudden, but I am in love with you. I never knew I could be as happy with anyone, as I am with you. I have been single for quite a while and busy with my work. I know I am older than you, I hope not too old for you to consider me as your partner for life."

Conrad went silent, his eyes searching Dale's face for her reaction. Her expression was non-committal, but it softened and a slight smile formed.

"Are you asking to marry me?" she asked softly.

"Yes!" Conrad croaked, anticipating her rejection.

Dale's mind was racing over the past few days, the time she had spent with Conrad and how much she enjoyed his company. Was this the man she could marry and settle down with? she asked herself. *It won't be long before I'm thirty. I don't want a bunch of one-night stands for the next few years! He's kind and gentle with a touch of class—a real gentleman. He's probably in his mid forties and looks younger. Nothing lacking in satisfying me in bed*, she thought. Finally, she realized that Conrad was in a state of anxiety, awaiting her reply.

"I won't say no," she said, "and I won't say yes. How about a maybe?"

Conrad swallowed and just nodded his head.

"I think we should have a chance to get to know each other better, don't you think?"

"You're right, of course," he acknowledged. "I just can't bear the thought of your returning to the Army and maybe getting shipped someplace far away."

Dale found that a tear or two ran down her cheek and she knew that here was a lonely man—one she could love—if their relationship could mature properly.

Regaining his composure, Conrad stated that he had given more thought about Dale leaving the Army and working for the law firm. Seeing the questioning look on Dale's face, he continued.

"What I have in mind is to train you in general law practice, and little by little phase you into such things as real estate legal work. Also investigative activities that would likely require you to move about, conduct personal interviews, get statements from witnesses or anyone involved or concerned with what we are investigating. The investigation part requires you to take the initiative with only a little assistance from the law office. With your background, army experience and ability to communicate, I think you could handle it quite well. Of course, I also have an ulterior motive," smiling at Dale, he went on.

"We would be sort of working together and if our relationship should blossom—as I hope it will, and then it would be just great. By the way," Conrad continued, "The starting salary would be eight hundred a week, plus expenses. Investigations that lead to winning our case would result in a bonus for their efforts."

Dale viewed this potential job as both challenging and varied—not the same old thing, day after day. She already decided to accept Conrad's job offer, but didn't say so. Instead, she said, "I am a little concerned about our personal relationship conflicting with the job. If I resign from the Army and take the position and then six months down the road our relationship goes sour, you could send me on my way and I would have nothing to fall back on. Would you be willing to negotiate an employment agreement, so that if you change your mind, I would at least get a severance to make a new start?"

"See!" responded Conrad. "You're already applying good logic and showing knowledge of legal matters. Sure! I wouldn't have it any other way!" Dale flashed a bright smile that brought a good feeling to Conrad.

Dale's mind was racing. Thinking out loud again, she said, "I shouldn't use up all my leave time, but go back early and put in my papers to resign. I will be paid for any unused leave time I have coming, and that is about fifty days. Let's see, I'll need to update my wardrobe with more civilian clothes," and seeing the amused expression on Conrad's face, she laughed and said, "I have to think about all these little things. Don't laugh!"

Conrad closed the distance to Dale and took her in his arms. "Dale, I have never been happier about anything in my whole life. Except when I discovered sex," qualifying his statement. "Getting married would be the next high point in my life."

Conrad thought about the VA problem concerning Erik.

"Dale, I think it would be a good idea for you not to go back to Fort Belvoir so soon. Wait until at least Tuesday. The reason is that I want to contact Dr. Sidney Perkins at the VA Hospital in Washington and arrange a meeting between Perkins and this R. R. Roberts. I would like you there when I confront Roberts. How about it?"

"Sure! I have no problem with that. I can handle Triple R Roberts without any problem."

"Okay, that's settled. How would you like to take a little drive out to Four Winds this afternoon so you can at least see the place and get a first meeting with Bernice and George Templeton?"

Dale's main concern was "How shall I dress?"

"You look great in everything I have seen on you"—*and off you,* he thought—"dress 'casual,' and you will look just fine."

Conrad made a courtesy call to Four Winds and asked if it was okay to drop in on short notice. The response was as expected. "We will get there around two or two thirty," he said. Dale dressed in a fawn-colored plaid skirt with a sweater and cardigan to match, complemented by a pair of penny loafers.

"You look like you are ready to play a game of golf," Conrad observed. "By the way, what sports do you like?" he asked.

"I'm a twenty-two handicap in the women's league and so-so on the tennis courts. I fenced in college, but never since. I like to go to the Skeet Range and shoot clay birds occasionally," she concluded.

Conrad was delighted! "I love to play golf, but haven't been working at it because I didn't have anyone to play with before. I also play a little tennis and racquet ball," he said, patting his stomach. Yes! The chemistry was working!

They arrived at Four Winds at two on the dot. Dale was amazed at the lovely approach to the house and the house itself. She knew it would be grand, but this was more than she expected. They were greeted by the household staff and directed to the enclosed terrace where the Templetons and Elizabeth were busy sorting out all kinds of wedding magazines and brochures.

"Looks like someone is preparing for a wedding," Dale observed. Conrad introduced Dale to Bernice and George Templeton.

"My, what a pretty girl," Bernice exclaimed.

Surprisingly, Dale blushed, and it did not escape notice.

Just then, Erik came in from outdoors. He was carrying a little plant that he had started from seed. He and Queenie had prepared a very rich and fertile soil for the seeds to germinate.

"Queenie wanted me to plant a dozen seeds, but I only planted one," he said. "These are special seeds, and I don't want to waste them!"

One stem extended six inches out of the soil.

"What kind of a plant or flower is that?" asked Conrad.

"I really can't answer that because I'm not sure myself," Erik responded. "I had the seeds in a little container, and I thought that they were very valuable. This seed germinated in only seven days and broke the surface two days ago, and just look at it, it's already six inches high. I am really curious to see what it will look like."

Martha arrived on the scene to ask what refreshments everyone wanted.

Conrad declined, saying that he and Dale had lunch an hour ago. "But I wouldn't say no to a gin and tonic."

"I wouldn't mind one also," Dale added.

Responding to Dale's questions, Elizabeth told her about the clothing, travel plans, and proposed wedding ceremony. Both women were soon engrossed in "girls" talk about the details. Conrad had been admiring Dale from where he sat; turning, he saw that Bernice was watching him with that knowing look on her face. Bernice then winked at Conrad, and he actually felt his face get warm and guessed that he had blushed.

Bernice got up and asked Conrad to accompany her around the garden area. As they strolled along, Bernice said, "I am a trained observer, and I see something nice brewing with you and that lovely creature, Dale. Am I correct?" she asked.

"Well … yes, sort of," he replied. "Dale is going to get out of the Army and come to work for the law firm."

"I think that there's more to that than meets the eye," Bernice chuckled.

"Well, I am very fond of her," he said somewhat lamely. "We will have to see how things go, I guess."

"Laddie," Bernice remarked, "you've been a bachelor too long. You need a fine, spirited woman to make an honest man of you, and I think that you have just met her!"

After a quick conference with Martha, Bernice announced that everyone was to stay for dinner and that they were going to have lobsters that came down from Maine. George selected two bottles from the wine cellar and put them to chill in preparation for dinner. After a while Dale detached herself from Elizabeth and joined Conrad, who was sort of pacing outside.

"You look like someone who needs company," she said. Conrad's face immediately brightened. They strolled through the massive garden area and stopped by the little bench and sat down. Dale reached out and turned Conrad's face toward hers and tenderly kissed his lips. She could feel the immediate and hungry response from Conrad as he returned her kiss.

Yes! I could love this man … maybe I do, already, she thought. It was peaceful and serene just sitting looking at the flowers and shrubbery starting to show the signs of spring. The bell at the house clanged a few times, and Conrad got to his feet.

"That's for us," he said. "Let's go back to the house."

Drinks were being served as they arrived, and Dale and Conrad helped themselves. Bernice reminded them both that they were expected on the coming Friday to her weekend party.

"If it is possible, it would be nice for you to get here around seven in the evening for dinner." Looking at Dale, she said, "I know that you would have a long way to drive from Fort Belvoir, so if you can't make dinner, come anyway; we will be waiting for you."

"I don't think that will be a problem," Dale said with a smile. "I am putting in my resignation from the Army, and Fridays are usually slow days, so I will leave after lunch time."

Erik and Elizabeth seemed surprised by the announcement that Dale would be leaving the Army.

"What are your plans for the near future then?" Erik asked.

"Well, I have a job opportunity that I am going to accept, and I will be working in the Baltimore area," she said, still not revealing everything.

"Well, I'll be! That's marvelous!" exclaimed George. "Then we'll get to see you out here more often!"

"You are so kind and hospitable," Dale demurred.

Conrad was close by and gently squeezed her elbow. Again, Bernice caught the little exchange. Conrad changed the subject and told Erik that he had contacted Dr. Sidney Perkins of the VA Hospital and that he has arranged a Tuesday meeting with this R. R. Roberts.

"R. R. Roberts? Boy, that name sounds familiar," Erik said.

"Try Triple R Roberts," Dale piped in.

"Triple R Roberts. What a pain! I seem to remember that he really abused his position, and of course, Dale told me how his career came to an end."

"I would like you to meet me at my office at nine-thirty in the morning, this Tuesday. We will be going over to the VA Hospital for a meeting and confrontation with this R. R. Roberts. Dale has agreed to be there also," Conrad announced.

Dale had to relate details about Colonel Robert's abrupt exit from the Army. George reminded Conrad that if they ran into trouble, they should let him know the details. He was not without high-level influence in the government.

"Dinner is being served!" Martha announced.

Everyone entered the dining area, and Bernice directed who should sit where. All the place settings at the table included picks and nutcrackers for the lobsters. Dale had never seen so many broiled lobsters at one table. They were bigger lobsters than the small lobster tails normally served in restaurants. They weighed around two pounds each. Garlic-infused drawn butter, heated by its own small candle, was placed before each dinner guest. George handled the serving of wine while Martha brought hot vegetables and rolls to the table. Following this memorable dinner, Martha served a special flan dessert that was flamed with a spot of cognac brandy. It was nearly eight-thirty before they pushed themselves away from the table and went onto the enclosed patio for a coffee and brandy.

Glancing at his watch, Conrad announced that he and Dale would have to get going.

"A work day tomorrow for me," he said.

Dale thanked the Templetons for their hospitality and said that she would be looking forward to the coming weekend party. Dale made a special effort to give Elizabeth a hug and whispered to her, "Can you keep a secret?" Surprised, Elizabeth nodded. She walked part of the way with Dale. Dale said, "Conrad has told me that he is in love with me and wants to tie the knot. Please don't tell anyone. I am trying to deal with that and the fact that I am going to get out of the Army. It's much to think about!"

Elizabeth was so surprised and delighted. "Conrad is such a nice guy. It's easy to see how you two get along. Are you engaged or what?" Elizabeth asked.

"No! He only asked me this morning, and I've spent most of the day trying to adjust to it all. I want to be sure, not so much for my sake, but for his. I wouldn't want him to get hurt. In some ways Conrad is kind of innocent and vulnerable, but that makes me like him even more."

Elizabeth gave Dale a hug and said, "Your secret is safe with me, but let me know when it is no longer a secret because I'll be bursting at the seams to tell Bernice."

CHAPTER 27

Business First!

Dale and Conrad were busy going over some documents when Erik arrived at the law office.

"Ah, there you are, Erik! Dale prepared a brief concerning both of your relationships with Colonel Roberts when you were stationed at Fort Lewis in Washington State. I have sent a letter to Dr. Perkins so that he can read it ahead of time!"

"Whose car are we going in?" Erik asked.

"It will take us over an hour to get there, and I know the way, so we'll take my car," Conrad said as they rose to leave. "Dale will be following in her car because she will go on to Fort Belvoir from the VA."

When they arrived at the VA Hospital, they took the elevator to Dr. Perkins office. The secretary was expecting them and showed them in to the conference room. "Dr. Perkins will join you in a few moments," she said. "I will tell him that you are here."

In a few moments the door opened and Dr. Perkins entered with two other men. Dr. Perkins made the introductions to all present in a business-like manner. Ex-colonel Ruppert R. Roberts looked flushed and uneasy. The other man was Matthew Crasko, R. R. Roberts' boss and the head of the VA Special Services Department.

Dr. Perkins then proceeded with the known facts.

"I have completed a week-long study of all details concerning First Lieutenant Neilsin. His injuries were sustained while he was serving in Korea. His entire medical history following his return to the US have been made available to us. I have not found anything inconsistent with how this case was handled, and I have great concern that the Veteran Administration has spent the time, money, and effort to make some sort of case out of this."

Ruppert Roberts tried his best not to look at Dale or Erik and just stared at the wall ahead of him.

"I have talked with Lieutenant Neilsin's attorney, Mr. Conrad Flemming, who brought this matter to my attention."

Dr. Perkins directed his next comments to Matthew Crasko. "As I have not found any justification whatsoever for this unfortunate situation, I have to be concerned about the motivation behind such actions. This is not the first complaint I have heard regarding how certain matters have been handled by

Mr. Roberts, and I have asked Mr. Flemming to present some matters that might explain the *why* in this matter."

Conrad cleared his throat and, looking at Ruppert Roberts, he started by stating how uncooperatively and rudely Roberts had spoken to him on the telephone. Next, he pointed out that Colonel Roberts had diverted Erik Neilsin and Dale Swan, both lieutenants at the time, from their overseas assignments.

"Further, Colonel Roberts was upset with Neilsin because of his friendly relationship with his fellow officer, Dale Swan. When Lieutenant Swan thwarted Colonel Robert's unwanted advances, Roberts became offensive and made a spectacle of himself before the deputy commander at Fort Lewis. The general gave Roberts the options: a general court martial or voluntary retirement. Roberts chose the retirement but has held a grudge ever since. I maintain that his coming across Erik Neilsin's file gave him an opportunity to seek some sort of revenge against him because he was a close friend of Dale Swan." Conrad paused and looked at Dr. Perkins.

"What do you have to say about that statement, Roberts?" Dr. Perkins asked.

Roberts was flustered and unable to get himself together. He had clearly not expected this sort of confrontation. He turned to Dale Swan, and his look had hatred written all over it. Consumed with loathing, Roberts murmured, "You bitch!" It was audible to everyone around the table.

Matthew Crasko finally spoke up and said, "As far as my department is concerned, this matter is finished, and I apologize for any aggravation and inconvenience this has caused you all."

Dr. Perkins acknowledged his statement with a nod of his head.

Matthew Crasko continued, "Roberts! Your tenure at the Veterans Administration is going to be ended. I am submitting a request for your dismissal from the VA. If you want to fight it—fine! But if you do, your reputation is at stake, not to mention that the attorney over there"—he pointed to Conrad—"might decide to personally take you to court and sue you. I want your response in my office by one o'clock today."

They got up, ready to leave, all, except Ruppert R. Roberts. They left the conference room, and Conrad shook Dr. Perkin's hand.

"You were absolutely marvelous in there, Sidney! Have you ever thought about becoming a real professional and taking up law?"

"You shyster, accident-chasing lawyers are all the same," Dr. Perkins responded. "You owe me a big dinner now—none of these rush-job, lunchtime meals."

"You got it, Sidney! I owe you a big one. Even a few drinks!"

They waved goodbye and left for the exit.

Erik was delighted at the outcome and relieved of the stress. He was eager to get back to Four Winds. Conrad asked Erik to wait for him in the car; he wanted to see Dale off on her trip back to Fort Belvoir. Dale sat behind the wheel of her Studebaker, and Conrad leaned in to kiss her.

"I will miss you so much until Friday rolls around," he said.

Dale kissed him back and touched his cheek gently. "I'll call you when I get back to Fort Belvoir. If I can't get you at the office I'll call you at home." Putting the car in gear, she pulled out.

Erik and Conrad rode back to the law office, and Erik got into his car and left for Four Winds.

Conrad had talked with his other law partners, and they went along with Conrad's wish to hire Dale Swan. They had seen Dale and told Conrad that she was certainly easy to look at—a nice addition to the office! The rest of the week went quickly for Conrad, who busily tackled cases that he had put on hold.

His legal secretary complained. "You leave me with little to do, and then you overload me! I hope you don't want me to work overtime?"

"No, no, no! You always complain. I either give you too much work or too little," he responded.

She changed the subject. "So, when is Lady Beautiful coming to work for us?"

"After she leaves the US Army, finds a pad, and is settled in. When that will be, I'm not sure," Conrad said.

Getting serious for a minute, Gloria asked, "Boss, it's getting serious isn't it? I can see it in your face, in your manner, and everything. If it is, it's a good thing! Everyone needs someone close. You have had no one, except me," she said jokingly, "and I'm married and spoken for!"

"For Christ's sake, Gloria." Conrad was blushing. "The way you go on!" He entered his office to get back to work.

"Conrad? A call for you on line two, Dr. Perkins," Gloria's voice announced.

"Hello, Sidney!" Conrad boomed. "You wanting to collect on that meal already?"

Dr. Perkins voice was serious. "Just thought I should let you know that Roberts resigned from the VA a few days ago. Apparently he started hitting the bars and drinking pretty heavily. The police found him last night in an alley in Georgetown. Looks like he was mugged and left for dead. He was taken to Emergency but didn't make it."

"That's a lousy way to go and a lousy conclusion," Conrad said. "Thanks for letting me know. The only good thing is that Roberts won't be around to cause any more grief. Okay, I'll be seeing you."

Conrad went back to work, trying to concentrate on finishing a legal brief. Glancing at the clock, he saw it was 3:30 already. It was Friday, and Dale would be on her way to Four Winds for the weekend party at the Templetons. He remembered suddenly that he had not packed anything for the weekend.

He made his mind up and quickly put his work back into the folders and announced to Gloria that he had to rush home to get ready for the weekend.

"You men!" Gloria scolded. "You leave everything for the last minute. I'm telling you, I hope that girl gets you straightened out."

"For Christ's sake, Gloria, give me a break! All you frustrated women think about is giving us single guys a hard time," Conrad responded.

"Well, someone has to keep you straight, and it might as well be me," she snorted.

He was not winning this verbal battle with Gloria, so Conrad left the office to go home.

The first thing he did was pack a small bag with clothing and left it open to put his toilet articles in after he showered, shaved, and changed. As he was toweling himself dry and splashing on some cologne, Conrad thought he heard his doorbell ring. Opening the bathroom door, he heard the doorbell ring again. Wrapped in his beach towel, he opened the door, and there stood Dale.

"Hi, lover! Are you Adam, dressed like that?" she asked.

"Dale! Come in, come in! I thought you might be going straight to the Templetons."

"I thought I might just ride there with you and keep my options open," she said with a glint in her eyes.

"I'll be a few minutes longer. Excuse me while I finish getting ready," he said and left for the bedroom.

A short while later he came out dressed, suitcase in hand, and found that Dale had made them both a drink. She brought over his drink, and as he reached for it, she said, puckering her lips, "Aren't you going to thank me for it?"

He thanked her for a long while until she pulled herself away from him. Once they finished the drinks, they left for Four Winds.

"When is the wedding date?" she asked.

Conrad nearly drove off the road. Stuttering a little, he asked, "Th-th-the wedding date?"

"Yes, when are Elizabeth and Erik getting married?"

"Oh ... s-sorry, it's a week after Easter. About three weeks away," Conrad said lamely.

Dale chuckled to herself because she realized that Conrad thought she was referring to themselves.

"Conrad, I submitted my resignation. In two weeks I will be a civilian. I really have to get my act together, because I will have so much to do. I have to find a place to live ..." She groaned. "And I don't even own a piece of furniture. I'll have to get a furnished place. What a mess!"

"Not to worry—you have a place to stay," he said. "You don't have to go rushing around trying to find a place just yet. You can stay here … permanently, if you want."

Dale flashed Conrad a smile but said nothing.

Four Winds was all lit up, inside and out, when they arrived. They were greeted by Penny and shown into the main living room, where others had already gathered. Elizabeth looked a little distressed, Dale thought.

"Anything wrong?" she inquired.

Bernice told them that Elizabeth had expected her sister to be her matron of honor, but that her sister called to say that her husband and family would not be able to participate in the wedding. Elizabeth's brother-in-law would be leaving for the Philippines for about three months. The whole family was going and would be leaving before the wedding date.

Bernice suddenly tugged Elizabeth's elbow and got her off to one side for a quick chat. Elizabeth rejoined everyone with a more cheerful and thoughtful look.

"Dale," she called. "Could I talk to you for a few moments?"

Both women walked into the dining room to talk, and Elizabeth asked Dale if she would do the honor of being her maid of honor.

At first Dale panicked a little. "I would be pleased to be your maid of honor, but I have nothing suitable to wear, and I'm getting out of the service in two weeks."

"That will not be a problem, because the gowns for all were ordered and only need the finishing touches or adjustments. If you have one day to spare, Bernice said we can get everything ready and fitted."

"Then I guess it's a go!" Dale said with a grin.

Elizabeth announced to everyone that Dale had agreed to be her maid of honor. Conrad was pleased, and Erik was surprised. George looked at Bernice and could see that his wife had been at it again. There was a lot of talk about the wedding plans. Dale would be a maid of honor and Penny would be the flower girl. Conrad was asked to be the best man, so the match would be perfect. Erik's family would be coming from Virginia, and an invitation, airplane ticket, and travel expenses had been sent to Nursing Sister Menckler in Heidelberg so that she could attend the wedding. A similar invitation was sent to Tante Marie, Elizabeth's aunt, who agreed to travel with Sister Menckler. They would arrive on the Wednesday three days before the wedding and would spend an extra week visiting in America.

Since Elizabeth had round-trip tickets to Hawaii for two—courtesy of her Las Vegas win at the big wheel—she and Erik decided they would go to Hawaii for their honeymoon. Examining the tickets, George snorted, "These are economy seats! Let me handle these arrangements for you." In typical

George Templeton style, he contacted the airline and upgraded the seats to first class and upgraded the hotel reservations in Hawaii to the honeymoon suite, along with a few additional perks.

The weather was cooperating and the temperature increased with a promise of a warm Easter and the hope for a nice day for a wedding, which was only a week later. Following a magnificent dinner, Erik presented Elizabeth with an engagement ring. It was a beautiful, three-quarter-carat blue-white diamond set in platinum and eighteen-karat gold. He had purchased it at Tiffany's. Elizabeth was thrilled with the ring, but when Erik discussed wedding bands, she insisted that she wanted to wear the gold wedding band she had kept and cherished so long. Erik was a little put out about it, as he wanted her to have something more substantial, but Elizabeth stood her ground and insisted that she wanted only the simple gold band to be put on her finger during the wedding. Bernice understood the details and significance and agreed with Elizabeth.

"You're letting me off cheap!" Erik quipped.

Elizabeth responded with a tender kiss. *He doesn't know that this was the ring that Pat gave me. I can't explain why it is so important,* she reasoned.

The weekend activities were nearly over. Elizabeth suggested to Dale that she could get fitted for her maid of honor dress a few days after she was discharged from the Army.

Conrad and Dale said goodbye Sunday evening and headed back to Baltimore. Dale advised him that she had asked for Monday off, so she did not have to drive straight back to Fort Belvoir.

"Since I only have another week, I'll have a light workload," she said.

Conrad was pleased that Dale would be staying over until the next morning. When they had settled down to relax in Conrad's apartment, he handed her a document to read. It was an employment agreement that he had prepared and signed; his law partners had also signed it. She read the entire document, which covered very broad and favorable conditions and a guarantee of employment for Dale. Conrad handed Dale a pen; she signed the two copies of the document, and he handed her back a copy to keep.

"There!" he said. "That makes it legal and binding!"

"You are a sweetheart, Conrad, and very generous as well! I hope that I measure up to your expectations."

"Let's sleep on it, shall we?"

Granville Mental Institution

The ward orderly unlocked Cliff Roberts's door and brought him the bad news that his brother, Ruppert, had died as a result of a mugging.

"Fortunately your brother left a trust fund to take care of your needs," the orderly said.

Cliff was quiet and did not show any emotion. The orderly left.

During the hours that passed, Cliff read his brother's last letter again, in which he told about Dale Swan and Eric Neilsin being at the hearing and that they were responsible for all his troubles. Gradually, his brother's death sank in, and Cliff's hatred and frustration focused on Dale and Erik. It dominated his every thought. Cliff had always been dependent on his older brother. Now he had to act on his own. He spent many months thinking of how to escape and he studied the guards daily routine and a plan to steal one of the dinner knives. The knives were dull and hardly could cut anything, but Cliff had a plan for that also - but first, get a knife.

When it was time for Cliff's section to eat, he managed to steal an extra knife, hiding it under his food tray. When he was not being watched, Cliff slipped the knife into his sock and pulled the trouser leg over it.

In the evening when the guards were at their station, which was away from his locked room, Cliff went to his cache of fingernail emery boards. He had asked for one several other times and kept them just for this purpose. He used the emery boards to file an edge in several places on the knife blade. It took all four emery boards to file four sharp sections. The blade had sort of a serrated edge and Cliff thought it would serve its purpose in his planned escape

After lunch, he went through all his belongings and found the little envelopes of money his brother sent him. He counted out the money, and it came to over five hundred dollars. He also had a key for a safe deposit box his brother had entrusted to him to keep.

When it was time for Cliff's evening meal, the orderly came, opened the door, and beckoned Cliff to accompany him.

"Just a minute, I have to tie my shoe laces," Cliff said.

The orderly was looking down the hall, his back to Cliff. Quietly and swiftly Cliff withdrew the hidden knife, grabbed the orderly from behind by his hair, and forcefully ran the blade across his throat. The orderly clutched at his throat as Cliff dragged him back into his room and kept slashing his throat. The orderly sank to his knees, and the only sound was the gurgling coming from the dying man. Cliff grabbed the keys chained to the orderly's belt. This was his way out!

CHAPTER 28

Getting a discharge from the military after six years was not a small task, Dale found out. She had to hand-carry documents and several types of clearance papers through the various branches. She had to be debriefed from her highly classified clearance of Top Secret and check with the Finance section for her full pay, unused leave time, and other pay details. She was advised that her status in the military would be automatically transferred to the US Army Inactive Reserve. This meant in times of national emergency, she could be recalled back to active duty. It was four o'clock in the afternoon before she had completed clearing the military installation and took her last look at Fort Belvoir before putting her car in gear and leaving for Baltimore.

It was after 10 p.m. when she finally arrived at Conrad's apartment, but the lights were on and the door opened as she approached. Conrad was waiting at the door, a big grin on his face.

"Welcome back to civilian life," he said, giving Dale a big hug and a kiss. "You look awfully tired."

"Yeah! It has been a long day, and I've never walked so much and waited so long for paperwork to get done," she said, collapsing on the couch.

"How about a hot shower and a nightcap?" Conrad asked.

"That sounds good! Make it a double scotch with a splash of soda, please," she said as she headed for the bathroom.

A short while later she emerged wearing Conrad's bathrobe. "I forgot to take my nightie. I'll change in the bedroom."

God! She looks terrific in just my bathrobe. Conrad juggled dates in his mind, thinking about wedding plans of his own. *Don't rush it*, he cautioned himself. *Let her adjust to the idea!*

A few minutes later Dale came out of the bedroom wearing a black lace nightgown with a matching negligee. Her blonde hair and fair features completed the vision. She was absolutely stunning. Conrad stood staring at her for a second or two before responding.

"You are beautiful!" was all he could muster.

The next morning Conrad called in to his office that he would be in later than usual.

"Is she with you?" asked Gloria.

"Give it a rest, Gloria! It was a long and late night for everyone."

"Everything's fine here. Take your time," Gloria said.

The day before, Conrad had managed to go to the supermarket, where he picked up breakfast items—fresh bread, eggs, and butter. He got the coffee brewing and set to making breakfast. He heard the shower going, so he knew Dale was up and about. She came into the kitchen while toweling her hair dry and wearing his white terrycloth bathrobe. She came up to Conrad and rose on her toes to kiss him. As they kissed, his hands explored the inside of his bathrobe.

Yep! Just as I thought, naked as a jaybird!

"Hey! Not so fast, mister. You have to feed me first," was her reaction. But she did not push herself away.

"Dale, God, how I love you," he said, expecting another kiss.

"You're burning the bacon," she admonished him, "and I'm hungry."

"Okay, okay! Anything for a peaceful life," he said as he started putting the breakfast on the table.

Without thinking, Dale said, "This apartment is a bit small for the two of us. We should get a bigger place." Realizing what she was saying, she looked at Conrad, and he was beaming all over.

"Does that mean what I think it means?" he asked.

Dale hesitated with a look of resignation on her face. "Welllll, I guess we could say we are engaged," she allowed.

Conrad suddenly thought, "You know wh-what," he stammered and then jumped up and ran to the telephone. He dialed a number and said, "Hey, Louis, Conrad Flemming here. The place upstairs, the penthouse. Yeah, I know it's not a penthouse, but it seems like one. How many rooms up there? Louis, do me a favor and bring me up the keys. I want to go up there and take a look. Okay? Fine!" Conrad hung up the phone.

Dale, who had overheard some of the conversation, gave Conrad a *So, explain* look.

On the top floor, he told her, was a large apartment that had its own terrace and more rooms than this place. Louis, the building caretaker would be bringing the keys so they could take a look at the place.

Within a few minutes the doorbell rang, and Louis was there with the keys.

"Don't make any mess, Conrad," he said. "It was repainted and cleaned last week."

After changing into casual clothing and slippers they walked up two flights of stairs. The top floor had only one apartment. The door opened to reveal a grand foyer with two closets: The foyer led to the living room area. The rooms were noticeably bigger than Conrad's were. There was a small dining room just off the kitchen. The kitchen, too, was bigger, and Dale said she liked that the kitchen had a bar countertop with ample space for a breakfast nook.

French doors off the living room led to a terrace about sixteen feet wide and eight feet in depth. *A nice lounging or dining area*, thought Dale. The bedroom was big and had its own bathroom and double closets. It also had a balcony with a different view of the city. There was another bedroom, a bit smaller than the master bedroom. Next to the kitchen was a powder room with sink and toilet. Dale was very impressed with the apartment. Yes, indeed! It was sort of a penthouse apartment. The rooms were bright with the morning sunshine, and it had a cheerful atmosphere.

"Well, what do you think?" Conrad asked.

Dale was quick to reply. "This place is simply gorgeous! One thing though," she commented. "It's a long hike up and down those steps every day."

"Not so, not so," chuckled Conrad, leading Dale to the apartment front door. Across the hall was another wide door. It was a small elevator. Conrad explained that the elevator went from the basement to the ground level and then to the third, fourth, and top floor. Conrad's apartment, on the second floor, did not have access to the elevator.

"You seem to be knocking down all my defenses," Dale said. "I guess I'm going to have to give in and marry you after all."

"That's the plan! There was never any doubt in my mind. Just the *when*!"

"I really like this apartment," Dale answered in response.

"If you agree, I'll put a deposit on it, and we can start to get it ready for when we get married, which I hope will be soon."

Dale grinned and said, "How about a June wedding?"

Conrad hugged the breath out of Dale in his enthusiastic response.

"If you don't mind, we'll have to change the decor a little. Let's see ... drapes, new set of dishes for everyday ... a better set for company."

Her mind was already racing with details to furnish and decorate. They returned downstairs, trying out the elevator. The elevator was a small Otis, not very wide, but had a little depth to it and was designed to carry three or four people.

Louis heard the elevator coming down and met them as the door opened. "Well, what do you think about the place?" he asked.

"We like it," Conrad said. "Now tell me what the damage is on it."

"It isn't cheap." Louis said, "It's three times what you're paying for your place. Taking the elevator usage into consideration and the privacy you will have, it brings a big rental."

"I want the place because Dale and I are getting married, and we will need a bigger apartment. Anyone spoken for it yet?" Conrad asked.

"Nope, not yet! Someone's looked at the place, but they haven't said anything yet."

"Okay," Conrad said. "We want the place, but I can't move in just yet. I will have to make arrangements for movers, some more furniture, and things like that."

"Well ... let's see. Seeing as you're already renting here and as soon as you move out I'll have to have your apartment redone, I can work something out, but you'll have to pay a holding fee for the apartment."

"That is very agreeable, Louis! I like your way of thinking," Conrad said. "You get some paperwork on the new lease arrangements, and we'll work out all the details."

Later, Conrad dropped by Louis' apartment and gave him an envelope containing a twenty-dollar bill. "It's for your trouble," Conrad said.

Louis liked Conrad, who was considerate and generous too.

Dale was off to Four Winds to meet with Elizabeth and Bernice to talk wedding arrangements. Bernice had the owner of a specialty bridal shop come out to the house along with the head seamstress to insure the dresses were fitted perfectly. Bernice didn't want to miss any of the excitement or input to the wedding plans. Dale was beaming with exciting news of her own. "You seem very excited about something that you're bursting to tell us!"

Dale gave a hearty laugh and said, "Yes—Conrad has asked me to marry him, and I said yes!"

Elizabeth, Bernice, and Penny squealed with excitement.

"Have you set a date yet?" Penny asked.

"We are talking about a June wedding," she announced.

"Splendid, just simply splendid," Bernice exclaimed, her mind now going into overdrive. Bernice went flying out of the room to track down her husband and tell him the news.

"Now, Bernice," George cautioned, "don't start making other people's plans for them. I can see your mind working and scheming. Conrad's a big boy and doesn't need our interference!"

"Yes, I know, darling," she said, "but I am just too thrilled for words!"

"Bloody hell!" Bill Cranfield said when he heard the news. "Around here it's either feast or famine!"

"They make a nice couple, don't you think?" George asked Bill.

"They do indeed. Dale is a handsome woman, to be sure, a real smasher!"

The fitting session took most of the day, and Dale was anxious to get back to Baltimore and her husband to be. Conrad gathered his law partners and all the staff into his office to make the announcement of his coming marriage to Dale Swan. After many questions and answers, he told them that a June wedding was planned, but no specific date as yet. Gloria, being practical, asked Conrad where he was going to get married.

"You do belong to some church, don't you?" she asked.

Noting the blank expression on Conrad's face, she said, "Don't worry. I'll help you sort things out. I told you how valuable I am to you. You still need nurturing," she finished.

"I swear, Gloria, you're like a nagging mother!" He was not annoyed, but pleased for all her help.

Gloria mentioned that Conrad had done a lot of legal work for one of the local churches for a pittance and more as a charitable accommodation. She suggested that he call on the minister of the church and see about making arrangements for the wedding.

"Good idea! Your are really on the ball," he said.

"Of course I am, and you're only just noticing," she shot back.

Conrad was in a great mood. Nothing could bother him today. He contacted the minister, Dr. Salazar, and announced his plans to get married and thought he might get married at Dr Salazar's Lutheran church. He was not a member of the church, but the minister had discretion on his side and did not hesitate to agree to marry the couple.

"It's about time, too," he added. They had known each other for over ten years. "Maybe I will get to see you sitting in my congregation. Saints be praised!"

Conrad mentally went over a list of guests to invite to the wedding. Then his thoughts turned to the wedding reception, and he found himself getting bogged down with all the details. *I will have to get Dale involved and helping me on this,* he thought. Conrad kept watching the clock and told Gloria that from now on not to make any appointments later than three o'clock. As a single person he had no commitments and often stayed late to accommodate clients, but now, it would be different! He was out of the office before Gloria even had her coat, and he was on his way home. He saw Dale pulling into the driveway as he arrived. She had several grocery bags, and he helped carry two of them.

"What did you do, buy out the supermarket?" he asked.

"Oh, just a few items to stock up the pantry," she said. "More than just breakfast stuff. I'm even going to start baking. I haven't done any baking for years. And," she added, "we are having supper here tonight. We are not going out to eat when we can eat at home."

Conrad couldn't be more pleased and marveled at the thought of coming home to someone, having dinner on the table and being married.

"I'm not saying we are going to eat at home all the time, because you need a little time to cook and prepare a decent meal. Besides, I will be a working gal, too, and you might be home before I am."

He helped Dale put the grocery items away. Fresh milk, steak for tonight, potatoes, vegetables, flour, sugar, spices. The small cabinets were full by the time they put everything away.

"By the way," Dale commented. "I didn't see a refrigerator upstairs, did you?"

"I don't think so, come to think of it," he said with a shrug. "We can shop for a big one. You can pick it out."

"While we're at it," Dale continued, "why don't we get a proper stove with a large oven, too?"

"Sure, why not!" Conrad was very agreeable.

Dale left the following morning on a shopping spree. First order of her several priorities was clothing. She knew what she wanted and did not waste time shopping. Next on her agenda was to check on a stove and refrigerator. She haggled with the appliance store for a better price including delivery and said she would be back to settle the order. Her last stop was at one of the better furniture stores and liked a king size bedroom suite that she thought would be perfect for their new bedroom. *We'll put Conrad's bedroom suite in the other bedroom,* she thought. She also looked at some all-weather outdoor furniture for the terrace.

All in all, she felt that she had a very productive day and was anxious to give Conrad all the news.

"That all sounds good to me," he said. "What kind of money are we talking about?"

"It's not cheap. Sort of middle of the road, but nice! I will chip in and help pay for it," she offered.

Conrad was surprised but pleased that she offered, nevertheless he said it was okay that he could handle it.

"We are going out tonight," Conrad said. "I have an appointment at seven tonight." He corrected himself, "*We* have an appointment tonight, and I don't want to be late."

They stopped by Chez Gustav for a fast, no-frills dinner and left for their appointment. Conrad entered a private parking area reserved "for customers only." Entering, Dale noticed that it was a very nice jewelry store. It was evident that they were expected. The attendant showed them to a display counter with tall, cushioned chairs. He then brought out a tray of very dazzling diamond rings.

"I want you to select several rings that take your fancy," Conrad encouraged. "Then you can narrow it down to the one you want as your engagement ring."

Dale was stunned and a little in awe, having not thought at all about an engagement ring.

"They are so big! Don't we want something a little less expensive?" she inquired.

"No, the size is just right, I think. I can't have you running around with a little chunk of glass on your finger," he said with pride. The jewelry salesman perked up at Conrad's comments.

However, Dale selected four rings with slightly smaller diamonds, but of exquisite design. She then narrowed down her choice to one ring and announced that she thought that was the ring she would like.

"That is a beautiful ring," the salesman said. Conrad raised an eyebrow, thinking that she selected the smaller one because of price.

The salesman said that she had a good eye for quality, as that ring was more expensive than several of the other larger diamond rings. Explaining, the salesman told them that the ring was from the "Empress Series" by Tiffany's. The diamond was the very best in clarity and color and was flawless. It was set in a unique and tasteful design.

"Great!" Conrad acknowledged. "How much?"

"Six thousand five hundred dollars," replied the salesman.

The ring fit Dale's finger perfectly. Conrad took out his checkbook and wrote the check and asked that a certificate of authenticity and appraisal be sent to their address. Dale was rather quiet and speechless as they left the jewelry store. She finally hugged Conrad when they were in the car, and he could see tears running down her cheeks.

"Please don't cry, my darling!"

"Oh, Conrad, the ring is so lovely, and you are so extravagant. That is a lot of money for a ring. I shall be fearful about misplacing or losing it," she said.

"Don't worry, sweetness," he replied. "That's what they have insurance for!"

Dale saw to it that Conrad's tuxedo went to the dry cleaners and that his shoes were up to snuff for Erik and Elizabeth's wedding. The day before the wedding Dale went to stay at Four Winds while Erik joined Conrad at the apartment. The day of the wedding, Erik woke, showered and dressed, and even made the coffee. Conrad, on the other hand, was a nervous wreck.

"My God! Where did I put the rings!"

"Relax, Conrad, they're right on the dresser in front of you," Erik said.

When it was time to leave for Four Winds, Erik volunteered to drive, but Conrad got himself together and said he would drive.

Arriving at Four Winds, they found the entranceway beautifully decorated. The main hallway was also lined with tall plants and flowers all beautifully arranged. Bill Cranfield escorted them into a small room next to the main room. There they waited.

"I'll come and fetch you when it's time for you to come out," he announced and then departed.

"The boys are here," Bill said to Bernice and Elizabeth. "Coo blimey! You do look loverly," he said.

"Thanks, Bill," Elizabeth said. "How's Erik holding up?"

"He's just fine. Can't say the same for Conrad though. He's nervous as a kettle of fish."

Bill left them to attend the arriving guests. A few minutes later, there was a tap on the door, and George Templeton popped his head in.

"Are we ready to get the show on the road?"

"Are we forgetting anything?" Bernice asked.

"Oh my God, yes!" Elizabeth said in near panic. "The gypsy's stone. I want to have it with me."

"You're right," Bernice said and brought the jewelry box to Elizabeth so she could take the stone out. Elizabeth had a tiny cloth bag into which she placed the magical stone. This she tucked away in the top of her wedding gown. All the anxiety seemed to pass and she felt herself in full control, announcing, "I'm ready now!"

CHAPTER 29

Trudy Backley, the organist at a nearby church, had been hired to play the electric piano-organ that the Templetons had in storage. Their daughter Jennifer used to play it, but when she passed away, it was put out of sight.

The ushers seated some of Erik's family members, and then Trudy began playing. The sound carried throughout the house. That was the cue for the groom and the best man to take their positions at the improvised altar, which was surrounded by beautiful flowers. Just to be sure, Bill knocked on the door and told Erik and Conrad that it was time.

Bernice and the rest of the household staff took their seats, and at the playing of "Here Comes the Bride," everyone stood.

George and Elizabeth stood waiting and watching while Penny, the flower girl, marched down the aisle, followed by Dale. Dale looked stunning; the bridal party looked strictly "first class." Next came the bride. Elizabeth looked beautiful and radiant as only a bride looks on her wedding day. Erik could not take his eyes from her as she approached, and neither could Conrad. The bride and groom took their place in front of Reverend Phipps, and the ceremony got under way.

"Who gives the bride away?" asked the reverend.

"I do," answered George, "on behalf of the bride's family."

George took his place next to Bernice. Dale took Elizabeth's bridal bouquet to hold while the ceremony continued. At the appropriate moment Conrad produced the wedding ring and nearly dropped it in his nervousness. Erik also had a wedding band and the minister blessed both rings and then Elizabeth and Erik made their vows. Elizabeth looked up to Erik's eyes as he placed the ring on her finger, saying, "With this ring I pledge you my ..." Elizabeth didn't hear the rest because she saw a momentary change in Erik's face that resembled Pat Duran. She recovered in time to make her pledge but was still a little shaken by the momentary appearance of Pat's image.

The minister continued. "... and what God has joined together, let no man put asunder. I pronounce you man and wife. You may kiss the bride." After the newly wedded couple did so, Reverend Phipps said, "Ladies and gentlemen, I present Mr. and Mrs. Erik Neilsin."

Everyone clapped, and the sound of the organ started the wedded couple back up the aisle. The Templetons had two professional photographers taking pictures throughout the ceremony, and they all posed for some formal pictures before joining the reception for the guests. Two newspaper photographers were also there. Bernice had not missed anything, and all the expected events took place.

Dale was taken aback when she looked at Conrad's face as they proceeded back up the aisle. He had tears running down his face. *He's very emotional.* She gave his hand a squeeze as a sign of encouragement. It was acknowledged by his smile. After that, Conrad settled back to his old self. Everyone kissed the bride, and all the women kissed the groom.

"Just think," Dale said to Conrad. "We get to do this again for ourselves in two months' time!"

Bernice and George hosted a magnificent reception, and everyone reveled in the good food, plenty of good liquor, and music from a local five-piece band called the Musical Notes. Conrad was delighted to see what a wonderful dancing partner he had in Dale as they took to the dance floor.

"This is our first dance," he said. "You dance very well!"

Dale was thinking the same of Conrad. Although he was a little rusty around the edges, he still knew the steps and had a good sense of rhythm.

Nursing Sister Menckler and Tante Marie were now good friends after making the trip from Heidelberg together. Both were a little in awe at the grandness and surroundings of the Templeton mansion. Sister Menckler tried to sample a little of each appetizer thinking that this was the main meal. She was amazed to see a large slice of roasted beef being carved for each guest. In addition, there was roast pheasant, Virginia ham, and turkey. Sister Menckler had never seen so much food in one place at the same time.

Bernice introduced her to a mimosa. Sister Menckler immediately liked the taste and sparkle of the champagne and orange juice cocktail. After her third glass, she quit counting and enjoyed herself as never before. She wandered over to one corner of the great room and recounted her exploits teaching young nurses. Later on, she was seen trying to do the Hokey Pokey with Bill Cranfield.

Elizabeth's Aunt Marie had her share of the bubbly also, and it was not long before she too was out on the dance floor with whomever she could get to dance with her. At one point she zeroed in on George because he spoke fluent German and dragged him out on the dance floor. He knew she'd had enough to drink when she asked him if he was "spoken for." Elizabeth had to rescue George.

Since they would not be leaving the party, Elizabeth and Erik retreated to their room upstairs to change into clothing less formal. When he helped Elizabeth out of her wedding gown, a little cloth sack fell to the floor. Erik reached down to retrieve the tiny bag and opened it to see a glowing gemstone. Taking the stone out of the tiny sack he asked, "What's this?" He held it up for Elizabeth to see.

For a moment she felt panic, but the stone was glowing with a radiance she had never seen before, and she reached to take the gemstone from Erik. When she did, she was immediately aware that she and Erik were not alone in the room. She glimpsed two men in white linen suits, but just as suddenly, they disappeared. It appeared that Erik had not seen the two men. She decided not to say anything because it was not uncommon for strange things to happen when the gemstone was handled. She remembered what the Gypsy woman had told her about not letting anyone touch the stone and wondered if the spell or influence of the stone might diminish.

They went downstairs to rejoin the wedding guests, and when Elizabeth had an opportunity she gave Bernice a nod that meant "we have to talk."

Elizabeth told Bernice what happened with the stone and what she saw. "I don't think it was anything bad," she said.

"What did they look like? What kind of expressions did they have?" Bernice asked.

"Well, it was only for a moment. One fellow was taller than the other. They looked pleasant enough, and they appeared to be interested in Erik and me, and then *poof*, they disappeared."

Bernice shook her head. "It doesn't sound bad to me."

"It is really strange the way the gemstone changes colors. I've never seen it that bright and radiant before, and when I took the stone from Erik it was almost too hot to handle."

"Where is the stone now?" Bernice asked.

"I put it back in my jewelry box for safekeeping."

They rejoined the celebration. Erik and Dale were relating some Army experiences to Conrad. Penny was very hyperactive, singing and dancing and laughing at the slightest things. That was when Martha found her sampling glasses of champagne and realized Penny was well into her cups.

"You are to go to your room now, Penny! The very idea, drinking alcohol at your age."

Penny went reluctantly, trying her best to look somber, but giggled all the way up the stairs to her room.

The reception lasted until almost midnight. Finally the majority of guests were leaving to go home.

"Bernice, George, a great reception," Conrad declared. "You should be in the catering business!"

Erik and Elizabeth started to head for their room and stopped to hug and kiss Bernice and George. "Everything was just grand," Elizabeth said. "You have been like a real mother and father to me. I love you both!"

"Goodnight, my dears," Bernice called after them and wiped a tear from her eye. Turning to George, she knew that he understood. "It's been such a joy to me. It's like our Jennifer and Jimmy was here with us. I know this is silly, but I think that God, or someone, brought them to us to fill the void and give us back our children."

George nodded his understanding, but said only, "Let's call it a day also, my dear. I'm getting kind of pooped."

The caterers took care of cleaning up under the supervision of the household staff. It was way past midnight before the household quieted down to rest.

Martha and Queenie were the first up and about. The house was quiet, and a smell of stale liquor hovered in the great room. Martha and Queenie opened the windows and doors, and soon the odor went away. Martha had some fresh bread baking in the oven, and the smell of it seemed to reach everyone. Soon, one by one, the guests came downstairs. Sister Menckler was one of the last, and without a word to anyone, she accepted a cup of black coffee and quietly sipped it. Queenie made the rounds to the less fortunates with a nip of Irish whiskey for the coffee.

"Will set you straight on course," she advised Sister Menckler. Not waiting for a reply, she put some whiskey in Sister's coffee. After her second cup of coffee, Sister Menckler could handle the food.

Erik and Elizabeth joined everyone for breakfast. With their bags packed, they were ready to leave for the airport. Hugs and kisses flowed as everyone saw the young married couple on their way.

They boarded the aircraft at Baltimore's Friendship International airport for Los Angeles, where they would connect with a direct flight to Hawaii. They were pleased with the first-class seating, and both of them dozed off after the meal. Before they knew it, the announcement came that they would be arriving in Hawaii within the next ten minutes. There was a five-hour difference in time, so when they arrived it was still early in the day.

They exited the aircraft and went into the terminal. There they saw a woman holding a paddle with a sign on that read "The Neilsins."

"Aloha" was the greeting, and beautiful leis of flowers strung into a necklace were placed over Erik and Elizabeth. They were escorted to a waiting limousine and taken to a beautiful hotel where they learned that George had them booked into the best honeymoon suite. The view was spectacular and overlooked the beach. Off to the left in the distance, they could see Diamond Head.

They heard a knock on the door, which they opened to reveal a waiter with a cart. He wheeled in a little trolley that had a big basket of fresh fruit, a bottle of chilled champagne in a silver ice bucket, and two glasses.

"Compliments of the hotel! Happy honeymoon," he said and departed.

The week was filled with casual sightseeing, swimming, and a typical Hawaiian luau on the beach. Like other tourists, they took the boat ride out to the sunken Battleship Arizona, where most hands were lost, but 355 survived during the attack on Pearl Harbor on December 7, 1941. Erik was interested in visiting Schofield Barracks, and they were permitted access to the post upon Erik showing his Army Inactive Reserve ID card.

They were told about the other islands, took boat rides there, and spent most of the day at each location. After the fifth day, Elizabeth had enough of the tourism agenda so they settled down to the beach, swimming, and making love. The days passed so swiftly that the time to head back to the mainland came as a jolt. They were nicely tanned and well rested for their return journey.

It was exactly four weeks since they had checked the progress of their new home in Rustburg, Virginia.

"The house should be completed and ready for us to move into," Erik said. "Conrad and Claudier were going up for the final inspection of the place."

Elizabeth said that she was eager to set up housekeeping but wondered if it was going to be a little lonely out there all by themselves.

"We are not going to be confined there, honey," he said. "We'll have plenty of travel and visits back to Four Winds, not to mention when Conrad and Dale tie the knot."

"I'm sure you're right," she allowed.

The flight terminated at Baltimore. They retrieved Erik's car from the long-term parking and drove out to Four Winds. When they reached the house they were greeted eagerly by George, Bernice, and the household staff.

"Here they are," yelled Penny, who had been watching for Erik's car.

There was much hugging and kisses to go around to everyone, and Elizabeth and Erik were eager to give the little gifts they had bought. George liked to smoke a cigar and even a pipe every now and then, so Erik and Elizabeth brought him a hand carved meerschaum pipe. George was very pleased with his gift. Bernice got an authentic Hawaiian native dress, complete with lei and Hawaiian bangles. They also had presents for all the household staff.

They ate, talked, and reminisced about their whole trip, and George showed them all the newspaper clippings about the wedding. It had made the society page in several papers.

Elizabeth noticed that Bernice looked a little tired and went to her and asked how she was feeling.

"I'm okay, darling," she said. "Just a little tired."

Elizabeth gave George a questioning look, and he said, "She's fine, Elizabeth. She had a thorough checkup, and the doctor said that she has made a remarkable and total recovery from that cancer."

Elizabeth was relieved and gave Bernice a kiss on the forehead. "Still, I think you should go to bed and get a good night's rest."

Once again, she was the nurse in charge!

The next morning, Conrad called to welcome the newlyweds home and to let them know that the house in Rustburg was "begging for some occupants." Erik was immediately excited and anxious to get there. Conrad also told them that he had instructed the interior decorators to coordinate the arrival of furniture and situate it in the rooms designated. It would be up to Elizabeth and Erik to "fine-tune" where everything was supposed to go.

"We are going to drive down there today," he advised Conrad.

Elizabeth had a pile of wedding presents, linens, and other items to take to the house. When the car was loaded, they made ready to leave.

"When we get everything in order, we want you both to come down and see the house and spend some time with us," Elizabeth said. "I am going to miss seeing you every day."

"That's okay, dear," Bernice was quick to respond. "As soon as you're ready we'll be down. Give us a call when you get there so that we won't have to worry."

Both Elizabeth and Erik responded with a "Yes, ma'am!"

There was a lot of activity going on when Erik and Elizabeth arrived at their new home. Three members of the interior decorators were busy putting the final touch on everything.

"You're just in time," the man in charge said. "We have just finished. Hope you like the way things have been set up. I expect you will move things around to suit your taste, but the heavy moving and arranging is taken care of."

They walked through each room of the house, and now that there was furniture, the rooms did not look too large. When they talked, the echo they'd heard before was no longer there. The carpeting was the best, and it felt good under foot. They were extremely pleased with everything and told the head decorator. The decorators left in a short while, and then Erik and Elizabeth ran through the house like a couple of kids yelling with enthusiasm. The kitchen captured Elizabeth's attention, and the sight of the big refrigerator brought her back to reality.

"Uh-oh! We didn't get any food. We'll have to go shopping for food," she said.

She opened the refrigerator and found a fresh container of milk, a dozen eggs, a package of lean bacon, a bottle of catsup, mustard, and butter. A loaf of bread was also on the bottom tray.

"Someone was thinking about us," Elizabeth ventured. She also saw a six-pack of beer with a note on it. The note read:

I'll bet you show up without any groceries. There's enough for breakfast and some other things in the pantry. Enjoy!
Love, Dale and Conrad

The pantry revealed a small stock of everyday spices, saltines, and cooking oil. There were also a few cans of soup, two tins of sardines, a can of tuna, and a can of coffee.

"How very thoughtful and sweet of them to do that for us," Elizabeth said to Erik.

"Yeah! Both of them are that way," Erik agreed.

"Are you getting hungry, Erik?"

He nodded his head as he was checking out the light switches. Elizabeth put a lunch together—a can of soup, tuna fish sandwiches, and beer. Erik went outside to inspect the greenhouse and was pleased when he entered because the greenhouse was nice and warm. *Good germination temperature,* he thought. Returning to the house, he found Elizabeth moving a few pieces of furniture to other locations in the room.

"We are going to need some pictures and things to decorate the walls. They look awfully bare, don't you think?"

Erik agreed and said that they would have to go to a bigger city to find the variety of things they wanted.

They spent their first night at the house, and they found that although they had enough of the basic furniture in the house, there was still a slight echo because of the large rooms and bare walls. Before retiring for the night, they both tried out the showers and found that there was plenty of hot water and good water pressure.

Erik was tired and went to sleep as soon as his head hit the pillow. Elizabeth lingered in the bathroom, blow drying her hair and then combing and brushing it out. Finished, she went to the dresser and got her handbag and looked for her small bottle of cologne. She found her gemstone and held it in her hand and mentally said, *Thank you for bringing Pat and Erik to me!* Still holding onto the gemstone, she entered the bedroom and started to place the gemstone on the nightstand next to her side of the bed. She was startled to see the same two men in white, standing next to the bed on Erik's side. They had a pleased expression on their faces as they looked down at Erik. Just as suddenly, they disappeared. Elizabeth marveled that, while startled, she had not been afraid. *Who are those two?* she wondered. *They seem to be interested in Erik, and they were not aware that I saw them.* She climbed into bed, and it was nearly an hour before she could close her eyes and fall off to sleep.

CHAPTER 30

The New Home

The following day the Neilsins set off to get the fill-in items for their new house. They came upon an art gallery and spent over an hour selecting a few painting reproductions and several prints that had to be matted and framed. Next they found another store that sold knick-knacks for the home, and they purchased some brass candlesticks with candles for the living room. Their last stop was to the supermarket to stock up on groceries, meat and paper products. The day soon passed and they were once again on their way home.

A week flew by as they set their home in order. Erik was viewing his plant that he had cultivated from seed while at Four Winds. The plant was growing and looked very healthy. It had sprouted several branches and on one, a small bud was evident. Erik had the notion to plant seeds for all the flowers that he and Elizabeth desired for around the property. Thus engrossed, Erik was busy in the greenhouse for several full days at a time. Another week flew by, and Elizabeth now caught up with getting all the little details squared away in their home, became a little restless. She was not used to having a lot of free time on her hands and she missed the activity at Four Winds.

"What about asking Bernice and George to come visit us now?" Elizabeth asked.

It was a Thursday, and they thought to ask the Templetons over for the weekend.

"I'll need to get some wine and stock of liquor in," Erik said. "I can get that tomorrow, and we'll be set!"

Elizabeth went to the phone and called Four Winds.

Penny answered the phone on the second ring. She had all kinds of questions for Elizabeth. "Are you all settled in now? How do you like it there?"

Finally Elizabeth was able to speak to Bernice. "What are your plans for this coming weekend?"

"I don't think we are doing anything in particular," she replied.

"How would you and George like to come and spend the weekend with us? I have missed you so much."

"We have also missed the two of you. It has been too quiet around Four Winds since you left," Bernice replied.

George and Bernice agreed to drive down on Friday for a long weekend visit. Elizabeth was delighted and set about planning the weekend menu.

They had found a seafood market that offered a large variety of fresh seafood. Elizabeth ordered two dozen large blue crabs for fresh crab salad as one of the appetizers. Stopping by the butcher shop, she bought some ham hocks for soup and a lovely prime rib roast. On second thought, she added some fresh cut-up chicken for grilling, hoping at the same time for good weather.

George and Bernice arrived with a flourish and the car horn blaring. Elizabeth and Erik rushed out to greet them.

"You know," George observed, "you haven't given this place a proper name yet. It looks very impressive."

"I haven't even thought about a name for the place. We just call it the farm. Let me show you around," Erik offered.

They went through the house, around the grounds and ended the tour at the big greenhouse.

"What do you think?" Erik asked.

"I think you have done a bloody good job—as Bill would say! What are all those things you're growing?" George asked, pointing to all the sprouts pushing their way through the soil.

"Over here, I have planted some vegetables, all from hybrid seeds. I have onions, parsley, carrots, snow peas, string beans, and cilantro. Outside, I have two varieties of corn growing. On this other side," he said, pointing, "I have flowers growing that I hope to transplant around the house and garden. Over here I have a few special things I am experimenting with. You remember the plant I started at Four Winds?" he asked.

George nodded.

"Well that big plant there is the baby! Look at how it is growing, and there are now several buds. I don't know when it will bloom, but at the rate it is growing, it should not be too long."

When the mailman made his rounds, Elizabeth found a letter from Dale Swan. She quickly scanned the letter and squealed with delight. She and Conrad had set a date for the twenty-first of June for their wedding.

"She wants me to be her matron of honor," Elizabeth announced.

Conrad's partners were selected as Best Man and groomsman. Dale had a special request to make of Erik. Because both her parents were dead and because she and Erik were like brother and sister—her words—would Erik agree to give the bride away? Elizabeth and Dale had become close friends, so she had no problem with Erik giving the bride away. The wedding was now three weeks away.

Elizabeth had an opportunity to talk to Bernice and tell her about what had happened a few nights ago. "These were the two same men I had seen before," she told her.

Bernice stole a quick glance around the room as Elizabeth related her experience. "I don't know what to tell you," she said. "It can't be bad, because they were only looking. You say that your impression is that they were not aware that you had seen them?"

"Yes, that's right. It was as if I could see them and they could not see me. It's all very strange, yet, I have to admit, I was not scared. Startled, yes! But not scared."

"You are keeping your gemstone handy, I hope?" asked Bernice.

"That's funny you should say that," Elizabeth said. "I remember that when I came out of the bathroom and went to sort out my handbag, I held the gemstone in my hand and that is when I saw the two men in white."

"If I were you," Bernice went on, "I would have that gemstone in my possession all the time. It seems that it is everything that gypsy woman told you."

The weekend passed, and Monday morning, the Templetons left to drive back to Four Winds. Erik was eager to get back to his work in the greenhouse. His vegetables and flower seedlings were bursting into healthy growth and with the weather warm and ideal, he started transplanting the flowers. He checked his "special" plant and saw that two flowers were emerging from the buds. He checked the soil for moisture, and was concerned that the plant got enough sunlight, without getting overheated. The greenhouse had top-opening windows that Erik opened to let excess heat escape. He had an electric thermostatic control for opening and closing the high windows; he had set the controls to regulate the greenhouse temperature.

Erik and Elizabeth spent the rest of the week transplanting the flowers around the exterior. She enjoyed working with Erik and noted with satisfaction that he was happy with what he was doing. Looking around the greenhouse, she was as pleased as Erik was that the vegetable seedlings were now big and hardy enough to be transplanted outdoors. Erik operated a power roto-tiller over the garden area and then made little trenches for transplanting the garden. Sets of onions, tomato plants, squash, beans, snow peas and others were planted. Once the plants were in the ground, Erik started his own developed irrigation system going. Within thirty minutes the garden area was quite moist as a fine spray of water covered the thriving vegetables. Two different types of corn were growing and looked very healthy. They got a good supply of water also.

Elizabeth needed to drive to Maryland to meet Dale, where she would be getting her outfit to wear for the wedding. She planned on being with Dale and Conrad for most of the day and then to avoid a long drive back, she planned to go on to Four Winds and spend the night there. Erik was left to his own devices.

Dale had started her new employment with the law firm and tried hard to absorb much of the legal procedures that were directed her way. She felt that she was holding her own—not in trouble yet! Conrad was very happy and proud of her progress. She had one small assignment to interview two people that concerned an insurance injury claim.

One interview was more or less easy and straightforward. The second interview was with a young man thirty years of age who was claiming a disabling injury that did not permit him to work. The claim stated that he was unable to move about freely without the aid of a cane or crutches.

When Dale arrived at the claimant's house, she rang the doorbell but did not get an answer. She left the pathway and walked to the rear of the house. There was a small swimming pool at the back and also an outdoor whirlpool tub. There was a young fellow in the whirlpool tub.

"Hi there!" she called. "Anybody at home?"

Dale hardly looked the role of an investigator. In fact she looked exceptionally attractive to the young man, who was quick to respond.

"Yeah!" he answered. "I'm here, just splashing away."

"That looks really inviting," Dale ventured. "Is there room for two in the tub?"

"You bet there is," the young fellow quickly replied.

Dale approached a bit and said, "I guess this is the wrong time to bother you." Turning, she started to exit.

"Hey, don't go," the young fellow called after her. But Dale had walked around the side of the house toward the front. Rick Casano, thinking that this lovely creature was probably selling some magazines or something like that, decided that he would like to see more of her. He sensed that she might be someone who would enjoy a little frolic in his back yard. And Rick Casano—Casanova to his friends—was not going to let this creature slip away. Quickly jumping out of the whirlpool, he grabbed his robe and went flying after Dale. He dashed around to the front of the house, but she had vanished, or at least that's what he thought.

He turned and walked back to his whirlpool and climbed back in. Leaning back to relax, he looked to his left and saw Dale who was on the other side of the fence. She had a camera in her hand and was talking pictures of him.

"Hey!" he called. "What are you doing?"

He did not yet realize that he had been caught moving about freely without any disability evident.

"I'm just taking some action shots," Dale replied.

Dale came around to the back of the house once again and introduced herself. "I'm an investigator, doing some field work for the insurance company you filed a claim with," she announced. "You don't seem to be having any difficulty moving around, Mr. Casano."

"Hey, wait a minute! Give a guy a break, honey, will you? So I fudged a little bit. What's the harm? I did hurt myself, you know. That was for real," he said, feeling he could win Dale over with his charm.

"I'm glad that you're not seriously hurt," Dale said with a touch of sincerity.

Rick figured that she would play ball and not blow the whistle on him. He was shrewd when it came to the opposite sex. He couldn't have been more wrong. In addition to recording his actions on her new camera, she also had recorded their little conversation on the tape recorder she held in her hand.

"I'm sorry, Mr. Casano. I earn my living as an investigator, and I have to report the facts."

"Oh, Christ!" Rick wailed.

"Want some good advice?" she asked him. "You would do yourself a favor if you withdrew your claim. If you don't, you could get prosecuted for trying to defraud your insurance company."

Dale then left an open-mouthed Rick Casano.

Conrad got a full report from Dale and congratulated her on exposing Casano. Within a few hours, Conrad took a telephone call from the insurance company that advised that Casano had formally withdrawn his claim, saying that he woke up that day and the pain was gone. Conrad reported Dale's visit to the claimant and how things turned out. Conrad didn't want to lose the law firm's fee for the job. The insurance representative agreed, and the matter was settled.

Dale took the following day off to meet with Elizabeth and go over the wedding costumes and other arrangements that had been made. Elizabeth told her all about what she and Erik had been doing to get the house in order. They spent most of the day together, and Conrad met them for lunch at their new apartment upstairs. Dale prepared a simple lunch for the three of them.

"What a lovely apartment!" Elizabeth exclaimed. "You really have a great view from here too!"

Conrad was quick to point out that Dale had given the place her woman's touch. Elizabeth left to beat the traffic during the rush hour and headed for Four Winds where she was expected.

As always, everyone received her with open arms. While she was there, Elizabeth told Bernice that she was going to give her a quick check-up in spite of her protests. Elizabeth prevailed and found that she was in reasonably good health. "Still," she said, "it is good to keep checking!"

Martha had prepared a nice, cozy supper for the two of them, since George was not expected until much later. This gave Bernice and Elizabeth time to talk about things they preferred not divulge to others. Elizabeth said she was amazed at Erik's intense interest in growing things.

"And I am so surprised that he seems to know so many things about plants. Conrad was also wondering how Erik acquired such knowledge about gardening and growing things. He told me that Erik graduated from college with an electrical engineering degree and never once talked about this new field, not until after he got hurt and spent such a long time in the hospital."

"I know, it all sounds strange," Bernice observed, "but after all the experiences you have had with the gemstone ..." Her voice trailed off.

Elizabeth glanced at Bernice, trying to understand what she was implying. "Do you think that there is some kind of connection between Erik's knowledge for growing of things and the gemstone?"

"Perhaps," was all Bernice ventured.

It was getting late, and Elizabeth excused herself to retire for the night. She wanted to drive back to the farm in the morning. "If I don't get back before supper time, I'm not sure that Erik will eat. When I'm away, he just snacks on junk food. Besides," she added, "he seems to like my cooking!"

Bernice saw Elizabeth off and cautioned her to drive carefully and to call when she arrived home. Stopping along the way, Elizabeth did her shopping for the evening's supper and picked up plenty of fruit so that Erik would have something good to snack on when he got caught up with work in the greenhouse. When she arrived home, Erik was not in the house, so she went to the greenhouse.

He looked up as Elizabeth entered. "Hi, sweetheart! I'm glad you're home. It's kind of lonely around here when you're not around."

They exchanged kisses and a fond embrace. Elizabeth noticed that Erik's special plant had grown even more branches bearing beautiful, multi-colored flowers.

"What beautiful flowers your plant has," she said.

She bent to smell the flowers. The fragrance was almost intoxicating. Delicate, yet strong.

Erik watched her reaction and said, "I know! I was wondering how those flowers could look so healthy and beautiful and have such a wonderful scent."

"I don't think I have ever seen a plant like this," Elizabeth confessed. "What is its name?"

Erik had the look on his face that she had come to recognize as his confused look. "I don't know. I have searched through all kinds of flower books, encyclopedias of gardening, and other references, and I can't find anything like it."

"Where did the seeds come from?" Elizabeth asked.

Again that look!

"I just can't remember! You said I had them with me when I arrived at the hospital."

"Yes! You had the seeds in a little metal box, and it was clutched in your right hand."

Changing the subject, Erik asked how the wedding preparations were going.

"Dale is a very organized person; she had everything ready, and we all got fitted nicely."

"How are Bernice and George?"

"Everyone's fine! I even gave Bernice a check-up, and she seems as healthy as can be."

"Are you getting hungry?" she asked.

"I'm practically starving! You can only go so far on potato chips, peanuts, and onion dip," he allowed.

"You come into the house and wash up while I make a nice supper." Catching his look, she said, "I got some really thick, juicy lamb chops to broil."

Erik headed for the bathroom, a quick shower, and a change of clothes. Elizabeth was an excellent cook and could prepare a meal quickly. The aroma of the broiled lamb chops drew Erik to the kitchen table as Elizabeth started to serve their dinner. Elizabeth presented Erik with a chilled bottle of wine to open, and that complemented their supper. For dessert, she had cut up fresh fruit and added some heavy whipped cream on top. Coffee followed, and when they were through eating she and Erik cleared away the dishes, loaded the dishwasher, and retreated to the living room to relax.

"Well, we have three days before Dale and Conrad will be tying the knot," Erik commented.

"Oh! You should see what a nice job they did fixing up the top floor apartment. It is really nice," Elizabeth said.

"How's Dale doing with her new job?" Erik asked.

"I guess she is doing well. She didn't say much about that, but Conrad was singing her praises."

Adopting the habits of the farming community, Dale and Erik turned in early for the night.

"Erik," she said, pushing his arm away. "I thought you were tired?"

"I am, but I need to relax before I can fall asleep," he said, moving closer to Elizabeth.

"Anything for a quiet life, I guess," she said with an exaggerated sigh.

The sun rose early in the morning, and so did Erik. Elizabeth felt a little tired and decided to stay in bed a bit longer. She didn't feel too good, and she thought that she probably ate too much for supper last night. It was around nine o'clock when Erik brought her a cup of coffee. Sitting up in bed, she started to sip her coffee, but all of a sudden she felt deathly sick. She jumped out of bed and ran to the bathroom, where she proceeded to throw up. Erik was alarmed and asked if she were all right.

"I think maybe the fresh fruit did not agree with my stomach. I feel much better now."

She felt a little better ... but not much more. *I won't say anything to Erik because he will just worry.* She had a little breakfast, just barely managing to keep the food down. Going outside, she sat in the sunshine and was gratified to feel herself getting better. Erik had retreated to the greenhouse to work and Elizabeth decided to write to her mother; she also owed a letter to Nursing Sister Menckler.

It was a balmy sunny day, and Elizabeth spent most of the morning outdoors. After glancing at her wristwatch, she went inside to make some lunch. She had made some soup and had put it in the freezer for Erik but discovered that he'd never taken it out. She heated it on the stove and started to make some sandwiches. She switched on the intercom that Erik had put in, and she called the greenhouse.

"Hey, you with the green thumb! If you're hungry for some lunch you better come now."

"I'm on my way!" came the response.

As they were having their lunch, a large delivery van pulled up to the house. It was the UPS truck with some packages for Erik. After lunch they opened the cartons that contained a collection of books, all on flowers, gardening and growing.

"This is the latest and largest collection of information on growing anything," Erik announced.

Elizabeth observed that his library of books was already filling their den. They both spent hours reading through the books and checking out pictures of flowers and plants to see if they could identify Erik's special plant. Their efforts were fruitless.

"Well?" asked Elizabeth. "What will you call your plant?"

"I'm not sure yet," Erik said, "but it's sure a keeper! That's it!" he cried. "I'll call it my keeper."

"Hmmm, you mean Erik's Keeper," Elizabeth ventured.

"Actually, that's an interesting name for the plant because it keeps so well," Erik commented. "Erik's Keeper it is, then!"

They both agreed.

"Oh, by the way, Conrad sent some of the newspaper clipping on our wedding. There are some nice photos of everyone and a great one of the four of us. It made several of the newspapers," she said. "Seems like you are some kind of celebrity!"

Erik glanced at the newspapers and saw that one of them was captioned

>Korean veteran and wealthy shipbuilder's son marries
>(Pictured L to R 1/Lt Erik Neilsin, wife Elizabeth,
>Captain Dale Swan and Attorney Conrad Flemming)

One of the photos was of Dale and Erik in uniform as first lieutenants.

"Wow! I guess a lot of people saw all these pictures and write-ups. I didn't know the papers could get this much information," he said.

CHAPTER 31

The following morning, Elizabeth woke up and felt terribly nauseous. *Uh-oh*, she thought, her nurse's mind starting to consider the facts. *When was the last time I had my period?* She decided not to say anything to Erik and retreated to the bedroom to retrieve the gemstone. Holding it in her hand, she felt the nausea fade away and in its place came a sense of well-being.

That afternoon they were to leave for Four Winds, where they would spend the night and attend Dale and Conrad's wedding the next day. Elizabeth had already had Erik's tuxedo cleaned and pressed and all his accessories packed away. They left on schedule and drove to Four Winds and were there before suppertime. As soon as was practical, Elizabeth gave Bernice all the high signs that she wanted to talk to her privately. Both retreated to the garden outside, and Bernice could sense Elizabeth's excitement.

"My dear, you are bursting to tell me something. What is it?"

"Bernice," Elizabeth gasped, "I think I'm pregnant!"

That caught Bernice completely unaware, as her response indicated. "No shit?"

Elizabeth explained how she felt and that she counted at least forty days or more since she last had her period. "Of course, I won't know for sure until I get a check up with an obstetrician at Johns Hopkins. I will call and make an appointment in a few days," she said. "It would be nice if I could be here at Four Winds on some pretext without Erik so I could have that check up and be sure."

"We can work something out," Bernice said, her plotting mind already at work.

"Please don't say anything to George or the staff—especially Queenie—or else it will be all over the village," Elizabeth said.

Elizabeth was startled when she saw Erik walking Dale down the aisle. They looked like a bride and groom! Conrad stood, waiting, with a big grin on his face, and his eyes reflected his excitement.

Dale was a beautiful bride, as pretty as seen in any bridal magazine. She had a touch of mischief in her, though. Just as they reached the altar she whispered to Erik, "This could have been you and me, you know," and gave a little chuckle as Erik nearly missed a step.

Erik gave the bride away and joined the Templetons. All of the Four Winds staff and the Templetons attended the wedding. Queenie was tearful as a waterfall throughout the ceremony.

"I pronounce you husband and wife," the preacher said and introduced Mr. and Mrs. Flemming to the congregation.

Gloria, Conrad's secretary, wiped a few tears from her eyes. Her husband soothed her, saying, "It's okay, honey. No need to be so sad!"

"Who's sad?" she bantered back. "These are tears of happiness—now someone else can take care of him!"

After the many photo sessions of the wedding party and guests, everyone set off for the reception at the Chez Gustav. Conrad had hired out the whole restaurant and had the terrace prepared for dancing. A five-piece band played the traditional selections, and the master of ceremonies talked everyone through all the typical wedding antics. Penny caught the wedding bouquet and a young man's attention too. Martha's comment got Penny back on track.

"Forget it!" was all she said.

The wedding celebration lasted until almost midnight. Dale and Conrad bid farewell to the guests and left to go home. They were leaving in the morning for a trip to England, Paris, and Spain, and would be gone for three weeks. Erik was a little concerned about getting back home to care for the flowers in the greenhouse, since the weather forecast called for a few days of hot weather. This gave Elizabeth hope for staying at Four Winds. Bernice jumped into the conversation, asking Elizabeth if she could possibly stay over for two days to help her. Elizabeth looked at Erik, who frowned.

"How will you get home?" he asked.

"Oh, don't worry," Bernice said. "I will have someone drive her back home."

Erik knew when he was licked and said okay. The following morning he left early for the farm.

"Now, my dear," Bernice said to Elizabeth. "You can make your appointment and see the OB doctor."

Elizabeth called the hospital and talked to the staff, and they said that they would squeeze her in without having to have an appointment scheduled. Bernice accompanied Elizabeth to the hospital and sat in the waiting room, trying to work on a crossword puzzle—and was not successful. Finally Elizabeth came out of the doctor's examination room. She looked a bit flushed, Bernice thought.

"Well?" she asked.

"The doctor says I am without a doubt … pregnant!"

"Hurray! Will it be a boy or a girl?"

"Good grief, Bernice, it's way too soon to make any kind of determination, let alone the sex of the baby."

"Yes, of course you're right. It's just that I'm so excited for you," she gushed.

They exchanged hugs and left the hospital.

"Next stop, the baby shop," Bernice advised.

"No! Bernice, you're just bursting at the seams to have the baby clothed before it's born. I can't do anything until I let Erik know that he's going to be a papa."

"You're right, dear. I must confess that it's like I am expecting a grandchild."

Elizabeth understood, and she hugged Bernice very tenderly. "You are like a mother to me," she said. "As far as I am concerned, this baby will be your grandson."

Bernice became all choked up, and tears ran down her cheek.

"Please, Bernice! Stop, or I will be crying next."

"Still," Bernice said, "it doesn't hurt to have a little look around and see what's in vogue for young tots. Don't you agree?"

"Okay, okay, you win! Where do we go for things for tots?" Elizabeth asked.

"First, we shall check at Toddlers and Tykes, and then we can run over to the Baby Barn. Then there are the major department stores."

"Wait a minute, Bernice! Let's just check a few places so I get an idea, and then let's go back to Four Winds."

They made a whirlwind tour of six baby clothes stores and then headed home thoroughly exhausted. The following day Chester Somers drove Elizabeth home. He stayed the night so he could have a good chance to look over the farm.

"Erik, you have done a great job here," he observed. Erik showed Chester the plant, which was now thirty inches high and had seven beautiful flowers blooming.

Chester whistled. "I'm not much for knowing about plants and flowers," he said, "but that one is sure a beauty!"

He bent over to smell the flower and was surprised by the exotic fragrance.

"I know what you're gonna say," Erik said, anticipating Chester's comment. "I don't know why it has such a strong fragrance. We did give it a name, however. We are calling it Erik's Keeper."

"That sounds like something Queenie would say," Chester said.

The following day Chester left to go back to Four Winds. Elizabeth didn't get up to see him off, as she had morning sickness again. Erik came into the bedroom and asked, "What's up, honey? Are you sick to your stomach again?"

"Yes, a bit," Elizabeth said.

She patted the bed and beckoned Erik to sit down next to her. "I have some news for you," she said.

Erik had a really confused look on his face, his mind ticking over and trying to anticipate why Elizabeth was so serious.

"What is it, honey?" he asked.

"Erik, my darling, we are going to have a baby. I'm pregnant," she announced. By the look on Erik's face she knew that it had not sunk in yet.

"What ... a baby?"

For the briefest moment Elizabeth feared that Erik might not welcome the news. Suddenly, fully realizing the fact, Erik jumped up and yelled, "I'm going to be a father! I'm going to be a father!"

He rushed back to Elizabeth and held her tight in his arms. "Darling, you just stay in bed. You just rest! I'll make you breakfast!"

"Erik, please! Pregnancy is not a disabling injury, and I'll be all right. Just a little morning sickness when I first get up," Elizabeth said in her most professional nurse's manner.

The rest of the day Erik popped in and out of the house to check on Elizabeth. She finally had to tell him to go back to his flowers and give her some peace. "I won't be having this baby until seven or eight months from now," she said. "You have plenty of time to get used to the idea!"

Still, Erik was on cloud nine and already thinking of boy names and visualizing things he could do with his son. At the supper table that night, Elizabeth burst his balloon by saying that it might turn out to be a girl. That brought Erik back down to earth.

"Hey," he said, quickly recovering, "we will have to make a nursery out of one of the rooms."

Elizabeth said that was a good idea and suggested that the color of the room should be neutral—neither pink nor blue. They settled on yellow with pink and blue motifs.

The next few weeks' interest concerned the right wallpaper for the nursery. Erik was ready to purchase a crib and a lot of other things suitable for a two-year-old.

"Let's wait awhile," Elizabeth suggested.

Erik's greenhouse was in full bloom, and the quality of plants and flowers was outstanding. A local florist came by the greenhouse to talk to Erik and was amazed at what he saw.

"Are you going to market these flowers?" he asked. "If you are, I'd like to take some of them off your hands ... if the price is right."

They negotiated a price, and the florist placed an order with Erik, with assurances that he could get more flowers and plants. The florist had his eye on Erik's Keeper.

"What is this?" he asked. "It is a beauty! I haven't seen this before. I wouldn't have any trouble selling that for a good price," he ventured.

"It's not for sale," Erik said. "It is something I have been working on."

Looking over the plant with an expert eye, the florist said, "You ought to enter this plant in the National Garden Show. It might win a prize, and it wouldn't hurt your business either."

"I'll think about it," Erik said thoughtfully.

"Honey," Elizabeth said to him a few days later, "look at this big flower show that's coming up. It's in Philadelphia. Remember what Harold the florist said? You should take a few of your best plants up there, especially Erik the Keeper."

"Oh, I don't know," Erik said, frowning. "I don't want to leave you and go away for a while. The show is a week long."

"Who said anything about leaving me behind?" Elizabeth protested. "I would like to go too!"

"Do you really mean it?"

"Sure I do!"

"Who would look after the greenhouse?" Erik asked.

"How about Harold the florist? Better still, why not ask Queenie and Bill to come and stay at the house for the week? They would love it, and Queenie would love to tend the greenhouse. I'm sure Bernice and George wouldn't mind."

Erik thought about it and said, "That's not a bad idea. Do you want to talk to Bernice first and then ask Queenie and Bill? If they say it's okay, I'll get entry forms and submit them to the Philadelphia Garden Show."

Elizabeth got on the telephone, and an hour later she informed Erik that everything was all set for Bill and Queenie to come up two days ahead of time. "Bernice said to tell you that she had high hopes for your Keeper plant."

CHAPTER 32

Flowers

Erik needed a suitable truck to carry flowers, plants, and gardening materials. He purchased a custom Jeep Wagoneer. A regular model would have suited him, but thinking about Elizabeth's pregnancy, he opted for the luxurious model instead. They loaded several of his quality plants and the Keeper, which now displayed yet another bloom. They set off for Philadelphia and arrived midafternoon. Only those displaying flowers were permitted access to the inner parking and unloading area. After getting his location assignment for display, Erik had to complete special forms with descriptive information and floral names. The main exhibit hall, Erik noted, had temperature conducive to support the flowers being displayed.

Erik placed his plants and the display card with each. He arranged them so that they were elevated; in the middle, he placed the Keeper. It was a nice effect, he thought. Erik and Elizabeth then left to check into their hotel nearby. They decided to dine early then turn in for a good night's rest.

Morning came soon enough, and after their refreshing rest they showered and dressed. Erik noticed that Elizabeth's tummy was beginning to show the swelling. She had bought some casual, loose-fitting outfits that were adjustable around the stomach area. After breakfast, they left for the exhibition hall. Admitted into the hall, they met many other growers at the coffee bar having a cup of coffee before admission of viewers. Elizabeth and Erik walked around and looked at all the other floral displays.

"They are very beautiful," Elizabeth observed.

They walked past their display and noted that several of the exhibitors were looking at Erik's Keeper and were in deep conversation.

"It's difficult to tell the fragrance of that Keeper plant," they overheard one exhibitor say. "For that matter, what is it?"

Finishing their walk around the exhibit hall, they returned to Erik's floral display. Erik excused himself to go make some inquiries about the show. When Erik returned, the doors were opened for thousands of viewers. Some viewers stopped to admire Erik's Keeper.

"What a beautiful plant! What beautiful flowers! What a delicate fragrance!" In fact, it was the fragrance of the Keeper that seemed to attract many people to linger for a while, admiring it. Others commented on the unusual and beautiful plant and its blooming flowers. As the day wore on, many were attracted to the Keeper, some coming back again for another look.

The exhibit went on for two more days, and then the certified Master National Garden Club judges made their rounds. Three times they came back to Erik's Keeper, and finally one judge came to Erik. "I do not know this plant. Is this a hybrid or something you created?" he asked.

Erik had no alternative but to say simply that it was something he created and nurtured.

Later in the day, official announcements were made and blue ribbon awards given to some very fine plants and flowers. Erik was not among the winners or honorable mentions.

"We also have a Grand Champion Award," the chairman of the judges announced. "We select the very best overall flower or plant that will qualify for national and international recognition. By unanimous decision of the judging, the award is given to Erik Neilsin for the 'Keeper.'"

The audience was pleased and went wild in agreement with the judgment. Elizabeth screamed her delight. Erik was practically speechless. Next came the award—a big silver cup. Photographers took pictures of the Keeper and then wanted one of Erik and Elizabeth with the trophy flanking the Keeper. They shook so many hands that their arms got tired.

Erik met several people who were interested in the Keeper and asked about acquiring some seeds. Erik stated that the new seeds would not be immediately available, and he was not yet sure of the market for such a plant as the Keeper. He was startled to learn that several of those questioning him were top officers in seed companies and a few were from Great Britain.

One distinguished gentleman asked Elizabeth and Erik where they were staying and discovered that they were at the same hotel as he. He was an Englishman, and he invited them to have a cocktail with him. He said he would like to talk to Erik about his future plans. Erik at first was inclined to refuse, but Elizabeth's instinct prevailed and she answered for both of them and said, "We accept your invitation!"

The Englishman introduced himself as Sir Byron Ankeny.

"One of my many functions in life," he said, "is to serve as a director for the Chelsea Garden Show in London. In addition, my main occupation is concerned with chemistry as pertains to perfumes and colognes. I am very impressed with your creation. The Keeper, is it? What an unusual and lovely fragrance! I would be very interested in testing the endurance of the Keeper's scent."

Sir Byron asked Erik all kinds of questions about the Keeper and expressed a keen interest in knowing how Erik had managed to keep the entire plant so uniform in size and shape while producing not one color of the flower, but different shades as well. Erik was a bit lost on how to answer all Sir Byron's questions. Sir Byron interpreted that it was Erik's guarded secret, and he really couldn't blame him for wanting to keep the details confidential. He left Erik with his card and took Erik's business card in return.

When Erik and Elizabeth arrived back at the farm, Queenie and Bill were very impressed with the award the Keeper won at the Philadelphia show. Elizabeth told them about meeting Sir Byron Ankeny and his interest in the flower's fragrance. The Keeper did not grow any taller, but it did grow two more branches that also flowered. The greenhouse was filled with the fragrance from the Keeper. Erik had to transplant the Keeper into a larger tub that he prepared with fresh soil, compost, and nutrients. He then prepared special soil beds to start a few more of the seeds from which the Keeper came.

CHAPTER 33

Summer was drawing to a close, and the weather was getting cooler. Elizabeth had an appointment with the doctor and had grown very large; she found it was becoming somewhat of a burden just moving about. When she arrived home, Erik saw the look of concern on her face.

"What is it, sweetheart?" he asked. "How did your doctor's visit go?"

"Sit down Erik," she said. "I hope you're ready for this. Everything is fine, health-wise, except ..."

"What is it, for God sake? Don't leave me hanging," Erik cried.

"We are going to have twins!"

Erik was flabbergasted. "Twins? Holy mackerel ... Twins! I should have guessed. You're getting so big. I thought that baby is going to be a whopper. But twins!"

Elizabeth burst into tears and Erik rushed to console her. "That's okay, dear. We can handle it, can't we?" he asked.

"I am getting so big. I don't know if I will be able to go the full nine months. The doctor said that I have to visit him every two weeks from now on. He doesn't think I will make it to Christmas and that he may have to bring them early," Elizabeth managed to get out.

"It's nothing that we can't handle. I want you to start taking things easier now. We will have to plan on only short trips and we might have to dash to the hospital on a short notice."

"The doctor was concerned about the long distance to the hospital. What are your thoughts?" Elizabeth asked.

"Let's sleep on it, and we can then make some firm plans."

Elizabeth's preference was to have the baby at Johns Hopkins, as she felt comfortable there in familiar surroundings and knew most of the staff as well. Sometime during the early morning hours, Elizabeth woke up. She could feel the twins moving about, and then they settled down. *Just changing their position for something more comfortable,* she guessed. She was wide awake now, and she noticed a soft, glowing light coming from on top of her dresser. She moved herself slowly to get out of bed and walked to the dresser. The glow was coming from her gemstone. She picked up the stone and felt a gentle and soothing current pass through her body. A thought popped into her head.

We should go and stay at Four Winds for the last week. I will be close to the hospital, and I will have people there to help me if needed. What about Erik? She would discuss that with him in the morning, she thought, returning to bed.

Oddly enough, Erik was somewhat relieved when Elizabeth suggested her idea. "I was getting concerned about the distance also," he said, "And you would have everyone at Four Winds to help out too."

"I hate to be away from you when the time is getting so short," she said.

"When the time gets close, I'll get someone to tend the greenhouse, and I'll be with you," Erik promised. "Having Dennis Faxton coming round a few days a week has been a great help in the greenhouse. He would be glad to work more hours tending the greenhouse and as you know, his dad is the sheriff for our area."

"Are you sure?" Elizabeth asked.

"Yes, having Dennis here is also having fringe benefits with his dad."

After breakfast, Elizabeth called Four Winds. The phone was answered on the second ring by a breathless Penny. Hearing Elizabeth's voice, she immediately asked if it was time yet.

"No, not yet, Penny. Can I please talk to Bernice?"

A few seconds later Bernice was on the phone, full of questions. "Is it time yet? Are you all right? How did your visit with the doctor go?"

Elizabeth advised Bernice of the news, and Bernice screamed loudly, "Twins!"

George heard Bernice scream and spilled his cup of coffee all over his shirt. He dashed to the phone and saw Bernice dancing about and waving her hands. At first he thought that Elizabeth had delivered already. He was eager to know what was going on, but Bernice waved him away. Finally she hung up the phone.

"Elizabeth is going to have twins! They will be staying with us in a short while, when the doctor thinks the time is getting close."

"When is the baby, I mean the twins, due?"

"Supposed to be in January, but the doctor thinks he may have to deliver in December. So far, we are planning for them to join us here for the month of December unless something happens sooner."

For months an APB (All Point Bulletin) had been circulating throughout the country for the capture of Cliff Roberts, who escaped from a mental institution after killing an orderly. So far, Cliff kept himself out of sight and started to make plans.

POLICE BULLETIN

The fugitive is twenty-three years old, weighs 155 pounds, has dark brown hair and green eyes, and is 5'11" tall. He is believed to have worn hospital orderlies clothing when he escaped. The fugitive is not known to be armed with a firearm; however, he is to be considered dangerous and unpredictable. The suspect's photograph follows.

Any information on this fugitive should be immediately transmitted to Central Police Control or to your state police.

Cliff Roberts did not gloat over his easy escape from the institution. In fact, he was quite cool and methodical about what he should do. *I may be crazy*, he thought, *but I'm not stupid!*

Cliff entered his brother's apartment house, searched the ledge above the door, and found the key that he knew would be there. He entered and took stock of his options. The closet had many items of clothing. Some of them were his. He got out of the hospital clothing and dressed in his own clothes.

Next, he went to the small desk and went through the drawers looking for his brother's papers. He then slid open a secret compartment that held the special papers he was looking for. He found the safety deposit box information and the bank address. He already had a copy of the key and since the safety deposit box was in both his and Ruppert's name, he would have no trouble getting the contents.

Cliff left the apartment and entered a fast food place for a meal. He wore his favorite baseball cap to cover his hair and put on a pair of Army sunglasses. His next stop was the bank. He carried an empty gym bag into the bank. After showing proper identification, he entered the vault area and opened the safety deposit box. He was left alone, and he examined the contents in the box. He took out the money, which after counting proved to be fifteen hundred dollars. He then withdrew an Army .45-caliber automatic pistol and the loaded magazine. This was his brother's weapon. After examining all the other items and paperwork, he closed the box and returned it to the waiting clerk, who placed it back in its place. Cliff then left on his mission.

Erik worked as much as he could in the greenhouse, and the first Keeper plant had sprouted a pod that opened to display an array of seeds. Erik extracted the seeds with an artist's paintbrush and placed them in a little dark container. The other Keeper seedlings had soon sprouted and the plants grew several branches and spread out with little buds on each of them. Erik marked a label and put it on the container. *The first seeds from Keeper number one!*

A police car with County Sheriff marked on it pulled up to the house. Dennis Faxton got out, and so did his father. Dennis introduced his father to Erik and Elizabeth.

"I just thought I would stop by to let you know that when you are away and Dennis is looking after things here, I will make it a point to check out the house and property frequently," he said.

"That is so kind and considerate of you," Elizabeth said.

Erik retreated into the greenhouse and returned with a beautiful plant. He gave it to Sheriff Faxton.

"This is for Mrs. Faxton," he said.

Dennis was scheduled to help out and set off to do his chores.

"I'll be back to pick you up when you're ready," his father called after him. "Just call the station, and they will pass on the message if I'm not there."

The morning mailbox was full; it included several advertisements and a few letters asking about the availability of the Keeper seeds.

That made the twenty-third request for seeds since the Philadelphia show.

Thanksgiving was just around the corner, and Elizabeth was finding it hard to sit or get into a comfortable position. She couldn't stand too long and found that when she did, her ankles would swell. During her last visit to the doctor, he'd suggested that she get her bags packed for a trip to the hospital and said that she might want to move closer to the hospital. Elizabeth advised him of their plan to go to Four Winds for the duration. He thought that was a wise idea.

The day before Thanksgiving they left for Four Winds. Bernice and George put on a grand spread for the holiday, but Elizabeth could only eat a small portion because of the doctor's warning not to over indulge. She had to keep her weight under control. Elizabeth understood this only too well!

When she found that she was too uncomfortable, she sought refuge on the reclining chair and held on to her gemstone. As always, the relief came gently and sure. It was during these moments that Elizabeth could take a nap and rest. Going into a deep sleep, she dreamed that she was walking in a field of beautiful flowers. A gentle old man was tending the flowerbeds, but he rose to his feet and went to greet Elizabeth.

"Welcome, Elizabeth," he greeted her.

She was surprised that he knew her name.

"Everything is going to turn out just fine," he said, as though reading the concern in her mind. "You and Erik are truly blessed," he went on. "I am very pleased with the work he is doing with the flowers. He has learned well, and he is a worthy person. Now, go in peace."

And just as suddenly her dream ended. Elizabeth awoke and did not get up. She felt very calm and contented. She sat for a long while, and eventually Bernice came to see if she was all right.

"We have two cribs set up in the large bedroom. George got a supply of disposable diapers also … ten packages! Enough for a year, I expect!"

"You are so good to me and Erik, Bernice."

"I don't know how many times I have to tell you. It is a joy to have you here with us, especially now!"

Elizabeth was now in the habit of keeping her gemstone by her side on the nightstand. She woke and heard the clock chimes indicating four o'clock. Her gemstone, she noticed, was glowing, a bright amber color. She grasped it in her hand and was again rewarded by the gentle soothing current.

She was somewhat startled at a sound. It sounded like babies crying! *I wonder if this is a sign,* she thought. No sooner had that thought passed through her mind that she felt the pain in her back starting to increase. This was what the doctor told her to expect. She gave Erik an elbow in his side to wake him up.

"Uh, what is it, honey?" he asked, sleepy eyed.

"I think we have to get ready to go to the hospital now. I think I am starting into labor," she said.

Erik stumbled out of bed and went racing to the door and down the stairs in his pajamas to the car. As soon as he opened the front door he realized that he'd forgot something important. Elizabeth started to laugh when this all happened. She turned on the intercom and softly called Bernice. Bernice was on the intercom in a second.

"I think I'm ready to go to the hospital," she announced. "I'm sorry to bother you so early in—"

Bernice cut her off. "Don't apologize! I'll be dressed and there to help you in a minute!"

The whole house was galvanized into action—like a military operation. Erik, feeling kind of stupid, got on the telephone and called the hospital to advise them that they were bringing Elizabeth in. The hospital said that they would notify Elizabeth's doctor. It was nearly five o'clock when they left for the hospital. Chester drove the big limousine with Elizabeth, Erik, and Bernice. George said he would come along in his own car a short while later. They were halfway to the hospital when the labor pains began. Elizabeth timed them. They were twelve minutes apart. When they arrived at the hospital, her pains were ten minutes apart. She was placed in a wheelchair and taken to the maternity ward while Erik went to the hospital registration office to have Elizabeth admitted. Her water broke while she was in her room, and the pains now came at regular six-minute intervals.

When Erik arrived at Elizabeth's room, he found that she was not there.

"She's in the delivery room now," the nurse advised him. "Better you sit in the waiting room," she told him.

Minutes later George arrived, so Erik had some company. He was extremely nervous, as this was a very new experience for him. For that matter, George was fidgety as well. Bernice came into the waiting room to join the two quaking men. It was now six-thirty in the morning.

"They have just taken Elizabeth into the delivery room," she announced.

Both men just nodded. Bernice chuckled to herself, and George and Erik looked at her.

"What's up?" George finally asked.

"Elizabeth wouldn't give up her gemstone and insisted that she wanted to hold it in her hand while she went into the delivery room. She and the doctor had words, but Elizabeth finally got her way."

"I don't know what it is about her gemstone," Erik said "She's got this thing about that chunk of quartz. It's something I don't understand."

"That is something that has great personal meaning for her," Bernice said. "Just go along with it and don't be too concerned."

George gave her the "raised eyebrow" look of his. He knew better than to argue with her and her mystic leanings.

"What do you think, Erik?" George finally asked. "Boys or girls?"

"Beats me! One thing for sure, they're not lightweights!"

They could tell there was a lot of activity going on. Several nurses went dashing past with a quick glance and a flashing smile to the waiting room gallery. Bernice started pacing the floor.

"What the hell is taking so long?" she said to no one in particular.

After a while the door swung open and a smiling doctor appeared. "Erik," he announced, "Mother is doing just fine! We delivered two beautiful babies. One is a boy and the other a girl!"

Bernice hugged Erik, George hugged Bernice, and they all hugged each other. The doctor stood and beamed at their antics. He had seen it all before.

"When can I see my wife?"

"Give us a short while. She is being cleaned up and getting settled to rest. We have examined the babies, and they are both healthy. The boy was delivered first. He is a little bigger than the girl. Have you thought up names for them yet?" he asked.

"No, we haven't. We just didn't know what they were going to be."

"Well, you will have two days to decide. We will have to enter the names on the birth certificates."

The doctor left them to go back to Elizabeth.

A short while later they were allowed to enter the room where Elizabeth lay in bed, a bundle in each arm. "Say hello to our two little ones," she said.

Erik peeked at one and then the other. He was in awe. He gently kissed Elizabeth and told her, "Well done, sweetheart!"

Bernice was beside herself when Elizabeth asked her to hold one of the twins. Bernice cooed to the baby, and the tears ran down her cheeks in happiness for Elizabeth.

Bernice and George left Elizabeth and Erik for a few moments so that they could call Four Winds and tell everyone the news. They bumped into Conrad and Dale at the front desk and brought them up to date. They waited their turn to visit Elizabeth.

"Darling," Elizabeth said to Erik, "are we in agreement on the names then?"

"Yes, I am," he confirmed.

Bernice and George had come back into the room, and Elizabeth said that she wanted to ask them something.

"Erik and I have agreed on names for the twins. I chose the boy's name, and Erik chose the girl's name. We want to call the boy James Patrick, and we want to call our daughter Jennifer Lillian."

There was a pause, and then Elizabeth went on. "I hope that you won't mind, but we would like to name the twins after Jimmy and Jennifer!"

Bernice and George both were teary-eyed and could only manage a nod of agreement. Elizabeth called the nurse and asked that the names of the children be recorded.

Conrad and Dale stayed a short while with Erik and Elizabeth; Dale was enchanted with the twins. She looked at Conrad. "I expect you're gonna want a couple of these also," she said, teasing Conrad.

The thought was a sobering one for him. He had not considered being a father. He cleared his throat and looked a little uncomfortable. "I think I could wait a little while," he was able to muster in response.

They all had to laugh at him.

"You're not bound in concrete for an answer," Dale said.

Elizabeth spent several days in the hospital before she was permitted to leave. Arriving at Four Winds proved to be a festive occasion for all. Bernice and Elizabeth practically had to demand equal time to hold the babies. The infants were passed from Queenie to Martha and then to Penny and back to Queenie.

"Hey, you guys!" Bernice yelled. "I want to hold my adopted grandchild."

Elizabeth beckoned for the one hollering the loudest and went to nurse it. The second one was nursed and put down in its bassinet. Martha was in charge of the formula. Penny saw to it that Elizabeth had plenty of fluids to drink—doctor's orders.

A date was set with the church to have the babies baptized. George and Bernice were chosen to be the children's godparents, a role that they both cherished. Bernice confided in George, "It's like we have our two children back, George. It is like, life is renewed!"

George was in agreement, but he could only nod his head because the emotion he felt ran deep.

Erik had to leave for a few days to go back to the farm and take care of some details. He had no worry about leaving Elizabeth and the twins in good, capable hands. Elizabeth had the good fortune to be able to nurse the twins and to have someone look after them while she had a restful nap in the afternoon.

The gemstone was rarely out of her possession. Taking a nap, she held it in her pocket of her housecoat. She went into a deep sleep and dreamed that she was walking along a road that was surrounded by beautiful trees and shrubs. The road led to an open area of grass with a small valley to her left side. She saw two men in white clothing walking toward her. They held hands with a boy and a girl. Elizabeth stopped walking and watched as the four approached her. When they were very close, she thought that she recognized the boy and then the girl. The two men in white were the same ones she had seen before. They smiled at her and said:

"Let me introduce you to Jennifer and Jimmy," the taller man in white said.

Elizabeth realized that these were Bernice's two children. Even in her dream, she wished that Bernice could share it. Almost reading her mind, the taller man said, "The children wanted to come to see the babies. It is not often that you can have this experience," he confided.

The girl spoke to Elizabeth. "Thank you for bringing this joy to my mother and father. Tell them that we are well and happy for them. Tell them that we are not gone, but only for a short while."

With that, the dream suddenly ended and Elizabeth woke up. Her eyes were moist from tears.

When she stirred, Penny came over to see if she could get her something. "Where is Bernice?" she asked.

"She's in the twins' room looking at the babies," Penny replied.

"Would you please ask her to see me right now?"

Bernice hurried to Elizabeth's side. "Hello, darling! Had a good nap?" she asked.

"Yes, I have. I also had another dream, and I have to share it with you."

Bernice was all ears. Elizabeth described the dream, the pathway, the meadow and the two men in white accompanied by the two teenage children. When she finished telling about her dream, Bernice was deep in thought and crying gently to herself.

"I didn't want to upset you," Elizabeth said, "but they wanted me to tell you! They were real as life itself." She then related every detail she could remember, the clothing worn, the expressions, manner of speaking and other details.

Bernice had not realized it, but somewhere in her being an unknown weight lifted from her mind and she at last found a reconciling peace.

"Thank you, Elizabeth. That means so much to me!"

The next few weeks flew by as they readied for the twins' baptism. George and Bernice, as godparents, were in attendance, along with Dale and Conrad and the rest of Four Winds staff. The children were baptized and only little Jimmy gave a frown when he was sprinkled with the holy water. When the baptism was completed, they all left the church to have a celebration luncheon. Following that, everyone returned to Four Winds. Conrad and Dale had plans of their own and said good-bye and left.

It was time for Elizabeth, Erik, and family to return to the farm. Elizabeth gave Erik a shopping list with groceries and other items to buy. Completing his shopping and returning to Four Winds, Erik helped Elizabeth ready the family to leave for the long drive home. Bernice insisted on kissing the twins several more times before they left for the journey.

Upon arrival back at the farm, Deputy Sheriff Faxton and his wife greeted them. They were anxious to see the twins. Dennis was not too crazy about babies and gave a respectful look at them both before catching Erik's eye.

"How did things go?" Erik asked.

"Everything is ship shape," he replied. "You have a bundle of mail though, and I have had all kinds of people coming by and calling about the Keeper. I hope you don't mind, but a man and woman said that they drove over a hundred miles to get here and wanted to see the Keeper. I took them out to the greenhouse and I could hardly get rid of them. They stayed for almost an hour and took all kinds of pictures of the plant."

"That's okay, Dennis. Where is all this mail we got?" He groaned when he saw the pile of mail in the cardboard box. "I'll have to sort through that stuff a little at a time."

"Oh, one other thing," Dennis said. "There was a fellow stopped by here twice. He wasn't interested in the flowers and when I asked him what he wanted, he just asked where you were and when would you be back. I didn't care too much about this guy, and I thought he looked awfully nervous. I mentioned it to my dad."

Dennis left with his parents. Elizabeth and Erik's first order of business was to prepare formula for the twin's feedings and to sort out their clothing and prepare the room for them to nap. Elizabeth was a bit tired from the long trip and still not fully recovered from her delivery. She retired for the night, anticipating that the twins would wake up during the night for a feeding. Erik stayed up later and waded through the piles of mail. He opened a letter postmarked from Great Britain. It was from Sir Byron Ankeny.

Enclosed was information about the Chelsea Garden Show and a form to complete if Erik was interested. He also indicated that Erik and his Keeper—a rare newcomer to the world of flowers and fragrances, one of the Keeper's unique features—was of great interest to his business.

Erik had an informational paper printed that he felt would answer the many requests about the Keeper seeds. By now, Erik had acquired around three hundred seeds that he sorted, into groups of six. He placed them in small bags and placed a label on each. He had also prepared planting and care instructions. The limited number of these seeds would dictate a high price that could be charged for those desiring to have a plant *if* he decided to sell the seeds. He advised interested people that he had not decided yet. This was the message he sent in response to the many inquiries.

All of the plants had produced pods of seeds, so Erik knew he would be able to accumulate a good starting quantity. They had to kept dry and be kept in darkness. Interestingly, as each plant grew and bloomed, it yielded a different variety of colors than the original Keeper plant. Erik had to identify the expected flower bloom colors on each packet of seeds. It was not long before potential orders started pouring in. In particular, Sir Byron Ankeny sent a special request and purchased one of the Keeper plants, which his company would do research on. Erik asked a very steep price for a plant, and Sir Byron was only too happy to pay it.

Early one evening, after they had eaten and the little ones were asleep, Elizabeth and Erik were reflecting on the past few years—about Erik's health recovery, their relationship, and their marriage.

"I am a really lucky guy. It has been like a fairy-tale experience," he said.

Elizabeth fondled the gemstone in her hand as they talked.

"Honey, I have to ask you about that stone of yours. You act like it is something mystical. Whenever we're faced with some kind of major decision, you immediately run and get it to hold."

He seemed to be waiting for an explanation.

"Well, my darling, I'll tell you this much," Elizabeth said, "this gemstone was given to me by an old Gypsy woman who told me that the stone was for me alone and that I should never part with it. It is like a good luck charm, and it has served me well."

Erik saw that Elizabeth was serious about it, so he decided not to make it an issue.

She went on and said, "I carried this gemstone with me when I had that terrible auto accident. If you remember what the state trooper said, his comments were that it was a miracle I escaped major injury, because the car was totally destroyed and they had to cut me out of the vehicle."

Erik's memory was jarred as he recalled the accident.

"I have had many good experiences while holding this stone in my hand," she told Erik. "It helped to bring you and me together, and it helped me through a very bad time of my life. Yes, I do think it has some kind of mystical power. I can't explain how or why, except that we are blessed to have it in our possession."

CHAPTER 34

London Dispatch

The front door bell chimed. Elizabeth opened the door, and a man from UPS who handed her a large envelope and asked her to sign for it. It was from Sir Byron!

"Sweetheart," she called into the intercom, "you have a large envelope that has just delivered … from London, England."

Erik opened the envelope, and inside was a letter from Sir Byron, a round-trip airline ticket and a certified check for the sum of ten thousand dollars. Sir Byron advised Erik that his chemist staff had run all kinds of tests on the Keeper and they were astonished by the resilience of the flowers to hold the magnificent fragrance. Sir Byron insisted that Erik come to London as his guest—airline ticket enclosed for a few days and that the certified check would compensate Erik for any loss of business during his absence. It was an offer that Erik could not refuse!

Erik was grateful that the seat next to his in the first-class section was unoccupied. After takeoff and a brief snack, he nodded off to catch up on his rest. He slept soundly, and the flight attendant did not disturb him until it was nearly time to land at Heathrow Airport in London. The flight attendant brought him a cup of coffee and advised that they would be arriving in about thirty minutes. Erik was glad for the nap and the coffee. Soon the flight attendant announced the preparation for landing as the aircraft turned on its final approach into Heathrow.

The thump and squeal of the wheels on the runway announced the aircraft's arrival.

Upon exiting the aircraft, Erik sought an attendant to inquire about transportation to London. Entering the baggage claim area he was surprised to see a man holding a sign with his name on it.

"I'm Erik Neilsin!"

"Welcome to London, Mr. Neilsin. I am Walters, your driver," he said. "Sir Byron directed me to meet you here and escort you to your accommodations."

Walters drove Erik to a very nice hotel. The reception desk clerk had anticipated his arrival and told him his room—suite, actually—was ready for him. The clerk did not ask for a credit card to pay for his room; Erik asked how he should make arrangements for payment.

"It is all taken care of, sir," she replied.

Erik looked over the majestic suite and saw an envelope with his name on it. Opening it, he saw it was from Sir Byron and asked that he call his number upon his arrival. Erik was not sure about the direct dialing from the hotel so he called the hotel operator, who put his call through to Sir Byron.

"Well, there you are!" Sir Byron bellowed. "I know it is a bit early for you because of the five hours difference in time; however, I would like you to take dinner with me this evening, and I can tell you all the news. Is that agreeable with you?"

"Yes, of course," Erik replied.

"Splendid! I will send a car round for you at six p.m. He will pick you up at the main entrance."

Erik looked at the time. His watch indicated four a.m., but in London it was nine in the morning. Erik headed for the front door and hung a *"Do Not Disturb"* sign on the door handle outside his room. Then he headed for the bedroom, shed his clothes, jumped into bed, and was asleep within a few minutes. Erik had left a message with the front desk for a wake-up call at three o'clock in the afternoon. The telephone rang, waking Erik, and it seemed that he had only slept for an hour.

"It is three o'clock, sir. You asked for a wake-up call."

"Thank you."

Erik headed for the shower to refresh himself and to wake up properly. He shaved and dressed. He had a few hours to wait so he turned on the television and caught the local news on BBC. Erik, noticing that the room had a mini fridge, opened it and found a variety of beverages, liquors, and snacks. He opted for peanuts and a British Pale Ale.

The driver was on time, and Erik was soon on his way to Sir Byron's house. The car drove through a gate with a driveway leading to a great mansion. A butler answered the door and ushered Erik in. Sir Byron was there immediately and greeted Erik.

"Well, well, Erik, so nice to see you again. Are your accommodations satisfactory?"

"Yes, very! Thank you for arranging everything, including the driver. Very considerate of you."

"Come, let us go to the drawing room for a cocktail before dining. I also have some very interesting news to share with you," Sir Bryon said. "Would you like a glass of sherry or something more stimulating?"

"Some sherry will be just right, thank you."

Erik looked around the room and admired the furnishings and the grand fireplace—noting the family coat of arms displayed above it. He sensed that his host was very anxious to discuss the reason why he asked Erik to come visit.

"Well, where shall I begin? I take it that you don't know very much about the perfume industry."

It was more of a statement rather them a question. He went on, "There are many categories in producing quality perfumes, colognes, etc., etc., etc. The really top-quality scents, as my people say, are derived from many fragrance sources. One of the substances for creating lasting depth and holding of a scent is extracted from the sperm whale. Did you know that?" Sir Byron asked.

Erik shook his head.

"Yes, that's true, and it is extremely expensive and not readily available. Your Keeper has the qualities that parallel what I just described. The essence we have extracted from the Keeper plant's flowers can provide that long-lasting quality while retaining that fragrance that is unique and very pleasing. I would like to offer you a contract to provide ten mature Keeper plants each month, and I will pay you top sterling, that is, top dollar. What do you say?"

"This is all very interesting. I have a backlog of people wanting Keeper seeds, and frankly I was not happy about getting into the seed business. The Keeper is special to me, and I was wondering how I might keep it select—so to speak," he replied. "And, yes, I would be interested as long as you agree not to exploit the Keeper and start retailing the seeds."

"Have no fear of that, my friend. In the perfume business we keep our sources and our production methods quite confidential. Once we have extracted the petals and other portions of the Keeper plant, the plant will die, that is why we need a replenishment of the Keeper to accumulate enough of the essence."

That being said, a gentlemen's agreement was arrived at, and Sir Byron gave Erik a copy of the contract and two-weeks to have Erik's attorney review it and then get it back to him.

The following day Erik did some shopping in London and confirmed his return flight reservations for the next day. Erik went up and down Oxford and Regent Streets looking at all the shops and made his way to Harrods. He had heard about Harrods being a rather elite shopping place, and Erik decided that this was the place to buy some gifts for the twins and Elizabeth. Not satisfied, he thought he should get something for the Templetons, the staff at four Winds, and then Conrad and Dale. His whole day was consumed with shopping. Erik had to buy another suitcase to put all the presents in.

Heathrow Airport was busy as usual, but Erik had first-class tickets on British Airways and was processed through quickly. The First Class Lounge offered a variety of refreshments and a relaxed atmosphere while waiting for his flight boarding time.

Airborne once again, he relaxed and reflected on his trip to London. Time passed quickly and the aircraft was on its final leg. They landed, and Erik picked up his luggage and cleared customs and immigration. He headed for his car and drove to Four Winds where Elizabeth and the twins were staying during his absence.

"Here comes Erik," Penny squealed as she peered out of the window. In a few moments the car pulled up to front of the house. Penny went to meet Erik and helped him with his luggage.

"How are the twins doing?" Erik inquired.

"They are having their afternoon nap right now. Elizabeth and Bernice are on the back terrace," she replied.

"Ah, there you are! The traveler returns at last," Bernice called out as Erik joined them on the terrace.

"How did things go, sweetheart?" Elizabeth asked.

"Couldn't be better. I am really pleased with the way things turned out. Matter of fact I was able to get in a little shopping. I had a one-day tour of the shopping district in London," he exclaimed.

Erik hurried to his luggage and started handing out the presents he got for everyone. Erik was very pleased with himself, and his gifts were well received by all.

"Oh, by the way," Bernice said. "That young man that tends your garden nursery called and said that a fellow came to the house again. He said he had mentioned it to you before. He said that the fellow was asking a lot of questions on where you were … when you were coming back, and he just told him that you were away and he was not sure as to when you would return. The odd thing, he said, was that when his father drove up in the sheriff's car this guy acted very nervous and left."

"I wonder who this guy is," Erik said, frowning. "Dennis said that he was asking questions before and was not interested in flowers."

A few minutes later the telephone rang, and Penny announced that it was Conrad and Dale on the phone. Elizabeth answered the call.

"Hello, Conrad. Hi, Dale!" She listened in silence for a few minutes and then looked toward Erik and beckoned him to the phone.

"You better talk to Conrad," she said to Erik.

"Okay! Hello, Conrad, what's up?"

"Erik, I got a call from the state police this afternoon advising me of something that might be important. Did you know that Ruppert Roberts had a brother? Well, his brother was in a mental institution for the criminally insane. He killed an orderly and escaped. The police investigating the homicide came across some of Cliff Roberts's personal affects at his brother apartment and found several newspaper clippings on your wedding and ours."

Erik just listened.

"Among his personal stuff, they found a letter from Triple R to his brother, and the police think that after Triple R was mugged and died that his brother went off the deep end and may somehow attributed his death to his being fired from the VA. He knows what you and Dale look like from the newspaper clippings, and the police say that this Cliff Roberts is dangerous. So if you see anything suspicious, the police want to know right away," Conrad concluded.

"You know, that is rather strange. A fellow has shown up twice out at our place when I wasn't there. He was asking a lot of questions about when I would be back. Did the police give you a description of this guy?" Erik asked.

"No, but I can sure as hell find out. When are you heading back to your house?" Conrad asked.

"Probably tomorrow morning because the twins are having a nap right now. How about Dale?"

"She said that she didn't know anything about Triple R's brother, and she wasn't really concerned … But I am!" Conrad responded. "Being armed with this information is better than walking around not knowing anything."

"I guess you're right. I would like to get a copy of this guy's description and run it by Dennis Faxton to see if this is the same guy. If it is, I will really be concerned. Anyway, thanks for the information, Conrad. As always, you're on the ball and thinking ahead."

Elizabeth looked at Erik, and her eyes asked the question *What's up?*

Erik didn't want to alarm her and said that Conrad was concerned about something and had brought it to his attention.

"Nothing to worry about."

CHAPTER 35

Penny accompanied Erik and Elizabeth back to Virginia, and she volunteered to stay over for a few days to help Elizabeth with the babies.

Elizabeth checked the twins, who were fast asleep and looking very content. Penny poked her head in the doorway and told Elizabeth that the babies were just little angels, so good while Elizabeth was out shopping. In the evening, Elizabeth retired to the bedroom and made ready for bed. She stripped down quickly to take a shower and had brought her purse into the bathroom, not knowing why, and tossed the purse on the bathroom counter. The purse popped open spilling out some of its contents, among them the gemstone.

Picking the gemstone up, Elizabeth felt the stone vibrating and emitting its warmth. In that instance Elizabeth had a thought, and almost immediately she felt the stone quicken its vibration as if in response to her thoughts. She put the gemstone down on the counter and entered the shower.

When Elizabeth woke in the morning she was puzzled. It was already so light outside and normally the twins would be wailing away for a diaper change and their breakfast bottle. She reached for the clock and saw that it was 8:30 in the morning. Erik was not in bed. She slid out from under the covers, put on her bathrobe, and went to the next room to check on the twins. They were not there. She went downstairs and found Erik and Penny with the twins.

"Good morning, sweetheart," Erik said. "You were sleeping so soundly that I decided to let you get some more rest and got the twins down here. They have been fed and changed."

"You're a good father," Elizabeth said and gave Erik a hug and kiss.

Penny left, and a short time later returned, carrying a tray with coffee, cups, and saucers. "Just made this fresh," she announced. "There are also some warm Danish pastries here. Dig in!"

The coffee helped to clear away the cobwebs from a long night's sleep.

"By the way, honey, a small special delivery package came for you this morning. The label says it's from Bernice."

Elizabeth opened the package and took out a note and a box. In the box was a gold chain with a gold sort of cage on the end. She read the note from Bernice, which said:

> *Elizabeth, enclosed is a specially crafted holder for your precious stone, fastened to the chain. When you put the stone inside, you can then seal the special clasp and you can wear*

it on your neck all the time and won't have to worry about losing it.

Love, Bernice

Elizabeth was thrilled with the gift and put the gemstone into the small, lantern-shaped container. It fit perfectly. That prompted a call to Bernice to thank her.

Elizabeth was deep in thought, Erik observed, and decided not to interrupt her. The twins thought otherwise and started to fuss and whimper. Elizabeth picked up baby Jennifer, who stopped crying right away. Elizabeth could smell the soft fragrance from the baby, a scent reflecting a freshly bathed and powdered little one. She returned the baby to her place beside the other twin. Elizabeth had a concerned look on her face.

She rose and paced the room briefly, and then, turning, she said, "Erik! I feel very uneasy about something, and I just don't know what it is. I can't put my finger on it, but since last night I've had a sense that something isn't right. I hope that the babies are not coming down with some illness," she muttered.

"I don't think so," Erik countered. "They look very contented and happy to me."

Secretly Erik marveled at Elizabeth's ability to key in on something as he was thinking about the possible threat from Cliff Roberts. He hoped that his concern was not evident to Elizabeth.

"You know, I have a pile of letters to answer and a number of orders to cancel. I will have to cancel them because of the contract I have with Sir Byron. I also have to go out for a few hours to get some things shipped. Penny is here with you. Would you mind?"

"No, of course not. You have to take care of business. I have a few things I want you to get for me ... like you say, a 'Honey Do' list."

Erik checked his mail and found a special delivery sent from Conrad. It was a copy of the police APB on Cliff Roberts. Erik placed it to one side to show Dennis Faxton.

"I'm leaving now, Elizabeth. I shouldn't be more than a couple of hours."

Erik drove into town and stopped at the sheriff's office to see if Dennis or his father was there. Sheriff Faxton was at his desk and rose to meet Erik.

"How's it going, Erik?"

"Fine! I wanted to run something by Dennis, but maybe I should check with you in any case," he said.

Erik handed Sheriff Faxton a copy of the police APB that Conrad had faxed to him. Erik proceeded to tell the sheriff about the fellow that came to the house twice before and wondered if it was Cliff Roberts.

"I'll talk to Dennis when he comes later this afternoon and see if the description fits. I will swing around to your place more often than I do, just in case this fellow is Cliff Roberts."

Erik nodded and then left to do his errands. Without thinking about it, Erik found himself checking his rearview mirror every so often. He drove into the hardware warehouse and went in for a supply of potassium pellets for the water softener. He loaded four bags into the back of his Jeep and then headed for his local supplier of fertilizer. Henry Ward, the owner, was always glad to see Erik come into his place because Erik always gave him a good order. Today was no exception.

"Hi, Henry. I need some supplies, and I have a list here. Can I just leave it with you and have it delivered in the next two days?" he asked.

"Sure thing. I can get it over to you in the morning if you like."

"Tomorrow morning will be fine. Just don't make it too early. Here's the list."

The next stop was at the UPS office. Erik knew he could call for a pickup, but he thought it would be more convenient to have a UPS account and have pickup and delivery service at the house. All that was arranged, and Erik was off again with his "things to do list."

Erik, thinking about Cliff Roberts, decided to give Conrad a call from a public phone booth and dialed his office telephone number.

"Just a minute, Erik, he's just off the phone!" the receptionist said.

"Hi, Erik," Conrad said. "I just got off the telephone with Dale. She's visiting a client of ours, and she said that she thought she spotted Cliff Roberts in a car that passed by her as she was entering the building. That was a few minutes ago. I'm going to give the local police a call and let them know. Dale gave me a very good description of the car, so that would help the police if it is Cliff Roberts."

The Stalking

Cliff Roberts had been driving around for several hours and found Conrad's law firm. He was not familiar with Baltimore so he parked in the street, a few buildings down from Conrad's office. Hunger pangs were playing hell with his digestive system. He was ready to leave to get something to eat when Dale Swan came out of the building's front door. She crossed the street, got into her Studebaker, and drove past Cliff. Cliff swore and had to drive to the end of the street in order to turn around and follow Dale.

He spotted Dale's car several blocks ahead of him and managed to speed through the light as it was changing. He caught up just as Dale pulled to the curb; Cliff had to drive past her.

Dale looked up briefly. Would her experience as an intelligence analyst crank into action?

It did, as she thought, *Could that be Cliff Roberts?* As soon as she reached her client's office she asked to use their phone and called Conrad.

Cliff Roberts was cunning enough not to be too obvious. He drove to the next street and parked near the corner so he could see when she came out and be able to follow. Dale was with her client for over an hour, and when she left she got into her car and drove down the street, taking a left turn and then left again as she headed back to the law firm. Cliff followed at a long distance behind Dale. He anticipated that she was headed back to the office so he turned at the next street and found another place to park. It was after five p.m. when both Conrad and Dale emerged from the building and drove off. Cliff put his car in gear and followed.

Dale drove the car and turned into their apartment complex parking lot. The regular parking area attendant was off duty, so the lot was unattended. They locked the car and took the elevator to the top floor. After waiting a few minutes, Cliff followed. He stopped at the mailbox and saw Conrad's name and apartment number. It was his former apartment; his name had not been switched to the upstairs apartment.

Miss Gracie Fletcher was the new occupant in Conrad's old apartment. Gracie was a forty-five-year-old unmarried librarian who worked at the local library. She was the type of person that if she didn't move or speak no one would know she even existed. Cliff saw someone delivering a pizza. The delivery boy rang the doorbell, and the buzzer sounded to admit him into the house. Cliff was out of his car in a flash and caught the door before it closed. He was now inside the building and made his way up to the second floor. The pizza delivery boy was collecting his money at a door, so Cliff walked up to the next landing and waited until the delivery boy left. He slipped back down to the second floor and found the apartment he wanted.

Removing the .45-caliber automatic pistol from his pocket, he pulled back the slide and put a round into the chamber. He listened at the door and heard sounds of movement. Cliff Roberts took an empty wax pint milk container from his coat pocket and placed it over the pistol, and he rang the doorbell.

Gracie was not expecting anyone and thought that it might be the building superintendent. Normally, Gracie would slip the chain onto the lock to open the door a crack, but she felt secure at her new apartment.

She opened the door, and Cliff fired as soon as she appeared. Even slightly muffled, the shot sounded like a cannon going off. Cliff realized too late that this was not Dale Swan and quickly ran down the stairs and out of the building. He dashed to his car and drove off immediately, cursing as he drove. He had planned every detail but this.

What went wrong? he asked himself.

Back in his room at the rooming house, Cliff pondered the whole situation. *Maybe it was the right place and that was an aunt or housekeeper*, he thought.

Now they will know that I'm after them.

"What the hell was that noise?" Conrad asked.

"Sounded like a gun or car backfiring to me," Dale replied.

Both Dale and Conrad looked out the window and could not see any car in the street.

Turning, Conrad said, "I didn't check the mailbox when we came in, did you?"

"No, I had my hands full, remember?"

"Okay, be back in a minute." Conrad went down the stairs instead of taking the elevator. As he reached the second floor he could smell gunpowder residue and glanced over to the door of his old apartment. The door was open, and on the floor lying on her back was Gracie Fletcher. She was dead and covered with blood.

Conrad dashed back upstairs to his apartment and rushed to the phone to call the police. He yelled to Dale to go downstairs and not touch anything or let anyone near Gracie Fletcher's place. Conrad gave a detailed report to the police and told of hearing what sounded like a shot about ten minutes earlier. The police were dispatched to the apartment house, led by a detective from homicide. They sealed off the premises and put on surgical gloves to avoid contamination. A second detective arrived, one whom Conrad had met in his previous inquiries about Cliff Roberts. One of the police found the spent .45-caliber shell casing outside on the landing, placing it in a plastic evidence pouch. After a few moments of questioning Conrad, Dale, and other residents of the apartment house, one of the detectives asked Conrad which apartment was his.

"Oh, we are on the top floor now. We used to have this apartment, but after we got married we took the place upstairs," he offered.

"I see that Miss Fletcher occupied that apartment but the name had not been changed. If that was Cliff Roberts, he wouldn't have known. He read the name above the button that indicated this apartment, assuming you both lived there," he surmised.

It was quickly established that the murderer had not entered the apartment but fired point blank when the door opened. The police broadcast a lookout for a suspect, possibly Cliff Roberts, who was now considered armed and dangerous.

The police detective identified himself as Detective Steve Krauss and said, "I don't think he will be back if it was Cliff Roberts. There is no motive for killing this poor lady, but on the other hand if he thought you or Dale would answer the door and realized too late it was not, and then he might try again but somewhere else."

Dale and Conrad were pretty shaken up by this experience, Conrad more so than Dale. Dale had seen combat in Korea and recovered her composure quickly. It wasn't until later in the day when Dale mentioned that they should contact Erik and Elizabeth and let them know what happened.

The telephone rang and rang, and then finally Dennis Faxton answered the phone from the auxiliary phone in the flower greenhouse. Conrad asked Dennis to have Erik call him as soon as he got back home.

Chester Somers pulled into the driveway and spent an hour with Elizabeth and Erik before leaving to bring Penny back to Four Winds. Erik spent some of that time showing Chester the progress of the plantings in the greenhouse. Erik selected one of his more mature Keeper plants and asked Penny to give it to Bernice.

After having a bite to eat and kissing the twins, they set off for the return trip to Maryland.

CHAPTER 36

Plan Revision

Cliff Roberts felt no remorse at killing the woman. He was upset with himself for acting too quickly. *This will not happen next time*, he promised himself. Picking up his coat and a few other articles from his brother's war trophies, he went down to his car and prepared to drive to Virginia.

Things will get a little hot around here with police all over the place. I will try again, but this time I'll go after Erik Neilsin in Rustburg, Virginia.

It was a long drive and well after seven o'clock before Cliff arrived close to Rustburg. He stopped at a donut shop for coffee and donuts to take-out.

It was getting chilly and although Cliff would have liked to be in a nice warm bed and be comfortable, he felt driven to get even for his brother, at all costs.

Cliff eased the car off the side of the road, just enough so that he could see the entranceway to Erik's house. Cliff tried to keep awake, but his body would not obey, and he soon fell asleep. Fifteen minutes later the sound of a passing tractor-trailer startled Cliff out of his sleep. He opened his door and stepped out to stretch. He nearly stumbled as he realized that his legs were stiff from a cramped-up position in the car. He took out a cigarette, lit it, and paced a few yards ahead to observe the Neilsin house.

He heard a door slam and saw Erik emerge into view then disappear into the greenhouse. *Am I ready to get him now?* He thought. The greenhouse door opened and Erik reappeared and returned to the house. Several cars drove past and Cliff realized that he was a bit obvious parked off the side of the road and that it might invite passing cars to stop or even the police. He climbed back in the car, turned on the ignition and engaged the gearshift and slowly drove past the Neilsin house. He caught a glimpse of a woman standing near the window. She was holding a baby up and appeared to be talking to it.

Cliff reached the next intersection and pulled into an old vacant gas station to consider what he should do next. A sudden thought entered his warped mind.

I could really get even for my brother if I take out Erik, his wife, and his kid. That would make up for not getting Dale Swan. Wouldn't that be a blast!

Searching through his brother's bag, he found what he was looking for. He took out the powerful binoculars and laid them on the seat next to him. He turned onto the road heading north and found a road that would take him west and maybe above the Neilsin place. Halfway down the road was a dirt road on his left that probably led to the back of the Neilsin property. He turned and slowly drove down the bumpy dirt road that became more like a pathway. He stopped the car and got out, taking the binoculars with him.

The pathway led down a slight hill. Cliff walked eagerly, anticipating a good view of the house. He was not disappointed. He could see the house and the greenhouse next to it. Looking around, Cliff saw a huge boulder off to one side and climbing onto it, he could see much more of the house. He focused his binoculars and scanned the windows. He could clearly see a woman in the kitchen. In the distance he once again heard the door slam and soon a car start up. He then saw Erik driving away. It was early evening and soon it would be dark. Erik stopped at the main road and turned right, heading back into town. Cliff didn't see any other cars and guessed that Neilsin's wife was alone with her kid.

This was his chance!

Cliff checked his .45-caliber automatic. There was a round in the chamber, and the safety was on. Glancing over the terrain, he decided that he could make his way down the slight hill and around the greenhouse to enter the house via a side door—all without being seen.

Elizabeth was talking to the twins, who were making sounds contented babies make when they have been fed and changed and are happy. She heard the kitchen door open and assumed that Erik had forgotten something and come back.

"I'm in the babies' room," she called out.

There was no reply. Only silence.

She saw a shadow coming from the doorway and turned to speak to Erik. She froze when she saw a man pointing a gun at her.

Cliff Roberts had a wild look on his face and appeared quite menacing.

"Where did Erik go?" he asked.

Elizabeth was silent, not because she didn't have anything to say, but because fear prevented her from answering.

"When is he coming back?" he demanded to know.

"I don't know. He had some shopping to do," Elizabeth replied, finally getting over the initial shock of a man holding a gun on her.

Cliff approached the baby's bed, and Elizabeth immediately placed herself in front of him, to protect the babies. Cliff sneered and then laughed.

"Sit on the bed over there." He pointed with his gun. "We'll wait for your precious Erik to get back."

"What do you want with us? Why are you threatening me with a gun?" Elizabeth asked.

"I am here on a mission," Cliff exclaimed dramatically. "You see, my brother was Ruppert R. Roberts, and your husband and that bitch Dale caused him to be forced out of the army and then the VA, where he worked. I'm gonna to see that they pay for that!"

Elizabeth felt her heart racing and realized that Roberts had to be unstable if he was threatening to kill Erik and Dale. She was trying to think what to do, but she knew there was no way she could because of the twins. She couldn't leave, with or without them. All she could think of was getting Roberts out of the children's bedroom.

"The babies have to sleep now. Please leave the bedroom now."

"Not without you, lady! What's your name, anyhow?" he asked.

"I'm Mrs. Neilsin."

"No! What's your first name?" he demanded.

"Elizabeth."

"Come out of the room and close the door. Go sit in that chair." He pointed to the easy chair facing him, its back to the front door where he expected Erik to come in.

It seemed like an hour had passed, but it was only twenty minutes. Cliff Roberts paced the floor in back of her, occasionally checking the window. Elizabeth clutched her necklace that held the stone and silently asked for help. None was forthcoming.

Suddenly she said, "I have to go to the bathroom," pointing to the small bathroom near the kitchen. Cliff walked over to the bathroom and switched on the light.

"Okay," he said, walking to the children's bedroom. "But if you try anything stupid your children will be history."

Elizabeth only nodded. She got up and went around the man, moving a few things on the kitchen counter as if to tidy up as she went by. Her hand moved to the intercom system and pressed the "on switch," and then she went into the bathroom. A few moments later she returned and sat down in the same easy chair.

I wonder if he saw me turn the switch on for the intercom?

Erik bought the few items he wanted and the baby formula that Elizabeth asked him to get. He also stopped at the newsstand and picked up the local newspaper before starting for home. Once he reached home, Erik drove up to the greenhouse and unloaded some of the things for gardening. He switched on the master greenhouse lights and started putting the items away.

Erik was startled to hear Elizabeth's voice talking to someone in the house. It was coming over the intercom, faint but distinguishable. He heard a man's voice and didn't recognize who it might be. Erik listened and heard the man mention settling the score for his brother. A chill ran through Erik, and he realized that it was Cliff Roberts.

He turned off the lights to the greenhouse and went out of the side exit and to the front door. The motion sensor automatically turned the lights on when Eric approached the house. Erik cursed himself for not thinking about that. When Erik heard Elizabeth cry out, he put aside all caution and rushed into the house. Cliff was waiting with his gun pointed at the front door as Erik burst in. Cliff swicthed off the safety, cocked the hammer back on the pistol and started to squeeze the trigger. In a fraction of a second a blinding light emitted from the pendant around Elizabeth's neck. Cliff, startled, moved his arm to ward off the light.

Erik's ranger training kicked into play, and he leaped forward, pushing the gun to his left side, and brought his right arm under and around Cliff's arm, forcing his arm backward. Cliff squeezed the trigger, and the shot was deafening in Erik's ear. Erik grasped part of the automatic as they fought each other Erik felt the clip ejection button and pressed it. The clip fell out of the gun handle. Erik shot his right leg behind Cliff and sent him flying onto his back. Cliff kicked out at Erik and caught him in the knee, and Erik tripped backward.

Fear now took the place of Cliff's quest for vengeance. He jumped to his feet and quickly scrambled out of the door and ran to the side of the greenhouse and up the path that led back to his car. Erik was ready to pursue him, but Elizabeth screamed at him to stop.

"He still has a gun. Call the police!" she urged.

The twins were screaming their heads off from the noise of the gunshot. Erik was shaking when he lifted up the phone and dialed Sheriff Faxon's number. The female dispatcher answered and Erik rushed to tell her what had happened.

"Slow down! Who is this?" she asked.

"Erik Neilsin! Is the sheriff there?" he asked.

"No, he's on patrol, but I'll get him on the radio. Stay put," she advised.

Within minutes the sheriff's car pulled up to the house. Gun drawn, Sheriff Faxton ran to the house and Erik met him at the door.

"It was Cliff Roberts! He's headed up that back path," Erik said, pointing toward the greenhouse.

"How long ago?"

"About five minutes ago. He's got a forty-five automatic. Looks like an army model," Erik said.

"Do you have a gun?" he asked Erik. Erik shook his head.

Reaching into his trousers leg, next to his boot, the Sheriff extracted a .32-caliber Berretta automatic.

"You know how to use this, don't you?"

Erik nodded.

"You call my dispatcher and tell her to get a couple of state troopers up here now," he yelled as he leaped to his car. The tires on his squad car squealed in protest as he shot away in pursuit.

Sheriff Faxton reached the side road that ran in back of Erik's house and sped down the road, his eyes looking left and right for a car or the suspect. He almost drove by the small dirt road that cut sharply to the left, and then he stopped and backed up his cruiser. He saw tire tracks on the dirt road and it didn't appear that any car had left. So he concluded that it must still be there. He parked his car into the dirt road with the lights off and pondered on how to deal with this situation.

He won't go back to the house, I'm sure. He's on foot, and I'm betting his car is down there.

He slipped the car into gear and slowly eased his way down the road. At the bend in the road he saw the car.

Cliff Roberts stumbled and grunted as he headed up the hill toward his car. There was no light ahead of him. Not like going down to the house. He stopped and looked back several times to see if Erik was chasing him, but saw no one nor heard anything. His right arm felt like it was sprained.

"That son of a bitch," he said out load, "nearly broke my damn arm."

Cliff saw the glint of reflection from his car and made his way toward it.

Suddenly a car's headlight turned on and Cliff was bathed in the headlights of Sheriff Faxton's police cruiser.

"Drop your weapon and put your hands behind your neck," a voice boomed out.

Cliff felt real terror now. He didn't know what to do, but at the same time frustration and anger moved him to be rash. He raised his hands, still holding the gun in his right hand.

"Put the gun down now," the voice commanded, "and put your hands behind your neck."

Cliff dropped his right hand and bent down to lay the gun on the ground. He could now make out the police car and he dropped to one knee and fired at the car. The bullet went wild and never hit anything.

Sheriff Faxton fired two rapid shots from his .38-caliber revolver. The first hit Cliff Roberts in the chest and the second in his left shoulder. Roberts was propelled backward into the dirt. He never realized that the clip was ejected from his weapon and that the only round he had left had been in the gun chamber. His last thought, as life vacated his body, was that flash of light that came from where Elizabeth sat. That light was like a laser beam, blinding him and numbing his brain.

Sheriff Faxton answered the state police call on his radio and informed them of the shooting. Ten minutes later a police cruiser followed by an ambulance pulled up. Sheriff Faxton had never shot and killed anyone before and as that realization now hit him it shook him up a bit. The state troopers were sympathetic to him, saying they, too, had similar experiences.

Cliff Roberts was dead on arrival, and was pronounced medically dead by the medical examiner. The state police notified the proper authorities that Cliff Roberts had been killed in a gunfight resisting arrest and was no longer a threat.

Case closed!

CHAPTER 37

It was December 21, and Dale was feeling down in the dumps, even though Erik, Elizabeth, and the twins were coming for an overnight stay on the twenty-third. They planned to get together for the whole day and then everyone would go to Four Winds and celebrate Christmas with the Templetons.

Conrad noticed that Dale was preoccupied and somewhat moody the past few days. She wanted to take a few days off from the work grind to get things ready for Erik and Elizabeth's visit.

"Sure! We are very slow at the office this time of year," Conrad said. "Oh, yeah! I invited Gloria and her husband over when Erik and Elizabeth are here. She wants to see the twins. That okay with you?" he asked.

"Certainly," responded Dale. "We should have had them over sooner."

Conrad left for work and Dale went out, did her grocery shopping and stopped by the liquor store to get stocked up. Returning to the apartment she had an idea for some Christmas decorations. She rummaged through a bunch of old boxes and cartons and found the old army footlocker she was looking for. Opening it up, she removed an old sawed off broom handle with holes drilled in it. She found the homemade tree branches that Erik had fashioned in Korea. They were very tattered, but Dale fixed them with a little scotch tape. Rummaging further, she found many of the little tree decorations she had made. She reconstructed the little homemade tree and put all the decorations she could find in the footlocker, onto the tree. *It looks a little sorry and sad*, she thought. She had some new tree tinsels and these she put on the little tree.

When Conrad came home and saw the tree he advised Dale that they were not on poverty road and they could afford a very nice Christmas tree. Dale then explained to Conrad how she and Erik had made that tree in Korea and that it was so special at that time. She told him about them all sharing their Christmas goodies.

She omitted Erik's special Christmas present.

"I think that Erik will really get a kick out of that," she purred.

"Anything you say my dear." Conrad smiled. "Your wish is my command!"

He noted that Dale seemed a little more like her old self that evening. Even though a few cocktails even made her more relaxed, Dale shrugged off Conrad's amorous advances saying she was busy right now. Conrad felt rejected and decided on a gin and tonic for consolation.

Just before noon on the twenty-third, Erik, Elizabeth, and the twins arrived. Conrad went down to help them with all the packages, cribs, and baby stuff.

Elizabeth apologized for all the baggage but said that the babies needed a lot of attention and went through diapers as fast as she could change them.

Conrad, although happy to see their guests, was still feeling grumpy and rejected. Dale prepared lunch for everyone while Elizabeth took care of the baby food. Following lunch Erik asked if it would be okay for him to take a short nap as he was tired from the trip and getting up extra early to see to the greenhouse and plants. But before he could, Elizabeth and Dale started talking about Cliff Roberts and his barging in with a cocked pistol.

"I still don't understand exactly what happened," Erik interjected. "When I came in, Roberts had that gun pointed straight at me, and then suddenly there was a flash of light—like a flash gun going off—and Roberts seemed to reel backward for a moment. That gave me time to shove his gun to the side."

"Where did the light come from?" Dale asked.

"I don't know. Everything happened so fast. Maybe it was reflection from a passing car. I can't be sure, but in any case it couldn't have happened at a better time."

Elizabeth's hand rose to clasp the gemstone on her necklace. She knew and would not reveal the secret. Changing the subject, she asked Dale about the odd little Christmas tree.

"Oh! This is a special Christmas tree that was created by no other than your husband while we were both in Korea," Dale said.

Erik took a close look at the tree. "I'll be darned. Is that really the tree?"

"Of course, silly! Even the decorations are authentic," she said bristling with pride.

Erik filled in the gaps on how he made the tree and Dale made the decorations from beer can tabs—which by now were rusted and corroded. Dale went into the other room and came back with the little cricket cage and a cotton bird inside.

"This," she announced, "was Erik's Christmas present to me. A Korean Kanary!"

They all had a good laugh and in a few moments of continued conversation, Erik said that following that Christmas, he left for the north. It was still a sobering memory for him.

Dale excused herself and left the room. Elizabeth could hear the sound of someone choking and left to find Dale. Dale was on her knees with both hands hugging the toilet bowl, throwing up.

"Dale, what's wrong?" Elizabeth asked in alarm.

Dale rose to her feet, washed her face, and rinsed her mouth with a mint mouthwash.

"I thought that I got a touch of stomach flu," she said, "but this has been happening almost every morning and sometimes later on."

Elizabeth sensed that she might know the cause and asked Dale when she had her last period.

"Oh, oh, shit!" She furiously checked the calendar. "About a month and a half ago," she wailed.

Elizabeth made a suggestion, and she and Dale informed the guys that they were going out for an hour and they were appointed joint babysitters. Elizabeth drove and headed for Johns Hopkins Hospital. Upon arriving, Elizabeth sought out one of the GYN medics and asked them for a favor. Dale completed a test. The medic said they would let her know as soon as possible. Elizabeth left the Four Winds telephone number.

On the way home they stopped for two six-packs of beer, Erik's favorite, so not to arrive back empty-handed. Soon after they got home, Gloria and her husband arrived. Much time was spent playing with the twins—cooing and dangling rattles to amuse the babies.

The following morning Erik and Elizabeth left for Four Winds with Conrad and Dale driving behind them. A light snow had fallen during the night making everything white and appropriate for Christmas. Arriving at Four Winds, they were greeted by Christmas decorations all the way up the driveway to the house. Two massive wreaths hung on the doors, which were framed with holly branches. The door opened immediately and Penny greeted them. The rest of the household joined them.

"Merry Christmas!" they all shouted.

Bernice burst through to the entranceway. "Where's my little babies? Come, let me take one of them," she begged of Elizabeth after a quick kiss on the cheek. Everyone unloaded the Christmas presents under the beautifully decorated, massive tree.

"Come and refresh yourselves! I have some very nice punch, suitable for a Christmas Eve afternoon," George boasted. This was accompanied with a variety of petite sandwiches and Christmas cookies. George was interested in what Erik was up to in the greenhouse now. Erik explained about his contract work for Sir Byron and that everything was going along smoothly. The women surrounded the twins and played with them for over an hour until the twins, yawning, were taken to have their afternoon nap.

The telephone rang, and Penny sought Dale. The call was for her. Dale answered the phone; it was the hospital GYN medic.

Suspicions confirmed! She was pregnant.

"Well, what say we start to open up some Christmas presents," Bernice said. She was anxious to have them open presents now.

Dale sought Conrad's eye and asked, "And what do you want for Christmas?"

Conrad was going to say *Baby, you know what I want!* But he only got as far as saying "Baby—"

"Your wish is my command!" Dale responded immediately.

Conrad had a confused look on his face. "What do you mean, my wish is your command?"

Dale, bursting with laughter, exclaimed, "You're going to be a papa. I'm pregnant!"

For the first time in his life, Conrad was speechless.

Erik was the first to react on the news. "You old goat, now you're into making babies."

Conrad was startled and looked to Dale to reconfirm the news. "Are you sure, or are you just pulling my leg?" he asked.

"It's for real, lover!" she responded. "That telephone call I got was from the hospital. They said it's positive."

The reaction set in, and Conrad had a silly grin on his face. "Well, I'll be. Christ! I'm going to be a father!"

Suddenly Conrad thought about his feeling rejection from Dale and gave her a silent, questioning look.

"I should have told you before now. I just didn't feel good and thought I had eaten some bad oysters or something," she allowed. "I never thought I had a bun in the oven."

Conrad swept Dale into his arms and gave her a big hug and a long kiss. "I thought for a while that your love for me was waning," he confessed.

"No, sweetheart! I was just feeling nauseous and trying not to be sick. It had nothing to do with you—that is, personally. But now that I think about it," she said, her voice trailing off and a smile on her face.

"Well, that is great news indeed," George said shaking Conrad's hand. Conrad suddenly recalled all that Erik and Elizabeth went through, planning for a baby. He was a man, and no exception as far as new prospective fathers was concerned. Dale recognized the signs and told Conrad to cool it.

"It is at least eight months down the road, so don't get anxious. Enjoy the moment!"

Presents were opened, and the majority of presents were for the twins. Bernice, not to be outdone, lavished them with beautiful and expensive presents. Elizabeth did not object, as she could see the joy on both the Templetons' faces. It was like bestowing gifts to their own children.

Later that night, after everyone turned in to greet Christmas the next morning, Elizabeth had to get up to tend to the twins. She was very tired and half asleep. She changed the babies and fed them their bottles. It was two-thirty in the morning. As Elizabeth was bending over the babies her necklace hung down, and the babies reached out for it, grasping the container with the gemstone inside. Elizabeth saw the gemstone glow a bright yellow color that slowly ebbed to amber and then faded to its natural color. It was at that moment that she became aware of someone standing in back of her. It was the two men in white.

"Do not be frightened," one of them said. "The gemstone spell has run its course, and you will no longer need its power. You have the man you love and are graced with two lovely children. We will no longer be visiting you," Brewster concluded.

Elizabeth was forming a question in her mind but never got to ask it.

"The gemstone was a gift, especially for you and Erik or, I should say, Pat Duran. Cherish that which has been provided for you. It is a gift from the Keeper."

EPILOGUE

Dale and Conrad Flemming had a baby daughter. They named her Erika.

The Neilsin twins seemed like they spent half of their childhood visiting and staying with "Grandma and Grandpa Templeton."

Penny Somers, now a young lady, left to go to college—all expenses paid by the Templetons. When she graduated she became a nutritionist.

The Keeper's essence was used to develop a new perfume and was given the French name of *"Providential"* (heaven sent). It was a huge success.

In the twilight of their retirement years, the Templetons went on a trip to Germany, taking Elizabeth, Erik, and the twins with them. The twins, in the care of their grandparents, visited many places in Germany, especially the Frankfurt zoo.

Erik and Elizabeth paid a visit to Heidelberg and rode on the streetcar to Handschuhsheim. Elizabeth noticed that the *"Nicht auf den Boden Spuken"* sign was no longer displayed in the streetcar.

That chapter of life had past a long time ago—along with the spell of Keeper's gift.

GLOSSARY

Other languages

Caldo gallego: soup
Gott am Himmel!: God in Heaven!
langosta: lobster
platz: A place
Schatze: Sweetheart
Leibling: Darling
Schnecken: Danish Pastry
Weihnachten: Christmas holidays
Kim-chi: a fermented Korean dish

Military terms

Divarty: Division Artillery
CONUS: Continental United States
FO: Forward Observer
NCO: Non-Commissioned Officers
O Club: Officers' Club
POC: Point of Contact
SOP: Standard Operating Procedure
APO: Army Post Office

Other terms

APB: All Points Bulletin
defibrillation: electrical shock to the heart
Hindenburg: A great German Zeppelin that ended its famous flight in flames at Lakewood, New Jersey in a terrible accident that ended the Zeppelin's era
ROK: Republic of Korea
UPS: United Parcel Service

ABOUT THE AUTHOR

Born and raised in the city of New York, the author, at the age of seventeen, entered the U.S. Army Air Corps in 1945. He participated in the occupation of Germany and the Berlin Airlift. He served two tours in Germany, three tours in England. Other duties were in Puerto Rico, and his last tour in Vietnam.

The Bronze Star Medal and three Air Force Commendation medals accompany a host of other service awards.

The author took up fencing in England and in 1963 he won the U.S. Air Force World-Wide Fencing Championship in Foil and Saber. He retired from the Air Force in 1972 after twenty-seven years active duty. He started his own business and retired in year 2000.

He resides in Somerset, Pennsylvania with his wife and Labrador, Rudy. He has four children, ten grandchildren and one great granddaughter.

He previously wrote a "Children's Country Trilogy" published in April 2000. Since then three novels have been published on Kindle Books: *The Blind Psychic*, *Alysia*, and *Maddie's Soldier Boy*.

His activities now include playing golf, fishing and writing. After forty years, he took up fencing again as a "Senior Veteran Fencer" but after two years he had to put that aside. The spirit was willing but the flesh was weak.

"dernier touché finale"